What Ho, Magic!

by

Tanya Huff

WHAT HO, MAGIC!

An MM Publishing Book
Published by Meisha Merlin Publishing, Inc.
PO Box 7
Decatur, GA   30031

Editing & interior layout by Stephen Pagel
Copyediting & proofreading by Teddi Stransky
Cover art by Todd Lockwood
Cover design by Neil Seltzer

ISBN: 1-892065-04-5

http://www.angelfire.com/biz/MeishaMerlin

First MM Publishing edition: March 1999

Printed in the United States of America
0 9 8 7 6 5 4 3 2 1

Table of Contents

Tanya Huff is...

This book is the first collection of some of Tanya's short stories, and the stories, bristling with an elegant wit that never becomes either self-indulgent or pretentious, speak more clearly for themselves than I ever could.

I'd like to concentrate on the work, and the work alone, but there's so much of Tanya *in* the work she does it would be like telling half a story when I know more of it: doesn't feel right. Besides, anyone who's reading this has already bought the book, a sure indication that I'd be singing to the choir.

So, briefly, Tanya Huff is scum. A maggot. Moreover, I mean both words in the nicest possible way.

Perhaps a little background is in order.

The first time I met Tanya, I was fifteen years old. I was at my first convention, and very nervous; she was at her umpteenth, and very confident. She was also dressed up as Belit. I couldn't think of anything clever to say to her—a recurring theme—so I didn't say anything at all because, well, I was intimidated. Nevertheless, I remembered her clearly.

The second time I met Tanya was as a customer at Bakka, the science fiction bookstore in Toronto where we'd later spend six of her eight-year tenure working together. She had just sold a novella to Pat Price at Amazing—the Kelly Chase story—and she was determined to sell a novel before she reached the other side of thirty.

At that time, I was scribbling poetry and editing fledgling attempts at my own fiction, and she seemed to have stepped across the impossibly wide divide that separates the published—and publishable—from the unpublished. She was very matter of fact about the sale and her future career. I was impressed—and intimidated—so I didn't mention the fact that I was writing.

I started working at Bakka very shortly after that, part-time to her full-time, and when I finally graduated to full-time, we overlapped on four of our five days. During those years, as most of you probably did, I read Tanya's fiction. But I got to read it *before* it was published.

It was torture.

Poets tend toward melodrama and abuse of the language; they're always at least a bit infatuated with words and the cadence of words, and before they find their feet...well, it isn't pretty. That was me.

Misery loves company. Unfortunately, I never did get any, not that way.

Tanya has never had that problem. I'm fairly certain she knows what purple prose is, but I guarantee she's also incapable of committing it.

"Here, Michelle," she'd say, "I think this is too slow. Or too boring. Or maybe not enough is *happening*." So I'd read her very polished, highly amusing and often deeply moving writing—and then I'd slink off to my computer with an inferiority complex the size of a small planet. *This* was her idea of *not good enough*?

Tanya, I thought, *you are scum.* But I wasn't about to say that because I didn't want it to be taken the wrong way.

Well, the years went by. I managed to figure out that I wasn't Tanya Huff, and I wasn't going to be Tanya Huff, so I settled into my own style of writing, rewriting and revising. I started, bit by bit, to feel less intimidated. Maybe it was because of the times I'd watch her spend twenty minutes—in the back room of the store—writing the same sentence over and over again until the cadence was *exactly* right. Maybe it was the month she spent writing the same four pages of a novel over and over again because she knew where the book was supposed to be going, but her instincts as a writer are far too strong—and too good—to let her hack her way paint-by-numbers style through the plot; if she blocks, it's for a reason. The book veered sharply to the left, and once she and her subconscious settled on a reasonable compromise, she took the driver's seat again.

I still read everything she wrote as she finished it. Novels were bad, as they came chapter by chapter; short stories came in a complete chunk.

When she finished "I'll Be Home For Christmas" I had yet to start a story for the same anthology. I read hers, and almost didn't start one. "No," I told her, "there's no way I'm writing anything contemporary; it'll only get compared to that, and I can't come close."

I was *very* glad that I didn't have that problem with "Shing Li-Ung", one of my favourite stories, because I wasn't asked to write a story for that anthology. As someone with some background in being a banana—white on the inside, yellow on the outside, in case you haven't come across the term—I found the story to be particularly moving and well thought out, and I liked the end.

In fact, I like the way most of Tanya's stories end. Although she's at home with a very dark edge—as the two horror stories in the anthology clearly show—for the most part, she deals in hope. In ideals. In what it takes to meet those ideals half way. Her characters know, like she does, that life is tough, and that people aren't perfect—but they don't use the excuse of imperfection to become self-indulgent, whiny jerks. They deal with their lives. They live up to their promise.

But I digress. I was speaking about scum.

As Tanya and I got more comfortable with each other's writing we began to depend, to some extent, on each other's opinion. And one day, when she'd handed me yet another excellent chapter with a mournful, "this is way too slow, nothing happens, and no one's going to finish the book if they even get this far," I was going through a complete throw-the-book-away-and-rewrite-from-the-ground-up revision. Misery, as I mentioned above, loves company.

I read the chapter.

In addition, when I finished it, I looked up, met her expectant gaze, and said, "You are a crawling maggot."

"What?"

"You are scum. You are vile."

"Is that good?"

"I am in the *middle* of the rewrite from *hell* and you have the nerve to give me this and tell me that it's *awful?*" Because, of course, it was wonderful.

She's not stupid. "Wow. Scum," she said.

It became our quick way of saying something was *really* good. It was shorthand for You've completely hooked me and I couldn't put this down.

When she finished *Blood Pact*, she was living three hours outside of Toronto, but I still got to read the book chapter by chapter, and when I finished it, I phoned her—this was before there were cheap long distance rates in Canada—to call her scum. It took a long time. I loved that book.

I also had to take three days off writing; I couldn't get it out of my head and when I went back to my own work I could clearly see just where the cadence and humour, the earthiness of her characters, the contemporary accessibility, were missing from mine. This happens every time I read a Huff novel.

Doesn't stop me from reading her books, though.

Nothing I can think of—short of the obvious—could do that.

So, Tanya Huff is scum.

And you're about to find out why; just turn the page.

—Michelle Sagara West
October 1998

"The Chase is On", the oldest story in this collection by a considerable margin, is pure space opera. I would never insult the many fine writers of science fiction by referring to this story as such. There is no science in it.

Space opera; fantasy with ray guns and space marines.

It's a sub genre I've always loved, space opera, and given the continuing reaction to Star Wars and Star Trek, so have a whole lot of people. I've actually pitched a couple of ideas for Star Trek novels but, unfortunately, they went nowhere.

As this collection appears, I'm working on my first novel-length space opera (untitled as yet) probably out from DAW in the spring of 2000. It has nothing to do with Kelly Chase or her universe.

THE CHASE IS ON

"Blundering, incompetent idiot!" roared the Atabeg of Rayanton, Guiding Light of Forty Star Systems. "A simple removal, and you fail dismally!"

The commander of the Atabeg's Immortals, some four thousand men whose loyalty was absolute, stared straight ahead, carefully emotionless, ignoring the spittle that dotted the front of his dress uniform—the physical evidence of his lord's rage. To show any emotion in the presence of the Atabeg was unwise, although groveling was acceptable after a certain point in the interview.

"Exalted One," began the officer, wishing that he dared wet his lips. "If I may be permitted...we had to deal with his escort first. There were a great many places he could hide, and we had a very small force."

"And may I remind you, Commander," the Atabeg snarled, "that we speak of an eight year old boy." Out of the corner of his eye, he saw tanned fingers fiddling with something on the desk. "Pay attention, Darvish," he snapped. "This concerns you."

Darvish sighed, sat up straighter, and tried to look as if he cared. When the Atabeg turned again to the commander, Darvish let the expression drop and returned to buffing his nails and brooding about the unfairness of his life.

"An eight year old boy," the Atabeg repeated, "who must be removed. When my fat fool of a brother finally gets what's coming to him, *my* son will be Shahinshah, Defender of Infinity. Do you understand me, Commander? Get rid of that boy!"

"Most assuredly, Exalted One." The commander bowed and backed quickly from the room.

"Uh, Father…"

The Atabeg took a deep breath and faced his son, wondering once again how this exquisite lump, this posturing fop, could be flesh of his. He cursed his brother for the mind blocks that kept him from taking the throne for himself. "I don't want to hear it, Darvish," he said sternly. "You're going to be Shahinshah, and that's all there is to it."

Darvish sighed again.

Some hours later, a nine-man squad of the Atabeg's Immortals moved into defensive positions around the perimeter of docking pit 90. Their squad commander walked slowly toward the docked freighter, gripping his weapon tightly, and trying not to let his nervousness show. He knew that any sign of weakness could precipitate an assassination attempt by one of his men, and at least half the squad felt ready for promotion.

His eyes swept across the gleaming enamel and chrome until they rested on the registration numbers set into the metal by the cargo hatch. He wished he could swear. The independent pilots of Company space were so damned unpredictable; they often shot back. As he closed in on the ship, an external video relay swiveled and pointed directly at him.

"Hold it right there, buddy," boomed a mechanical but still definitely female voice. "Kelly, we've got company."

The squad commander glanced hastily from side to side. He saw no Kelly. A sudden noise brought his eyes back to the ship. He tightened his finger on the trigger as an access panel clanged back, exposing a pair of shapely legs.

The shapely legs kicked, jerked, and emerged, followed by an equally shapely body.

"Who the blazes are you?" she snarled, tossing the wrench she carried into a tool kit and dropping a hand to her sidearm.

This was not the reaction the squad commander usually evoked in tall, blonde, and strikingly beautiful young women. It almost startled him into taking a step back; a move his men would surely misinterpret, with fatal results. She moved closer, showing apparent disregard for his superior firepower. His men moved closer as well, although, admittedly, a very little closer. If they had no intention of being reported for cowardice, they had less of being caught in a crossfire.

The squad commander pulled a sheet of hard copy from his belt pouch and handed it over.

She scanned it quickly. "And just why does the Atabeg of Rayanton, Guiding Light of Forty Star Systems, et cetera, et cetera, want to run an energy scan of my ship? His customs brokers searched it when I landed. Everything is in order."

"A search is not an energy scan." He glowered forebodingly, an expression which never failed to strike terror into the hearts of subordinates. The woman didn't appear to notice. His eyes flicked over the sleek lines of the freighter. A pity that simple confiscation no longer remained an option. The empire needed the imports too much to scare the independents off with the one thing that outweighed their desire for profit: the possible loss of their ships. The squad commander sighed. The old ways had been easier. "The Atabeg, may he live forever, thinks you have something on board he wants."

A golden eyebrow rose. "Would you believe me if I said I don't know what you're talking about?"

"No."

"I didn't think so."

She dropped to the ground and a raking line of blue fire from the ship turned all ten men into smoldering piles of carbon.

Kelly Chase glanced around at the bodies and shook her head ruefully as she dusted off her knees. Her nose wrinkled in distaste as she stepped over the ruins of the squad commander.

"I've always wondered why they call them Immortals. Nice shooting, Val. A little overdone, but nice shooting."

"Dead's dead, Boss. They don't care how cooked they get." The gun ports closed and a hatch hissed open as the self-aware computer that ran the ship, that was the ship, began to warm the engines for lift-off. "Looks like we'd better blow this joint, huh?"

"Yes," agreed Kelly, "looks like we'd better."

The Atabeg and his son still sat at dinner when the dispatch came in from the commander. Scowling, the Guiding Light of Forty Star Systems snatched the hardcopy from his aide's grasp.

"Morons!" He threw the thin sheet of plastic down into the remains of the first course.

"Did he get away again, Father?" Darvish asked, his perfect brow furrowing as he plucked the message out of the white sauce.

A muscle jumped in the Atabeg's jaw. The aide stepped back. "Yes. He got away. Again."

"Oh, good." The young man favored his father with a dazzling smile. "Now I don't have to be Shahinshah."

"You don't have to be..." The Atabeg sputtered into silence then began again, his voice rising to a shriek. "For the last time, Darvish, you *will* be Shahinshah!"

"But..."

"Not another word!" He glared up at his aide, his anger a sizzling presence in the room. "Get me that ship and everyone on it. Call out the fleet if you have to!"

"Why me?" Darvish asked of no one in particular.

"What I don't understand," Kelly murmured, her booted feet up on the control console, "is how he knew I had the rocks on board."

"Maybe he was watching our dealer," the ship suggested.

"The Atabeg can't keep spies in Company space," the independent scoffed. "His men sell themselves too cheaply."

"Lucky guess?"

Kelly yanked both hands up through her loose curls. "Maybe." The only alternative, that one of their own had sold them out, didn't stand considering. Independents trusted few enough people as it was. If they couldn't trust each other, the whole system would fall apart. "How are repairs coming?"

"I'm running final systems checks now. Give me a few minutes, and I'll have full internal sensory input again."

The ship fell silent and Kelly amused herself by watching lights flicker on the control board as one by one the systems damaged in a small argument with a Company patrol boat came back on line.

"Uh, Kelly. Maybe they weren't after the rocks."

"What?" Kelly's feet hit the deck.

"I've just picked up an intruder in the lounge; within human parameters but small."

Kelly was out of the control room almost before the ship finished talking. She raced into the lounge and skidded to an abrupt halt. Backed against a bulkhead was a red-haired boy with a runny nose, a dirty face, and an energy weapon pointed at the general area between her chin and her navel.

"Come one step closer," said the youngster calmly, "and I'll blow you into a greasy smear on the deck."

"Lovely," said Kelly. "Just what I needed to round out my day." She took a step forward but stopped when the boy showed every indication of carrying out his threat. "Couldn't we talk about this?"

He shook his head, lips compressed into a thin line.

Suddenly, alarms shrilled and lights flashed. As the boy jerked, Kelly dove to the deck, seconds before an energy blast boiled the paint on the metal behind her head.

"I feel," commented Val, the boy and his weapon safely wrapped in the extensile arms she used in the lounge, "like a child molester."

"Child, hell!" Kelly snapped. "That little monster nearly fried me."

The little monster in question stopped struggling and relaxed against his bonds, frustration giving in to fatigue.

"This ship's self-aware," he said sulkily. "That's against the law."

"So, sue me." Kelly gingerly touched the blistered paint and shook her head. "Why didn't you grab him before I was in his line of fire?"

A shrug was implicit in the computer's sheepish tone. "I didn't think of it."

Kelly's brows rose. "You didn't think of it? The best interfaces money can buy, and you didn't think of it? Maybe I should turn you in for a good abacus, then if I get shot at, at least it'll be my own fault."

"My old man'll get you for this," the boy blurted out suddenly, more peeved at being ignored than confined. "You'll see."

Kelly sighed. "Listen brat, I don't know why you're on my ship, and I don't care if you're the Shahinshah's only son…"

"Yeah? Well, I am."

"Am what?"

"I am the Shahinshah's only son."

"All right, Ahrikhartoum Gafer…Gaaf…Giff…" Kelly threw up her hands in defeat. "What did you say your name was again?"

"Ahrikhartoum Gaafar Nimeiry Umma al-Mahdi, Heir to Infinity." He stopped mashing his food into interesting piles long enough to add: "Most people call me Your Magnificence."

"They do?"

"Yeah."

"Well, forget it." She considered a moment, absently sculpting her own dinner into mounds and hollows. "Ahrikhartoum …Ahrikhar…Erik…I'll call you Erik. If," she added mockingly, "the Heir to Infinity approves."

The boy shrugged, more interested in whether or not he could stand an eating utensil up in the mess on his plate.

She took that as an affirmative. "Okay, Erik, let's see if I've got this straight. Your uncle, the Atabeg, wants to kill you so that his son Darvish inherits the throne. He destroyed the troops escorting you from your grandmother's but you slipped by his Immortals, stowed away on my ship, almost killed me, and now want me to take you to your father. The Shahinshah. The King of Kings. He Whose Slightest Whim is Law in a Thousand Star Systems."

Erik nodded. "Grandmother says I'm old enough to start protecting myself."

Kelly remembered the squad commander and sighed. Perhaps she'd been just a tad hasty. "Well, I can't take you back, that's for sure."

"Surer," broke in Val. "We've been followed."

"Followed?" Kelly ran for the control room. "What did you do, stop and admire the scenery?"

"You don't like the way I move, get out and walk."

"Maybe half a dozen self-aware ships in the galaxy," Kelly muttered as she slid into the pilot's couch, "and I get the one who thinks she's a comedienne. C'mere, brat."

"I'm here."

"Right." She waved him into the other couch and indicated two brightly-lit screens. "Those ships belong to your uncle?"

"A ship this size doesn't carry trackers for Susumu space."

"That's not what I asked you."

Erik shrugged and studied the displayed schematics. "Yeah. So?"

"They're just D-class cruisers," Kelly said thoughtfully. "What do you think, Val?"

"We can't outrun them," the ship pointed out. "They're built for speed. We've got to fight."

Kelly's fingers danced over a bank of pressure-sensitive switches. "Val, I'm bringing us into real space. Raise the shields, and swing us about when we've switched. Maybe we can talk to them first."

"My uncle always says shoot first, ask questions later."

"Easy for him to say. He has the heavy artillery."

The screen flared through a complete spectrum, filled with a blaze of wheeling stars, and then showed a distant view of the two cruisers.

"You didn't lose them," Erik mentioned, rather unnecessarily.

"Didn't intend to."

"They're separating, Boss. They'll probably try to flank us." The Valkyrie rocked as a blast from one of the cruisers grazed her shield. "Still think we should talk to them?"

Kelly shrugged. "So the one time I don't assume the worst, I'm wrong. Line us up, Val."

"Aligned."

"Then fire."

An energy beam fountained out from the freighter and splashed explosively against the nearest cruiser. Light flowed over the cruiser's bow but left no visible damage.

"Hey," Erik cried as the Valkyrie deflected another shot. "It didn't work."

"Guess again. Her front shields folded."

"How can you tell?" the boy asked suspiciously, scanning the screens and finding no answer.

The board blurred under Kelly's fingers. "There isn't a shield in the imperial fleet built to take on a T-ray."

"Cargo freighters don't carry T-rays!"

Kelly grinned. "This one does."

Erik's jaw dropped and his eyes grew round. "You..." he choked. "You're a pirate!"

"Am not. Hurry up a bit, Val."

The boy bounced gleefully on his couch. "If you're not a pirate, you've got to be a smuggler!"

"Do not. Careful, Val. She doesn't need shields to shoot at us. I'm an independent freighter captain, carrying legitimately contracted cargo."

"Then what about the tracker and the gun?"

"I like to stay competitive. Val! Move it!"

"Aligned."

"Fire!"

The forward shields of the second cruiser went the way of the first.

"Oh yes, I'm good," Val muttered.

"All right!" Erik's whoop echoed around the control room, and he flung a grimy fist into the air. "Now let's take the T-ray and finish them off."

"Great idea, kid, but we just used the last charge."

Val rolled hard to starboard and the boy grabbed for support.

"You only carry two charges?" he yelped incredulously.

"Have you any idea how much one of those things costs...?" Kelly began, but broke off as a near miss lit up the room. "Watch what you're doing!" she ordered her ship. "We're not out here on a Company picnic, you know. How much longer until you've got them lined up?"

"Ready now."

"Then why are we hanging around?"

The two humans slammed up into their harnesses as Val dropped straight down out of the battlefield. The cruiser commanders had barely enough time to stare at each other across empty space before the twin blasts, meant for their quarry, tore their ships apart.

"Someday," Kelly mused, watching the twin explosions, "the empire will realize that space has three dimensions...and then what'll I do?"

Erik's eyes widened and his jaw dropped. "Wow! Teach me to do that!"

"You think I'm crazy?" Kelly sat back and swung her feet up. "First thing I know, you'd use it on me."

"No, I wouldn't." He reached over and grabbed her arm. "Honest."

Kelly plucked his hand free, grasping it between thumb and forefinger as though it was a particularly noxious growth. "I don't like to be touched," she said sternly and dropped it back in his lap.

The boy's lower lip went out, and he rocked back and forth in the copilot's couch. "You gonna take me to my father now?" he asked at last.

"Well, I've got a cargo to get rid of." She ran a hand through her hair and studied the boy, her brown eyes thoughtful. Traditionally, stowaways were spaced. Traditionally, stowaways were not snot-nosed kids. Traditionally, snot-nosed kids were not under attack by the most powerful man in the sector. Kelly's lip curled. And she'd be fried if she let the Atabeg have him, not after that malignant tumor ordered her destroyed without even checking to see if she could be bought. "You stay with me for now," she said at last. "I'll figure out what to do with you later."

Erik considered it and grinned. "Great, you can teach me to be a smuggler."

Kelly closed her eyes and counted to ten. What had she done? *The whole point is to keep him alive,* she reminded herself, turning to the controls. "Back to Susumu space, Val. Previously plotted course." The stars streaked and ran. "We've got business on Elite."

"Elite?" repeated the Atabeg. "What makes you think anyone would go to that wretched scum hole?"

"We have reason to believe that the woman is smuggling Susumu crystals, Most Exalted. Elite is at present the only place she can possibly dispose of them."

"Who commands our garrison on Elite?"

"Company Commander Gripe, Most Exalted."

"Inform him of what's going on. He will hold both the woman and my nephew until I arrive." The Atabeg stood, an unpleasant smile of anticipation creasing his face. "We leave immediately."

The alley was narrow and dirty. Black stone buildings blocked out most of the light. The gloom seethed with sentient races of every description—buying, selling, being sold.

Erik, muffled in an old cloak of Kelly's, stared, eyes wide. A cuff on the side of his head caused him to stumble and he glared up at his companion.

"Don't stare," Kelly said shortly. "It's rude."

"I can stare if I want to," declared the Heir of Infinity, running his nose over his sleeve. "What're you going to do about it?"

"Nothing. But whoever you're staring at will likely rip your head off."

"Really?" Erik looked around with new interest. "I wish I had my blaster."

Kelly forged ahead. "I wish I'd left you with Val."

Erik's short legs and low line of sight made progress slow and the time spent standing still, waiting for him to catch up, made Kelly very nervous. Used to being alone, she didn't like crowds at the best of times. In this neighborhood, in this crowd, she much preferred to present a moving target. She was almost relieved to turn and come eye to eye to eye with something large and hairy and disinclined to let them pass.

"*Gur lampic signa bac,*" it crooned, wrapping an anonymous appendage around her waist.

Kelly smiled, locked her hands together, and clubbed the being where its head met what served it for shoulders. With a surprised "*Crik,*" it collapsed to the ground.

"Wow," breathed Erik, stepping over the body. "What did it say?"

"How should I know? Now stay close, we're here."

Here was a rusty metal door, guarded by something that either had been human once but wasn't now or was trying to be human but hadn't made it yet.

Kelly dropped two units of the local currency into what, given its relative position, had to be a hand. "Gaby expecting me?"

The being nodded, more or less, and moved away from the door.

Kelly placed her palm flat against the metal and set her teeth as current trickled down her arm. If the grid read her as an enemy, she'd die where she stood. After two or three seconds— that took hours to pass—the door slid open. With a backward glance at Erik, she started up the narrow stairs. "Well, come on. And what did I tell you about staring?"

The room at the top of the stairs had little connection with the squalor of the street below. It was light, spacious, exotically furnished, and, at the moment, rather crowded.

Kelly bounded through the door and slid to an abrupt halt.

Erik pushed past her. "Hey, Kelly, what's…"

Company Commander Gripe rose to his feet and inclined his head in greeting. "Your Magnificence. We meet again, Captain Chase."

"You know this guy?" Erik's head swiveled between Kelly and the slightly portly officer in the Atabeg's colors.

"We've met." If Gripe was coolly polite, Kelly was ice. "I spent some time with the satrap a couple of years ago." She scanned the room; a well-armed Immortal stood between her and each of the room's exits.

"It's only company commander, now," Gripe corrected gently. "And I worked my way back up to that. My superiors were most displeased when I let you get away."

"I broke a chair over your head," Kelly pointed out as an Immortal relieved her of her sidearm. "You were hardly aiding and abetting."

Gripe smiled, most insincerely, and moved so close his weapon tip grazed Kelly's belt. "Oh, I agree with you, Captain. It was entirely your fault." He placed his free hand on Erik's shoulder. "And now, young sir…"

Erik swung his head and sank his teeth into the older man's hand.

Gripe shrieked.

Kelly made a grab for his gun.

She regained consciousness with her head on something soft and several loud explosions going on inside her skull. "Medic," she muttered and instantly regretted it as the noise bounced back and forth, back and forth, between her ears. Slowly, very slowly, she opened her eyes. Through dancing patterns of light, she saw Erik bending over her, then realized her head rested on his lap. Her jerk away was involuntary and instantly regretted.

"Are you alright, Kelly?" He sounded worried.

She sat up carefully. "No," she decided as the room spun. "I'm not all right. I'm not even a little bit right." She gingerly touched the swelling lump on the back of her head. "Where are we?"

"In a storage vault, I think."

The ceiling of the small, square room glowed softly. The walls were identical, blank, and featureless, with no sign of a door.

Kelly pulled herself to her feet. The screaming pain dulled to a persistent throb, which was an improvement. Unfortunately, each throb was accompanied by a wave of nausea, which wasn't. "Vault's a good guess," she agreed slowly. "This looks like one of Gaby's walk-in safes. I wonder why Gripe didn't take us back to the Citadel?"

Erik turned from his own scan of the vault and studied her face. "Why are you smiling?" he asked at last.

"Because Gripe's made a very serious mistake here, kid." She took a deep breath, lifted her arms, and began to run her fingers along the joints between walls and ceiling. "Gaby built these vaults, and Gaby builds nothing without a way out. He's shown me more exits out of this building than...aha!"

A small section of the wall flipped down, exposing a tiny circuit board and a tangle of colored wire.

"Wow, just like when you escaped from that detention cell on Shalamar," Erik said with awe. "Val says you can get out of anywhere."

"Val exaggerates."

"Maybe." Erik shrugged. "You don't seem too worried about your friend."

"Gaby's probably two systems away by now, selling somebody's mother for a tidy profit. This isn't the first time he's had Immortals drop in. Nothing takes Gaby by surprise."

"You weren't surprised either."

Kelly snorted. "And your grandmother thought you could take care of yourself...." She ran a hand through her hair and winced as it tugged on the lump. "You never let the enemy know you're surprised, kid. You lose the initiative."

Erik rolled his eyes and slapped the wall. "Right. Some initiative."

The panel he'd hit slid aside, the cover of the door-release snicked shut, and Company Commander Gripe swaggered into the vault. Two of his men followed. One carried a long, slender, black wand.

Kelly fought down another rush of nausea that had nothing to do with the lump on her head and everything to do with that long, slender, black wand. She shoved Erik behind her.

"I see you remember what this is," Gripe said dryly. "And a very touching gesture on your part, Captain Chase."

Kelly forced her eyes away from the deadly little machine. "Yeah. Well, I've grown fond of him in a masochistic sort of way."

"A pity to part you, then." Gripe turned to the larger of the Immortals. "Escort the Heir to Infinity to the office where he can await the Atabeg, may he live forever, in comfort."

"I'm staying with Kelly," Erik glowered.

"As I said, Your Magnificence, a pity."

The larger Immortal carried Erik, kicking and screaming, from the room. As the door hissed shut, the Immortal appeared to be getting the worse part of the deal.

"Actually, I hope persuasion will be unnecessary." Gripe thrust his hand forward. "Just tell me where I can find the rest of these." On his palm lay a red crystal that pulsed with light. As it picked up more heat from Gripe's hand, it grew brighter until it looked about to burst into flame.

Kelly reached into her belt pouch. Empty.

"Yes, it's yours," agreed Gripe. "Until I found this, I wondered why you dared to return to this section of space, considering what happened the last time." He rubbed the crystal softly with his thumb. It flared. "A Susumu crystal, a perfect lattice. Too perfect for a ship's drive where only mass amplification is necessary. This is a precision amplifier. For energy weapons. Carrying even a dozen of these would make the risk worthwhile."

"I was carrying circuit boards for the gravity field of Vagna. They had no return contract. That's not cost efficient, so I dropped in on Gaby to pick up a cargo. I'm licensed to carry arms. The rock is a spare." Kelly bit off the words, her tone one she kept for minor customs officials and other bureaucratic time-wasters.

"I don't believe you." Gripe flipped the now uncomfortably hot crystal into his own pouch. "I want the rest of the rocks, and I haven't the time to take your ship apart piece by piece…"

"…before the Atabeg arrives." Kelly finished his sentence and managed a grin. So that was why he hadn't taken them to the Citadel; official interrogations were recorded. "Setting up a retirement fund?"

Gripe's smile showed teeth right back to the molars. "I suggest you talk."

Kelly made a rude suggestion in return.

The company commander sighed. "Have it your way, then."

The black wand hummed, a thin beam of energy came from one end, and Kelly screamed.

When Kelly regained consciousness for the second time that day, she was alone in the vault. She struggled to her hands and knees, paused, and spewed greenish yellow bile all over the floor. Eyes watering and teeth clenched against continuous spasms of painful retching, she dragged herself up onto her feet, swayed, and nearly fell.

She concentrated on breathing for a moment. And then another moment. When she finally seemed able to tell up from down, she forced her arms above her head and pushed her fingers along the ceiling seam until they snagged on the hidden catch. When the cover flipped open, she clutched at a wire, took a step backward, and collapsed. The wire pulled free. The door panel slid open. She stared up at it in surprise. "This must be my lucky day."

She spat to clear her mouth of blood and acid, then lurched to freedom.

The heavy footsteps of the Immortals indicated areas to avoid and she staggered unopposed downward and deeper into the building, heading for one of Gaby's numerous back doors. In a dead-end corridor, she fell to her knees before a lurid mosaic and began pushing at the bottom row of tiles. It took her three tries to get the sequence right, but finally a section of the floor behind her lifted up on silent hinges.

Gagging, she swung her legs into the hole. "It would have to lead into the sewers." She slid over the edge and disappeared. The floor section snapped back into place.

Moments later it lifted again and Kelly heaved herself up into the hall.

"Damn that kid anyway."

"We'll reach Elite at 2100 hours, Most Exalted. Have you any orders?"

"I want that boy," the Atabeg growled without looking up from the sharpening of an antique skinning knife. "I want him brought to this ship where I will personally see that the job of removing him is not botched again."

The aide inclined his head in understanding and began to back from the room. At the door, he paused and dropped to his knees. "Most Exalted, if one who is nothing may presume, have you considered that the Shahinshah, your brother, may make an attempt on the life of your son?"

"Of course, I've considered it, you idiot!" the Atabeg snapped. "Even now, my son and a trusted pilot speed out of my brother's reach." He tested the point of the knife against his thumb and smiled at the burgundy bead. "My son is safe, but his son is mine."

Gripe had appropriated Gaby's office for his own and looked as though he belonged behind the satiny rinzewood desk that dominated the room. Erik, on the other hand, appeared sadly out of place amid the lush wall hangings and erotic sculptures.

"If you hurt me," Erik sneered, turning from a thoroughly educational study of the room's artwork, "Kelly'll skin you for a rug."

Gripe smiled almost fondly at the boy. "Don't be ridiculous, Your Magnificence."

Erik bridled at his tone. "Kelly's the bravest, strongest, best pilot in the galaxy, and any minute now she'll break in here and blast you in zillions of little pieces!"

Rising, Gripe leaned over the desk and said with bored precision, "Your Kelly is the end product of a society founded by hucksters and con men. She's no more than a common merchant, a scruffy trader, a peddler of lies. You'd best forget about her help, boy."

"Oh yeah? Kelly and Val and me could take out your whole fleet!"

"Val?" Gripe's eyes narrowed.

"Yeah, Val. She's Kelly's ship and she's almost as good as Kelly and..."

"Val is the ship?"

"That's what I just said. Stop interrupting me!"

"My apologies, Your Magnificence." Gripe smiled and came around the desk. If Val was the woman's ship, it explained a great deal of the nonsense she'd babbled when she broke. He opened his mouth to call for the guards, but never got the chance as the chair he'd just vacated crashed down across the back of his head.

"Kelly!" Erik dove around the desk and flung himself on her. He flung himself off her almost as fast. "You smell terrible."

"Yeah, well, it's been a trying sort of day." After retrieving her own weapon from the desk, she rolled Gripe over and pulled his sidearm free. "Here, brat, catch. Let's see if you shoot as straight at other people as you shoot at me."

Erik deftly fielded the gun out of the air, flicked off the safety, and checked the charge. He slipped his finger over the trigger guard in a businesslike manner and looked curiously at his rescuer. "Now what?"

"Now, we leave." She lifted a tapestry away from the wall. "Come on."

"Oh, wow! A secret passageway!" Erik sighed with satisfaction. "You smugglers know about the neatest stuff."

"I'm getting tired of telling you this, kid, I am not a smuggler." Kelly leaned down and retrieved her crystal from Gripe's belt pouch. Rubbing it to a searing radiance, she grinned. "At least not usually."

* * *

"And so I said to her, 'If you went to all this trouble to find me, the least I can do is…' Say, Leo, are you listening to me?"

The pilot rolled his eyes and made a minute adjustment in the ship's gravitational field. "Yeah, Exalted One, I'm listening."

"Good." The Atabeg's son settled deeper into his couch. "So I said, 'The least I can do is show my appreciation,' and she said…Leo, what are you doing with that gun?"

"Nothing personal, Exalted One," Leo told him, thumbing off the safety, "but I'm going to kill you."

"But father pays you to protect me," Darvish protested.

Leo smiled. "Someone topped his price." His finger tightened as Darvish dove for him. The shot went wild, destroying the communications board. Darvish's knee came down on the Susumu controls and the small ship leapt forward out of real space. The violent jerk flung the older man into his intended victim's arms and then flung them both to the floor.

In the cramped quarters of the control room, the fight ended quickly.

Darvish stood, tossed the gun onto an acceleration couch, and studied the ship's controls. The communications board was a smoking ruin; he couldn't call for help.

"Too many buttons," he sighed and pushed one he vaguely remembered as being important.

The Susumu drive shut down, and Darvish looked out at a pattern of stars he couldn't remember ever seeing before.

"Okay, Leo," he muttered, "what am I supposed to do now?"

Leo, being dead, didn't answer.

Kelly wormed her way back from the edge of the docking pit and sat up in the shelter of the door alcove. "Those irradiated morons scratched the enamel trying to break open the hatch," she growled.

Erik peered over the edge, then up at Kelly. "Don't you think we should worry more about getting past two full squads of my uncle's men?" he asked.

"That's my livelihood we're talking about, kid. No one wants to hire a ship that looks like a piece of junk." She ran her hand through her hair and her brow furrowed. "Oh yeah, speaking of business." With a minimum of contact—a white-knuckled grip on his shoulders and a quick release—she turned the boy to face her and looked him in the eye. "Do you know what a contract is?"

He nodded. "It's where you promise to do something if the other person does something for you."

"Basically," Kelly agreed. "But where I come from it's more. Contracts are about the only law we have in Company space and no one ever, ever, breaks one." She searched his eyes, making sure he understood. "You and I, we need to make a contract."

"I don't have anything to promise."

"Not now you don't, but you will. Someday, you'll be Shahinshah." Shahinshah of a decaying empire, perhaps, but over five hundred stars remained under the Imperial flag and Kelly liked doing business in the empire; it was a system absurdly easy to take advantage of. "I'll take you home and you'll pay me when you're Shahinshah. Deal?"

He thought about it. "But I don't want to go home. I want to stay with you and be a smuggler."

Kelly gritted her teeth and stopped herself from throttling in the boy. "You can't," she said shortly.

His lower lip went out. "I can do what I want. I'm the Heir to Infinity."

"But if you're the Heir to Infinity, then you have to go home and be Shahinshah."

"Why?"

"Because that's what the Heir to Infinity does. And if you're not the Heir, then you can't do what you want and you can't stay with me but you still have to go home." Taking a deep breath, she realized that the logic appropriate for an eight-year-old rather remarkably resembled the logic appropriate for customs agents.

His eyes narrowed as he considers it. "Oh, all right," he said at last. "Deal."

She held out her hand. "Touch your palm to mine." When he did, she breathed a sigh of relief. If anyone ever found out she'd gone back for the kid before they had a contract, she'd never hear the end of it. Smiling suddenly, she plucked Gripe's gun from his hand. "Now, go down there and turn yourself in."

"What!"

"They won't shoot—your uncle seems to want you alive—but they will group around you. That'll let Val know we're here and give her a clear shot a both squads at once. I'll finish off any she misses."

"What if they don't recognize me?"

"So it's a good idea, not a great one." She scrambled out of his way and swept a gracious hand toward the stairs. "Don't forget to duck."

At the top of the stairs, Erik paused and looked down into the docking pit. The twenty men in the black and blue of the Atabeg's livery were very large and very well armed. He glanced back at Kelly who gave him a thumbs-up. "No one ever, ever, breaks a contract," he reminded himself, and started his descent.

He'd left the stairs and swaggered out onto the cracked bedrock floor of the pit before anyone noticed him. Suddenly, all weapons pointed in his direction.

"Hi, guys," he chirped brightly, raising his hands above his head. "Remember me?"

"It's the Heir," breathed an Immortal and received a backhanded rebuke from his squad leader.

"It's the enemy of the Atabeg, may he live forever," corrected the leader. "Take him."

So intent were they on the boy, not one of the Immortals noticed the freighter's externals follow them as they ran. They didn't notice but Erik did. When the covers snapped off the gun ports, he hit the dirt. Nineteen of the twenty had no time to wonder why as energy beams burned them where they stood.

Missed me! thought the twentieth, diving for cover. A shot from the edge of the pit corrected him and finished the fight.

"Holy suns." Erik stood and looked around. "It worked!"

"Of course, it worked," Kelly snorted as she swerved around a pile of char. With a sharp, impatient toss of her head, she propelled him toward the ship. "But whatever your uncle pays these guys, it isn't enough."

The Atabeg stepped over the trembling and abased body of Company Commander Gripe. "Demote him," he said coldly.

His aide hurried to catch up. "Demote him to what, Most Exalted?"

"Compost."

"At once, Most Exalted."

"And when you've done that," the Atabeg's voice was inhumanly calm, "you find me that woman and the boy."

The smoke from a dozen sticks of incense rolled languidly through the air of the Shahinshah's private quarters. The Defender of Infinity lay stretched out on a massage table, receiving the loving ministrations of three of his wives while his vizier paced the length of the room and tried not to sneeze.

"...our agent has not reported in so I can only conclude he failed. As we still have no idea who harbors your son, may His Magnificence never dim; getting to your nephew may be his only hope. I suggest we put a tracer in space at the point where we received the last broadcast from our agent and follow the energy residue of his ship. That should lead us straight to your nephew and we can proceed with eliminating him from there."

He paused and pinched his nose, his face purpling with the suppressed explosion of air. It was a capital offense to sneeze in the presence of the Beloved of the Multitudes.

"Do I have your approval, Oh Greatest of Kings Who Stops the Planets in Their Turning?"

The Shahinshah raised a pudgy hand, heavily encrusted with rings, and waved it aimlessly in the vizier's general direction. "Do what you wish, Sakar," he sighed. "Whatever happens, it won't be the first son I've lost. Perhaps I shall try to get another this evening."

Two of his wives giggled. The third, safely out of sight, rolled her eyes.

Kelly had just brought the Valkyrie back into real space when Erik crashed into the control room.

"Val says you once broke the bank at Cortellno three nights in a row!"

Kelly sighed. "Val makes it sound more interesting than it was."

"My grandmother has played there and she says that Cortellno can't be broken." Erik threw himself into the other couch, eyebrows red exclamation points. "You must be some kind of a cardsharp!"

"Not me, kid." Her lips twisted into a strange sort of a smile. "My brother's the cardsharp in the family; I'm strictly amateur. Now, sit still. We're coming up on a ship."

Against a backdrop of stars, and not many of them, the other ship showed as a tiny silver triangle.

"Where are we?"

"It's sort of a trading center for ships out of Company space," Kelly explained. "Sometimes we need to meet away from...from..."

"Away from the law," Val finished dryly.

"Smugglers," Erik declared with evident satisfaction.

"Erik, how many times do I have to tell you..."

"You're not a smuggler." The boy winked broadly. "I know, I know." He snuggled back into his couch, grinning like an idiot. "Hadn't you better check out that ship?"

As Val approached, the ship grew from a speck to a small vessel hanging motionless in vacuum. "That's just a private yacht," Val said, moving closer still. "Made over for deep space."

"And that's the Atabeg's crest on her bow," Kelly added, lips in a grim line. "Bring us alongside, Val. Let's take a closer look."

"Do you think it's a trap?" Erik asked, sounding as though he rather hoped it was.

Kelly snorted. "If it is, it isn't much of one. Yachts that size carry weapons or Susumu drive—they haven't room for both."

"Sensors read one life form, and all systems but drive and communications operative, Boss."

"You know, it looks like..." Erik stopped and shook his head. "Nah, it couldn't be. Not out here."

"Couldn't be what?"

"Well, my cousin Darvish used to visit Grandmother a couple of times a year, and that looks like his yacht."

"Darvish? The Atabeg's son? The reason people keep shooting at us?"

Erik nodded.

"I think," said Kelly, rising and heading out of the control room, "I'd better go investigate this one life form."

"No need."

Val's voice stopped her.

"It seems the life form is coming to investigate us."

The air lock in the yacht opened and a suited figure jetted across the narrow void between the two ships.

Kelly glanced at Erik, who shook his head.

"How can I tell in that suit?" he asked.

She studied the screen for a moment. "Let him in when he gets here, Val," she instructed finally. "But don't open the inner door until you've checked him for weapons. His Magnificence here can ID him when he comes through."

By the time they reached the Valkyrie's air lock, the outer door had shut and the pressure was cycling up. A few moments later, the light went green.

"No weapons, Boss. I'm opening the door."

"Why does Val have extensionals in the air lock?" Erik wanted to know.

"It helps us get the jump on creditors and insurance salesmen," Kelly explained as the door slid open. She pushed the boy out of the direct line of fire.

The suited figure stepped out of the lock and removed his helmet. Kelly sucked in air. She hadn't seen a man that attractive since...well, not for a long time.

Darvish smiled a dazzling and vacant smile. "Hello, Ahrikhartoum." He tossed blue-black hair out of violet eyes. "What are you doing on my father's rescue ship?"

Erik sighed.

"I keep telling him I don't want to be Shahinshah," Darvish protested, "but he never listens."

Kelly rubbed at her forehead. She was getting a headache. "Let's try this another way," she sighed. "If you don't want to be Shahinshah, what do you want to be?"

"A dilettante," Darvish replied promptly.

"A what?"

"A dilettante. You know, a…"

The headache arrived. "I know what a dilettante is. It's not usually considered a career move. Why do you want to be a dilettante?"

Once again, Darvish bestowed on them the light of his smile. "Because it's what I'm good at."

Kelly indulged in a brief moment of sympathy for the Atabeg. "I can understand why your father has trouble with this."

"When you take me back to him, you can help me explain."

"I'm not taking you anywhere."

Violet eyes looked puzzled. "But you have to. I'm Exalted."

"Forget it, Darvish," Erik broke in. "I'm more Exalted than you and she's taking me home."

"I may space both of you and let you walk," Kelly snarled and stomped out of the lounge. "Val, get us out of here and then get me a drink. Preferably something illegal."

Darvish turned to his young cousin. "Where are we going?"

Erik looked smug. "Beats me; but I've got a contract with her and you don't."

"Maybe not…." Darvish stood, made a minute adjustment in the tight tunic that covered his broad shoulders and started toward the control room.

"Where are you going?" Erik asked suspiciously.

"To talk to the captain. I want to go home and women are putty in my hands."

"Forget it, Least Exalted," the boy scoffed. "You're more likely to be broken bones in hers."

Darvish merely grinned and continued on his way.

Erik shrugged at his departing back. "So finish telling me about how you and Kelly single-handedly wiped out Hamish O'Shawnessy and his pirates," he prompted Val.

Val didn't need much prompting. "Well, old Hamish had four full sectors terrified of him. Kelly and I felt that wasn't right. The murdering hijacker had tied up trade, making it impossible for an honest businessman to turn a profit. You paid his prices or you paid with your life. Now Kelly refused..." Val slid into the story, Erik squirmed into a more comfortable position, and neither paid any attention to the sound of a large body slamming into a bulkhead with some force.

"Most Exalted." The aide stepped into the room and fell to his knees. "We've calculated the probable course of that freighter if it hopes to reach the Imperial Seat with your nephew."

The Atabeg's eyes lit up. "How accurate is the projection?"

The aide consulted the hardcopy in his hand. "Slightly better than 96%, Most Exalted."

"Good." The Atabeg rubbed his hands together and cracked his knuckles. "Have my cruiser prepared and ready six dreadnoughts for full battle alert."

"Six dreadnoughts? But, Most Exalted, for one small freighter?"

The look on the Atabeg's face caused the aide to reconsider his protest, swallow nervously, and begin backing from the room.

"At once, Most Exalted. Six dreadnoughts at full battle alert."

"Vizier, sir, we've found the yacht."

Sakar, not trusting any hand but his own to eliminate this threat to the throne—and his personal power—leaned toward the screen. He stared at the yacht drifting aimlessly in space. "It looks dead," he said at last.

"Sensors indicate that all systems but drive and communications are operative, sir. We're sending a man over to check it out."

On the screen, a tiny figure jetted over to the yacht and in through the open hatch. Moments later, he emerged, a body tucked under his arm.

Sakar hurried to the air lock. Even at that distance, the body had not looked like that of the Shahinshah's nephew. He arrived just as the soldier cycled through and dumped the body on the deck.

The assassin. With a hole in his chest that the vizier could stick both hands into.

"I found him tangled in the control-chair webbing, sir," the soldier explained, removing his helmet.

Sakar swore.

"Vizier, sir!" The pilot's shout blasted out of the intercom. "The tracers picked up another trail! A very recent one!"

"Follow it," Sakar ordered. "It must belong to the ship that rescued the traitorous whelp. When we catch it, destroy it."

"I'm sorry, Kelly," Erik spread his hands helplessly, "but no one ever taught me the safe access codes. I guess they thought I'd never need them. Couldn't we just blast our way in?"

"And get blasted ourselves by your father's defense squadrons?"

"Probably wouldn't," Erik offered philosophically, studying his reflection in the polished metal of the webbing buckle. "They don't shoot very straight."

"We're a pretty big target," Val interjected sharply.

"I thought you were keeping Darvish busy?"

"I quit. I'm telling you, Boss, the man's a menace. If he pushes one more button back there, I'm going to give him a couple of thousand volts to remember me by."

"You make a mess, you clean it up." Kelly turned back to Erik, who'd begun to giggle. "Would the commander of your father's fleet recognize your voice?"

"If I got a chance to say something before they got in a lucky hit."

"Who got a lucky hit?" Darvish wanted to know, swaggering in. He noticed both couches were occupied. "Out of the chair, junior."

"Go space yourself, neutron brain," Erik advised, staying put. "I was here first."

"Move it!"

"Make me!"

"Share it," Kelly snapped. "We're coming up on the Shahinshah's home sector and I want both of you in here where I can keep an eye on you."

"We have them on sensors now, Most Exalted. They've just returned to real space and will be in range in twelve minutes."

"Wonderful!" The Atabeg leapt to his feet, almost knocking over the aide in his rush to the control room. "Get those dreadnoughts to battle stations. We've got them this time!"

"Vizier, sir, the ship has just come onto our sensors. Computer identifies it as a K-class freighter registered to one Kelly Chase, an independent from Company space."

"Excellent, excellent. And the reinforcements I sent for?"

"They're approaching the ship from the other side, sir. Six dreadnoughts, heavy class."

"Boss, rear sensors indicate a ship approaching."

Kelly scowled as the board lit up. "Type?"

"Cruiser, L-class. And there's another coming in from the front." Val sounded worried.

"Two L-class cruisers are no trouble," Kelly snorted, glancing over at her passengers who'd somehow both managed to get strapped into the copilot's couch.

"Maybe not, but twelve dreadnoughts are."

"What!"

"We seem to be surrounded."

"Seem to be, nothing! We *are* surrounded." A sweep of her hand threw all ship to ship frequencies open. "Erik, tell them who you are."

Freckles standing out like tiny copper beacons, Erik took a deep breath and told them.

* * *

"I don't know what good he thinks that will do him," grunted the Atabeg. "Line up the target."

"It's a trick," snorted Sakar. "The Shahinshah's son is nowhere near this sector. Line up the target."

"Kelly! Half those ships carry the Atabeg's crest!" Erik cried.
"What is this?" Kelly demanded. "Are we the new imperial sport or something?"
Darvish leaned toward the console. "Father," he called. "Father, it's me."

"I don't know what good he thinks that will do him," Sakar grunted. "Prepare to fire."

"It's a trick," snorted the Atabeg. "My son is nowhere near this sector. Prepare to fire."

"Kelly, they're preparing to fire. Do something!"
"Don't rush me, I'm thinking!"
That reassured Erik but it didn't do much for Val.
"What we need now," said the ship calmly, "is a miracle."

"Most Exalted, we've picked up six other dreadnoughts!"
"What?" The Atabeg whirled to face the screen. "My brother! Damn his interference! Hold your fire!"

"Vizier, we've picked up six other dreadnoughts!"
"What?" Sakar whirled to face the screen. "The Atabeg! What's he doing out here? Hold your fire!"

For a moment, the twelve dreadnoughts and two cruisers hung in space. When it became apparent to their commanders that neither intended to provoke a civil war by firing the first shot at the other, they turned their attention again to the freighter.
But by then, the freighter was gone.

"Kelly?"

"Yeah, kid?"

"Was that a miracle?"

After flying a course guaranteed to send a human pilot into strong hysterics, Val swung into orbit around a gas giant with nine moons.

"Orbit?" Darvish asked incredulously. "Shouldn't we run for our lives?"

"Run where?" Val demanded. "I can't outrun, outshoot, or even evade hardware that size for long."

Kelly sighed and ran a hand through her hair. "Then we'll have to out-think them."

"That leaves you, me, and Val," Erik said with a disdainful glance at his cousin. "Darvish isn't very strong in the think department." He tapped a finger against his forehead. "Man's got a black hole for brains."

"I can think circles around you!"

"You wouldn't know a circle if you tripped over one," Erik sneered. "I've seen dwarf stars less dense."

"Listen runt…"

"Runt?" Erik fought with the webbing that kept him from getting his hands on his cousin. "I don't have to take that from a dork who had his teeth capped."

Darvish's face flared red. "That does it!" His position was less confining than Erik's. Bronze fingers wrapped around the boy's throat.

"Val!"

"You got it, Boss." Cables wrapped around the combatants, trapping their arms at their sides.

Kelly leaned back in her chair and regarded the cousins coldly. "I've had just about as much as I'm going to take from both of you," she told them, her voice ice. "From now on, if anyone does any hitting around here, it's going to be me."

To her surprise, Erik's face broke into a broad smile as he bounced as high as possible within the confines of the cables. "That's it!" he cheered. "We'll go to Grandmother. She's the only person my father's ever listened to."

"Mine too," Darvish added, enthusiastically. "She'll get us out of this."

"Grandmother's the greatest!" Erik's eyes glowed. "She can do anything."

Blonde brows rose. Realizing that Erik thought more of his grandmother than he did of her, Kelly felt a completely irrational stab of jealousy. She waved a hand and Val released her captives. "What brought this on?"

"Grandmother always says…" Darvish began.

"…that if anyone does any hitting, it's going to be her." As Erik finished, they smiled at each other, for once in complete accord.

Kelly sighed. "I think I like her already. Do either of you know her co-ordinates?"

"I always had a pilot," Darvish admitted. "But I'd recognize the planet if I saw it."

"The Okmar IV system," Erik said, with a disgusted look at his relative and a careful move out of his reach. "Sixth planet. It's on the charts as uninhabitable 'cause Grandmother wants to be left alone. She fields her own army and everything."

"You get that, Val?"

"Plotted."

"Good. As soon as these two have strapped themselves in…" She paused for effect. "…in the lounge, we'll leave orbit."

Darvish—who'd learned that when the captain said leave, she meant it—sidled out of the control room.

Erik leaned against Kelly's couch and stared up at her with big, adoring eyes. "Can't I stay, Kelly?" he pleaded. "I could help."

Kelly snickered.

Erik sighed. He hadn't expected the helpless little kid act would work but it was worth a try. He straightened. "I'd rather be where the action is," he pouted.

"I'd rather you keep an eye on Darvish," Kelly told him dryly. "I don't trust Val not to space him."

"Wish she would," Erik muttered as he scuffed out of the control room.

* * *

In spite of Val's best efforts, her scanners picked up the tracer and its accompanying imperial dreadnought while the fugitives were still a fair distance from Okmar IV.

"I can't lose it," the ship said at last. "It's on me too tight."

"Then outrun it," Kelly suggested.

"I'm not sure I can."

"You have to."

"Another dreadnought just reached the edge of my sensor range."

"The Atabeg?"

"Probably. They appear to be ignoring each other."

"Pity. Too bad they haven't the decency to blow each other up."

For over an hour the three ships moved toward Okmar IV, the distance between them steadily closing.

"It's no use," Val admitted. "By my calculations, we'll still be an hour out when they catch up. I'm just not fast enough. Looks like we've had it."

"Not yet." Kelly's jaw set. "Get our problem children into the control room and seal off the rest of the ship. Keep the life support going up here, but feed everything else into the Susumu drive."

"Everything?"

"Everything. Don't even think too hard. Just pick up enough extra energy to buy us that hour."

"What about the shields?"

"The shields go first; they drain more than the other systems combined."

"And if they catch up to us?"

"If they catch up to us," Kelly said, looking down at the screen where the enemy showed as angry red blips, "the shields would only prolong the inevitable."

Erik and Darvish jostled their way into the control room. The door sealed shut behind them.

"What's up?" Erik asked shooting a curious glance back at the door.

"Maybe us. Both of you sit down and shut up."

"In my opinion," Darvish began.

"I said both of you!"

Exchanging puzzled glances, the cousins contorted themselves into the copilot's couch.

"We're pulling away, Boss. We can't lose them but they can't catch us unless they divert power from their shields."

Kelly looked considerably more cheerful. "No chance of that."

"Why not?" Darvish asked, a frown creasing his perfect brow.

"Because, ditz head," Erik told him, trying to put his feet up in imitation of Kelly and missing the console by a good half meter, "if they lower their shields, there'll be nothing to protect them from each other."

Darvish spent a moment figuring out who they were. "Oh," he said at last.

Time passed. The dreadnoughts gained marginally but they were still out of firing range when Val dropped back to real space and swung into orbit around the sixth planet of Okmar IV.

"This is it, Boss. Nothing appears to be waiting for us."

"Nice change," Kelly commented, straightening and studying the readouts. "Hail the planet on a tight beam. Identify us and our passengers and sweep for a reply."

"Don't expect a reply from Grandmother."

Kelly turned to stare at Darvish.

"Grandmother only answers when she feels like it," he explained. "And that isn't often."

"Swell," Kelly sighed. "If we get down in one piece, she's on our side?"

"That's about it," Erik agreed.

"Atmosphere in seven minutes, Boss. No reply to our identification, but a landing beacon just came on." Val sounded almost jubilant. "Looks like we're in the clear."

Kelly's expression suggested she doubted it, but she remained silent. Briefly, she regretted not spacing Erik back on Rayanton when she had the chance.

As the Valkyrie slid into the atmosphere, the pursuing dreadnoughts came into firing range. Both ships let fly a futile barrage of shots then, still warily apart, followed the freighter down.

"They're still after us, Boss. I'm raising the speed and shortening the angle of descent. It's going to get a little warm in here."

"It's going to get a lot warmer if they catch up," Kelly pointed out. "Just get us down in one piece."

The dreadnought's pilots were good but only human and their margin of error was comparatively large. Without the ability to split seconds into infinitely smaller units and navigate accordingly, they could only watch as their prey sped down toward the planet while they followed at a much more sedate pace.

"It's been months since I visited," Darvish protested when Kelly tried to find out how to get to his grandmother's from the landing site. "Jungles change a lot in months."

"Jungles?" Kelly repeated weakly.

"Jungles," Erik confirmed. "And swamps."

"Swamps?"

"Yeah, but we didn't usually go out in them because of the shkiys."

"Shkiys?"

"Large slugs," Erik explained.

"With large teeth," Darvish added.

"And large appetites," Erik finished. "Grandmother says they're better than Immortals for getting rid of unwanted visitors."

"Lovely," said Kelly as the braking jets screamed. "I take it the air is breathable?"

"Breathable," Val told her. "But it's raining."

"That should be the least of our worries."

It wasn't.

The rain fell, not in drops, but in solid sheets of water.

They were wet before they stepped out of the airlock.

Ten meters away, they couldn't see the ship.

Twenty meters away, Darvish proved all those lovely muscles rippling under his tunic were functional when he pulled Kelly out of a sinkhole.

Forty meters away, Kelly and Erik returned the favor.

"Kelly," Val boomed from the remote on Kelly's wrist. "Sensors pick up a large cluster of life forms two and a half kilometers ahead. Head about ten degrees to your right."

"Two and a half kilometers?" Kelly pushed a wet strand of hair back off her face. "Val, you've got to be kidding."

"I'm not. And you'd better get moving, Boss. Those dreadnoughts just landed shuttles."

"The only bright spot in this mess is that they'll have as much trouble as we are."

"Both ship's parties have disembarked with swamp gear," Val informed them, "and are heavily armed."

"And monitoring our position from the remote, not doubt," Kelly muttered. "Sit tight, Val. I'm switching you off."

The three slogged on. For about another ten meters. Then Kelly hit another sinkhole.

"I don't believe this is happening," she sighed as the sludge rose up her legs. "Darvish, throw me your belt."

He obliged.

Kelly sighed again. "Keep hold of one end."

"Oh." He grabbed the flailing end and started to pull. The mud rose to Kelly's waist. "You're stuck tighter this time."

"Then pull harder," Kelly snapped as the mud reached her chest.

Darvish gritted his teeth and managed to get her clear to her hips.

"What was that?" Erik asked suddenly, whirling and pointing his weapon back the way they'd come. "Something's back there!"

Darvish let go of Kelly's lifeline and turned to look. "Nothing's back there," he scoffed.

"And nothing's going to be here if someone doesn't get me out," Kelly said sharply as the mud regained its lost territory.

"Huh?" Darvish turned back. "Oh, sorry."

He grabbed the belt, Erik grabbed him, and, with a sucking sound, the mud reluctantly released Kelly to solid land.

"Now then," she said, scraping off her sidearm. "What's wrong?"

"I heard something." Erik's lower lip went out. "I did."

"I don't hear anything." She wrinkled her nose in disgust. "But I sure smell something. What stinks?"

"That," said Darvish calmly. He pointed over her shoulder. She twisted and almost fell.

No more than three meters away, four meters of slug rose into the air. Shkiy. A large slug, Erik had said, with large teeth and a large appetite. The first two points were self-evident. Kelly didn't want to make any bets on the third. The rain made no impression on its slime and the sinkhole it rested in didn't bother it at all.

"Hold it right there," came a command from the jungle. "We have you under our guns."

"No," broke in another voice. "We have you under our guns."

"The Atabeg," began the first voice but the second cut him off.

"We serve the Shahinshah!"

Kelly peered from one groups of Immortals to the other and then back at the shkiy. "Is this a joke?" she asked of no one in particular.

"Kelly." Erik danced around her. "Let's make a run for it while they're arguing."

"Run? Swim, maybe."

The shkiy slithered a little closer.

"I think it's going to..." Kelly grabbed Erik's arm and the two of them dove out of the way.

With a speed contradicting its flaccid appearance, the slug launched itself forward. Darvish was flung clear on a muddy wave. The Immortals weren't so lucky. One went before he had time to react. Another went while those remaining lifted their guns.

Ten energy beams sliced up from the jungle floor.

The shkiy reared in pain.

Three, six, twelve meters it rose, exposing more and more of its surface to the searing fire. The slime covering boiled away. The stench turned from merely bad to unbelievable; rotten egg mixed with ruptured bowel mixed with noxious odors less easily identified. Greasy smoke, weighted down by the rain, rolled sluggishly over the ground. Whole sections of the slug were destroyed before it would die. And when it did, twelve meters of smoking shkiy, falling in death, took four more Immortals with it.

Darvish splashed out of the jungle. Kelly and Erik got slowly to their feet. Six Immortals, weapons steaming, faced them over the body of the slug.

"Drop those guns!"

The nine survivors turned as one. A swamp buggy, barely visible through the rain, churned toward them, its single gun swiveling to cover the entire area.

"If anyone does any shooting around here, it's going to be me."

Darvish and Erik exchanged relieved grins.

"Grandmother!" they chorused.

Kelly sat down with a splash and started to laugh.

"My sons," said Quintella Osear, dowager Shabanou, "are fools. They have no concept of power—what it means or how to use it."

Kelly watched the older woman maneuver the unwieldy swamp buggy with no apparent effort. Although she'd found the last two days fascinating—as fascinating as spending two days with a dozen shkiy—she wasn't sorry to return to her ship.

"My husband," the tiny, grey haired woman continued, "grew lax in later years. Had it not been for me, the empire would have been eaten away by the rot and corruption."

"You held the rot and corruption together?"

The dowager smiled. "I still hold the rot and corruption together. The satraps report to me. I run the empire."

Kelly had a few thoughts on the way the empire had been run lately, but wisely, she kept them to herself. "Even with rejuvenations, you won't live forever," she said instead.

"I won't," the dowager agreed. "So I train my grandson."

"Erik?"

"Ahrikhartoum. Not even I could create a Shahinshah out of that other imbecile. I had intended this trip to dip him into the intrigues of the court. It became something else but I am not displeased. He survived. That is more than the Shahinshah's previous sons have done."

"Erik has brothers?"

"Had. The Defender of Infinity is permitted only one heir at a time. Ahrikhartoum is the sixth."

"You're a little hard on your relatives, aren't you?"

The old woman speared Kelly with her gaze. "Only the strong are fit to rule." An eyebrow rose. "I'm surprised the boy is not here to bid you farewell."

"We said good-bye already."

"Looks like you're out of the contract," Kelly had told him. *"I never did get you to your father."*

"You never said you would," Erik had replied. *"You said you'd take me home."* He'd spread his hands and grinned. Sometime in the last few days, he'd lost one of his front teeth. *"This is home."*

Kelly'd thought back over the terms of the deal. The kid was right. The contract held. She'd grinned back at him.

"You grew fond of the boy?" the dowager asked.

Kelly snorted. "Not likely." The smile came slowly. "But he's a good kid."

"He is my immortality." She stopped the vehicle. "We are here."

Standing, Kelly peered out at her ship then headed for the door.

"Captain Chase."

She turned.

"You have not requested payment for returning my grandson—both my grandsons—to me."

Kelly met the dowager's eyes squarely. "I have a contract with your immortality. When Erik is Shahinshah, I'll be back to collect."

The older woman spread her hands. "I will have him for many years yet. When you return, who can say if he will remember your...contract?"

Kelly's lips lifted off her teeth. "I'll take that chance," she said, and left.

"What's the big idea?" Kelly gasped; peeling herself out of the acceleration couch as the Valkyrie lifted into space at full power.

"Just ridding myself of the stink of that place, Boss. Another minute down there and I'd have rusted solid."

"You don't rust," Kelly reminded her. "But I know what you mean."

"We're clear for Susumu. Where to?"

"I seem to recollect we have rocks to sell." She ran her hand through her hair and swung her boots up on the console. "Plot a course for Elite."

"Elite?" Had Val possessed eyebrows, they would've gone up. "Does that mean people won't be shooting at us anymore?"

"No more than they used to," Kelly said with a grin. "We're free and clear."

"Not exactly."

"What do mean, not exactly?"

The ship hesitated before answering. "Technically, there's an intruder in the lounge."

"An intruder?"

"Within human parameters but small."

"Val!" Kelly's feet hit the floor. "How could you?" she demanded racing for the lounge.

"Come one step closer and I'll shoot."

"Erik! What are you *doing* here?"

"I want to go with you."

As the Valkyrie moved farther away, two dreadnoughts whipped around from the far side of the planet.

"You can't. Put the gun down."

Val picked the ships up on her scanners then switched to visual. At the moment, they showed as shadows against the planet but they were catching up fast.

"I don't want to be Shahinshah."

"We've been through that already."

"I want to be a smuggler like you."

"For the last time, Erik, I am not a smuggler. Now put…the gun…ERIK!"

This story is a classic example of how people are a writer's best resource. While I was working at Bakka (an SF bookstore in Toronto, Ontario) one of our customers who worked as an inspector for the Toronto Transit Commission told me the story of a little known but real disaster that occurred during the construction of the Toronto subway system.

Essentially, UNDERGROUND is the sequel to that story. I've always thought it would make a good Outer Limits episode.

UNDERGROUND

He always preferred being under things—under the covers, under the bed, under the porch in the cool damp hollow that smelled of earth and wood and secrets. When, on his fourteenth birthday, an Uncle took him spelunking, he slid down through the narrow entrance to the first cave like he was going home. Not once did he worry about the weight of rock pressing down from above, not once did he think that there might be dangers in the caverns. It took threats of violence to get him to leave.

Had his parents lived in the right place or had he received the right encouragement, he would have been a miner, going joyfully into the embrace of the earth, going topside reluctantly at the end of his shift. Unfortunately, his parents lived in Scarborough, a suburb engulfed by the urban sprawl of Toronto, and there wasn't a high school guidance councilor in the country who'd consider mining an intelligent career choice.

He found the next best thing.

"Pick up your feet, kid. Trip down here and the next thing you know one of the old red rockets comes by and slices, dices, makes julienne fries—whatever the hell they are—and your career in subway maintenance ends real fast. You know what I mean?"

He shrugged. "Yeah. I guess."

"You guess?" Carl Reed rolled his eyes and pounded gently on the wall with one massive fist as he walked. "No guessing down here, kid. You gotta know. Know when it's safe to move, when to stay out of the way. Mostly, we work the tunnels after the system shuts down and all the trains have been put to bed but since tonight's your first night, well, I thought I ought to let you in on the first lesson a subway man learns if he's gonna survive."

The kid wet his lips. The air stirred. The roar of a thousand pounds of machinery blew into his face, filling his nose and throat with the smell and taste of iron and oil and ozone. "Uh, Carl, isn't that…?"

"The train? Yeah. Come on, it hasn't even hit the curve yet, we've got plenty of time."

"But…?"

"Kid, I've been doing this for almost fifteen years; goin' down under the ground at night, resurrecting myself every morning." Carl turned and waggled bushy eyebrows, the motion barely visible under the edge of his hard-hat. "Trust me." Up ahead, the outside wall of the curve lit up. Carl calmly stepped over the single rail to his right and leaned back against the wall. "Tuck up tight," he bellowed, "turn your feet sideways. And it might help if you held your breath."

Then the train was there.

Impossibly large, impossibly loud, the rims of the great edged wheels just below eye level going around and around and around—although the movement couldn't really be seen. The train became the world. The world became the train. The urge to reach out and touch the passing monster fought with the urge to press back into the concrete farther than either concrete or bone would allow. Everything shook and screamed and swallowed him up and spit him out.

Then the train was gone.

* * *

"Jesus Christ, Carl, you're gonna get fuckin' fired, union or not, if the supervisors find out you're sandwiching your apprentices with the trains again."

"Hey!" Carl protested, shoving his hard-hat onto the almost-too-small shelf of his locker. "After I finish with 'em, my boys know they got nothin' to fear in the tunnels. They keep their heads, don't panic, and everything's okay. That kinda confidence means more than some pussy rules. Besides, what've they got to complain about, I haven't lost one yet."

"What about Hispecki?"

Carl looked hurt. "How was I supposed to know he had a weak heart?"

"Well, you wouldn't have found out if you hadn't sandwiched him!"

"Yeah? Well just remember, I turn out some of the best tunnel men in the system." Carl reached over and clapped his newest apprentice on one thin shoulder. "Right kid?"

He started. "Yeah. Sure."

"Jesus, Carl, leave him alone. He's probably still got that damned train rockin' and rollin' between his ears."

He had almost forgotten the train. It had come and gone and left no lasting impression. Of his first night's work, only the tunnels remained. Mile after mile of tunnels burrowing under the city. His body might be going through the motions that came with the end of shift but his head was still down there. In the tunnels.

He had a basement apartment just west of Davisville and Yonge. On the short walk from the subway home, he never raised his eyes from the concrete under his feet and tried not to think about how high up the sky went without stopping. He showed up half an hour early for work the next day and on the days that followed never once complained about long hours or the length of time he went without seeing the sun.

"Carl? What's that noise?" They were working downtown, east of St. George Station on the lower level where the University line runs under Bloor for a ways.

"Wind in the tunnels, kid. You've heard it before."

"No, not that noise." He cocked his head. "It sounded like moaning."

"Wind moans in the tunnels, kid."

"It sounded like people moaning."

"Oh. People." Carl straightened, pushed his hard-hat back and grinned. "Then you're hearing them."

"Them…"

"Yeah. Two guys. Construction workers. Fell into the wet concrete back when they were buildin' the system. You know what wet concrete's like; sucked 'em right in." After appropriate sound effects, Carl continued. "Nothing the crew could do for them. They're still in there."

"No…"

"Yup. Trapped for eternity. Sometimes the wind moans in the tunnels, kid. Sometimes it's them."

He stood at the edge of the empty platform and listened, blocking out the noise of the train receding into the distance. He couldn't sleep. So he came back.

Heart pounding, he moved quickly down the half dozen stairs and into the welcoming twilight.

"Hey, Carl? I found the place."

"What place, kid?"

"The place where those two guys are."

"What the hell are you talking about?"

"Those two guys you told me about, the ones who moan…"

Carl snickered. "That's just a story, kid. Somethin' we old timers tell to scare greenies like you."

"It's not just a story."

"Sure it is." Carl's shadow reached elongated fingers around the curve of the wall.

"No. I found the place. Yesterday."

"Jesus Christ, kid. You have any idea of the trouble you can get into wandering around down here on your day off? How deep in shit you'll be if anyone ever finds out?"

He shook his head, not paying attention. "They've become a part of the structure, part of what's holding everything together. They want to leave, but they can't, not until someone takes their place. That's why they moan."

Carl squinted into the young man's face. "And who told you that?"

"They did."

"They did...Dammit kid but you had me going for a second there. They did." The laugh bounced off the concrete and metal, around the curves, through the tunnels and over any protest that might have been made.

He sat in his basement apartment and stared up at the window. Up at the sky. Up at infinity.

"This is the place."

"What place?!" Carl considered himself to be a man of infinite good humor but three days flagging trouble spots on an area that seemed nothing but trouble spots had left him a little short.

"Where they are."

"Drop it, kid. I'm not in the mood for ghost stories tonight. I wanna get this section done and get my ass out of here and into bed. I wanna hear my old lady snorin' beside me and I wanna..." Carl frowned and fell silent. In almost fifteen years working down in the tunnels, it had never been so quiet. So still. "Kid?"

The kid laid one hand against the concrete, arm held straight out before him, drew in a deep breath and released it slowly. Then he took a step forward. His hand disappeared up to the wrist.

Beside him, a hand emerged.

"Jesus Christ, kid!" Astonishment, terror, something less easy to define, held Carl motionless through a second step and the beginning of a third then courage, stupidity, something equally less easy to define, pulled him into motion and had him fling a beefy arm around a skinny chest. "You're out of your fuckin' mind, kid! I'm not gonna let you do it!"

He wanted to tell Carl that it was all right, that he was all right, but the wall embraced him the way the world never had and he lost the words.

When the concrete closed around Carl's arm, he remembered there had been two men trapped.

Sometimes the wind moans in the tunnels.
Sometimes, it shrieks.

The guidelines for *The Christmas Bestiary* said we were to write about mythological creatures enjoying and/or celebrating Christmas. Well, two out of three of my mythological creatures weren't enjoying Christmas very much but I can assure you that the third one had a very good time.

The part of Sid-cat is being played by the eldest member of my personal menagerie. Unfortunately, Revenue Canada refuses to agree that this makes him a deduction.

I'LL BE HOME FOR CHRISTMAS

"...yes, you'll be dressed in holiday style if you come down to Big Bob's pre-Christmas clothing sale. All the fashions, all the frills, all major credit cards accepted..."
"Are we there yet?"
"Soon, honey."
"How soon?"
"Soon."
"I'm gonna be sick."
Elaine Montgomery took her eyes off the road just long enough to shoot a panicked glance at her daughter's flushed face. "We're almost there, Katie. Can't you hold on just a little bit longer?"
"No!" The last letter stretched and lengthened into a wail that completely drowned out the tinny sound of the car radio and threatened to shatter glass.
As Elaine swerved the car towards the shoulder, an echoing wail rose up from the depths of the beige plastic cat carrier securely strapped down in the back seat. The last time she'd assumed Katie could hold on for the two kilometers to the next rest stop, it had taken her over an hour to clean the car—which

had allowed the cat's tranquilizers to wear off long before they arrived at their destination.

Neither Katie nor the cat were very good travelers.

"Mommy!"

Wet gravel spun under the tires as she fought the car and trailer to a standstill. "Just another second, honey. Grit your teeth." *How many times can you throw up one lousy cheese sandwich?* she wondered unbuckling her seatbelt and reaching for her daughter's. *Thank god she's not still in the kiddie car seat.* It had taken a good twenty minutes and an advanced engineering degree to get Katie in and out of the safety seat and all signs indicated she had closer to twenty seconds.

"It's all right, baby. Mommy's got you." She slid them both out the passenger door and went to her knees in a puddle to better steady the four year old's shaking body. December rain drove icy fingers down the back of her neck and, not for the first time since leaving Toronto that morning, Elaine wondered what the hell she was doing heading into the middle of nowhere with a four year old, a very pissed off cat, and all her worldly goods, two weeks before Christmas.

Trying to survive, came the answer.

I knew that. She sighed and kissed Katie's wet curls.

"Ms. Montgomery?" Upon receiving an affirmative answer, the woman who'd come out of the house as the car pulled up popped open an umbrella and hurried forward. "I'm Catherine Henderson. Your late aunt's lawyer? So nice to finally meet you at last. I was afraid you weren't going to make it before I had to leave. Here, let me take the cat…"

Elaine willingly surrendered the cat-carrier, tucked Katie up under one arm and grabbed for their bag of essentials with the other. The two-story brick farmhouse loomed up out of the darkness like the haven she hoped it was and, feeling more than just a little numb, she followed the steady stream of chatter up onto the porch and into the kitchen.

"No need to lock the car, you're miles away from anyone who might want to steal it out here. I hope you don't mind going around to the back, I can't remember the last time the front door was opened. Careful on that step, there's a crack in the cement. The porch was a later addition to the original farmhouse which was built by your late aunt's father in the twenties. You'll have to excuse the smell; your aunt got a bit, well, eccentric later in life and kept a pair of pigs in here over last winter. I had the place scoured and disinfected after we spoke on the phone but I'm afraid the smell is going to be with you for a while." She dropped the umbrella into a pail by the door and heaved the carrier up onto the kitchen table. "Good heavens he's a big one isn't he? Did he wail like that all the way from Toronto?"

"No." Elaine put Katie down and brushed wet hair back off her face. "Only for the last one hundred kilometers or so."

"I'll let him out, Mommy." Small fingers struggled with the latch for a second and then a grey and white blur leapt from the table and disappeared under the tattered lounge by the window.

"Leave him be, Katie." A quick grab kept her daughter from burrowing beneath the furniture with the cat. "He needs to be alone for a while."

"Okay." Katie turned, looked speculatively up at the lawyer and announced, "I puked all over the car."

"I'm sorry to hear that." Catherine took the pronouncement in stride. "If you're feeling sick again," she crossed the kitchen and opened one of four identical doors, "the bathroom is through here." Reaching for the next door over, she continued. "This is the bedroom your aunt used—I suggest you use it as well as it's the only room in the house that's insulated. This is the hall, leading to the front door and the stairs—another four bedrooms up there, but as I said, uninsulated. And this is the cellar."

Elaine took an almost involuntary step forward. "What was that?"

"What was what?" the other woman asked carefully, closing the cellar door.

"The music. I heard music…just for a second. It sounded like, like…" Obviously, the lawyer hadn't heard it, so Elaine let the explanation trail off.

"Yes, well, these old houses make a lot of strange noises. There's an oil furnace down there but it must be close to twenty-five years old so I wouldn't count on it too much. I think your aunt depended on the woodstove. You do know how to use a woodstove, don't you?"

"I think I can figure it out." The question had hovered just on the edge of patronizing and Elaine decided not to admit her total lack of experience. *You burn wood; how hard can it be? Whole forests burn down on their own every year.*

"Good. I've left a casserole and a liter of milk in the fridge, I don't imagine you'll want to cook after that long drive. You've got my number, if you need anything don't hesitate to call."

"Thank you." As Catherine retrieved her umbrella, Elaine held open the porch door and wrinkled her nose. "Um, I was wondering, what happened to the pigs when my aunt died?"

"Worried about wild boars tearing up the property? You needn't; the pigs shuffled off this mortal coil months before your aunt did. There might still be packages marked Porky or Petunia in the freezer out in the woodshed."

Elaine closed the door on Catherine's laugh and leaned for a moment against the peeling paint. *Porky and Petunia. Right.* It had been a very long day. She started as skinny arms wrapped around her leg.

"Mommy? I'm hungry."

"I'm not surprised." She took a deep breath, turned and scooped her daughter up onto her hip. "But first we're both putting on some dry clothes. How does that sound?"

Katie shrugged. "Sounds okay."

On the way to the bedroom, Elaine dropped the overnight case and pulled the cellar door open a crack, just to check. There was a faint, liquid trill of sound and then the only thing she could hear was water running into the cistern.

"Mommy?"

"Did you hear the music, Katie?"

Katie listened with all the intensity only a small child could muster. "No," she said at last. "No music. What did it sound like?"

"Nothing honey. Mommy must have been imagining it." It had sounded like an invitation, but not the kind that could be discussed with a four-year-old. It probably should have been frightening, but it wasn't. Each note had sent shivers of anticipation dancing over her skin. Elaine was willing to bet the farm—well maybe not that, as this rundown old place was the only refuge they had—that she hadn't been imagining anything.

The forest was the most alive place she'd ever been; lush and tangled, with bushes reaching up and trees reaching down and wild flowers and ferns tucked in every possible nook and cranny. She danced through it to the wild call of the music and when she realized she was naked, it didn't seem to matter. Nothing scratched, nothing prickled, and the ground under her bare feet had the resilience of a good foam mattress.

Oh yes! the music agreed.

The path the music led her down had been danced on before and her steps followed the imprint of a pair of cloven hooves.

She could see a clearing up ahead, a figure outlined in the brilliant sunlight, pan pipes raised to lips, an unmistakable silhouette, intentions obvious. She felt her cheeks grow hot.

What am I thinking of? Her feet lost a step in the dance. *I'm responsible for a four-year-old child. I can't just go running off to...to...well, I can't just go running off.*

Why not? the music asked indignantly.

"Because I can't! Yi!" She teetered, nearly fell, and made a sudden grab for the doorframe. The cellar stairs fell away dark and steep and from somewhere down below the music made one final plea. It wailed its disappointment as she slammed the cellar door closed.

A little dreaming, a little sleepwalking, a little...Well, never mind. Elaine shoved a chair up under the doorknob and tried not to run back to the bedroom she was sharing with Katie. *I'm just reacting to the first night in a new house. Nothing strange about that...And old furnaces make a lot of...noises.*

Of course, she had to admit as she scrambled under the covers and snuggled up against the warmth of her sleeping daughter, old furnaces don't usually make lecherous suggestions…

"How much!?"

The oilman wiped his hands on a none-too-clean rag. "You got a 200 gallon tank there Ms. Montgomery. Oil's thirty-six point two cents a liter, there's about four and a half liters a gallon, that's, uh…" His brow furrowed as he worked out the math. "Three hundred and twenty-five dollars and eighty cents, plus G.S.T."

Elaine set the grubby piece of paper down on the kitchen table and murmured, "Just like it says on the bill."

He beamed "That's right."

She had just over five hundred dollars in the account she'd transferred to the local bank. Enough, she'd thought, given that they no longer needed to pay rent, to give her and Katie a couple of months to get settled before she had to find work. Apparently, she'd thought wrong. "I'll get my cheque book." If her aunt kept the house warm with the woodstove she must've been re-lighting the fire every half an hour. Which was about as long as Elaine had been able to get it to burn.

The oilman watched as she wrote out his cheque then scrawled paid in full across the bill and handed it to her with a flourish. "Don't you worry," he said as she winced. "Your late aunt managed to get by spendin' only twelve hundred dollars for heatin' last winter."

"Only twelve hundred dollars," Elaine repeated weakly.

"That's right." He paused in the door and grinned back at her. "'Course, not to speak ill of the dead, but I think she had other ways of keepin' warm."

"What do you mean?" At this point any other way sounded better than twelve hundred dollars.

"Well, one time, about, oh, four, five years ago now, I showed up a little earlier than I'd said, and I saw her comin' up out of the basement with the strangest sort of expression on her face. Walkin' a bit funny too. I think," he leaned forward and nodded sagely, "I think she was down there having a bit of a nip."

Elaine blinked. "But she never drank."

The oilman tapped his nose. "That's what they say. Anyway, Merry Christmas, Ms. Montgomery. I'll see you in the new year."

"Yes, Merry Christmas." She watched the huge truck roar away. "Three hundred and twenty-five dollars and eighty cents plus G.S.T merrier for you anyway..."

"Mommy!"

The wail of four-year-old in distress lifted every hair on her head and had her moving before her conscious mind even registered the direction of the cry. She charged out the backdoor without bothering to put on a coat, raced around the corner of the building, and almost tripped over the kneeling figure of her daughter.

"What is it, Katie? Are you hurt?"

Katie lifted a tear-streaked face and Elaine got a glimpse of the bloody bundle in her lap. "Sid-cat's been killeded!"

"Ms. Montgomery?"

Elaine moved Katie's head off her lap and stood to face the vet, leaving the sleeping child sprawled across three of the waiting room chairs. There'd been a lot of blood staining the white expanse of his ruff but Sid-cat had not actually been dead— although his life had been in danger a number of times during the wild drive into the vet's. There are some things Fords are not meant to do on icy backcountry roads.

Dr. Levin brushed a strand of long dark hair back off her face and smiled reassuringly. "He's going to be all right. I think we've even managed to save the eye."

"Thank god." She hadn't realized she'd been holding her breath until she let it out. "Do you know what attacked him?"

The vet nodded. "Another cat."

"Are you sure?"

"No doubt about it. He did a little damage himself and fur caught in his claws was definitely cat. You've moved into your aunt's old place, haven't you?"

"Yes..."

"Well, I wouldn't doubt there's a couple of feral cats living in what's left of that old barn of hers. You're isolated enough out there that they've probably interbred into vicious, brainless animals." She frowned. "Now, I don't hold with this as a rule but housecats like Sid don't stand a chance against feral cats and you've got a child to think of. You should consider hiring someone to clear them out."

"I'll think about it."

"Good." Dr. Levin smiled again. "Sid'll have to stay here for a few days, of course. Let's see, it's December 20th today, call me on the 24th. I think we can have him home for Christmas."

When they got back to the farmhouse, a line of paw prints marked the fresh snow up to the porch door and away. In spite of the bitter cold, they could smell the reason for the visit as soon as they reached the steps.

"Boy pee!" Katie pronounced disdainfully, rubbing a mittened hand over her nose.

Every entrance to the house had been similarly marked.

The house itself was freezing. The woodstove had gone out. The furnace appeared to be having no effect.

Elaine looked down at her shivering daughter and seriously considered shoving her back into the car, cramming everything she could into the trunk and heading back to the city. *At least in the city I know what's going on.* She sagged against the cellar door and rubbed her hand across her eyes as a hopeful series of notes rose up from below. *At least in the city, I wasn't hearing things.* But they didn't have a life in the city anymore.

Come and play, said the music. *Come and...*

I *can't!* she told it silently. *Shut up!*

"Mommy? Are you okay?"

With an effort, she shook herself free. "I'm fine Katie. Mommy's just worried about Sid-cat."

Katie nodded solemnly. "Me too."

"I know what we should do, baby. Lets put up the Christmas tree." Elaine forced a smile and hoped it didn't look as false as it felt. "Here it is December 20th and we haven't even started getting ready for Christmas."

"We go to the woods and chop it down?" Katie grabbed at her mother's hand. "There's an axe in the shed."

"Uh, no sweetheart. Mommy isn't much good with an axe." Chopping wood for the stove had been a nightmare. "We'll use the old tree this year."

"Okay." The artificial tree and the box marked decorations had been left by the dining room table and Katie raced towards them, stopped and looked back at her mother, her face squeezed into a worried frown. "Will Santa be able to find me way out here? Does he know where we went?"

Elaine reached down and laid a hand lightly on Katie's curls. "Santa can find you anywhere," she promised. Katie's presents had been bought with the last of her severance pay, the day she got the call that her aunt had left her the family farm. No matter what, Katie was getting a Christmas.

The six-foot fake spruce seemed dwarfed by the fifteen-foot ceilings in the living room and even the decorations didn't do much to liven it up although Katie very carefully hung two boxes of tinsel over the lower four feet.

"It needs the angel," she said stepping back and surveying her handiwork critically. "Put the angel on now, Mommy."

"Well, it certainly needs something," Elaine agreed, mirroring her daughter's expression. Together, very solemnly, they lifted the angel's case out of the bottom of the box.

Carefully, Elaine undid the string that held the lid secure.

"Tell me the angel story again, Mommy."

"The angel was a present," Elaine began, shifting so that Katie's warm weight slid under her arm and up against her heart, "from my father to my mother on the day I was born."

"So she's really old."

"Not so very old!" The protest brought a storm of giggles. "He told my mother that as she'd given him an angel…"

"That was you."

"…that he'd give her one. And every Christmas he'd sit the angel on the very top of the Christmas tree and she'd glow."

When Elaine had been small, she'd thought the angel glowed on her own and had been more than a little disappointed to discover the tiny light tucked back in-between her wings. "When you were born, my parents…"

"Grandma and Grandpa."

"That's right, Grandma and Grandpa…" Who had known their granddaughter for only a year before the car crash. "…gave the angel to me because I'd given them another angel."

"Me." Katie finished triumphantly.

"You," Elaine agreed, kissed the top of Katie's head and folded back the tissue paper. She blew on her fingers to warm them then slid her hand very gently under the porcelain body and lifted the angel out of the box. The head wobbled once, then fell to the floor and shattered into a hundred pieces.

Elaine looked down at the shards of porcelain, at the tangled ruin of golden-white hair lying in their midst, and burst into tears.

Come and play! called the music. *Be happy! Come and…*

"No!"

"No what, Mommy?"

"Never mind, pet. Go back to sleep."

"Did you have a bad dream?"

"Yes." Except it had been a very good dream.

"Don't worry, Mommy. Santa will bring another angel. I asked him to."

Elaine gently touched Katie's cheek then swiped at her own. *Isn't it enough we're stuck in this freezing cold house*—only the bedroom was tolerable—*in the middle of nowhere with no money? I thought we could make this a home. I thought I could give her a Christmas at least…*

But when the angel had shattered, Christmas had shattered with it.

"I'm tired of eating pigs."

"I know, baby, so am I." Porky and Petunia had become the main course of almost every meal they'd eaten since they arrived. Elaine had thought, had hoped they could have a turkey for Christmas but with the size of the oil bill—not to mention oil bills yet to come—added to the cost of keeping the cat at the vet for four days it looked like a turkey was out of the question.

"I don't *want* pigs anymore!"

"Well there isn't *anything* else."

Katie pushed out her lower lip and pushed the pieces of chop around on her plate.

Elaine sighed. There were only so many ways to prepare...pigs and she had run out of new ideas. Her aunt's old cookbooks had been less than no help. They were so old that recipes called for a pennyweight of raisins and began the instructions for roasting a chicken with a nauseatingly detailed lesson on how to pluck and gut it.

"Mommy. Mommy, wake up!"

"What is it, Katie?"

"Mommy, tomorrow is Christmas!"

Elaine just barely stopped herself from saying, *So what?*

"And today we bring Sid-cat home!"

And today we pay Sid-cat's vet bill. She didn't know what she was looking forward to less, a cold Christmas spent with Porky and Petunia or the emptying out of her checking account.

Bundling a heavy wool sweater on over her pajamas she went out to see if the fire in the wood stove had survived the night and if maybe a cup of coffee would be possible before noon.

Not, she thought as a draft of cold air swirled around her legs through the open bedroom door, *that I have very high hopes.*

"Katie!" A layer of ash laid a grey patina over everything within a three-foot radius of the stove. "Did you do this?"

A small body pushed between her and the counter. "You said, stay away from the stove." Katie swung her teddy bear by one leg, the arc of its head drawing a thick, fuzzy line through the ash on the floor. "So, I stayed away. Honest truly."

"Then how...?"

Teddy drew another arc. "The wind came down the chimney whoosh?"

"Maybe. Maybe it was the wind." But Elaine didn't really believe that. Just like she didn't really believe she saw a tiny slippered footprint right at the point where a tiny person would have to brace their weight to empty the ash pan. Heart in her throat, she stepped forward, squatted, and swiped at the print with the edge of her sweater. She didn't believe in it. It didn't exist.

The sudden crash of breaking glass, however, couldn't be ignored.

Slowly she turned and faced the cellar door.

"That came from downstairs," Katie said helpfully, brushing ash off her teddy bear's head onto her pajamas.

"I *know* that, Katie. Mommy has ears. Go sit in the chair by the window." She looked down at her daughter's trembling lip and added a terse, "Please."

Dragging her feet, Katie went to the chair.

"Now stay there. Mommy's going down to the cellar to see what broke the window." *Mommy's out of her mind...*

"I want to go too!"

"Stay there! Please. It's probably just some animal trying to get in out of the cold." The cellar door opened without the expected ominous creak and although Elaine would have bet money against it, a flick of the switch flooded as much of the cellar as she could see with light. *Of course, there's always the part I can't see.*

The temperature dropped as she moved down the stairs and she shivered as she crossed the second step; until this moment the furthest she'd descended. From the bottom of the stairs she could see the cistern, the furnace, wheezing away in its corner, and the rusted bulk of the oil tank. An icy breeze against her right cheek pulled her around.

Probably just some animal trying to get in out of the cold, she repeated, taking one step, two, three. *A lot it knows...*By the fourth step she was even with the window and squinting in the glare of morning sun on snow. *Oh, my god.* The glass had been forced out, not in, and the tracks leading away were three pronged and deep. She whirled around, caught sight of a flash of color and froze.

The feather was about six inches long and brilliantly banded with red and gold. She bent to pick it up and caught sight of another, a little smaller and a little mashed. The second feather lay half in shadow at the base of the rough stone wall. The third, fourth and fifth feathers were caught on the stone at the edge of a triangular hole the size of Elaine's head.

Something had forced its way out of that hole and then out of the cellar.

Barely breathing, Elaine backed up a step, the feather falling from suddenly nerveless fingers.

"Mommy?"

She didn't remember getting to the top of the cellar stairs. "Get dressed, Katie." With an effort, she kept her voice steady. "We're going in to get Sid." *And we're going to keep driving. And we're not going to stop until Easter.*

"…I don't expect anyone to have that kind of cash right at Christmas." Dr. Levin smiled down at Katie who had her face pressed up against the bars of the cat carrier. "I'll send you a bill in the new year and we can work out a payment schedule."

"You're sure?" Elaine asked incredulously.

"I'm very sure."

The vet in Toronto had accepted credit cards but certainly not credit. Under the circumstances, it seemed ungracious to suggest that they might not be around in the new year. Elaine swallowed once and squared her shoulders. "Dr. Levin, did you know my aunt?"

"Not well, but I knew her."

"Did she ever mention anything strange going on in that house?"

Ebony eyebrows rose. "What do you mean, strange?"

Elaine waved her hands helplessly, searching for the words. "You know, strange."

The vet laughed. "Well, as I said, we weren't close and the only thing I can remember her saying about the house is that she could never live anywhere else. Why? Have *strange* things been happening?"

"You might say that…"

"Give it a little while," Dr. Levin advised sympathetically. "You're not used to country life."

"True…" Elaine, admitted, slowly. *Was that it?*

"If it helps, I know your aunt was happy out there. She always smiled like she had a wonderful secret. I often envied her that smile."

Elaine, scrabbling in the bottom of her purse for a pencil, barely heard her. Maybe she just wasn't used to living in the country. Maybe that was all it was. "One more thing, if you don't mind, Doctor." She turned over the cheque she hadn't needed to fill out and quickly sketched the pattern of tracks that had lead away from the basement window. "Can you tell me what kind of an animal would make these?"

Dr. Levin pursed her lips and studied the slightly wobbly lines. "It's a type of bird, that's for certain. Although I wouldn't like to commit myself one hundred percent, I'd say it's a chicken."

Elaine blinked. "A chicken?"

"That's right." She laughed. "Don't tell me you've got a feral chicken out there as well as a feral cat?"

Elaine managed a shaky laugh in return. "Seems like."

"Well, keep Sid inside, make sure you give him the antibiotics, call me if he shows any sign of pain, and…" She reached into the pocket of her lab coat and pulled out a pair of candy canes. "…have a merry Christmas."

"Mommy?" Katie poked one finger into her mother's side. "Sid-cat doesn't like the car. Let's go home."

Elaine bit her lip. Home. Well, they couldn't sit in the parking lot forever. Dr. Levin had said it was a chicken. Who could be afraid of a chicken? It had probably been living down in the basement for some time. It had finally run out of food so it had left. There was probably nothing behind that hole in the wall but a bit of loose earth.

Her aunt had never said there was anything strange about the house and she'd lived there all her adult life. Had been happy there.

Where else did they have to go?

The fire in the woodstove was still burning when they got home. Elaine stared down at it in weary astonishment and hastily shoved another piece of wood in before it should change its mind and go out. The kitchen was almost warm.

Very carefully, she pulled Sid-cat out of the carrier and settled him in a shallow box lined with one of Katie's outgrown sweaters. He stared up at her with his one good eye, blinked, yawned, gave just enough of a purr so as not to seem ungracious, and went back to sleep.

Katie looked from the cat to her half-eaten candy cane, to her mother. "Tomorrow is Christmas," she said solemnly. "It doesn't feel like Christmas."

"Oh, Katie…"

Leaving her daughter squatting by the box, *"standing guard in case that federal cat comes back,"* Elaine went into the living room and stared at the Christmas tree. If only the angel hadn't broken. She thought she could cope with everything else, could pull a sort of Christmas out of the ruins, if only the angel still looked down from the top of the tree.

Maybe she could glue it back together.

The ruins lay on the dining room table, covered with an ancient linen napkin. A tiny corpse in a country morgue…

That's certainly the Christmas spirit, Elaine… She bit her lip and flicked the napkin back. One bright green glass eye stared up at her from its nest of shattered porcelain. *Oh god…*

"MOMMY!"

She was moving before the command had time to get from brain to feet.

"MOM-MEEEE!"

Katie was backed into a corner of the kitchen, one arm up over her face, the other waving around trying to drive off a flock of…

Of pixies?

They were humanoid, sexless, about eight inches tall with a double pair of gossamer wings, and they glowed in all the colors of the rainbow. Long hair in the same iridescent shades streamed around them, moving with an almost independent life of its own. Even from a distance they were beautiful but, as Elaine crossed the kitchen, she saw that her daughter's arms were bleeding from a number of nasty looking scratches and a half a dozen of them had ahold of Katie's curls.

"Get away from her!" Elaine charged past the kitchen table, grabbed a magazine, rolled it on the run, and began flailing at the tiny bodies. She pulled a pink pixie off Katie's head and threw it across the kitchen. "Go back where you came from you, you overgrown bug!" It hit the wall beside the fridge, shook itself, buzzed angrily and sped back to Katie.

"Mom-meee!"

"Keep your eyes covered, honey!" They swarmed so thick around the little girl that every swing knocked a couple out of the air. Unfortunately, it didn't seem to discourage them although they did, finally, acknowledge the threat.

"Be careful, Mommy!" Katie wailed as the entire flock turned. "They bite!"

Their teeth weren't very big, but they were sharp.

The battle raged around the kitchen. Elaine soon bled from a number of small wounds. The pixies appeared to be no worse off than when they'd started, even though they'd each been hit at least once.

A gold pixie, gleaming metallically, perched for a moment on the table and hissed up at her, gnashing blood stained teeth. Without thinking, Elaine slammed her aunt's old aluminum colander over it.

It shrank back from the sides and began hissing in earnest.

One down... The kitchen counter hit her in the small of the back. Elaine smashed her wrist against the cupboard, dislodging a purple pixie that had been attempting to chew her hand off, and groped around for a weapon. *Dish rack, spatula, dish soap, spray can of snow...*

Katie had wanted to write Merry Christmas on the kitchen window. They hadn't quite gotten around to it.

Elaine's fingers closed around the can. Knocking the lid off against the side of the sink, she nailed a lavender pixie at point-blank range.

The goopy white spray coated its wings and it plummeted to the floor, hissing with rage.

"HA! I've got you now, you little…Take that! And that!"

The kitchen filled with drifting clouds of a chemical blizzard.

"Mommy! They're leaving!"

Although a number of them were running rather than flying, the entire swarm appeared to be racing for the cellar door. With adrenaline sizzling along every nerve, Elaine followed. They weren't getting away from her *that* easily. She reached the bottom of the stairs just in time to see the first of the pixies dive through the hole. Running full out, she managed to get in another shot at the half dozen on foot before they disappeared and then, dropping to her knees, emptied the can after them.

"And may all your Christmases be white!" she screamed, sat back on her heels and panted, feeling strong and triumphant and, for the first time in a long time, capable. She grinned down at the picture of Santa on the can. "I guess we showed them, didn't we?" Patting him on the cheek, she set the empty container down— "Good thing I got the large economy size"—and turned her attention to the hole. The rock that had fallen out, or been pushed out, wasn't that large and could easily be maneuvered back into place. She'd come down later with a can of mortar and…

Now that she really took the time to look at it, the hole actually occupied the lower corner of a larger patch in the wall. None of the stones were very big and although they'd been set carefully, they were obviously not part of the original construction. Squinting in the uncertain light, Elaine leaned forward and peered at a bit of red smeared across roughly the center stone.

Was it blood?

It was Coral Dawn. She had a lipstick the same color in her purse. And the shape of the smear certainly suggested…

"Sealed with a kiss?"

Frowning, she poked at it with a fingertip.

The music crescendoed and feelings not her own rode with it. Memories of…She felt herself flush. Sorrow at parting. Loneliness. Welcome. Annoyance that other, smaller creatures broke the rules and forced the passage.

Come and play! Come and...

A little stunned, Elaine lifted her finger. The music continued but the feelings stopped. She swallowed and adjusted her jeans.

"I think she had other ways of keeping warm. Walkin' a bit funny too."

"She always smiled like she had a wonderful secret."

"A wonderful secret. Good lord." It was suddenly very warm in the cellar. If her aunt—her old, fragile aunt who had obviously been a lot more flexible than she appeared—had accepted the music's invitation...

The scream of a furious cat jerked her head around and banished contemplation.

"*Now* what?" she demanded scrambling to her feet and racing for the stairs. "Katie, did you let Sid-cat outside?"

"No." Katie met her at the cellar door, eyes wide. "It's two other cats. And a chicken."

Elaine gave her daughter a quick hug. "You stay here and guard Sid-cat. Mommy'll take care of it."

The pixie trapped under the colander hissed inarticulate threats.

"Shut up," she snapped without breaking stride. To her surprise, it obeyed. Grabbing her jacket, she headed out through the woodshed, snatching up the axe as she went. She didn't have a clue what she was going to do with it but the weight felt good in her hand.

The cats were an identical muddy calico, thin with narrow heads, tattered ears, and vicious expressions. Bellies to the snow and ragged tails lashing from side to side, they were flanking the biggest chicken Elaine had ever seen. As she watched, one of the cats darted forward and the chicken lashed out with its tail.

Up until this moment, Elaine had never seen a chicken that hadn't been wrapped in cellophane but even *she* knew that chickens did not have long, scaled, and apparently prehensile tails.

The first cat dodged the blow, while the second narrowly missed being eviscerated by a sideswipe from one of the bird's taloned feet. Elaine wasn't sure she should get involved, mostly—although the chicken had obviously come from her cellar—because she wasn't sure whose side she should be on.

Growling low in its throat, the first cat attacked again, slid under a red and gold wing, and found itself face to face with its intended prey. To Elaine's surprise, the bird made no attempt to use its beak. It merely stared, unblinking, into the slitted yellow eyes of the cat.

The cat suddenly grew very still, its growl cut off in mid note, its tail frozen in mid lash.

All at once, choosing sides became very easy.

Still buzzing from her battle with the pixies, Elaine charged forward. The not-quite-a-chicken turned. Eyes squeezed shut, knuckles white around the haft, she swung the axe in a wild arc. Then again. And again.

The blade bit hard into something that resisted only briefly. Over the pounding of the blood in her ears, Elaine heard the sound of feathers beating against air and something stumbling in the snow. Something slammed against her shins. Opening her eyes a crack, she risked a look.

The headless body of the bird lay, not entirely still, at her feet. She leapt back as the tail twitched and nearly fell over the stone statue of the cat. Its companion glared at her, slunk in, grabbed the severed head, and, trailing blood from its prize, raced into a tangle of snow laden bushes.

"I am not going to be sick," Elaine told herself sternly, leaning on the axe. Actually, the instruction appeared unnecessary for although she was a little out of breath she felt exalted rather than nauseous. She poked at the corpse with her foot. Whatever remaining life force had animated it after its head had been chopped off, appeared to have ebbed. "And it's really most sincerely dead," she muttered. "Now what?"

Then the crunch of small bones from the bushes gave her an idea and she smiled.

Elaine watched Katie instructing Sid-cat in the use of her new paint box and decided that this could be one of the best

Christmases she'd had in years. The woodstove seemed to be behaving, throwing out enough heat to keep the kitchen and the livingroom warm and cosy. She'd found a bag of frozen cranberries jammed under one of Porky's generous shoulders and a pot of cranberry sauce now bubbled and steamed on top of the stove. Thanks to the instructions in her aunt's old cookbooks, the smell of roasting...well, the smell of *roasting*, filled the house.

Her gaze drifted up to the top of the tree. Although the old angel had been an important part of her life and she'd always feel its loss, the new angel was an equally important symbol of her fight to make a new life and find a new home for herself and her daughter. Tethered with a bit of ribbon, its wings snow-covered in honor of the season, the pixie tossed glowing golden hair back off its face and gnawed on a bit of raw pork.

"Mommy?"

"Yes, Katie."

"Didn't Santa bring *you* any presents?"

"Mommy got her present early this morning. While you were still asleep."

"Did you like it?"

"Very, very much."

On the stereo, a Welsh choir sang Hosannas. Rising up from the cellar, wrapping around a choirboy's clear soprano, a set of pipes trilled out smug hosannas of their own.

Short fiction usually explores a single idea and most of the ideas I have for short stories are clever, not deep. This is one of the exceptions. In many ways this is one of the stories I stretched the farthest in. Writing from the point of view of a culture I am not actually a part of, I had to be sure that, regardless of content, I respected that culture.

When I wrote "SHING LI-UNG," I was living in the heart of Toronto's Chinatown and there was an incident just outside the Jade Garden Restaurant. No one saw the dragon.

SHING LI-UNG

"Donna. Your grandmother has asked to see you."

Incipient panic thrust Donna Chen up out of the chair and nearly pushed her voice over the edge to shrill. "Me?" She waved an agitated arm towards the backyard where her three cousins were playing a subdued game of croquet. "What about them?"

Her Aunt Lily, her mother's younger sister, stepped back out of the family room and shook her head. "You're the oldest. And besides, she asked to see you."

Donna recognized the tone; her mother had one just like it. Ears burning, she stood and headed for the stairs. With her aunt marching close behind, she felt as though she were being escorted to her own execution. *There's someone dying in my house. That just doesn't* happen *in the suburbs.*

Just outside the master bedroom, she paused, resisting the pressure of a small hand between her shoulder blades. "What if she dies while I'm with her?"

"Oh for heaven's sake, Donna, you're almost eighteen; you're not a child. And you'll be in a lot more trouble if she dies before you get there. Now go."

The bedroom had been her parents' until eight months ago when her grandmother had fallen, broken her hip and been unable to live alone any longer. She had been frail then. Now, with eight months of pain behind her and death so near, she looked ethereal, no longer real.

To Donna's surprise, the curtains were open and, instead of the gloom she'd been expecting, the afternoon sun filled the room with golden light. Father Xiangao, the priest from Our Lady of Sorrows, sat to the right of the bed, her mother to the left. She paused just inside the door but her grandmother saw her and, murmuring something in Mandarin, beckoned her forward. Determined to make the best of a bad situation—given that she had no choice—Donna moved to the end of the bed and paused again, her knees pressed up against the mattress.

"Yes, grandmother?"

The bird-claw hand beckoned her closer still.

Eyes on the neutral landscape of the yellow blanket, its surface barely rippled by the wasted body beneath, Donna shuffled past her mother's knees and jerked to a stop when fingers of skin and bone clutched suddenly at her wrist. Heart in her throat, she somehow managed not to pull away.

"Chun Chun, woh yu ishi don-shi ne shu-ino."

Although her grandmother spoke fluent English, in the last few months she had reverted solely to the language of her childhood. As Donna spoke no Mandarin, Father Xiangao translated.

"She wants to give you something. She brought it with her from Kweilin. It carries very powerful..." he paused and asked a question before continuing. "It carries very powerful protection."

Donna allowed her hand to be pulled forward and, curious in spite of herself, leaned down for a closer look. Although she didn't understand the words, she understood the tone. Her grandmother considered this to be very, very important.

Three inches long and about one high, a red and gold enamel dragon on cheap tin backing—the kind they sold for less than a dollar at most of the junkier Chinatown stores—lay on Donna's palm, still warm and slightly damp from her grandmother's hand.

This was it? Donna turned it over. Meant to be worn as a brooch, the pin had been bent and straightened more than once and rust pitted the clasp that secured it.

"Shing Li-ung."

Startled, Donna glanced over at the priest. Maybe she was missing the point of this.

"That's its name," the priest said softly. "It means, Shining Heart."

Donna could feel her mother's presence behind her and knew what was expected. "Thank you, Grandmother." It could have been a lot worse.

The grip the old woman had on her wrist relaxed a little and then surprisingly, convulsively tightened again. Her eyes opened very wide and she appeared to be staring at a patch of sunlight on the ceiling. Then thin lips curved up in a wondering smile and, just for that moment, Donna realized that this woman had once been eighteen too.

She breathed out the name of her husband, long dead, and never breathed in again.

Trying very hard not to freak, Donna pulled her hand out of the circle of slack fingers as Father Xiangao reached over and gently closed the old woman's eyes. The imprint of the death grip clung to her wrist. Frantic scrubbing against her jeans did nothing to erase the feeling.

Then behind her, over the drone of the priest's prayers, she heard her mother crying. Puzzled, she turned. She had seen her mother cry before but never like this. Understanding came slowly. The dragon dropped to the blanket, momentarily forgotten, as Donna drew the older woman's head down to her shoulder and held her tightly while she wept. Her own tears were not so much for her grandmother as for the sudden knowledge that someday, she would be the daughter who grieved.

"So this is the family heirloom, eh?" Bradley grinned down at the dragon and then up at his sister. "Boy are you ever lucky that you're the oldest and it went to you. I mean, this must be worth, oh, seventy-nine cents."

"Very funny."

"Maybe you should rent a safety deposit box. Wouldn't want it to be stolen…" He rubbed a thumb over the enamel. "Hey, it looks kinda sad."

"What are you talking about?" Donna took the dragon pin back and frowned down at it. It did look sad; its eyes were half closed and its great golden mustaches appeared to be drooping around the downturned corners of its mouth. Its whole posture spoke of melancholy. "Yeah, I suppose it does. Do you miss grandma, Shing Li-ung?"

"Shing Li-ung?" Bradley repeated.

"That's its name."

"Oh great. You've got a piece of junk jewelry with a name." He reached out one finger and stroked the red scaled curve of its tail. "So, grandma didn't mention she had a pair of ancient family chopsticks or anything for me to guard and revere did she?"

"No." Donna sighed. "Just one seventy-nine cent dragon."

"For you."

"I was there."

"Yeah, well, if you don't want old Shing Li-ung, I suppose I'll take it."

She stared at him in surprise. "You'll what?"

"I'll take it." He looked disinterested in his own words—the way only a young man almost seventeen could. "It'll look kinda cool on my jean jacket. Very ethnic. And besides, Chinese dragons are supposed to bring you luck."

"Grandma said it was for protection…" *And she died giving it to me…*Just for an instant Donna felt the clasp of dead fingers around her wrist. "I think I'll hang onto it." She scooped her canvas shoulder bag up off the floor and forced the pin through the thick fabric. "Besides, I'm the one who's starting university in six days; I'm the one who's going to need the luck."

"Suit yourself," Bradley shrugged, his expression unreadable, and slouched out of the family room.

"Shing Li-ung?"

Three inches had become thirty feet; thirty feet of shimmering scarlet and gold in constant flowing motion. Tooth and claw gleamed, strength and power in every curve, in every edge, in every point. Its eyes were deep and black and the light from a thousand stars shone in their depths. The air around it smelled strongly of ginger and when she drew it into her lungs, it burned just a little.

It was frightening but she wasn't frightened—which made perfect sense at the time.

Then it bent its great head and asked her a question.

She spread her hands. "I don't speak Mandarin."

It frowned and asked again.

"If you don't speak English, how about French?" She felt it sigh, the warm wave of its breath rolling over her, sweeping her away until the dragon was no more than a red and gold speck in the distance.

And then she woke up.

The red and gold speck remained and for a moment the dream seemed more real than her bedroom. But only for a moment as normalcy fell quickly back into place. A narrow beam of light from a street-lamp at the curb spilled through a crack in the curtains and across her shoulder bag propped on the top of her dresser. It illuminated the pin, igniting the enamel into a cold fire.

Pretty but hardly mystical, Donna decided, and padded across the room to twitch the curtains closed. With one hand full of fabric, she paused, frowned, and took a closer look at the dragon. Shing Li-ung no longer looked sad.

It looked disgusted.

"Hey Bradley, have you seen my bag, I had it when I got home this afternoon but I haven't seen it...oh, there it is." She moved her brother's feet and scooped the bag up off the end of the couch. "What are you watching?"

"Television."

"Very informative." A quick glance at Shing Li-ung showed it still looked disgusted. Its expression hadn't changed in the last four weeks and Donna was beginning to believe she'd imagined the whole thing. Although, considering that it had just spent three hours pointed at primetime programming, it had reason for looking disgusted tonight. "This show any good?"

"It's crap."

"Then why are you watching it?"

"What else am I supposed to do?" Bradley jabbed at the remote. The new program didn't look significantly different; same dizzy blonde, same square-jawed hunk, same disgustingly cute kid.

Donna sighed and sat down on the arm of the couch. Always prickly, since Labor Day Bradley had been developing a noticeable attitude. "Is everything all right at school?"

"Why shouldn't it be?"

"I don't know, you just seem kind of, well, cranky." Not the right word but she couldn't think of a better one.

"Cranky?" He spat it back at her. "Little kids get *cranky*."

"Look, I just wondered…"

"Well, you can stop. You don't know shit anymore about what's going on with me."

She should have remembered. He'd been impossible when the year between them had left him behind in junior high. God only knew what he'd get into now. And now, he was old enough to get into things that could have serious consequences. She *was* the oldest. He was, to a certain extent, her responsibility.

"So," she tried again, "how's Craig?"

"How should I know?"

"But he's your best friend."

"Was. I have other friends now."

Great. "Bradley…"

"Kae Bing."

Donna blinked, brought to a full stop. Finally she managed a weak, "What?"

"Kae Bing. It's my name."

"But you hate that name, you never let *anyone* use it. You told Aunt Lily it sounded like a chicken puking."

"Maybe I changed my mind. Maybe I want to get in touch with my Chinese heritage."

"Bradley...Okay," she raised a hand in surrender, "Kae Bing, that makes as much sense as black guys in the seventies calling themselves Kunta Kinte."

"African-Canadian."

"What?"

"Nobody says 'black guys' anymore. You're the *oldest*, I thought you would have known that. Everybody has a hyphen now. Oh, pardon me, everybody who isn't white has a hyphen now."

The laugh sounded forced, even to her. "Oh come on, we live in Don Mills, the definitive suburb, you can't get any whiter than that."

He didn't smile. "Looked in a mirror lately, Chun Chun? Well I hate to break this to you, but you aren't white. *You're* what's known as a visible ethnic minority. And what's really disgusting, you go out of your way to fit the stereotype." He began ticking points off on his fingers, the edge in his voice sharping with every point. "You're quiet, you're polite. I've never seen you lose your temper. You don't smoke, you don't drink, and you probably don't even kiss with your mouth open. You're a dutiful daughter, a good student—especially in all those subjects us Asians are supposed to be good at like math and physics. You even play ping pong for chrisakes."

Donna opened and closed her mouth a few times but all she managed to get out was, "What's wrong with playing ping pong?"

"Not a damn thing. It *is* the only sport we slants excel at after all." He threw the remote to the floor and flung himself up onto his feet. "Well, you can keep playing by their rules if you want to, Donna..." He weighted the name and threw it at her as he stomped out of the room, "...but I quit."

"But Mom, you should have heard him. He was really angry."

"Young men his age are always angry."

"Not like this." Donna paced the length of the kitchen trying to think of some way to make her mother understand. "He
wanted me to call him Kae Bing."

"It is his name."

"But he hates it!"

"He's just looking for something to believe in. That's common enough."

"But he's hardly ever home anymore and when he is he
spends all his time sulking in front of the television."

"Leave him be, Donna. It's harder for boys."

"What is?"

"Finding out who you are."

"I know who *I* am."

"You're a girl. And, you're the..."

"...oldest. Yeah, I know."

"But Dad, what do you know about these new friends of his?"

"Your brother is almost seventeen years old, Donna. He's
capable of choosing his own friends."

She couldn't believe she'd heard correctly. "You wanted to
know the family background of every person I ever spoke to."

"You're a girl. Boys need more freedom."

The habit of being a dutiful daughter closed her mouth on
the reply she wanted to make, but only just.

"Was that all, honey? I really have to get this report done for
tomorrow."

"That's all, Dad. Good night."

If they wouldn't listen, what could she do?

It moved like fire and air and water all at once and its beauty
brought a lump to her throat. It lowered its head until she could
see into the diamond-strewn blackness of its eyes and it asked,
"WHAT IS EVIL?"

Shing Li-ung seemed to have learned English in the last
month. She hoped it hadn't picked up any bad habits from all
the television it had been exposed to.

It didn't seem to mind having to wait for an answer.

"Evil is hurting someone else," she told it at last.

"So," golden brows drew down and light glinted off a thousand pointed teeth, "BY YOUR DEFINITION IT IS SOMETIMES NECESSARY TO DO EVIL."

She had a sudden vision of taking a baseball bat to the side of her brother's head. "To prevent a greater evil, yes."

It cocked its head. "THE YOUNG LIVE LIFE SO SIMPLY," it said thoughtfully.

"And the old complicate life with the past."

It laughed then and the sound vibrated through her body, shaking blood and bone and tissue. While not exactly an unpleasant feeling, it wasn't one she was in any hurry to repeat.

"YOU ARE WORTHY," it told her, twisted back on itself and disappeared.

"Well, whoop de do," she muttered and fell deeper into sleep.

Donna had taken the special eight week night course at Victoria College over her parents' objections and would have thrown that small act of defiance in Bradley's face—except she never saw him any more. She left early every morning for the long transit ride downtown and, as Bradley had no classes until ten, she was gone before he got up. He was never home in the evenings, having suddenly acquired more freedom than she'd ever been allowed.

She'd seen his new friends only once when they'd dropped him off late one Saturday—or early one Sunday—and the noise of their talking and laughing had woken her up. From her window, she'd seen the red glow of a trio of cigarettes and heard how "they wouldn't be allowed to take over our town. They can just fucking get back on the boats and go back where they came from." She didn't care who "they" were; she wasn't impressed.

"What?" Bradley had demanded the next day when she'd approached him. "You think they're not good enough for me 'cause I don't have an accent? 'Cause they know what it's like to be Chinese? 'Cause they're living with their heritage not hiding and pretending?"

"No one except you cares that you're Chinese!"

"My point exactly," he sneered and flicked the dragon pin with a fingernail. "You think you're so smart…"

"No," she snapped, "but I think Dad's going to kick your butt if he finds out you're smoking. You know how he got about it after Uncle Karl."

Uncle Karl had been a two pack a day smoker and had died at fifty-one, both lungs eaten away by cancer.

The new friends never dropped him off at the house after that but Donna was sure nothing else had changed. Maybe next year, when he'd pulled even with her again and was at university too, they'd be able to talk. Meanwhile, she could only hope he didn't get into anything he couldn't get out of.

She was thinking of transverse vectors, not her brother, when she came down the steps of Victoria College and realized that, except for her, the night was empty. What had happened to the other thirty-seven students in the class? She'd stayed to ask a couple of questions but she hadn't stayed that long. Had she? The echo of a stereo drifted down from the student residence to the east but the paths were deserted and dark and the subway a long, lonely distance away.

I'm being ridiculous. She settled her bag more firmly on her shoulder and clamped it securely down with her elbow, the edge of enameled tin cutting into her upper arm. The soles of her shoes made a soft squelching sound against the mat of fallen leaves that covered the pavement as she started towards Queen's Park Circle and the security of street-lights and traffic. *Once I get out onto the street, everything will be…*

Will be…

Between her and the street, a shadow moved. It could have been the trees, tossing in the wind…

One foot lifted to step forward, she paused, and turned and started moving quickly along the darker paths that cut between the university buildings. *I'm being ridiculous,* she told herself again but she couldn't make herself believe it.

"Hey, China doll."

The voice came from behind her, from the way she had so suddenly decided not to go. Her legs moved faster; not running, not yet. The buildings around her were locked and dark. The only safety lay three hundred twisting meters away where the paths came out into the blaze of light that was University Avenue. Three hundred meters.

She started to run.

A hand grabbed hold of her jacket and jerked back hard. She went down, arms flailing wildly in an effort to keep her moving forward. Moving away. Moving to safety. Then a larger, heavier body landed on top of her.

"Hey, China doll, I don't want to hurt you. I just want us to have some fun."

The hand he clapped over her mouth when she opened it to scream smelled of deodorant soap and the cuff button of his leather school jacket dug into her cheek. He was blonde. He was clean-shaven. He was smiling. His breath smelled like peppermints and beer. He shifted his weight, grinding her head through the pad of dead leaves and into the concrete.

"Now, we can get something going here if you'll just stop…"

She didn't so much stop fighting, as stop moving. In fact, at that moment, she doubted she was capable of movement. Her eyes were open so wide, they hurt.

"Hey! What're you staring at?"

Red and gold it towered up behind his shoulder. Beautiful. Terrible. Impossible.

Real.

Blood splashed against her face as talons dug deep and lifted him skyward. He twisted against their grip for a second, staring down at her in disbelief. Then he screamed.

Donna screamed with him. And when he stopped, she went on screaming.

"ARE YOU HURT?"

The voice rang through her head like a gong, impossible to ignore. "I, I don't think so."

"THEN WHY DO YOU MAKE SUCH A NOISE?"

"I, uh, I…" She got slowly to her feet, head craned back, eyes still open painfully wide. It was like sitting too close to the screen in a movie theater; too much to take in all at once. The smell of ginger made her want to sneeze. *I'm not afraid,* she realized. *I was, but now I'm not.* She took a step back, and then another, and then, in the red/gold light that came off the dragon, caught sight of the broken body crumpled across the path, one massive taloned forefoot still resting negligently across its back. "Oh my god, you killed him!"

"Yes."

Her exclamation had been purely instinctive. Shing Li-ung's placid confirmation transferred her growing sense of wonder into outrage. "You can't *do* that!"

It cocked its head to one side and regarded her with mild curiosity. "WHY NOT? I HAVE PROTECTED YOU AS I PROTECTED YOUR GRANDMOTHER."

"You just can't kill somebody like that!"

It looked down at the body. "YES I CAN."

"Well," she threw her shoulders back, "if that's the kind of protection you offer, I don't want it."

Great golden brows drew in. "BUT I MUST PROTECT THE HOLDER OF THE TALISMAN."

"Do you have to *kill* people?"

"I MUST PROTECT YOU."

"But you don't have to kill people!"

The shrug rippled the full thirty-foot length of Shing Li-ung's serpentine body. It didn't look convinced. "YOU HAVE BEEN GIVEN THE TALISMAN."

"Then you must obey me?"

"NO. I MUST PROTECT YOU."

"I don't believe this," Donna muttered and brushed her hair back off her face. Her hand came away damp and sticky. Her heart back in her throat, she held it out and in the dragon's light she saw it smeared with blood. "I don't believe this!" But this time the words were wailed as whatever cocooning the dragon's presence had offered peeled away.

An echoing wail came from behind the surrounding buildings, from the street.

The sound brought a new panic.

"The police! Someone called the police."

"You were making a great deal of noise," Shing Li-ung observed.

"But what do I do? He's dead!"

"Are you in danger?"

Her laugh hung on the edge of hysteria. "I am if I stay here. I'll end up in the psycho wards. I didn't kill him, Your Honor, my grandmother's dragon did."

"If you are in danger, I must protect you."

In the next instant, she stood on the front porch of her parent's house in Don Mills, safe in the suburbs, miles away from the savagely murdered body of a young man. *And barely a month ago I was freaked by my grandmother dying peacefully in bed...*

Her hands shook too violently for her to open the door so she leaned against the bell.

"Keep your pants on, jeez, I'm...Donna?"

"Mom? Dad?"

Bradley dragged her inside and managed to hang onto her as she sagged against him. "Mom's at Aunt Lily's and Dad's working late. Christ, Donna, you're covered in blood!"

"Not mine."

"Not yours!?" His voice which hadn't cracked in years shifted an octave on the second word. He lowered her onto a chair and gripped her shoulders so tightly she squeaked in pain. "What happened to you!?"

"What happened to me?" Donna shrugged his hands away and dragged the canvas bag down onto her lap, turning the dragon pin into the light. The tiny golden claws were red. "What happened to me?" she repeated, just barely holding on to coherency. "Oh, nothing much happened to *me*."

"...and then I was home."

Bradley sighed, a long exhalation that released all the interruptions he'd wanted to make but hadn't throughout her story. She wouldn't let him touch the dragon so he sat and stared at it as she turned it over and over between fingers puckered by almost thirty minutes in the shower.

She looked up at the sound and waited for him to speak, wondering what he was thinking. Would he think she'd gone crazy? Had she? But he didn't speak and she couldn't read his expression. The silence lengthened until she broke under the weight of it. "Well?"

"I need a smoke."

"No, you don't!" The response was automatic older sister and it snapped her past some of what she supposed had to be shock. She sighed in turn and felt the knot in her stomach begin to ease with the wavering breath. "Bradley, please…"

He spread his hands. "I want to believe you," he said simply.

And he did. Donna recognized his expression now. Hope. A desperate hope. She thought she'd done all the crying she could in the shower. She was wrong.

"Jeez, Donna, don't. I mean, you're all right, right? Like that guy didn't hurt you and you're okay. You said, Shing Li-ung came in time. I mean, jeez, please Donna, stop crying."

Because it was upsetting him, she tried. It took a few minutes. "Why don't you believe me?" she asked when she finally regained control.

He shrugged, watching her nervously in case she should break down again. "Well, I mean…a dragon?"

She rubbed her nose on the fuzzy purple sleeve of her old bathrobe. "You're the one who's always going on about Chinese heritage. Dragons are a part of that."

"Yes…" He turned that over, accepted it.

"And you know I never lie. Not even when it would keep me out of trouble. Even when it would keep us out of trouble. You always said it was one of my most annoying habits. If I never lied before, why now? And why about something so…so extreme."

"Why indeed?" His sudden smile illuminated the room. "Donna, this is awesome. A dragon, a real dragon."

"No, Bradley…"

"Kae Bing. And what do you mean, no?"

"It isn't awesome, at least not like you mean…that boy is dead."

"So?"

"Dead!" she repeated. "And Shing Li-ung killed him."

"He deserved to die."

"It's not that simple," she began but she saw suddenly for Bradley, for Kae Bing, it was that simple. "Look, you can't just go around saying that some people deserve to die."

"Can't I?" He jerked to his feet, hands balled into fists. "Well, maybe Saint Donna can't, but I can. Get some sleep and forget about that round-eye punk, he got what he deserved." Half out of the room, he paused and looked back. "Oh, and I wouldn't tell Mom or Dad about this. *They* wouldn't understand."

Then to Donna's surprise he bowed to the bit of enameled tin she still held in her hand.

The boy's name had been Alan Ford and all three city papers had a full report of his death. The tabloid even had color pictures. Not one of the papers mentioned a thirty-foot long, scarlet and gold Chinese dragon although all of them mentioned multiple knife wounds.

To her parent's relief, Donna dropped out of the night school course and unless she had a crowd of friends around her, she stayed off the paths in the daytime as well. But even crowds couldn't stop her reaction to blond hair and leather university jackets.

Shing Li-ung stayed at home on her dresser, watching its own reflection in the mirror. Donna had no intention of being responsible for releasing the dragon again.

"I MUST PROTECT YOU."

"No!"

"WHY DO YOU FEAR ME?"

"Because you burn too brightly."

"I MUST PROTECT YOU."

"Get out of my dreams!"

"Mr. Chen?"

"Yes, I'm David Chen. What is it Officer?"

"Are you the father of Bradley Chen?"

Donna came out of the family room, one finger holding her

place in a physics text, heart beating so loudly she was certain the two police constables at the front door must hear.

"I'm Bradley's father, yes."

"Your son has been injured, Mr. Chen."

"Injured? Bradley? How?"

Standing just behind her father's shoulder, Donna saw the look they exchanged. *How much do we tell him?*

"There was a gang fight, in the Dragon Mall, on Spadina..."

"And my Bradley got caught in it?"

No, Dad...

"No, Mr. Chen. Your son was part of a Chinese gang attempting to force a Vietnamese gang off their turf."

"That's impossible!" She could feel the indignation coming off him in waves. "My son would never get involved in something like that."

"There's no doubt about his involvement, Mr. Chen."

"Well, you're wrong!"

No, Dad...

"We're sorry, Mr. Chen but..."

"You said he's injured, where is he?"

"He's been taken to Wellesley Hospital."

"Well, I'll go to him. I'll talk to him. You'll see. He wasn't involved in this. You're wrong."

Again, Donna saw the silent exchange between the two constables.

"Dad, I'm going with you." She knew without looking that the dragon pin would be missing from her dresser.

Bradley had remained quiet and unresponsive throughout their father's questioning. He had admitted being part of the gang, his lower lip thrust out in what looked to Donna like a defiant pout, but he had refused to co-operate any further. Finally, the police took their father aside for a private discussion and Donna was left alone with her brother.

He'd had a hundred and thirty-seven stitches, mostly in his right arm and side. She thought the bandages and the tubes made him look ridiculously young and she couldn't think of what to say.

Bradley finally broke the silence.

"It's in the drawer."

She pulled the pin out of the jumble of personnel effects—the contents of his pockets, his watch, an earring; *When had he gotten his ear pierced?*—and brought it back to the bed.

"You really sucked me in." His voice had the rough rasp of unshed tears behind it.

"What?"

"I believed you. Believed your stupid story about the dragon. There isn't any dragon. There never was."

Donna closed her fingers so tightly around Shing Li-ung the edges cut into her palm. Anger she could have dealt with but not this black despair.

"Oh, stop crying. I've learned my lesson."

"Good." Donna drew in a long shuddering breath and swiped at her cheeks with her empty hand. "So you'll come home and stop seeing these people and stop this gang stuff. Bradley, I…"

"Kae Bing!" He spat the name at her. Now, the anger showed. "Shall I tell you what I've learned? I've learned that if we're going to make a place for our people in this country, and hold it, we're going to have to do it one drop of blood at a time." He couldn't move his right arm but his left came up off the bed and his fist punched the air. "If they use knives, we'll use knives. If they use guns, we'll use guns."

"You sound like a bad remake of West Side Story." She couldn't believe she was hearing this. "You haven't learned anything."

"I learned the lesson your *dragon* taught me; we can't count on outside help. We have to do this ourselves." He turned his head on the pillow. "Now get that piece of junk jewelry out of my room. I'm tired."

"Bradley…I mean, Kae Bing, I want to help…"

The glimmer of silver between his lids was her only answer. She watched one lone tear roll onto his pillow then, slipping the pin in her bag, she left the room. She didn't know what else to do.

* * *

"Why didn't you protect him?!"

"I WAS NOT GIVEN TO HIM."

"But you were with him! And he only acted so foolishly because he thought you'd protect him."

Shing Li-ung looked somewhat taken aback. "YOU DO NOT KNOW THAT."

"I do know that. You inspired his recklessness."

"I DID NOT."

"You did."

"DID NOT."

"Did. And now because you didn't show up, he's convinced that the gang answer is the right answer."

"THE YOUNG CAN CONVINCE THEMSELVES OF ANYTHING."

"Well, you should have protected him against that too!"

"THERE IS NO PROTECTION AGAINST YOUTH SAVE TIME. AND BE-SIDES, I WAS NOT GIVEN TO HIM. I MUST PROTECT THE ONE I HAVE BEEN GIVEN TO." It snorted and the smell of ginger became al-most overpowering. "IF THAT ONE IS WORTHY."

"Oh that's it. You didn't find my brother worthy so you let him almost die?"

"IT DID NOT COME TO THAT. I MUST FIRST BE GIVEN." Obviously considering that to be the final word on the matter, it twisted back on itself and disappeared.

"Come back here! This is my dream and I'll tell you when you can leave! Shing Li-ung! Shing Li-ung!"

Her anger almost woke her but she fought her way deeper into sleep, searching for the dragon, chasing a gleam of scarlet and gold.

Winter broke before Bradley left the hospital and Donna sus-pected the weather, not his injuries or the terms of his probation, kept him home. He spent long hours on the telephone, talking, she was sure, with his *friends* from downtown, keeping the an-ger alive. It didn't help that most of the kids at school consid-ered him some kind of hero.

Donna tried to understand what he was angry about but it seemed directed at being Chinese—not because he didn't want to be, but because he did. Her own anger she reserved for her family, who seemed to think that by ignoring the problem, it'd go away.

She buried Shing Li-ung in her underwear drawer.

In March, when the snow stopped and the air began to warm, the patterns of the previous autumn reappeared.

"Say, Donna, isn't that your brother?"

If it was, he'd skipped his afternoon classes again. "Where?"

"On the corner, with those other two guys. I didn't know he smoked."

"He doesn't."

"He is."

The other two guys were all angles and edges with slicked back hair and muscles pulled tight over bone. Inside their expensive clothes and heavy jewelry, they moved with the boneless grace of alley cats anticipating a fight. What bothered Donna the most was not how different Bradley looked, but how much the same.

"I better go over and talk to him."

"He doesn't look like he wants to be bothered."

"Tough." But by the time she got across the street, they'd already begun to move and she had to hurry to catch up.

"...be there tonight."

"I'll be there." Bradley tossed his cigarette in the gutter. "Jade Garden Night Club Restaurant. One-thirty in the am."

"Why don't you just tell the world?" hissed the taller of his companions.

Bradley's laugh scraped at the hair on the back of Donna's neck. "We'll have the guns," he pointed out. "Who's going to stop us?"

That's my cue, Donna thought, feet suddenly rooted to the sidewalk as the trio pulled ahead and turned the corner onto Beverly without ever seeing her. Jade Garden Night Club Restaurant. One-thirty am. We'll have the guns.

I could tell the police; if nothing else, Bradley's breaking probation. Except that he was her brother and, as much as it was the sensible, right thing to do, she couldn't do it.

I could tell Mom and Dad, and they'd say boys will be boys and insist he's given up all that gang nonsense, that he swears he's given it up. "And it would never occur to them that someone who gets into knife fights in shopping malls could be lying."

"What?"

"Nothing…" She flushed and started walking, ignoring the worried looks shot her way by the two elderly women who'd heard her talking to herself. Their parents expected both her and Bradley to fit neatly into the lives they'd devised for them. That she did made it even harder on Bradley who didn't. The incident last fall had shaken their belief in the system only for a moment.

So. It looks like it's up to me. She fought with a sudden irrational desire to rip open her jacket and yell, This is a job for, Shing Li-ung!

If the dragon deigned to make an appearance. It had already refused to rescue her brother once.

And what are you going to do if Shing Li-ung doesn't show? Donna asked herself later that night, emotions trembling on the edge of hysteria. *Stick the bad guys with the rusty pin and hope they get tetanus?* She'd told her parents she had to go back downtown to use the library. It was the first time she'd been out after dark on her own since…

A tall young man across the subway gave her a speculative look. Donna jerked her head away and stared fixedly at her reflection. *Don't try anything, buddy. I've got a dragon in my pocket.*

She stayed at the library until it closed at eleven and then closed down the coffee shop across the street at twelve. The Jade Garden Night Club Restaurant was on Baldwin between Beverly and McCall, right in the heart of Chinatown. The library—and the coffee shop—was only five blocks north—five short blocks—so she arrived just before twelve thirty, the dragon clutched in a sweaty hand, heart leaping into her throat at any and every noise.

The restaurant was locked although she could see people moving around inside, lifting chairs onto tables, sweeping the floor.

Am I too late? Has it happened?

Moving slowly and carefully, trying to see everything at once, she backed to the edge of the sidewalk. The health food store across the road had large empty plywood bins out front, a perfect hiding place if she wanted to watch and wait for Bradley then…then…then what? She still didn't know.

This is ridiculous. I should have told someone. I don't know what I'm doing here.

But she went and hid in the bin anyway, crawling through the open back, trying to ignore the rotting bits of vegetable on the pavement. She was the oldest. He was her responsibility. Just for an instant, she envied Bradley his ability, or at least his attempt, to break free of the conditioning they'd faced all their lives. *But if I break free, little brother, where does that leave you?*

The car pulled up at twelve fifty, when only one light remained on in the restaurant and most of the staff had left. It cruised by not two feet from where Donna knelt, turned into the alley way beside the store, and cut the engine.

No.

It hadn't happened.

This was it.

The silence thickened until it lay over the street like a fog, enclosing it, isolating it. The steady traffic on Beverly, only two short blocks to the west, sounded muffled and distant. She wouldn't have heard the car doors, or the footsteps approaching, had she not been listening so desperately for them.

"He's still inside. That's his car down the street."

They were leaning on the outside of her bin. Donna peered through the crack where moisture had warped the boards apart. Her brother looked like a stranger, all angles and edges.

"Remember, full automatic. Don't worry about accuracy. We've got to do them and get out of here."

"Them?" She could see the curve of a black tube cradled in Bradley's arms. It took her a moment to realize it was part of a gun. She'd never seen a gun before. "What do you mean *them*? I thought we were after Bui? We take out the leader of the most powerful Vietnamese gang and the gang falls apart. I mean, that was the plan."

"Hey, Kae Bing, chill out. Bui owns this place and the guy who manages it for him is in gang business up to his balls. He launders the gambling money, stores the dope, pimps for the whores. We do him too."

"Besides," the second of Bradley's companions took a long pull on his cigarette, "they'll come out together. It's all or nothing."

Nothing, Donna prayed. *Please God, nothing.* Her brother's jacket brushed up against the bin. She could slip the dragon pin through the space between the boards and drop it into his pocket. Give him the dragon. There was nothing she could do about the two men in the restaurant but at least Bradley would be safe.

"What's taking them so long?"

"You scared, Kae Bing?"

"Fuck you."

He was scared. She could hear it in the bravado. Holding Shing Li-ung by the very end of its tail, Donna pushed the other end at the crack. There'd be just barely enough room—if only there'd be enough time. Then the clasp caught on a sliver of wood and jerked the dragon out of her grip. It twisted back on itself, hit her shoulder, her knee, and rang against the pavement under the bin.

"Hey, what was that?"

She froze, too frightened even to blink.

"What was what?"

"I heard something under here." Bradley slapped his palm down and the wood over Donna's head boomed.

"Probably a rat. Or a cat, or something."

"Well, I'm going to look."

"No time. Here they come."

It suddenly didn't matter if they heard her. She pressed her face up to the boards as the door to the restaurant opened and three people came out onto the step.

"Hey wait!" She saw Bradley's arm go out, stopping the surge forward. "There's a waitress with them."

"So?" They shook free of his restraint. "Come on. We've got to do them before they reach the bottom of the stairs."

"You can't shoot her!"

"Wanna bet?"

Donna, eye tight against the hole, saw her brother break into a run towards the three figures on the steps and knew without a doubt what he was going to do. Desperately, she scraped the pavement with her fingers, searching for the dragon.

He'd gone four steps when she found it.

Six when she threw herself out of the bin.

Seven and the guns came up.

Eight, he grabbed the terrified woman by the arm.

Nine, he threw her out of the way.

On ten, they opened fire.

"No!" Donna's scream got lost in other screams, in the spitting roar of the pair of submachine guns, in lead impacting with flesh. She didn't feel the pavement rip through her jeans and into both her knees as she flung herself down by Bradley's side. Two crimson rosettes blossomed and spread across his chest and a line of them stitched color down his leg.

But he was breathing. And conscious.

"Donna?"

"Shut up!" She snatched his hand up off of the ground, forced the bent fingers straight, and pressed Shing Li-ung into his palm. "Here, this is yours now, I'm giving it to you."

He blinked. Tried to focus on his hand. Couldn't do it. "Wha…?"

"Fucking stupid, Kae Bing."

And the world came back.

"You just signed your death warrant, you know." The quiet conversational tone was infinitely more terrifying than an attempt to terrify would have been. "You *and* your girlfriend."

"My…sis…ter."

"Rough luck for your folks," said one, shaking his head.

"Say good-bye," said the other.

The guns came up. Donna saw their fingers tighten on the triggers and afterwards, although she knew it was impossible, she swore she saw the first bullets emerge.

Then the street between them became filled with thirty feet of scarlet and gold dragon.

"Ho...ly...fuck."

Shing Li-ung bent its massive head down until its golden mustaches brushed the pavement and just for an instant Donna saw her brother reflected in the starlit depths of its eyes. "YOU RISKED YOUR LIFE FOR ANOTHER," it observed. "YOU ARE WORTHY."

"Awe...some."

The dragon smiled. "YES."

Then it turned and faced the gunmen.

Donna closed her eyes. The wail of a police siren snapped them open again. She should have realized. Fifty-two division was barely four blocks away. They must have heard the shots.

"Shing Li-ung! Look out..."

Then she was looking through red and gold after-images at a police car and an empty street. Two submachine guns lay by the opposite curb and a rain of bullets dropped harmlessly to the pavement between. An Asian police constable stood half out of the car, staring wide-eyed at the space where Shing Li-ung had been, murmuring *Tien Lung* over and over.

"Jesus H. Christ!" His partner obviously saw only the bodies and the blood.

The next little while became a kaleidoscope of flashing lights, loud voices, and the lingering scent of ginger. Gently, but firmly, the ambulance attendants moved Donna away from her brother and she found herself standing beside the young woman whose life he'd saved.

Cold fingers clutched at her arm. "The dragon can't let him die."

"It doesn't work like that."

"Then tell me his name, I'll pray to the Buddha for him."

Donna closed her hand around the enameled pin that had slid to the pavement, the curved loop of Shing Li-ung's tail cutting into her palm. It took a moment for her to find her voice. "His name," she said, swallowing tears, "is Kae Bing."

* * *

The graveyard was still and quiet, the only sound a cicada high in one of the surrounding trees. Donna laid Shing Li-ung down on top of the tombstone and dug a stick of incense out of her purse, her hand a little unsteady as she bent and pushed one end into the grass.

She stepped to one side as Kae Bing knelt and pulled out a disposable lighter.

"Not very traditional," he muttered, "but it'll have to do."

Donna slipped a hand under his elbow to steady him as he stood. Over a month in hospital had left him weak and pale, tiring easy, still in pain, but alive. His trial was scheduled for October 6th, over thirteen weeks away, but everyone concerned seemed to think his dramatic change of heart combined with a willingness to co-operate would keep him out of prison.

No one mentioned the dragon.

The bodies of the two gunmen still hadn't been found.

"Are you sure this is going to work?"

"Look," Donna sighed and pushed her hair back off her face, "we agreed that Shing Li-ung is too much for one person to handle."

Kae Bing patted the warm marble of the tombstone, brows drawn down. "Grandma managed."

"Grandma knew who she was. She had centuries of history behind her. What do we have? We're not white, we're not Chinese..."

"But we have a dragon." Shaking off the melancholy, her brother grinned. "Let's get on with it."

They each gripped one corner of the dragon pin between thumb and forefinger and held it over the rising column of blue-grey smoke.

"If this doesn't work, we're going to feel like idiots," Kae Bing pointed out, nervously licking his lips.

"If this doesn't work," Donna reminded him, squinting through the smoke, "we've got something much bigger to worry about."

"Yeah. About thirty feet bigger." His brows dipped down again. "I wonder where it came from."

"Maybe, it came from where we're sending it."

He blinked and shook his head. "Deep Donna. Very deep. So let's do it on three..."

Their unison sound a little ragged and, over her brother's deeper, measured tones, Donna could hear her voice shaking.

"We give Shing Li-ung, Shining Heart, to the spirit of Chinese-Canadians so that spirit might be protected."

They'd argued for weeks about the wording.

The colors of the pin began to move; to throb to the beating of a pair of hearts; to swirl about in a pattern too complicated to understand.

And then all they held was memory as the smoke from the incense rose over their heads and disappeared.

Kae Bing swallowed audibly. "Holy shit. It worked."

"Yeah." Donna stared down at her fingertips then slowly raised them to brush at the tears trickling down her cheeks. She didn't know why she was crying. It wasn't as though they'd actually given the dragon away.

"Uh, Donna? We forgot, I mean, how are we going to know if it considers them...us...worthy?"

"Mommy! Look at the kite! Look at the dragon kite."

A number of people at the First Annual Chinese Heritage Festival squinted skyward, heads turned by the piping cry of the child. High overhead, far above the other kites, a scarlet and gold celestial dragon gleamed iridescent in the sunlight and danced with the wind. It swept over the crowd, then rose on a hundred breaths exhaled in wonder.

Donna, her fingers white around the frame of the kite she carried, felt as though her ribs were suddenly too small to contain her heart. Faces all around her seemed lit from within. Even her parents, pulled protesting out of the suburbs by the determination of both their children, watched the dragon with a new awareness shining from their eyes. Kae Bing lifted one hand to the sky in salute.

She bit her lip, afraid she might cry out. *So, Shing Li-ung,* she gave the thought to the wind. *Does this mean we're worthy?*

From deep within, and from high above, and from all the people around came the answer.

DID YOU EVER DOUBT IT?

When we expanded our property, the additional 25 acres came with an old car that a previous owner had dragged out into a clearing in the woods. I'm the only one in the family who thinks it looks like a 1976 Saab 900…

I loved that car.

FIRST LOVE, LAST LOVE

"Hey Dad! There's a robin the size of a Buick on that round cement thing in the lawn."

Back bowed under the weight of half a sofa, Nigel Richards groped for the first of the cement steps with the toe of his work-boot. "Admire the wildlife later," he grunted at his oldest son. "For now, can we get this thing inside?"

"Sure, Dad. No problemo."

"Easy for you to say." Nigel shifted his grip and braced the heavy piece of furniture against his knee. "Your back is twenty-three years younger than mine." As they moved the sofa up the four steps and in through the front door he tried to remember why not hiring professional movers had seemed like such a good idea at the time. *"Raymond and I can do the heavy lifting; think of the money we'll save."* Next time, they'd spend the money.

And it's not like we don't have it to spend. Two days of Lynn's consulting fees would've covered it. After all, Lynn's consulting fees had bought them the house and the twenty-five acres of land it sat on.

"You okay, Dad?"

"Fine, Ray. Just fine." Maybe their savings could buy him a new back.

The sofa, which had dominated their living room in the city, was in turn dominated by the room it now found itself in. "Nigel, just look at this." Box braced against her hip, Lynn Richards indicated the ceiling with a lift of her chin. "That's the original patterned tin, I'm sure of it."

"Sweetheart, as long as it stays where it is, it can be the original carved stone for all I care." He pulled himself erect on his wife's shoulder. "We have too much stuff. We should treat this place like a new beginning and simplify."

"We should have simplified before we packed it all into boxes and moved it."

"Good point."

Ray looked up from the floor where he'd thrown himself to better sort a stack of cd's. He'd personally seen to it that the stereo had been the first item unloaded and had immediately set it up; just in case it had been damaged in transit. "Yeah, Dad, no point in locking the garage after the bike's been stolen."

"Words of wisdom for our time." Nigel sank down onto the end of the sofa. "Which, oh fruit of my loins, is one of the reasons we moved. You don't have to lock the garage door out here."

"It's not a garage," declared a new voice, authoritatively. "It's a shed. And it doesn't have a door. Or much of a roof."

Nigel twisted around to face his daughter. "It doesn't need a roof, Dorrie…"

"Doris!"

"Right. Sorry." The instance on her full name had been a recent phenomenon. He still wasn't used to it. "It doesn't need a roof because there's less acid in the rain out here and the cars don't need the protection."

"I don't think that's right and besides, what about my baseball equipment?"

"What's wrong with the big old room behind the kitchen?"

She snorted.

Only a thirteen-year-old, Nigel reflected, who'd recently discovered that her parents weren't perfect could stack so much meaning on a single sound.

"You do realize, father…"

Use of the word *father* was recent vocabulary addition as

well. Nigel supposed it was a protest against authority. As protests went, he could live with it.

"...that we can't get cable out here. No cable means no TSN.
How am I supposed to watch my baseball games?"

"It won't hurt you to miss a few. You'll have more time to
practice." Girls in his day wanted to grow up to be...well, he
supposed he didn't actually know what girls in his day had
wanted but he was pretty sure they hadn't wanted to play short-
stop in the major leagues. "Where's your brother?"
Finger quivering with disdain, Doris pointed across the room.

"I meant the other one."

"Oh. Petey ran off to explore. I told him he should help
unload but he *never* listens."

"Speaking of unloading." Lynn shoved at her husband's
shoulder. "We have to have that truck back to the rental place
by five and there's still two dressers and the oak buffet left to
carry in."

"No problem, Mom." Ray rocked back on his heels and shot
to his feet. "Me and dad'll each take a dresser and that buffet's
not as heavy as it looks." Cranking the volume up on the stereo,
he danced out the door, yelling, "Come on, Dad!" back over one
gyrating shoulder.

Nigel sighed and rose considerably more slowly. "I feel old,"
he groaned and shuffled through drifts of crumpled newspaper
to the stereo where he slid the volume down.

"DAD!"

Recognizing the protest as a fair one—Ray *was* doing at least
half of the work—he eased it back up to a compromise position.
"Whatever happened to music?" he shouted over the heavy metal
pounding of a Metallica ballad. When his wife shrugged and his
daughter sneered, he decided he'd probably meant it as a rhe-
torical question anyway and followed Ray out into the yard.

"Hey Dad! You gotta come and see what I found!"

Wondering how the hell they'd gotten the buffet *into* the truck,
Nigel didn't bother to turn. "Shouldn't you be helping your
mother in the house, Peter?"

"But Dad, this is great! It's a car. A really, really old car."

"How old?" It was the wrong shape to fit on the dolly; maybe they'd turned it sideways.

"Really old." The metal truck bed echoed as Peter bounced up the ramp. "At least as old as you."

Had they laid it down?

"Dad!"

Nigel finally turned to face his youngest and found, as usual, his resolve couldn't stand against the enthusiasm in Peter's hazel eyes.

"Hey Dad!" Having taken both dressers into the house, Ray was ready to start on the buffet. "Where are *you* going?"

"Pete's found an abandoned car on our property. He's taking me to see it."

"Cool." Ray fell into step beside his brother and shoved him sideways. "Way to go, squirt."

Peter shoved back. "I'm not a squirt," he protested. "You're an orangutan."

"Bet you don't even know what an orangutan is."

"Do too. It's a big orange ape that lives in Madagascar. And you're a big orange ape that lives...ow! Dad!"

As Nigel knew Peter was in no danger, and would in fact protest even more strongly should he interfere, he ignored the noisy battle and kept walking in the direction indicated. Ray got his carrot top from his mother but neither of them had any idea where he'd got the accompanying bulk. At fifteen he was already pushing six-foot and still growing. *Taller than his father already...Wasn't it just yesterday we brought him home from the hospital?*

A few moments later, the boys caught up.

"It's through these trees. You can't even see it 'til you're right on top of it." Peter leapt over a fallen log and charged through a break in the bushes. "Come on!"

Four months short of his sixteenth birthday and automotive freedom, Ray looked thoughtful as he shoved a sapling aside. "Maybe if it's in okay shape I could restore it. You know, like it could be my car."

"Don't get your hopes up," Nigel warned him as they passed the last barricade. "It's probably..."

"...a piece of junk," Ray finished as they emerged into the clearing and got their first look at Peter's discovery.

Behind the facade of a nearly complete body, white paint gleaming in the late afternoon sun, little more than rust remained. Unidentifiable bits of flaking red metal filled the roofless trunk, a sapling grew up through the space where the engine had been, wild grape vines buried the radiator, the only thing left under the hood—had there been a hood—and the tires had long since rotted down to collapsed rims. The back seat had been completely removed and large holes had been excavated in most of the front seat. The steering wheel and dashboard were in reasonably good shape although not one piece of glass had escaped destruction.

"Watch where you're walking, squirt." Ray grabbed the back of his brother's tee-shirt and hauled him to his side. "There's enough busted glass and metal around here to slice and dice and make julienne fries." He sighed and kicked at a door panel. "Not enough to make a car though. Come on, Dad. We better get that buffet unloaded before Mom blows. Dad?" He stared at his father who was staring at the car. "Dad?"

Nigel reached out and gently ran his fingers along the warm metal of the roof. "Boys, do you know what this is?"

"Yeah, it's industrial waste."

"No. It's a 1966 Ford Galaxy, seven-liter. It was a special upgrade on the regular Galaxy and there weren't that many sold. I had one just like it. It was my first car. Christ, this could *be* that car."

"Language, Dad."

"What? Oh, right, sorry." He shook himself, pushing away the memories that had crowed around. "Come on, we'd better get that buffet unloaded." At the edge of the trees, he stopped and looked back, murmuring again. "It could be that car."

"Don't see what you're getting so excited about. It doesn't look like it was that great a car."

"Not great?" Nigel turned to face his sons. "The Ford Galaxy seven liter was a 428 cubic inch, V-8 automatic, four speed, dual exhaust..." His expression softened as he looked into the past. "She had heavy duty suspension and held the road like she was holding her one true love. She handled like a charm, and fast...I'm telling you boys, there's nothing like the expression of shock on a guy's face when your family sedan peels away from his flashy muscle car."

Ray looked shocked. "You drag raced? My dad? The guy who's never even got a speeding ticket?"

"Not exactly drag race, no." Nigel cleared his throat. While he didn't want to set a bad example, neither did he want his teenage son to think of him as stuffy and old; not when he'd been suddenly reminded of how it felt to be young. "I bought her from my Uncle—your great-Uncle—Frank. Paid him two hundred and fifty dollars for her and even in 1971 that wasn't a lot of money. He cut me a deal because he loved the car himself."

"You couldn't get a good set of hubcaps for two hundred and fifty bucks today," Ray pointed out, slapping at a bug.

"Well, she didn't come with hubcaps but boy did she have heart. I loved that car. We *all* loved that car because I was the only one in my gang of friends with wheels. We called her the Jelly-roll."

"The what?"

Even Peter stopped trying to shinny up the uncooperative trunk of a beech tree and turned to stare at his father, repeating, "Jelly-roll?"

"Sure." Nigel smiled a little self-consciously. "My nickname when I was a kid, well, right up until I moved away to university—was Jelly."

"Dad," Ray frowned. "Nigel and jelly don't rhyme."

"It's a derivative son. Ni-*gel*. *Jel*-ly." He shook his head as the boys exchanged expressions of identical disbelief. "Never mind." Twisting protesting muscles for one final look at the wreck, he sighed. "My buddies and I cruised all over town in that car, windows down, radio up. We even had a set of fuzzy dice; red ones 'cause the car was white. Wimbleton white."

"That's a tennis tournament."

"No, no, it's the shade of white that Ford did their cars in '66. We thought it was *very* classy, *very* hip." He could feel the car behind them as they headed back to the house; and the buffet; and the unpacking; and the starting over somewhere new. "I haven't thought of the old Jelly-roll in years."

While Peter ran on ahead, Ray patted his father on the shoulder. "Yeah well, Dad, do me a favour would you? Never tell that story around any of my friends. It is so majorly uncool."

"Uncool?"

"Sure. I mean, a four-door sedan? Jelly-roll? Fuzzy dice?"

"And what would *you* consider to be cool?"

"A Firebird." Ray's hands sketched a long, low silhouette in the air. "Royal blue. I'd call it something like Road Warrior or Maverick Machine. And *no* fuzzy dice."

"Cost you more than two hundred and fifty bucks..."

"Yeah. Well, actually, I was meaning to talk to you about that."

Nigel punched his son lightly on the arm. "Should've thought of that before you called my Jelly-roll uncool."

"Dad!"

"You still have four months to save. Talk to me on your birthday." He waggled his eyebrows as they emerged out onto the lawn. "Maybe I'll have forgiven the insult by then."

"Dad!"

"Where's your mother?"

Ray glanced up from his second bowl of cereal and nodded towards the front of the house. "Office. One of her papers called with a problem."

Nigel poured himself a cup of coffee and glared down the hall. "I thought she was supposed to be on vacation until the middle of July?"

"Yeah, well, I guess it's an emergency. Something about a hard drive eating a graphics program she'd installed and they need it right away."

"Still. You'd think the world could manage without her for more than two lousy days."

Ray shrugged and swallowed.

"When I say I'm taking two weeks off," Nigel dropped into a chair. "I don't go into the office until my vacation is over."

"Yeah, well, Mom's essential." Grabbing his empty bowl, Ray pushed away from the table. "Most of these corporate guys couldn't even underline without her."

"Mom's essential. Right." Listening to the hollow boom of his son pounding up the stairs, Nigel scowled into his coffee and tried very hard not to grind his teeth.

"Hey sweetie, what're you doing out here?" Picking a careful path between the brambles, Lynn made her way to her husband's side and tucked herself under his left arm. She felt rather than heard him sigh.

"I was just having a little think about the good old days," he admitted.

"The good old days?"

"Yeah, you know. Before SAT's and job searches and mortgages and diapers and braces and little league."

She snaked an arm around his waist and tucked her thumb through a belt loop. "Before me?"

He turned to look at her then. He hadn't met her until after university. Long after the Jelly-roll had been sold. "Never before you," he said, knowing she'd believe the lie.

"Definitely before poison ivy."

"Poison ivy?"

"Uh huh. Peter found a patch of it out behind the garage."

"How bad is he?"

"Well…" Pivoting on one foot she turned him around and began to herd him from the clearing. "…you can take him to Dr. Patton's after you've dropped Doris off at her ball game."

Pushing through the screen of bushes meant single file. While Lynn went on ahead, Nigel shot one last glance back over his shoulder at the Galaxy.

Before poison ivy, before ball games…

Time is relative. Vacation time, doubly so. Nigel pulled into the driveway, turned off the motor, and let his head fall forward onto the steering wheel. The drive from country home to city job took fifty minutes on traffic free secondary highways for most of the trip. Before they'd moved it had taken thirty—although that half hour stood more in theory than fact. He'd once spent ninety minutes moving two kilometers. Fifty minutes of clear driving was a fair exchange. The problem wasn't the drive. The problem was the destination.

He'd returned to a job that hadn't changed in the week he'd been away. The same memos were still stuck to the bulletin board, his boss was still having the same problems with the tenants in the three story building she owned downtown, supply and distribution still weren't talking to each other. And nothing would change now he was back.

Exhaling noisily, he climbed out of the car and stretched, leaving his briefcase lying on the front seat. His job and his car were much alike, dependable and dull. He was halfway to the clearing before he realized he'd decided to go look at the wreck.

As nobody bounded out to meet me, I guess they can wait a few more minutes for the pleasure of my company.

Wading through the knee-high grass to the driver's side, he wrapped his fingers around the handle and it almost felt as though the warm chrome confirmed to the contours of his palm. To his surprise the mechanism depressed under his thumb. He jerked his arm back to break the rust. Screaming like a tormented soul, the door swung open.

The actual place where the driver would rest butt and back had barely been touched although the rest of the front seat had been extensively scavenged for nesting material. He could get in. Sit down. Remember.

After the graduation ceremonies were over, practically the entire senior class had ended up at a party out in the suburbs. For the last time as a cohesive group, they'd danced, drank, and necked. Couch rugby, they'd called it then, although most of them had never seen a rugger game. The party had finally broken up, just before dawn, and as one of the few remaining with a car, Nigel had packed the old Jelly-roll for the trip back into town. Four guys were shoe-horned into the back-seat, three girls were tucked in on their laps, and Mitchel Hughes sprawled across the stack, feet out one window, head resting on the other. Ron

Allen sat on the front seat, a girl supported in each arm. As Nigel remembered, Ron never had much luck with girls. With no room left in the car, Jim Elliot folded his lanky, six foot one frame into the trunk. The girls were all in long gowns, the boys were in suits, none of them were exactly sober.

Nigel had eased the Jelly-roll, straining under the weight but gallantly responding, away from the curb and out onto the empty streets. At the first stop light, Jim climbed out of the trunk, over the roof, and slid down the windshield to rest, legs akimbo, grinning stupidly, on the hood. In the interest of safety, Ron had helped him thread the happy wanderer through the back window on top of Mitchel. Mitchel protested but not as loudly as the four guys on the bottom of the pile who'd suggested that they put Jim back into the trunk and, this time, latch it.

The sun was up by the time everyone had been safely dropped off and his father had found him, three hours later, sound asleep on the front seat of his car.

"Those were the days," he said quietly to his reflection in the rearview mirror. "People had to get home so we did it, me and the Jelly-roll. We didn't worry about it, about the doing or the consequences, we just took them home." A simpler time or a simpler sense of responsibility? Probably both.

He hadn't thought about Mitchel, or Ron, or Jim for years. His parents had moved just after he'd left town for university and that had pretty much shattered all remaining ties. "Wonder what they're doing now? Wonder if it's as basically senseless as what I'm doing now." He raised a hand to brush sweat-damp hair back off his forehead, the reflection making it appear thicker and darker than it had in years. The tiny lines around his eyes had all but disappeared. The longer he looked, the more he like what he saw.

"Hey, Dad, whatcha doin'?"

When he turned, Nigel was astonished to find his oldest leaning on the car's open door. The question had seemed to come from much further away.

"We saw you drive in but then you never came into the house. How come?"

He shook off the warm layer of memory. "Because I came down here instead."

"Oh." Ray squinted into the car, scratching at an insect bite. "What're you lookin' at?"

Nigel laughed self-consciously and slid out from behind the steering wheel. "Just my reflection in the rear view mirror," he said. *Thicker. Darker. Wrinkle free.*

Leaning around his father, Ray frowned. "But Dad, there's no mirror in the frame."

"No mirror?" Confused, Nigel looked into the car at the rusted, rectangle of metal. Just for a second, his reflection, stripped of the marks that three kids, a mortgage, and a dead-end job had left, looked back. "No mirror..." Then it was gone.

"Come on, Dad. I think you've had a hard day and too much sun."

"Too much sun..." Maybe that was it. The nose of the car pointed west. He'd been staring into the sun...

"Or maybe you're losing your marbles, getting old."

"I am not getting old."

The force of the protest pushed Ray back a step and he stood, staring at his father in astonishment.

"I am not getting old," Nigel repeated. He brushed at his face. It felt as though there were cobwebs hanging from his lashes.

"I've been thinking about restoring that old Galaxy." Nigel capped the salad dressing and set the bottle down on the table. "What do you think?"

"Me?" Lynn frowned. "Is it worth it?"

"Depends on how you measure worth, doesn't it?"

She turned to stare at him, puzzled by his tone. "I wasn't criticizing, Nigel. I was just wondering."

He refused to be mollified. "Well, it's worth it to me."

"Then do it, by all means. I've always said you needed a hobby."

"Little boys and old men have hobbies," Nigel snapped.

Lynn surrendered. Obviously, she couldn't say anything right.

* * *

He remembered the summer trips to the drive-in and tentative kisses that became the first feel of someone else's tongue caressing the inside of his mouth. Sweaters were best although the middle buttons on blouses could be undone enough to allow access to a questing hand while still maintaining appearances. Front closing bras were a godsend. In a car the size of the Galaxy, the steering wheel left plenty of room for serious maneuvers while the rear view mirror allowed a voyeur's eye view of Mitchel's or Jim's or Ron's successes.

He didn't remember many movies.

Leaning his head back against the seat, he breathed deeply, savoring the smell of sweetly scented flesh and the distinct metal and vinyl and young male odor of the old Jelly-roll. If he stretched his arm out, he could almost feel the rounded shoulder of Marianne Lewis, soft and warm and yielding under his hand.

"But Mom, he's not actually doing anything to it. He hasn't even cut down that tree that's poking up."

"He got the book…"

"Yeah but he isn't using it. When he gets down there he gets all stupid." Ray handed her another stack of paper. "I mean, geez Mom, Jelly-roll?"

Lynn refilled the feed on the laser printer. "The original Jelly-roll was very important to your father," she said, as the first page rolled through. "And men of your father's age very often attempt to hold onto a piece of the past."

"I wish he'd act his age," Ray muttered.

"Raymond, that's no way to talk about your father."

"Yeah, well he's not acting much like my father. If you'd just go out there and see what he's like around that stupid car…"

"Oh no, you're not getting me back out there. I've quite enough to do handling the wildlife that Peter brings home." She squinted at the printout, sighed, and pulled the keyboard down onto her lap. "Now, please go away; the Post's graphics have just screwed up again and I have lots of work to do."

"But Mom…"

"Not now Ray. We'll talk about this later, okay. Okay?"

"Yeah. Okay."

The streets had to be almost empty of traffic, that was part of what made the game so cool.

"That one!" Mitchel yelled. "Follow that one. The blue two door."

With Jim hanging over the seat between them—guys didn't ride three in the front—he pulled out of the parking lot and tucked the Jelly-roll exactly three lengths behind the designated leader. When the blue car turned, he turned. When the blue car slowed, he slowed. Maintaining the distance was a crucial aspect of the game.

"Has he figured it out yet?" Jim hitched his elbows behind the headrests and flattened himself against the back of the seat.

"I don't think so."

The blue car sped up suddenly at the traffic circle. They'd been spotted.

"This is great!" Mitchel carolled as they squealed around the long outside curve.

It was great. He put his foot down and...

...nearly shoved it right through the rotten bottom of the car. A jagged metal point etched a line between sneaker top and jeans and the pain jerked him back to the front seat of a wreck, abandoned and nearly overgrown with bush.

Nigel swallowed and ran the tip of his tongue over dry lips. He'd been there. With Jim and Mitchel. He'd felt the Jelly-roll respond. Turn when he said turn. Go when he said go. Stop when he said stop. His heart was pounding so hard that it drowned out the sound of the birds and the insects and left him isolated in the car.

He almost broke his ankle in the panicked scramble out into the sunlight and somehow managed not to look back as he hobbled as fast as he was able towards the house.

He hadn't realized that the wreck could be seen from the road. Rounding the corner at the top of the hill, at just the right angle, and just for an instant, he could see it every evening as he came home from work.

On the fourth day, he went back to the clearing.

"Doris, you think Dad's been acting weird lately?"

"He's always acted weird. Throw me some grounders."

"No, I mean really weird." Ray skimmed the ball in the general direction of his sister, not really paying attention as she dove for it, rolled, and whipped it back. "Like he goes down to that wreck every night after work and he's there almost all weekend. I mean, last Saturday afternoon he sat there for two hours in the rain."

"So he's restoring it. Let me have one on the other side."

"There's nothing to restore. The best thing you could make out of that heap of junk is a half a box of rusty razor blades." He had to jump to catch her return throw. "Most catchers are not seven foot tall," he pointed out. "Anyway, I'm worried about Dad."

"Dad's fine."

"I don't think so..."

"Just throw the ball!"

"That kind of an obsession isn't natural!"

"Are you going to throw the ball or am I going to come down there and pound you?"

He threw the ball. Was he the only one who felt that something was wrong? Peter was too young but at thirteen Doris should be nearly sentient. *'Course she's not interested in anything that isn't wearing a baseball uniform. Not the best person to talk to about obsession.*

Maybe it was the heat. He'd read somewhere that people did crazy things in the summer because of the heat.

He wanted to believe it was the heat.

But he didn't.

He loved the smell of the wax as he rubbed it into the sun-warmed paint. Loved the way his reflection rose up through the streaks and the smudges until it grinned up at him from a mirror perfect finish. Other guys might only concern themselves with what went on under the hood but he took care of his car.

* * *

"Mom, he was out there all afternoon, rubbing wax into the one spot on the roof that isn't all hacked to ratshit."

"Language," Lynn cautioned.

Ray ignored her. "Mom, he called me Jim. Said it looked like I was finally getting some muscle to match what I had between my ears. Mom, he didn't know it was me until I shook him."

Lynn sat back on her heels, trowel dangling from one hand. "He called you Jim?"

"Yes!"

"Maybe I'd better talk to him…"

"That's what I've been saying all along!"

She stood and dusted bits of grass and dirt off her knees. "Is he down there now?"

"No. He's in the room behind the kitchen. Going through that old trunk of his."

"Well, at least I don't have to go get my machete." When Ray refused to smile, she reached up and touched his cheek with some concern. "This is really bothering you, isn't it?"

He jerked his head away from her fingers. "It's just that car is all he ever thinks about anymore. And nobody seems to think that's strange but me!"

"Ray, I think you're over-reacting…"

"Just talk to him, Mom. Please."

She handed him the trowel. "Don't worry, I'm on my way."

Fingers twisting the wooden handle, he watched her walk to the house. He knew she didn't really think there was anything wrong. Behind him, even through the insulating distance of lawn and field and bush, he could feel the car waiting.

"You haven't opened that trunk in years, sweetie. Are you looking for something?"

Nigel continued to rummage in the depths of the rusty blue trunk. "Yes," he said shortly.

Lips pursed, Lynn peered over his shoulder, one hand resting lightly on the curve of his back. "Can we talk for a minute?"

"About what?"

"Oh, your son. That car…"

Nigel straightened. "What about the car?"

"Well, Ray seems to think you're spending too much time with it." She perched on the edge of an old wooden table they'd inherited with the house. "You know how it is at fifteen, not quite a boy, not quite a man…"

Fifteen. Almost sixteen. In mere months he'd have his license then Uncle Frank had promised, promised he'd sell him the car.

"…and I think he might be jealous. It hasn't been easy for him moving out here, away from his friends. Oh, I know Jeff was out for three days last week and he rides his bike into the rec center most days, but until school starts he's pretty much on his own. I don't know, maybe you should spend more time with him. What do you think?"

Nigel blinked. "Spend more time with who?"

"Raymond. Your son."

His son? He frowned. Son…"He'll be okay." Maybe they were under all those old racing magazines. He bent back into the trunk.

Lynn frowned. It wasn't like Nigel to brush off one of the kid's concerns like that. Maybe he was a little too involved in that old wreck. Still, a lot of men developed eccentricities as forty approached. *I suppose I should be glad it's not another woman…*

"Found them." String clutched tightly in his hand, Nigel rose.

"Fuzzy dice?" She stared at the faded pinky-red ornaments, not really fuzzy or very dice-shaped anymore. A number of their black felt dots had come unglued and, under the matted plush, they were far from square. "That's what you were looking for?"

He nodded and headed for the door. "Gonna put them in the car. Don't know why I took them out."

"Nigel!"

Although he had to have heard, he continued to head straight for the clearing. Lower lip caught between her teeth, Lynn watched him until he disappeared into the bush, all at once less than certain that everything was all right.

* * *

"Mom, didn't Dad go to work this morning?"

Lynn paused at the door to her office, coffee cup raised half-way to her mouth. "As far as I know he did. Why?"

"Well 'cause his car's still in the driveway." Peter leaned forward until his nose indented the screen. "Don't see Dad though."

She took a step back towards the kitchen. "Is my car there?"

"Uh huh." Peter turned and headed for the fridge. "He's probably down at that dumb ol' jelly car."

"You're probably right. Ray…?"

Ray looked up from his cereal. "You want me to go get him?"

"Please." The expression on his face anchored her where she stood. "No, never mind. He's already late for work. You might as well finish your breakfast."

"It's okay." He pushed the bowl aside. "I'm not real hungry." He paused at the door and turned, looking younger and more vulnerable than she could remember seeing him look in years. "What if he doesn't want to come?"

"Don't be silly, of course he'll come." Her laugh sounded more hollow than reassuring. "Just tell him I want to talk to him. That it's important."

He didn't seem convinced but he nodded and said, "I'll tell him."

From her office window, Lynn watched him cross the yard and disappear into the bush, like his father had the day before.

"Now is that the finishing touch or what?"

Jim leaned over the front seat, stretched out a long arm, and flicked at the dice with one finger. "Definitely very cool."

"Outa sight," Mitchel agreed.

Nigel closed the driver's door then reached up to brush his hand over the plush. "I got red because the car's white."

"You're one classy hombre, Jelly." Jim pulled on a pair of mirrored sunglasses. "So are we out of here or what?"

"It's time," Mitchel declared. "Come on, Jelly. Let's hit the road."

* * *

Stomach in knots and wishing he hadn't eaten even as little as he had, Ray pushed through the brush towards the clearing. Although there wasn't a cloud in the sky, the world felt as though it were waiting for a storm, trembling on the edge of thunder and lightning and wind and hail.

"Mom wants to talk to him, she should go get him herself."

He hated the way his father was around the wreck. He didn't want to go near him. But he didn't want to leave him there either.

"Heck, I'm bigger than he is. If he doesn't want to come, I'll drag him."

Just behind the last barricade of brambles, he paused. Every leaf, every twig, every blade of grass stood out in sharp relief. He could hear his own heart slamming up against his ribs but that was all. No birds. No insects. It was so quiet, he could almost hear the trickle of sweat running down his back.

Why isn't there a path? There should be a path by now.

As he stepped out into the clearing, a trick of the early morning sun made the car seem almost whole. Eyes watering, he squinted, tripped, and flung out both hands to stop himself from falling. They smacked against the hood with a metallic boom.

But this thing doesn't have a hood...

Sprawled half over the car, Ray twisted and found himself staring through the windshield at his father.

"Dad?"

Nigel frowned. "Did you guys hear something?"

Jim lifted his sunglasses. He and Mitchel exchanged a long look. "No," he said. "We didn't hear anything."

"I'm sure I heard something..."

Mitchel shrugged. "Okay. Heard what?"

What *had* he heard? It was important. He knew it was important. "I heard...I heard someone calling for their father."

"Nothin' to do with you, Jelly." Jim's hand closed on his shoulder. "Now can we blow this popsicle joint?"

"No...I...I have to..."

"All you have to do is get in the old Jelly-roll and hit the road." Mitchel bounced against the seat, setting the shocks gently rocking. "You don't have a care in the world, Jelly old bean. Not a care in the world."

"Not a care…"

"That's right." Jim hooked his elbows behind the headrests. "So crank her up and let's go man go!"

Nigel glanced up at the review mirror. His reflection grinned down at him.

Something wasn't right…

His fingers closed around the key.

"DAD!"

Dad. Nigel shook his head. *He* was Dad. "Ray?"

The engine turned over.

Ray grabbed for the sapling and just barely managed to keep from pitching over the side of the wreck and into the rusted remains of the engine compartment. With trembling fingers he reached out and stroked the air where the windshield should have been. His ears were ringing and over the early morning sounds of birds and insects, he thought he heard his father scream his name.

"D…dad?"

Pushing himself erect, he fought to breathe. There wasn't a hood. There wasn't a window. He hadn't seen his father in the car.

Hadn't seen his father.

Hadn't.

He swallowed hard and staggered back a step.

The car had been white. The pitted paint was now blue. Royal blue. Its shape, warped only a little by time and neglect, was long and low.

I'd call it something like Road Warrior or Maverick Machine. And no fuzzy dice.

Blood roaring in his ears, he turned and ran for the house.

* * *

"Honey, you'll never guess what I just found out in the woods."

Christine Naylor smiled fondly at her husband. "You're right. I'll never guess. What did you find?"

"It's a 1973 Dodge Dart." He dropped to his knees beside her lawn chair. "Some moron just left it there."

"Well, I'm glad that a man with a brand new mortgage who's about to be a brand new father can find such joy in a wreck in the woods."

He pushed his cheek up against the curve of her belly. "You don't understand, Chris. A 1973 Dodge Dart—my first car was a 1973 Dart.

"I loved that car."

"WORD OF HONOR" is the only story appearing in the collection that has been changed slightly since its original appearance. There's two reasons for that.

The first reason is Katherine Kurtz. I'd be willing to bet cash money that Katherine Kurtz knows everything there is to know about the Templars. In *Tales of the Knights Templar*, in her afterword to my story, she mentioned that the splinter of the True Cross the Templars were said to have was encased in gold and jewels. In the original version of this story, I had the splinter encased in gold without jewels so, for the sake of historical accuracy, I've added a few in this version. Katherine also mentioned in her afterword that the splinter was one of the Templar "hallows" that fell into the hands of Philip of France. Clearly I couldn't have that happen or I wouldn't have a story and Katherine very kindly allowed me to play fast and loose with the facts.

The second reason for changes involves my broadening world view. When I wrote this story, I hadn't been to Inverness so I was working out of guide books and a long distance phone call to the minister at Petty (who was very helpful if a tad confused). Having spent five days in Inverness after the Glasgow WorldCon, I've changed the reference to the Station Hotel—which I couldn't afford to stay at—to match reality.

Small changes really, but I thought you should know.

WORD OF HONOR

The prayer became a background drone without words, without meaning; holding no relevance to her life even had she bothered to listen.

Pat Tarrill shoved her hands deep in her jacket pockets and wondered why she'd come. The moment she'd read about it in the paper, attending the Culloden Memorial Ceremony had become an itch she had to scratch—although it wasn't the sort of thing she'd normally waste her time at. *And that's exactly what I'm doing.* Wasting time. Sometimes she felt like that was all she'd been doing the entire twenty-five years of her life. Wasting time.

The prayer ended. Pat looked up, squinted against the wind blowing in off Northumberland Strait, and locked eyes with a wizened old man in a wheelchair. She scowled and stepped forward but lost sight of him as the bodies around the cairn shifted position. *Probably just a dirty old man,* she thought, closed her eyes and lost herself in the wail of the pipes.

Later, while everyone else hurried off to the banquet laid out in St. Mary's Church hall, Pat walked slowly to the cairn and lightly touched the damp stain. Raising her fingers to her face, she sniffed the residue and smiled, once again hearing her grandfather grumble that, *"No true Scot would waste whiskey on a rock."* But her grandfather had been dead for years and the family had left old Scotland for Nova Scotia in 1770.

Wiping her fingers on her jeans, Pat headed for her car. She hadn't been able to afford a ticket to the banquet and wouldn't have gone even if she could have. All that *Scots wha hae* stuff made her nauseous.

"Especially," she muttered, digging for her keys, "since most of this lot has been no closer to Scotland than Glace Bay."

With one hand on the pitted handle of her car door, she slowly turned, pulled around by the certain knowledge that she was being observed. It was the old man again, sitting in his chair at the edge of the churchyard and staring in her direction. This time, a tall, pale man in a tan overcoat stood behind him—also staring. *Staring down his nose,* Pat corrected for even at that distance the younger man's attitude was blatantly obvious. Flipping the two of them the finger, she slid into her car.

She caught one last glimpse of them in the rear view mirror as she peeled out of the gravel parking lot. Tall and pale appeared to be arguing with the old man.

"Patricia Tarrill?"

"Pat Tarrill. Yeah."

"I'm Harris MacClery, Mr. Hardie's solicitor."

Tucking the receiver between ear and shoulder, Pat forced her right foot into a cowboy boot. "So should I know you?"

"I'm Mr. *Chalmer* Hardie's solicitor."

"Oh." Everyone in Atlantic Canada knew of Chalmer Hardie. He owned…well, he owned a good chunk of Atlantic Canada.

"Mr. Hardie would like to speak with you."

"With me?" Her voice rose to an undignified squeak. "What about?"

"A job."

Pat's gaze pivoted towards the stack of unpaid bills threatening to bury the phone. She'd been unemployed for a month and the job hadn't lasted long enough for her to qualify for Unemployment Insurance. "I'll take it."

"Don't you want to know what it's about?"

She could hear his disapproval and frankly, she didn't give two shits. Anything would be better than yet another visit to the welfare office. "No," she told him, "I don't."

As she scribbled directions on the back of an envelope, she wondered if her luck had finally changed.

Chalmer Hardie lived in Dunmaglass, a hamlet tucked between Baileys Brook and Lismore—the village where the Culloden Memorial had taken place. More specifically, Chalmer Hardie *was* Dunmaglass. Tucked up against the road was a gas station/general store/post office and then up a long lane was the biggest house Pat had ever seen.

She swore softly in awe as she parked the car then swore again as a tall, pale man came out of the house to meet her.

"Ms. Tarrill." It wasn't a question, but then, he knew what she looked like. "Mr. Hardie is waiting."

"Ms. Tarrill." The old man in the wheel chair held out his hand. "I'm very happy to meet you."

"Um, me too. That is, I'm happy to meet you." His hand felt dry and soft and although his fingers curved around hers, they didn't grip. Up close, his skin was pale yellow and it hung off his skull in loose folds, falling into accordion pleats around his neck.

"Please forgive me if we go directly to business." He waved her towards a brocade wing chair. "I dislike wasting the little time I have left."

Pat lowered herself into the chair feeling as if she should've worn a skirt and resenting the feeling.

"I have a commission I wish you to fulfill for me, Ms. Tarrill." Eyes locked on hers, Chalmer Hardie folded his hands over a small wooden box resting on his lap. "In return, you will receive ten thousand dollars and a position in one of my companies."

"A position?"

"A job, Ms. Tarrill."

"And ten thousand dollars?"

"That is correct."

"So who do you want me to kill?" She regretted it almost instantly but the richest man in the Maritimes merely shook his head.

"I'm afraid he's already dead." The old man's fingers tightened around the box. "I want you to return something to him."

"Him who?"

"Alexander MacGillivray. He led Clan Chattan at Culloden, as the chief was, at the time, a member of the Black Watch and thus not in a position to support the prince."

"I know."

Sparse white eyebrows rose. "You know?"

Pat shrugged. "My grandfather was big into all that..." She paused and searched for an alternative to *Scottish history crap.* "...heritage stuff."

"I see. Would it be too much to ask that he ever mentioned the Knights Templar?"

He'd once gotten into a drunken fight with a Knight of Columbus..."Yeah, it would."

"Then I'm afraid we'll have to include a short history lesson or none of this will make sense."

For ten thousand bucks and a job, Pat could care less if it made sense but she arranged her face into what she hoped was an interested expression and waited.

Frowning slightly, Hardie thought for a moment. When he began to speak, his voice took on the cadences of a lecture hall. "The Knights Templar were a brotherhood of fighting monks sworn to defend the holy land of the Bible from the infidel. In 1132, the patriarch of Jerusalem gave Hugues de Payens, the first Master of the Knights, a relic, a splinter of the True Cross sealed into a small crystal orb that could be worn like a medallion. This medallion was to protect the master and through his leadership, the holy knights.

"In 1307, King Philip of France, for reasons we haven't time to go into, decided to destroy the Templars. He convinced the current Grand Master, Jacques de Molay, to come to France, planning to arrest him and all the Templars in the country in one fell swoop. Which he did. They were tortured and many of them including their Master were burned alive as heretics."

"Wait a minute," Pat protested, leaning forward. "I thought the medallion thing was supposed to protect them?"

Hardie grimaced. "Yes, well, a very short time before they were arrested, de Molay was warned. He sent a messenger with the medallion to the Templar Fleet with orders for them to put out to sea."

"If he was warned, why didn't he run himself?"

"Because that would not have been the honorable thing to do."

"Like dying's so honorable." She bit her lip and wished just once that her brain would work before her mouth.

The old man stared at her for a long moment then continued as though she hadn't expressed an opinion. "While de Molay believed that nothing would happen to him personally, he had a strong and accurate suspicion that King Philip was after the Templar's not inconsiderable treasure. Much of that treasure had already been loaded onto the ships of the fleet.

"The fleet landed in Scotland. Maintaining their tradition of service, the Knights became a secular organization and married into the existing Scottish nobility. The treasure the fleet carried was divided amongst the Knights for safekeeping and, as the centuries passed, many pieces became family heirlooms and were passed from father to son.

"Now then, Culloden…In 1745 Bonnie Prince Charlie returned from exile to Scotland and suffered a final defeat at Culloden. The clans supporting him were slaughtered. Among the dead were many men of the old Templar families." He opened the box on his lap and beckoned Pat closer.

Resting on a padded red velvet lining was probably the ugliest piece of jewelry she'd ever seen—and as a fan of the home shopping network, she'd seen some ugly jewelry. In the center of a gold disc about four inches across, patterned with what looked like little specks of gold and inset with colored stones, was a yellowish and uneven crystal sphere about the size of a marble. A modern gold chain filled the rest of the box.

"An ancestor of mine stole that before the battle from Alexander MacGillivray. You, Ms. Tarrill are looking at an actual sliver of the True Cross."

Squinting, Pat could just barely make out a black speck in the center of the crystal. *Sliver of the True Cross my Aunt Fanny.* "This is what…" She searched her memory for the name and couldn't find it. "…that Templar guy sent out of France?"

"Yes."

"How do you know?"

"Trust me, Ms. Tarrill. I know. I want you to take this holy relic, and place it in the grave of Alexander MacGillivray."

"In Scotland?"

"That is correct. Mr. MacClery will give you the details. I will of course pay all expenses."

Pat studied the medallion, lips pursed. "I have another question."

"Perfectly understandable."

"Why me?"

"Because I am too sick to make the journey and because I had a dream." His lips twitched into a half smile as though he realized how ridiculous he sounded but didn't care. "I dreamt about a young woman beside the cairn at the Culloden Memorial Service—you, Ms. Tarrill."

"You're going to trust me with this, give me ten thousand bucks and a job based on a dream?"

"You don't understand." One finger lightly touched the crystal. "But you will."

As crazy as it sounded, he seemed to believe it. "Did the dream give you my name?"

"No. Mr. MacClery had your license plate traced."

Her eyes narrowed. Lawyers! "So, why do you want this thing returned? I mean, if it was supposed to protect MacGillivray and Clan Chattan at Culloden, giving it back isn't going to change the fact that the Duke of Cumberland kicked butt."

"I don't want to change things, Ms. Tarrill. I want to do what's right." His chin lifted and she saw the effort that small movement needed. "I have been dying for a long time; time enough to develop a conscience if you will. I want the cross of Christ back where it belongs and I want you to take it there." His shoulders slumped. "I would rather go myself but I left it too long."

Pat glanced towards the door and wondered if lawyers listened through keyholes. "Is Mr. MacClery going with me?"

"No. You'll go alone."

"Well what proof do you want that I actually put it in the grave?"

"Your word will be sufficient."

"My word? That's it?"

"Yes."

She could tell from his expression that he truly believed her word would be enough. Wondering how anyone so gullible had gotten so rich, she gave it.

Pat had never been up in a plane before and, as much as she'd intended to be cool about it, she kept her face pressed against the window until the lights of St. John's were replaced by the featureless black of the north Atlantic. In her purse, safe under her left arm, she carried the boxed medallion and a hefty packet of money MacClery had given her just before she boarded.

Although it was an overnight flight, Pat didn't expect to sleep; she was too excited. But the food was awful and she'd seen the movie and soon staying awake became more trouble than it was worth.

A few moments later, wondering grumpily who'd play the bagpipes on an airplane, she opened her eyes.

Instead of the blue tweed of the seat in front of her, she was looking down at an attractive young man—tall and muscular, red-gold hair above delicate dark brows and long, thick lashes. At the moment he needed a shave and a bath but she still wouldn't kick him out of bed for eating crackers. A hand, with rather a great quantity of black hair growing across the back of it, reached down and shook the young man's shoulder. With a bit of a shock, she realized the hand was hers. *Well, this dream obviously isn't heading where I'd like it to...*

"Alex! Get your great lazy carcass on its feet. There's a battle to be fought." Her mouth formed the words but she had no control over either content or delivery. It appeared she was merely a passenger.

Grey eyes snapped open. "Davie? I must've dozed off..."

"You fell asleep but there's no crime in that. Lord John is with his Highness in Culloden House and Cumberland's men are up and about."

"Aye, then so should I be." Shaking his head to clear the sleep from it, Alexander MacGillivray, lieutenant-colonel of Clan

Chattan, heaved himself up onto his feet, his right hand moving to touch his breast as he stood.

His fair skin went paler still and his eyes widened so far they must've hurt. He dug under his clothing then whirled about to search the place he'd lain.

"What is it, Alex? Have you lost something?" Pat felt Davie's heart begin to race and over it, pressed hard against his skin, she felt a warm weight hanging. All at once, she knew it had to be the medallion. *That son of a bitch!* Stuffed into Hardie's head, she could access what it held; he'd known the medallion had been in the MacGillivray family for a very long time but had only recently discovered what it was. More a scholar than a soldier, he'd found a reference to it in an old manuscript, had tracked it back to the Templar landing in Argyll where the MacGillivrays originated, had combed the scraps of Templar history that remained, and had discovered what it held and the power attributed to it. He hadn't intended to take advantage of what he'd found—and then Charles Edward Stewart and war had come to Scotland.

Pat could feel Davie Hardie's fear of facing Cumberland's army and touched the memory of how he'd stolen the medallion's protection for himself—even though he'd known that if it were worn by one with the right it could very well protect the entire clan. *That cowardly son of a bitch!*

When Alexander MacGillivray straightened, Pat could read his thoughts off his face. By losing the medallion, he'd betrayed a sacred trust. There was only one thing he could do.

"Alex?"

The young commander squared his shoulders, faced his own death, and tugged on his bonnet. "Come along, Davie. I need to talk to the chiefs before we take our place in line."

You need to talk to your pal Davie, that's what you need to do! Then the dream twisted sideways and she winced as a gust of sleet and rain whipped into her face. The Duke of Cumberland's army was a red blot on the moor no more than 500 yards away. When Hardie turned, she saw MacGillivray. When he turned a little further, she could see the companies in line.

Then the first gun boomed across the moor and Hardie whirled in time to see the smoke. A heartbeat later, there was nothing to see but smoke and nothing to hear but screaming.

I don't want to be here! Pat struggled to free herself from the dream. Her terror and Hardie's became one terror. Dream or not, she wanted to die no more than he did.

The cannonade went on. And on.

Through it all, she saw MacGillivray, striding up and down the ranks of his men, giving them courage to stand. Sons were blown to bits beside their fathers, brothers beside brothers. The shot killed chief and humblie indiscriminately, but the line held.

And the cannonade went on.

The clansmen were yelling for the order to charge so they could bring their broadswords into play. The order never came.

And the cannonade went on.

"Sword out, Davie. We've taken as much of this as we're going to."

Hardie grabbed his colonel's arm. "Are you mad?" he yelled over the roar of the guns and shrieks of the dying. "It's not your place to give the order!"

"It's not my place to stand here and watch my people slaughtered!"

"Then why fight at all? Even Lord Murray says we're likely to lose!"

All at once, Pat realized why a man only twenty-five had been chosen to lead the clan in the absence of its chief. Something in his expression spoke quietly of strength and courage and responsibility. "We took an oath to fight for the prince."

"We'll all be killed!"

MacGillivray's eyes narrowed. "Then we'll die with honor."

Pat felt Hardie tremble and wonder how much his colonel suspected. "But the prince!"

"This isn't his doing, it's that damned Irishman, O'Sullivan." Spinning on one heel, he scrugged his bonnet down over his brow and made his way back to the center of the line.

A moment later, Clan Chattan charged forward into the smoke hoarsely yelling "Loch Moy!" and "Dunmaglass!" The pipes screamed the rant until they were handed to a boy and the Piper pulled his sword and charged forward with the rest.

Davie Hardie charged because he had no choice. Pat caught only glimpses of the faces that ran by, faces that wore rage and despair equally mixed. Then she realized that there seemed to be a great many running by as Hardie stumbled and slowed and made a show of advancing without moving forward.

Cumberland's artillery had switched to grape shot. Faintly, over the roar of the big guns, Pat heard the drum roll firing of muskets. Men fell all around him, whole families died, but nothing touched Davie Hardie.

Then through a break in the smoke and the dying, Pat saw a red-gold head reach the front line of English infantry. Swinging his broadsword, MacGillivray plunged through, leapt over the bodies he'd cut down, and was lost in the scarlet coats.

With his cry of "Dunmaglass" ringing in her ears, Pat woke. She was clutching her purse so tightly that the edges of the box cut into her hands through the vinyl.

"Death before dishonor my butt," she muttered as she pushed up the window's stiff plastic shade and blinked in the sudden glare of morning sun. That philosophy had got Alexander MacGillivray dead and buried. Davie Hardie had turned dishonor into a long life in the new world. So he'd had to live knowing that his theft had been responsible for the death of his friend—at least he was alive.

Chill out, Pat. It was only a dream. She accepted a cup of coffee from the stewardess and stirred in double sugar, the spoon rattling against the side of the cup. *Dreams don't mean shit.*

But she could still feel Hardie's willingness to do anything rather than die and it left a bad taste in her mouth.

Customs at Glasgow airport passed her through with a cheery good morning and instructions on where to wait for her connecting flight north to Inverness.

At Inverness airport, she was met by a ruddy young man who introduced himself as Gordon Ritchie, Mr. Hardie's driver. After a few moments of exhausted confusion while they settled *which* Mr. Hardie, he retrieved her suitcase and bundled her into a discreet black sedan.

"It was all arranged over the phone," Gordon explained as he drove towards A96 and Inverness. "Here I am, at your beck and call until you head back across the pond."

Pat smiled sleepily. "I love the way you talk."

"Beg your pardon, Ms. Tarrill?"

"Never mind, it's a Canadian thing, you wouldn't understand." A large truck passed the car on the wrong side of the road. Heart in her throat, Pat closed her eyes. Although she hadn't intended to sleep she remembered nothing more until Gordon called out, "We're here, Ms. Tarrill."

Yawning, she peered out the window. "Call me Pat, and where's here?"

"Station Hotel, Academy Street. Mr. Hardie—Mr. Chalmer Hardie, that is, booked you a room here. It's pretty much the best hotel in town..."

He sounded so tentative that she laughed. "You're not the only one who wonders if Mr. Hardie knows what he's doing." She could just see herself in some swanky Scottish hotel. *Likely get tossed out for not rolling my r's.*

Her room held a double bed, an overstuffed chair, a small desk spread with tourist brochures, and a chest of drawers. There was a kettle, a china teapot and two cups on a tray next to the color TV and the bathroom had both a tub and shower.

"Looks like Mr. Hardie blew the wad." Pat dragged herself as far as the bed and collapsed. After a moment, she pulled the box out of her purse, flipped it open, and stared down at the medallion. It looked the same as it had on the other side of the Atlantic.

"Well, why wouldn't it?" Setting the open box on the bedside table, she stripped and crawled between the sheets. Although it was still early, she'd been travelling for twenty-four hours and was ready to call it a night.

"Bernard? Is that you?"

Who the hell is Bernard? Yanked back to consciousness, Pat opened her eyes and found herself peering down into the bearded face of a burly man standing in the center of a small boat. The combination of dead fish, salt water, and rotting sewage smelled a lot like Halifax harbor.

"Quiet, Robert," she heard herself say. "Do you want to wake all of Harfleur?"

I guess I'm Bernard. She felt the familiar weight resting on his chest. *Oh no, what now?* She searched through the young man's memories and found enough references to hear Chalmer Hardie's voice say, *"In 1307 King Philip of France decided to destroy the Templars."*

Pat tried unsuccessfully to wake up. *First Culloden now this! Why can't I dream about sex, like a normal person?*

The wooden rungs damp and punky under callused palms, Bernard scrambled down a rickety ladder and joined the man in the boat. Both wore the red Templar cross on a dark brown mantle. They were sergeants, men-at-arms, Pat discovered delving into Bernard's memories again, permitted to serve the order though they weren't nobly born. Bernard had served for only a few short months and his oaths still burned brightly behind every conscious thought.

"I will suffer all that is pleasing to God."

How do I come up with this stuff? She looked over Robert's shoulder and saw, in the grey light of pre-dawn, the eighteen galleys of the Templar Fleet riding at anchor in the harbor.

Covered in road dirt and breathing heavily, Bernard grabbed for support as the boat rocked beneath the two men. "I've come from the Grand Master himself. He said to tell the Preceptor of France that it is time and that he gives this holy relic into his charge."

The crystal orb in the center of the medallion seemed to gather up what little light there was and Pat could feel the young man's astonished pride at being chosen to bear it.

Over the soft slap, slap of the water against the pilings came the heavy tread of armed men.

Scrambling back up the ladder, Bernard peered over the edge of the dock and muttered, "The seneschal!" in such a tone that Pat heard, *"The cops!"*

Right, lets get out of here.

Chalmer Hardie's voice, murmured, *"...burned alive as heretics."*

To her surprise, Bernard raised the medallion to his lips, kissed it devoutly, turned, and dropped the heavy chain over Robert's head.

Pat's point of view shifted radically and her stomach shifted with it.

"Row like you've never rowed before," Bernard told his companion. "I'll delay them as long as I can."

If they close the harbor, the fleet will be trapped. It was Robert's thought, not hers. Hers went more like: *He's going to get himself killed! There's five guys on that wharf! Bernard, get in the damned boat!*

Deftly sliding the oars into the locks, Robert echoed her cry. "Get in the boat. We can both..."

"No." Bernard's gaze measured the distance from the dock to the fleet and the fleet to the harbor mouth. "Wait until I engage before moving clear. They'll have crossbows."

Then Pat remembered Davie Hardie. *Put the medallion back on, you idiot. It'll protect you!*

But this time Robert said only, "Go with God, Brother."

A calm smile flashed in the depths of the young Templar's beard.

You know what the medallion can do! she screamed at him. *So the fleet leaves without it; so what? Is getting it on that boat more important than your life?*

Apparently it was.

When the shouting began, followed quickly by the clash of steel against steel, Robert pulled away from the dock with long, silent strokes. As he rowed, he prayed and tried not to envy the other man's opportunity to prove his devotion to the Lord in battle.

The sun had risen and there was light enough to see Bernard keep all five at bay. Every blow he struck, every blow he took, moved the boat and the holy relic that much closer to the Templar flagship. With his blood, with his life, Bernard bought the safety of the fleet.

A ray of sunlight touched his sword and the entire dockside disappeared in a brilliant flash of white-gold light.

Pat threw up an arm to protect her eyes. When the after images faded, she discovered that the sun had indeed risen and that she'd forgotten to close the blinds before she went to bed.

"Shit."

Something cold slithered across her cheek. Her reaction flung her halfway across the room before she realized it was the chain of the medallion. During the night, she'd taken it from its box and returned to sleep with it cupped in her hand.

Moving slowly, she set it carefully back against the red velvet and sank down on the edge of the bed. Wiping damp palms on the sheets, she sucked in a deep breath. "Look, I'm grateful that you seem to be translating these violent little highlights into modern English and all so that I understand what's going on but...

"But I'm losing my mind." Scowling, she stomped into the bathroom. "I'm talking to an ugly piece of jewelry." Obviously, Chalmer Hardie's history lesson had made an impression. "I'm not stupid," she reminded her reflection. "I could take what he told me and fill in the pieces. I mean, I could be making all that stuff up out of old movies, couldn't I?" She closed her eyes for a moment. "And now I'm talking to a mirror. What next, the toilet?"

She went back into the bedroom and flicked the box shut. "You," she told it, "Are more trouble than you're worth."

Worth...

In a country where the biggest tourist draw was history, there had to be a store that sold pieces of the past. Even back in Halifax there were places where a person could buy anything from old family silver to eighteenth century admiral's insignia.

Gordon assumed jet-lag when she called to say she wouldn't need him and Pat didn't bother to correct his assumption. "Oh aye, Mr. Hardie said you might want to rest before you went off to do whatever it is you're doing for him."

"You don't know?"

He laughed. "I assumed you would."

So Chalmer Hardie hadn't set up the driver to spy on her. Why settle for ten thousand and job when she could have ten thousand, a job, and whatever the medallion would bring? No one would ever know and Mr. Hardie could die happy, believing she'd been fool enough to stuff it into MacGillivray's grave. With the medallion shoved into the bottom of her purse, Pat headed out into Inverness.

She found what she was searching for on High Street where shops ranged from authentic Highland to blatant kitsch, all determined to separate tourists from their money. The crowded window of *Neal's Curios* held several World War II medals, a tea set that was obviously regimental silver although Pat couldn't read the engraving under the raised crest, and an ornate chalice that she'd seen a twin of in *Indiana Jones and the Last Crusade.*

An old ship's bell rang as she pushed open the door and went into the shop. The middle-aged woman behind the counter put down her book and favored her with a dazzling smile. "And how may we help you taday, lassie?"

"Are you the owner?"

"Oh aye, Mrs. Neal, that's me."

"Do you buy old things?"

The smile faded and most of the accent went with it. "Sometimes."

"How much would you give me for this?" Pat dug the box out of her purse and opened it on the scratched glass counter.

Mrs. Neal's pale eyes widened as she peered at the medallion. "There's a piece of the True Cross in the crystal."

The older woman recovered her poise. "Dearie, if you laid all the so called pieces of the True Cross end to end you could circle the earth at the equator. Twice."

"But this piece comes with a history..."

"Have you any proof?" Mrs. Neal asked when Pat finished embroidering the story Chalmer Hardie had told her. Both her hands were flat on the counter and she leaned forward expectantly.

"Trust me," the old man said. "I know."

Pat sighed. "No. No proof."

It wasn't exactly a snort of disbelief. "Then I'll give you five hundred pounds for it but that's mostly for the gold and the gem stones. I can't pay for the fairy tale."

At the current exchange rate five hundred pounds came to over a thousand dollars. Pat drummed her fingers lightly on the counter while she thought about it. It was less than what she'd expected to get but she could use the money and Alexander MacGillivray certainly couldn't use the medallion. She opened her mouth to agree to the sale and closed it on air. In the glass cabinet directly below her fingertips was a red-enameled cross with flared ends about three inches long. Except for the size, it could have been the cross on the mantle of a Templar sergeant who fought and died to protect the medallion she was about to sell.

Unable to stop her hand from shaking, she picked up the box and shoved it back into her purse. She managed to stammer out that she'd like to think about the offer then turned and nearly ran from the shop.

Before the door had fully closed, Mrs. Neal half-turned and bellowed, "Andrew!"

The scrawny young man who hurried in from the storeroom looked annoyed about the summons. "What is it, Gran? I was having a bit of a kip."

"You can sleep later, I have a job for you." She grabbed his elbow and hustled him over to the door. "See that grey jacket scurrying away? Follow the young woman wearing it and, when you're sure you won't be caught, grab her purse."

"What's in it?"

"A piece of very old jewelry your Gran took a liking to. Now go." She pushed him out onto the sidewalk and watched while he slouched up the street. When both her grandson and the young woman disappeared from sight, she returned to her place behind the counter and slid a box of papers off an overloaded shelf. After a moment's search, she smoothed a faint photocopy of a magazine article out on the counter. The article had speculated about the possibility of the Templar fleet having landed in Argyll and had then gone on to list some of the treasure it might have carried. One page held a sketch of a jewel encrusted, gold medallion that surrounded a marble sized piece of crystal that was reputed to contain a sliver of the True Cross.

Mrs. Neal smiled happily. She knew any number of people who would pay a great deal of money for such a relic without asking uncomfortable questions about how she'd found it.

"I don't believe in signs." Pat threw the box down onto the bed and the medallion spilled out. She paced across the room and back. "I don't believe in you either. You're a fairy tale, just like Mrs. Neal said. The delusions of a dying old man. I should have sold you. I will sell you."

But she left both box and medallion on the bed and spent the afternoon staring at soccer on television. When the game ended, she ordered room service and spent the evening watching programs she didn't understand.

At eleven, Pat put the medallion back in the box, wrapped the box in a shirt and stuffed the bundle into the deepest corner of her suitcase.

"I'm going back there tomorrow," she announced defiantly as she turned off the light.

"Tomorrow, his Majesty intends to arrest the entire Order."

What's going on? I don't even remember going to sleep! Pat fought against opening her eyes but they opened anyway. Bernard?

The young sergeant was on one knee at her feet, his expression anger, disbelief, and awe about equally mixed.

I don't want any part of this! Pat could feel the weight of the medallion and knew the old man who wore it as Jacques de Molay, the Grand Master of the Knights Templar. *Last Grand Master*, she corrected but like all the others, he couldn't hear her. She could feel his anger as he told Bernard what would happen at dawn and gave him the message to pass on to the Preceptor of France—who with fifty knights had all but emptied the Paris Temple five days before. She touched de Molay's decision to stay behind lest the king be warned by his absence.

"There will be horses for you between Paris and Harfleur. You *must* arrive before dawn, do you understand?"

"Yes, Worshipful Master."

De Molay's hands went to the chain about his neck and he lifted the medallion over his head. He closed his eyes and raised it to his lips, much as Bernard had done—would do, Pat amended. "Take this also to the Preceptor, tell him I give it into his charge." He gazed down into the young sergeant's eyes. "In the crystal is a sliver from the Cross of our Lord. I would not have it fall into the hands of that *jackal…*" Biting off what would have become an extensive tirade against the king, he held out the medallion. "It will protect you as you ride."

Bernard leaned forward and pressed his lips against the gold. As the Grand Master settled the chain over his head, Pat—who settled into his head—thought he was going to pass out. "Worshipful Master, I am not worthy…"

"I will say who is worthy," de Molay snapped.

"Yes, Worshipful Master." Looking up into de Molay's face through Bernard's lowered lashes, Pat was reminded of her grandfather. *He's a stubborn old man. Certain he's right, regardless of the evidence.* And he was going to die. And there was nothing she could do about it. *Because he died over six hundred years ago,* she told herself. *Get a grip.*

Given the way Bernard had died—would die—Pat expected to hear him declare that he would guard the medallion with his life but then she realized there was no need, that it was understood. *I don't believe these guys. One of them's staying behind to die, and one of them's riding off to die and neither of them has to!*

If de Molay had left Paris with the rest…

If Bernard had got in the boat…

If MacGillivray had refused to charge…

She woke up furious at the world.

A long, hot shower did little to help and breakfast sat like a rock in her stomach.

"You're worth five hundred pounds to me," she snarled as she crammed shirt, box, and medallion into her purse. "That's all. Five hundred pounds. One thousand…"

Her heart slammed up into her throat as the phone shattered the morning into little pieces. "What?"

"It's Gordon Ritchie, Ms. Tarrill. Pat. I'm in the lobby. If you're feeling better, I thought I might show you around..." His voice trailed off. "Is this a bad time?"

"No. No, it's not." This was exactly what she needed. Something to take her mind off the medallion.

"So where are we going?"

"Well, when he hired me, Mr. Hardie suggested I might take you to Culloden Moor." Gordon held open the lobby door. "The National Trust for Scotland's visitor's center just reopened for the season."

Culloden? Pat ground her teeth. *Been there. Done that.*

Catching a glimpse of her expression, Gordon frowned. "I could take you somewhere else..."

"No." She cut him off. "Might just as well go along with Mr. Hardie's suggestion. He's paying the bills." Although she was beginning to believe he might not be calling the tune. *Yeah right. As I've said before, Pat, get a grip.*

Swearing under his breath, Andrew ran for his car.

A cold wind was blowing across the moor when they reached the visitor's center. Pat hunched her shoulders, shoved her hands deep into her pockets, and tried not to remember her dream of the slaughter. She watched the AV presentation, poked around old Leanach Cottage, then started down the path that ran out onto the battlefield, Gordon trailing along behind. She passed the English Stone without pausing, continued west, and came to a roughly triangular, weather-beaten monument.

"'Well of the Dead.'" Her fingers traced the inscription as she read. "'Here the Chief of the MacGillivrays fell.'"

The wind slapped rain into her face. Over the call of the pipes, Pat heard the guns and men screaming and one voice gathering up the clan to aim it at the enemy. *"Dunmaglass!"*

"Pat? Are you all right?"

At Gordon's touch, she shook free of the memory and straightened. "I'd like to go back to the hotel now." He looked so worried that she snarled, "I'm tired, okay?"

He stepped back, quickly masking his reaction, and she wished that just once she'd learn to think before she spoke. *He only wanted to help*...But she couldn't seem to find the apology she knew he deserved.

"But Gran!" Andrew protested, raising a hand to protect his head. "The first time she even left the bloody hotel, she had this guy driving her around. He never left her."

Mrs. Neal threw the rolled magazine aside and grabbed her grandson's shirt front. "Then get a couple of your friends and, if you have to, take care of the guy driving her around."

"I could get Colin and Tony. They helped with that bit of silver..."

"I don't care *who* you get," the old lady spat. "Just bring me that medallion!"

On the way back to the hotel, Pat had Gordon stop and buy her two bottles of cheap scotch. He hadn't approved, she saw it in the set of his shoulders and the thin line of his mouth but he took the money and came back with the bottles. When she tried to explain, the words got stuck.

Better he thinks I'm a bitch than a lunatic.

She couldn't remember where she'd read that alcohol prevented dreaming and after the first couple of glasses, she didn't care. As afternoon darkened into evening, she curled up in the overstuffed chair and drank herself into a stupor.

"You don't understand, Ms. Tarrill." The old man stroked the crystal lightly with one swollen finger. "But you will."

Before Pat could speak, Chalmer Hardie whirled away; replaced by a progression of scowling old men in offices, shipyards, and mills all working as though work was all they had. Clothing and surroundings became more and more old fashioned and by the time she touched a mind she knew, she had realized she was tracing the trail of the medallion back through time.

"Dunmaglass!"

Once again, she watched Alexander MacGillivray lead the charge across Culloden moor. Then she watched as the MacGillivrays, son to father, returned the clan to Argyll. There were more young men than old in this group for these were men willing to take a stand in a dark time. There were MacGillivrays on the shore when the Templar fleet sailed into Loch Caignish.

"Go with God, Brother."

Bernard smiled and climbed to his death.

"In this crystal is a sliver of the Cross of our Lord. I would not have it fall into the hands of that jackal—"

The Masters of the Knights Templar had not lived an easy life. In spite of the protection of the Cross, many of them died in battle. She saw William de Beaujey, the last Master of the Temple before the Moslems regained the Holy Land, fall defending a breach in the wall of Acre. She saw de Sonnac blinded at Mansourah and de Peragors dying on the sands of Gaza. Master, before Master, before Master, until an old man slipped a medallion over the head of Hugues de Payens.

All at once, Pat could hear pounding and jeers and was suddenly lifted into dim light under an overcast sky. She could see a crowd gathered and a city in the distance but she could feel no one except herself. Then she looked down. The sliver had been taken from near the top of the cross. She saw a crown of thorns, dark hair matted with blood, and the top curve of shoulders marked by a whip.

NO!

For the first time, someone heard her.

Yes.

Tears streaming down her face, Pat woke, still curled in the chair, still clutching the second bottle. When she leapt to her feet, the bottle fell and rolled beneath the bed. She didn't notice. She clawed the box out of her purse, clawed the medallion out of the box, and stared at the crystal.

"All right. That's it. You win." Dragging her nose over her sleeve, she shoved the medallion into one pocket of her jacket, shoved her wallet in the other, and grabbed the phone.

"Gordon? I'm doing what Mr. Hardie wants me to do, now, tonight."

"Ms. Tarrill?"

"Pat. Do you know where the church is in Petty?"

"Oh aye, my uncle has the parish but.."

"I'm not drunk." In fact, she'd never felt more sober. "I need to do this." She checked her watch. "It's only just past ten. I'll meet you out front."

She heard him sigh. "I'll be right there."

The car barely had a chance to slow before she flung open the door and threw herself into the passenger seat.

"Ms. Tarrill, I…" He broke off as he caught sight of her face. "Good God, you look terrified. What's wrong?"

Pat found a laugh that didn't mean much. "Good God indeed. I'll tell you later. If I can. Right now, I have something to get rid of."

"And you wanted to call it a night." Andrew let the car get two blocks away then pulled out after it. The large man crammed into the passenger seat of the mini said nothing and the larger man folded into the back merely grunted.

The church in Petty stood alone on a hill about seven miles east of Inverness just off the A96. A three-quarter moon and a sky bright with stars sketched out the surrounding graveyard in stark silver and black. Gordon pulled into the driveway and killed the motor.

"At least it's stopped raining," Pat muttered getting out of the car. "No, you wait here," she added when Gordon attempted to follow. "I have to do this alone."

Lips pressed into a thin line, he dropped into the driver's seat, reclined it back, and pointedly closed his eyes.

Chalmer Hardie's instructions had been clear. *"The MacKintosh mausoleum is against the west side of the church. Close by it, you'll find a grave stone with only a sword cut into the face. MacGillivray's fiancée managed to bury him but with Cumberland's army squatting in Inverness, she could find no one who dared put his name on the stone. There are MacGillivrays buried in Kilmartin graveyard under similar stones—Templar stones. Put the medallion in the grave."*

Keeping a tight grip on her imagination, Pat found the ancient mausoleum, skirted it, and stared down at the grave of Alexander MacGillivray. Then suddenly realized what *put the medallion in the grave* meant.

"And me without a shovel." Swallowing hard, she managed to get her stomach under control although at the moment the possibility of spending another night with the medallion frightened her more than a bit of gravedigging. She pulled it out of her pocket and glared down at it. All she wanted to do was get rid of it. Why did it have to be so difficult?

"Hand over the jewelry and nobody gets hurt."

Fear clamped both hands around her throat and squeezed her scream into a breathy squeak. When she turned, she saw three substantial shadows between her and the lights that lined Moray Firth. If they were ghosts, Hell provided a pungent aftershave. Two of them were huge. The third was a weasely looking fellow no bigger than she was.

The weasely fellow smiled. "I won't say we don't want to hurt you because me pals here rather like a bit of rough stuff. Be a smart lady; give it here." While he spoke, the other two closed in.

Pat laughed a bit hysterically. "Look, you have no idea how much I want to get rid of this. Go ahead and..."

Then she stopped. All she could think of was how Davie Hardie had been willing to do anything rather than die.

"Your word will be sufficient."

"My word? That's it?"

"Yes."

She'd given her word that she'd put the medallion in Alexander MacGillivray's grave. Her chin rose and she placed it carefully back in her pocket. "If you want it, you'll have to take it from me."

"You're being stupid."

"Up yours." Pat took a deep breath and was surprised by how calm she felt.

The man on her left jerked forward and she dove to the right. Fingers tangled in her hair but she twisted free, fell and scrambled back to her feet. *If I can just get to the car...*

Her ears rang as a fist slid off the side of her head.

A hand clutched the shoulder of her jacket. If she slid out of it they'd have the medallion so she stepped back, driving her heel down onto an instep.

One of them swore and let go. The other wrapped his arm around her neck and hung on. When she struggled, he tightened his grip.

"Right then." The weasely fellow pinched her cheek, hard.

Pat tried to bite him.

"That'll be enough of tha...ahhhhhhhhh!"

He sounded terrified.

The arm released her neck and Pat dropped to her knees. Gasping for breath, she watched all three of her assailants race away, tripping and stumbling over the gravestones.

"Good...timing...Gordon," she panted and turned.

It wasn't Gordon.

Alexander Macgillivray had been a tall man and although it was possible to see the church and the mausoleum through him, death hadn't made him any shorter. Pat looked up. Way up. This time the scream made it through the fear. She stood, stumbled backwards into a gravestone and fell. Ghostly fingers reached out towards her...

When she opened her eyes, Pat discovered there was no significant difference between a private hospital room in Scotland and one in Canada. They even smelled the same. Ignoring the pain in her head, she pushed herself up onto her elbows and discovered her clothes neatly folded on a chair by the bed.

Teeth clenched, she managed to snag her jacket. Although she half expected the ghost of Alexander MacGillivray to have claimed the medallion, it was still in her pocket. Closing her fingers around it, she stared at the ceiling and thought about what had happened in the graveyard. About what she'd done. About what she hadn't done. About what had sent her there.

About the medallion. By the time the nurse came in to check on her, she'd made a decision.

When she fell asleep, she didn't dream.

They'd just cleared the breakfast dishes away—she'd been allowed a glass of juice and hadn't wanted much more—when Gordon, looking as though he'd spent a sleepless night, stuck his head into the room. When he saw she was awake, he walked over to the bed. "I'm not a relative," he explained self-consciously. "They made me go home."

"The nurse said you nearly drove through the doors at emergency."

"It seemed the least I could do." His expression shifted through worry, relief, and anger. "I came running when I heard the screams. When I saw you on the ground..."

"You didn't see anyone else?"

"No." He frowned. "Should I have?"

If she said she'd been attacked, the police would have to be involved and what would be the point?

"Pat, what happened?"

"I saw a ghost." She shrugged and wished she hadn't as little explosions went off inside her skull. "I guess I tripped and hit my head."

Scooping her clothes off the chair, he sat down. "I guess you did. The nurse at the desk told me that if you'd hit it two inches lower, you'd be dead." He colored as she winced. "Sorry."

"S'okay. Gordon, last night you said your uncle had the parish of Petty. Does that mean he's the minister there?"

It took him a moment to get around the sudden change of topic. "Uh, yes."

"Is he a good man?"

"He's a minister!"

"You know what I mean."

Gordon considered it. "Yes," he said after a moment, "he's a good man."

"Could you call him?" Pat lightly stroked the crystal with one finger. "And ask him to come and see me..."

* * *

Sunlight brushed the hard angles off the graveyard and softened both the grey of the stones and the red brick of Petty church. Released from the hospital that morning, Pat looked out over the water of Moray Firth then down at the grave of Alexander MacGillivray.

"I gave my word to Chalmer Hardie that I'd put the medallion in your grave." She sighed and spread her hands. "I don't have it anymore. I tried to call him but he's in the hospital and MacClery won't let me talk to him. Anyway, I'm going home tomorrow and I thought you deserved an explanation."

When she paused, the silence waited for her to continue. "So many of the Templars died violently that I was confused for a while about the medallion's power to protect. You gave me the clue. If you'd thought it could stop shot, you'd have torn the country apart to find it before you sacrificed the lives of your people. Davie Hardie wanted the medallion to protect him from dying in battle so that's what it did—but the Templars expected to die in battle so they wanted protection against the things that would cause them to break their vows."

Her cheeks grew hot as she remembered how close to betrayal she personally had come and how much five hundred pounds sounded like thirty pieces of silver. "Chalmer Hardie wanted me to right the wrong his ancestor did you by having the medallion returned where he thought it belonged. But I don't think it belongs with the dead. I think we could really use that kind of protection active in the world right now.

"Gordon's uncle says there's still Templar organizations in Scotland, even after all this time. I thought you'd like to know that." The gravestone was warm under her fingertips as she traced the shallow carving of the sword. "He gave me his word that he'll give it to the person in charge.

"So I'm bringing you his promise in place of the medallion."

Shoving her hands into her pockets, she turned to go. Then she remembered one more thing. "I could still lie to Mr. Hardie. Tell him you got the medallion back, pick up that ten grand and the job—but I won't. Because it isn't dying honorably that counts, is it? It's living honorably, right to the end."

As she reached the corner of the church and could see Gordon waiting by the car, the hair lifted off the back of her neck. The silence pulled her around.

Standing on the grave was a tall young man with red-gold hair and pale skin in the clothing of the Jacobite army. Pat forgot to breathe. He hadn't been wearing the medallion the night he'd driven off the three thugs but today it hung gleaming against his chest.

The air shimmered and she saw a line of men stretch into the distance behind him. They all wore the medallion. Many wore the white mantle and red cross of a Templar Knight. For an instant, she felt a familiar weight around her neck then both the weight and all the shades but Alexander MacGillivray's disappeared.

Tell Chalmer Hardie, he said to her heart as he faded, *that you kept your word.*

I'd intended this story to be about Alison's mother but realized, about half way through, it just didn't work with a female protagonist. I'm not sure why.

We have a number of very strange holes out toward the back of our property but, familiar as I am with Alice in Wonderland, I'm hesitant about investigating any of them too closely.

This, by the way, is the story the collection's title comes from. You'll understand why when you get there. What ho.

THE HARDER THEY FALL

"Daddy?" Alison put her glass in the sink and stared out the kitchen window. "Daddy?" she repeated a little louder. "There's a dragon at the hummingbird feeder."

"You mean a dragonfly, sweetie."

"No, I *don't*." She was as certain as only a nearly-five year old could be. "I mean a *dragon*."

Colin Ostrander put his screwdriver down amidst the ruins of the toaster and stood, sternly repressing a preoccupied, *"That's nice, dear."* Just last night, he and his wife had agreed that they had to become more involved in their daughter's life. Granted, Alison was always seeing the weird and wonderful but didn't any magic his daughter could find in the mess that adults had made of the world deserve to be investigated? Besides, the toaster had, for the moment, completely defeated him.

"All right, Ali, let's see your dra..."

There was a dragon at the hummingbird feeder.

Coiled once around the neck of the bulb, it clung to the overloaded feeder with tiny, hand-like front claws, nose pressed tight against one of the plastic flowers. Green scales gleamed iridescent in the summer sunlight and its folded wings enclosed it in a shimmering gossamer tent. Its dangling tail traced lazy arcs of obvious contentment.

"Oh my lord, that's a dragon."

Alison sighed. "That's what I *said*, Daddy. Isn't it pretty?"

The wasps that perpetually plagued the hummingbirds were nowhere in sight. Neither, for that matter, were the hummingbirds.

The level of red sugar-water in the bulb dropped noticeably as they watched.

Colin found himself clutching the edge of the counter so tightly it creaked a protest. "Where could it have come from?"

Just then the dragon lifted its head. Topaz eyes stared into the kitchen while a scarlet tongue tasted the air.

"Where's your mother?" Janet would never believe this if she didn't see it for herself.

"Mommy's in the garage."

With a sudden slither, the dragon dropped from the feeder, spreading its wings barely in time to avoid impact with the flowers below. About two feet long from nose to tail tip, stomach visibly rounded, it flew laboriously across the backyard.

No time to get Janet, Colin decided. "Come on, Ali. Let's go after it!"

"Nah." She shrugged and headed for the livingroom. "I'm gonna play Super Mario."

No time to argue. The dragon had almost reached the rail fence and once it got into the fields and woods beyond the row of neat suburban/country houses, he'd lose it for sure. The screen door slamming shut behind him, Colin leapt off the back porch and raced across the lawn. Here was actual proof of magic and myth still in the world and he wasn't going to let it get away.

Clearly straining, the dragon managed enough altitude to crest the top cedar rail then locked its wings and dropped into a long shallow glide.

Colin scrambled over the fence after it, sank into the weeds on the other side with an audible squelch, stumbled sideways, and drove the thorns of a wild rose through his sock and into his ankle. Caught up in the chase, he hardly felt the pain.

The dragon peered back over its shoulder, turning its head almost a complete one hundred and eighty degrees so that its nose pointed down the valley between its wings. Even almost fifteen feet away, Colin was sure he saw its eyes widen. Facing front, it put on a frantic burst of speed.

Sneakers sinking into wet ground, brambles snagging bare flesh between socks and shorts, Colin sprinted after it. "This is amazing," he panted, pushing through a stand of dog-willow fast enough to raise welts. "What am I going to do if I catch up to it?"

The question seemed moot as up ahead the dragon flashed once in the sun, dove towards the ground, and disappeared.

"Oh no you don't!" He fought his way past a clump of prickly ash with only a minor loss of blood and came to the edge of a small clearing just in time to see the tip of a green tail vanish into the shadowed recess below a fallen cedar. Sucking at a laceration on his wrist, Colin raced towards the downed tree; as the dragon hadn't reappeared it must still be under there.

"Hey, dragon. It's okay." He dropped to his knees. "I'm not going to hurt you. I just want to..." With no idea of what it was he just wanted to do, he let the reassurance trail off. Bending almost double, he peered eagerly into the shadows.

The dragon was nowhere in sight but the tree was covering a cleft in the earth about thirty inches long by eighteen inches wide.

Colin stretched out a hand then, rational again for a moment, paused and sniffed the breeze. Not much—not even the magic of an actual dragon—could stand against the reality of a skunk. The whole family had learned that lesson just after they'd moved out here from the city and it wasn't one he was anxious to re-peat. As his nose declared the hole unoccupied, he balanced awkwardly on his knees, bent under the edge of the fallen tree, and squinted into the earth.

Was that light? A flash of green?

Inching ahead, he stretched both arms down into the hole. It appeared to continue, with no significant change in dimension, far deeper than he could reach. A faint light rose up from the bottom. He could see the outlines of rock below in spite of the fallen tree above blocking the sun.

"Just a little farther…"

In the best tradition, it proved just a little too far.

The loosened dirt at the lip gave way. The rock he tried to brace his hands against crumbled out of the wall. Unable to prevent it, he tumbled forward—not quickly, for the passageway was barely wider than he was, but inevitably.

Gravity spilled him out of the cleft and into a passageway brilliantly lit by light reflected from thousands of pieces of embedded quartz where a bewildering array of tiny rainbows danced in the air. A little stunned—*At least Alice didn't land on her head*—he pushed himself along with elbows and toes, squinting against the glare. As he hadn't landed on the dragon when he fell, squashing it into an iridescent smear on the rock, he reasoned, somewhat muzzily, that he had to still be following it.

He'd traveled between ten and fifteen feet when the world tilted sideways. Perceptions scrambled, he threw himself forward until the physical structure of the passage reformed itself around him. When his head emerged into a circular cavern about six feet in diameter, he collapsed, panting. Half out of the tunnel, leaning his weight on the less abraded of his arms, he lifted the other hand to shade his watering eyes from the sunlight pouring in through a fissure directly across from him.

There was still no sign of the dragon but piled against the curve of the cavern wall was a curious collection of chunks of quartz and bits of strangely shaped metal that could only be its horde.

Inching the rest of the way out of the passage, Colin carefully got to his feet. Nothing seemed to be too terribly damaged. *Okay, first of all, find out where you are.* They'd been living in that house for three years and none of the neighbors had ever mentioned finding a cave in the area. *Of course, they've never mentioned finding a dragon either…*

Shoving aside a strangely shaped bush, Colin ducked and stepped out into the open air.

And very nearly tripped over the dragon stretched out on a rock ledge, basking in the sun.

Up close, it reminded Colin of nothing so much as an elongated cat for its expression said clearly, *Oh, puh-leez, I've just gotten comfortable. Surely you don't expect me to move?* When he stepped forward, it managed to look simultaneously disgruntled and wary, wings spreading slightly, forked tongue flicking out to taste the air. Colin froze, worried that, frightened, it might fly away. Heart racketing about in his chest, he slowly slid his hand into the pocket of his shorts.

The dragon's head whipped back, eyes locked on the movement.

His fingers closed around a sticky, plastic wrapped rectangle. Still moving slowly, he drew it out. Two days ago, in town, he'd bought Alison a large grape sucker. Six or seven licks into it, when the stick had snapped, she'd decided she no longer wanted it and it had ended up stuffed in Daddy's pocket for later.

"Well, we know you've got a sweet tooth..."

A second later he was counting his fingers as the dragon devoured sucker, wrapper, and remnant of stick with obvious enjoyment.

Which was when it hit him.

His legs buckled and he sat down suddenly, painfully, on a pointed rock. He'd just fed a two-day-old sucker to a dragon a little smaller than the family cat. This was not the sort of thing that happened to boring, thirty-something software analysts.

"Maybe I slipped on my way across the kitchen," he said thoughtfully to the dragon as it climbed onto his lap and began nosing through his clothes, "and all this is just my subconscious keeping me amused while I'm being rushed to hospital in a coma. Ouch! Watch those claws!"

Setting the dragon aside with one hand, he rubbed at the four bleeding, parallel scratches dug into his thigh with the other. This dragon, this wondrous, miraculous dragon, was painfully real. "Maybe," he told it, stroking the warm curve of an offered belly with something very close to reverence, "you're the sort of thing that happens to fathers of almost-five year olds."

"What ho, dragon! Thou art named arrant and most pernicious worm. Come hither and fight!" The voice, thinned by distance and strangely high pitched, held the distinct sound of threat.

The dragon flipped back onto its feet, scrambled over Colin's legs, and dove into the cave.

"If that's one of the Dushane kids..." Colin leaned forward until he could see off the ledge.

About twenty feet away was a sort of a plateau and on that plateau was a meadow fifteen feet square and in that meadow was a knight in armor on a horse, also in armor. The sun gleamed off polished steel and although the breeze snapped the pennant on the lance tip gaily back and forth, the weapon itself appeared grimly businesslike. The only problem was, the mounted knight wasn't much more than a foot high.

Which explained the high-pitched voice but not much else.

Colin wiped suddenly sweaty palms on his shorts as he finally realized that the strangely shaped bush beside the cave entrance was a full-grown tree. That all the bushes surrounding the meadow were trees. *There's only one logical...*No, somehow logical wasn't the right word...*one possible explanation. I'm definitely not in Kansas anymore.* It didn't seem to matter that he'd never been to Kansas. *It had to have happened back in that tunnel when things slipped out of whack.* The hair on the back of his neck lifted. *I went through a magical portal.* Somehow, he seemed to have been flung into one of the fairy tales he read to his daughter. *I thought that sort of thing only happened in wardrobes!*

Although he realized that perhaps he should be, he wasn't afraid. He'd trust the magic that had brought him through to get him home again. It was Alison's magic after all.

"What ho, dragon!" the knight called a second time, rising in his stirrups. "I, Sir Jorrin of Barrowford, do challenge thee to single combat for the sake of honor and in the name of his most gracious majesty, King Bryant. Come hither and fight!"

Colin felt the dragon's wedge-shaped head push under his arm, and he almost thought he heard it sigh as it also gazed down at the knight. "I wouldn't worry about it," he murmured comfortingly, "there's no way he can climb up onto this ridge in that outfit."

"What ho, dragon! By the avouchment made in the exordium of time, that which pledges the great worms to answer when summoned thrice, I challenge thee for the third and final time. Come hither and…"

"Hold it buddy!" Colin leapt to his feet, tumbling the dragon behind him. While he had no idea what an avouchment was, no diminutive St. George was forcing *this* dragon to fight. "Just what do you think you're doing?"

It took Sir Jorrin a moment to regain control of his horse and he lost his lance in the process. Finally managing to draw his sword, he yanked his mount around until it faced up the mountain again.

"What ho, giant!" he yelled, voice even higher pitched than it had been. "Thou art named, uh, megatherian and uh, most, uh, well, uh, most prodigious great. Come hither and fight!"

"I will not!"

"What ho, giant! I, Sir Jorrin of Barrowford, do challenge…"

"Look, you stay right there. I'm coming down." Shooing the dragon back inside the cave and telling it to stay put, Colin climbed down the ridge to the plateau, Sir Jorrin continuing his challenge in the background.

As Colin stepped onto the meadow and his size became apparent, the knight's horse reared and headed for the trees at full gallop, reins trailing and rider left lying helmless on the grass. Colin reached down to help but an expression of terror stopped his hand a foot from the ground. "Are you all right?" he asked instead. "Are you hurt?"

Golden curls in disarray, Sir Jorrin pushed himself into a kneeling position and searched frantically about in the grass.

"Sir Jorrin?"

At the sound of his name, his search grew more frantic still.

Well, we're not going to accomplish anything until he finds it. Colin scanned the grass from his superior vantage point and plucked the miniature sword from out of the sod. "Here." Carefully holding the three-inch blade between thumb and forefinger, he squatted and offered the knight the hilt.

Still on his knees, Sir Jorrin grabbed for it with both hands.

Colin released the blade. "Now, put it away before you hurt someone."

Driving the point into the ground, Sir Jorrin used it to lever himself laboriously to his feet

"Well?" Colin insisted pointedly as the blade remained unsheathed.

"God's teeth, giant!" Panting slightly, Sir Jorrin glared up at him, terror shoved aside by indignation. "I am *not* a child. I am an anointed knight and a man full three and twenty years old!"

Somewhat taken aback, Colin spread his hands in a conciliatory gesture. "Did I say you weren't?"

"Thou art treating me as though I were but moments back pulled mewling from the tit!"

"I am?"

"Thou art!"

"Sorry. It's that you're so, so…" He was eleven inches high is what he was and prejudices said adults were not eleven inches high. Colin felt heartily ashamed of himself. *All right. So lets say he's vertically challenged and leave it at that.*

"I have never heard of giants in this place before." Sir Jorrin's tone made it an accusation.

"I'm not exactly from around here."

"Then where?"

Why not tell him? "I came through a magic portal in the mountain."

"This mountain?"

"Yes."

"Thy home is on the other side?"

The *other side*; seemed accurate enough in the classical sense. "Yes."

"Hast thou come then to be the dragon's champion? To answer the challenge in its place?" Without turning his back, Sir Jorrin moved to where his helm had fallen and scooped it up.

"Well…" Well, somebody had to do it or the poor dragon would end up looking like those pictures of slaughtered baby seals that Greenpeace had plastered North America with back in the seventies. Except of course that the dragon had scales instead of fur and didn't look at all like a seal and it was about to be spitted not clubbed. Actually, he had to acknowledge, it wasn't a very good analogy. More importantly, what would Alison say if she knew her Daddy had allowed the dragon to be killed? "Okay, what will it take for you to go away and leave the dragon alone?"

"If it is thy desire that I leave, giant, thou must first defeat me in single combat." Apparently undaunted by the prospect of fighting someone almost six times his size, Sir Jorrin cheerfully clapped his helm on his head took a deep breath and bellowed, "What ho, giant! Thou art named megatherian and most prodigious great. Come hither and fight!"

"Is that your answer to everything?" Colin asked sharply. "Fighting?"

Sir Jorrin looked confused. "I am a knight. It is what we do."

"Well, I am *not* a knight and it's *not* what I do." *What do I do? Got any programs you need debugged? This is ridiculous.* But since he'd opened his big mouth…"I, uh, negotiate."

"What means this, negotiate?"

"It means that instead of fighting, we talk."

"Ah. If it is thy desire to talk, go ahead and while thou art talking, I shall fight the dragon. Although," the knight added peevishly, taking a few practice cuts at the air, "it would be a great deal easier if my niddering horse and equally niddering squire had remained. No doubt the two of them are back at Kiramar by now." He took one final swing then turned to face up the mountain. "What ho, dragon!"

"Sir Jorrin. We *have* to talk about this."

"I have no time for talk, I must needs rid the land of this arrant and pernicious worm."

"Oh." Colin hadn't considered that. "Does it eat maidens then?"

"Maidens?" Sir Jorrin laughed. "*I* never found any maidens in these parts. No," he continued, oblivious to the tatters of chivalric myth, "no maidens. But it flies over the villages, affrighting persons and livestock. Oftimes in the year, it takes a sheep or calf."

"A sheep or calf?" That was all? "And you're going to kill it for that?"

Sir Jorrin snorted. "Not likely. His Majesty has offered a Dukedom to the knight who can best the beast."

"You're going to kill the dragon for personal profit?" Like the rest of his generation, Colin had no problem with upward mobility but, as an archetype, Sir Jorrin was becoming a bit of a disappointment. "What about honor?"

Under his armor, Sir Jorrin shrugged. "What about it?" he asked.

Colin sighed. Eleven inches of knight braced himself against the gust. "This is getting us nowhere fast." He checked his watch. He should be getting home but Janet could look after Alison for a little while longer. "I think I need to talk to someone in charge."

"Thou art desirous of speech with his Majesty?"

"If he's the one who makes things happen, the local CEO, then yes."

"No!"

"Why not?"

"Thou art a giant!"

"So?" Colin resisted the urge to throw in a Fe, Fi, Foe, Fum— which was the only giantspeak he could remember.

"It is not what is done with giants!"

"Why not?"

Tiny golden brows drew down. "If I take thee to my King, what will stop thee from destroying him?"

"Destroying him? I just want to *talk.*"

"Again, talk." Sir Jorrin chopped absently at a buttercup with his sword, obviously deep in thought. After a moment he looked up and asked, "How can I be *certain* thou wilt but talk?"

How indeed. *I suppose a citation from the Chamber of Commerce for civic responsibility won't cut it.* Then suddenly Colin had a truly brilliant idea. "I tell you what, Sir Jorrin, I'll take the most sacred oath of my people." Straightening to his full height, he solemnly traced an ex across his chest. "Cross my heart and hope to die, stick a finger in my eye, my nose drops off if I tell a lie." Alison had come up with the last phrase herself and been inordinately proud of it. It seemed like the sort of thing that a man enamored of shouting *What ho!* might be impressed by.

"Quite the oath, giant." Sir Jorrin turned it over a moment longer, seemed to settle an internal argument, and sheathed his sword. "Very well. Let us waste no time."

"How far is it?"

"A three hour gentle ride." The knight looked disgusted. "A longer walk."

"Three hours!"

"Hast thou better things to do?"

"I have to get home." Colin looked back up at the dragon's cave and caught a glimpse of sunlight reflecting off iridescent green scales. It was the color of the leaves in Sherwood Forest. It was the color of the Emerald City. It was the color of his little girl's eyes—well, actually Alison's eyes were more hazel but in some lights they looked sort of green. *And Alison's daddy can't quit now.* "I guess I can be a little late." He'd have to tell Janet he'd got lost in the woods. While she'd believe that, she'd never believe this.

"Perhaps," Colin suggested after he'd crossed the meadow in three long strides and then waited fifteen minutes for Sir Jorrin to catch up, "I should carry you."

"Carry me?" panted Sir Jorrin. "I tell thee again, giant, I am no...uh..." He wiped a sweaty brow with an equally sweaty hand and sighed deeply. "Mayhap thou should."

Sir Jorrin's "three hour gentle ride" took about forty minutes of steady walking. They paused once, Colin regretting the four cups of coffee he'd had that morning before leaving home. Unfortunately, the rocky ground was unable to absorb such a quantity of liquid and the steaming stream washed away a section of the path. *I guess I should've aimed downhill.*

"Incredible!" exclaimed Sir Jorrin when he was retrieved.

During the speculation that followed, Colin tried not to feel smug.

When they reached the first of the farms, he became too preoccupied with finding a place to safely put his feet to pay Sir Jorrin much attention. Fortunately, there were few fences, a great deal of fallow land, and most of the people either barricaded themselves inside squat stone buildings or screamed and ran for the woods. The one exception raced towards him and jabbed a pitchfork through the top of his running shoe.

"A stupid man," observed Sir Jorrin as the next step left the farmer far behind. "But a brave one."

"Right," Colin agreed tightly, shaking the pitchfork loose.

"If thy foot-coverings were not thick enough to keep it out, thou hast better hope there was no shit on the prongs. Shit will cause a wound to putrefy most wondrously."

"Thank you, Sir Jorrin."

With his brain attempting to operate on the scale it was used to, it seemed that next to no time passed between spotting Kiramar in the distance and arriving in the cleared area outside the waist-high wall. It looked, Colin decided, just the way a city in a fairy tale should. *Kind of like Barbie and Ken do Camelot.*

"Unless thou art impervious to arrow fire," Sir Jorrin told him dryly, "I should wait here."

"For how long?" He couldn't look at his watch without dropping his hitchhiker but the sun seemed nearly straight up. It had to be close to noon.

"Not long. Watch the Dragongate."

"The what?"

"The gate we face in the wall."

A few moments later, the Dragongate opened just far enough for a mounted knight to ride out. The gleaming figure stopped about ten inches from the wall and set his lance.

"What ho, giant! Thou art named ponderous and most minacious calumniator! Come hither and…" The knight broke off, raised a gauntleted hand, and lifted his visor. "Sir Jorrin?"

Explanations took a while. At the request of the city council, Colin tried not to fidget. Sir Jorrin disappeared, leaving him staring at the crowds who'd climbed to the top of the city wall to stare at him. Eventually, a man no more than nine inches tall and trying desperately hard to make up for it, came out to tell him that the king had graciously agreed to grant him an audience.

"As the wall is too high for thee to step over and climbing would damage both it and the buildings against it, mayhap thou canst squirm though the Dawngate. Surely th'art not wider than four wagons."

"Can't his Majesty talk with me out here?" Colin wondered.

Apparently not.

He wasn't wider than four wagons, but it was close. While squirming, he tried to ignore the embarrassingly frank suggestions from the watching crowds and tried harder to ignore what he was squirming in. By partially dislocating one shoulder, he got through the gate and standing again without doing any more than a very minor bit of destruction. An escort of mounted knights waited for him inside and Colin made his way carefully from gate to palace behind them, his sense of wonder fighting for survival against the stench of open sewers.

The wall around the palace was more decorative than functional and reached only just above knee high. He cautiously stepped over it and into a courtyard where he was, once again, told to wait.

Just like home. He eased down onto the cobblestones, back to the wall, in the one position he could manage without crushing anything. *They tell you that you've got an appointment then make you wait some more.*

Under shadowed scrutiny from every window, Colin went over the argument he intended to present to the king, wishing that he'd paid more attention to the boys in marketing. All he could remember was a mouthful of teeth that had to have been capped and a lengthy justification of expense accounts, neither of which would be of much use under the circumstances.

After what seemed like hours, the officious little man reappeared followed by an anthill's worth of servants who swarmed over a balcony by Colin's head laying carpet, hanging tapestries, and finally setting up what had to be a small throne.

"Will it take much longer?" Colin asked.

The official didn't even bother to look at him. "His Majesty will see thee shortly."

A less magical tone could not be imagined. His dentist's receptionist had one just like it.

Then, as suddenly as they'd appeared, servants and official disappeared. A trumpet sounded, the balcony doors swung open, and out stepped a man Sir Jorrin's size but older, his hair and beard liberally streaked with grey. *Actually, he looks like Sean Connery in a good rug and a crown. I hope my breath is okay.*

Settling himself on the throne, King Bryant gripped intricately carved wooden arms tightly enough to turn his fingertips white. "So, giant, Sir Jorrin hath told me much about thee. It is thy desire to speak with me concerning the dragon?"

Colin approved of his Majesty getting straight to the point. He'd always been terrible at small talk. "Right. The dragon." Fortunately, he'd just received the quarterly package from the World Wildlife foundation and while dragons weren't exactly snail darters or black footed ferrets and the destruction of the Brazilian rainforest certainly didn't affect them, the text could be adapted to fit. Becoming increasingly impassioned, he wrapped up with an emotional plea for wonder and diversity in the universe, lifted in its entirety from a classic Star Trek episode.

When he finished, King Bryant, looking much less tense, leaned forward and said, "If th'art saying the dragon is magical, th'art wrong. It is nothing more or less than a giant flying lizard."

Kings, Colin decided, should be less literal. "No your Majesty, I'm saying the dragon represents all the things that are magic and wonderful in the world and you shouldn't allow people like Sir Jorrin to keep trying to kill it."

"Allow?" Tiny brows rose imperiously. "Giant, I did not allow Sir Jorrin to challenge the dragon. I encouraged him."

"Encouraged him? But why?"

"Because Sir Jorrin is young and strong and ambitious and deserves a chance to win a Dukedom."

"But you should be *protecting* the dragon!"

"From what?"

"Well, essentially, from everything. And you should be finding a mate for it. Trying to get it to breed."

King Bryant stared up at him in astonishment. "Then we should have more than one."

"And just think what that would do for the tourist industry."

"The what?"

"People would pay to see a family of dragons in their natural habitat. You could open a theme park. Sell t-shirts. Finance civic improvements."

"Thy words are strange, giant." Shaking his head, the king stood. "Thy thoughts are stranger. I shall consider them. We will speak again when thou hast been refreshed."

"But..."

The balcony door swung shut.

Colin could only wait.

And wait.

Finally, a door opened by his left knee and what appeared to be the same crowd of servants rolled out half of a huge wooden barrel which they then filled with buckets of water. As attempting to talk to them only brought panicked retreats and a damp courtyard, Colin gave up and tried, not very successfully, to stretch his legs.

With the barrel full, a bucolic looking young man dragged a confused and protesting cow out into the courtyard by a rope halter and left it there.

Colin gratefully drank the water. After a few moments of terror, the cow settled down and began chewing a bit of topiary.

There wasn't a bush ungnawed in the courtyard by the time the king returned. "Thou wast not hungry?" he asked, indicating the cow with the sweep of his hand.

Colin winced. He was supposed to eat the cow? Alive? "Uh, no. Thank you." Whatever happened to a dozen tiny loaves of bread; roast turkeys the size of chickadees; great bowls of custard, sweet and creamy and swallowed whole? Obviously, some fairy tales had better catering than others.

"I have considered your words," King Bryant told him solemnly, "and have decided that my knights will no longer hunt the dragon."

"Your Majesty! That's wonderful!" By God, he'd done it! The dragon was safe! A traditional happy ending and *he* was responsible. Alison was going to be so proud of her daddy.

The king regarded him speculatively. "Is it true that thou carried Sir Jorrin down the mountain?"

"Well, yes. His horse had run off and he couldn't walk very quickly in armour and I didn't have much time...and good grief, is that the time?" Carefully, so as not to step on the cow, Colin got to his feet. "You've made the right decision, your Majesty, you'll see." Pins and needles exploded up his right leg, a thousand tiny points of pain. In the interests of diplomacy, he hid the grimace in a smile. "Thank you for your time. Now, if you'll excuse me, I've *really* got to go."

"Home?"

"Yes, home."

"As thou hast carried Sir Jorrin, wouldst thou carry his king to the city wall on thy way out?"

Colin smiled. From playgrounds to battlefields, people didn't change. If one kid had a sucker then all the kids had to have a sucker. If one country had nuclear capabilities then all the countries had to have nuclear capabilities. If Sir Jorrin had been carried by a giant then the king had to be carried by a giant. "Of course, your Majesty."

It was much easier to squirm out of the city than it had been to squirm in. At the king's request, Colin carried him around the outside of Kiramar to the Dragonsgate and set him down on top of the wall, the line of guards that stretched around a quarter curve, parting to let him in.

"The giant," the king announced, "is going home."

The guards cheered, waving their bows over their heads. Colin smiled and waved back, reassuring King Bryant that he could find his way to the meadow without a guide.

The king seemed to approve. "Then good-bye, giant. It has been..." He paused, appeared to discard several words, and finally finished with, "...interesting."

With his hands free of knight, Colin made better time on the way up than he had on the way down and, although people still screamed and ran, no one tried to stick a pitchfork in him. Humming *Puff the Magic Dragon* as he walked, in a little under half an hour, sweating and with a stitch in his side, he arrived back at the meadow.

All in all, it had been the sort of day that dreams were made of. Still favoring the pulled muscle in his left shoulder, he bent and scratched at some of the dried blood on his knee—whether it came from the prickly ash, the shards of quartz, or the dragon's claws he wasn't entirely certain but every bump, every bruise had been worth it. He couldn't wait to see Alison's eyes light up when he told her what he'd done.

"What ho, giant!"

"Sir Jorrin!" Colin grinned down at the knight. "How did you get back up here so quickly?"

"As thou was entering the Dawngate, I rode from the Dragongate with the city between us. His Majesty kept thee long enough for me to return to this place."

"Have you come to see me off?"

"In a manner of speaking," the knight replied. Behind him, a line of archers rose to their feet, and continued to rise until the meadow was almost completely enclosed in a circle of longbows. "I have come to see that thou art stopped."

"What?"

"I have come to kill thee."

"What!"

"Kill thee," Sir Jorrin repeated. Then, just in case there might still be some confusion, he added, "Dead."

"But why?" A fantasy land of miniature knights and dragons he could manage to cope with but this was something else again.

"Because thou art a giant." Tone and manner added a clear, *Why else?*

"That's hardly a good enough reason!" They weren't actually going to kill him. That sort of thing happened in books and movies but not in the real world.

"If thou must needs have an explanation," Sir Jorrin sighed, "know that as thou wilt not be bound by challenge, thou art dangerously unpredictable, creating a grave threat to the kingdom. This I told my king. But of more danger is the certainty that where there is one giant there must be others and unless we would have the kingdom overrun, something must be done. When I told him of thy vow, his Majesty agreed to keep thee talking—and this desire to talk is, I vow, the strangest thing about thee—whilst I, with a company of archers, returned to the place I first saw thee to wait and kill thee before thou canst go back under the mountain and lead thy people through."

"But I wouldn't! Cross my heart and hope to die!"

"Precisely," said Sir Jorrin. "The arrows," he added, "are poisoned. We could, of course, have shot thee from the city walls as thou didst leave but that would have meant thy great corpse would rot before Kiramar bringing pestilence and no doubt plague as well. Here, the dragon will devour thy carcass and the sun will bake thy bones clean and they shall lie as silent witness to challengers of the worm."

"Challengers? Hold it right there! The king promised me his knights would stop hunting the dragon!"

"The king's word shall stand. We have no need to hunt the dragon for we *know* where it is."

Why that royal... "So you're going to keep trying to kill it?"

"It is a dragon. *That* is what one does with dragons. Ready the bows."

Colin stared down at the ring of archers, or more specifically at the ring of metal points that tipped each angled shaft, and suddenly realized that the safety of the dragon had become a secondary concern. "Hang on! You're kidding, right?"

"Thou art a giant," Sir Jorrin pointed out reasonably. "*This* is what one does with giants. Aim."

Apparently, he wasn't kidding. The arrows were three, maybe four inches long. Not really very threatening except that Colin had recently seen a National Geographic special about some tribe in the Amazon basin that used poison darts half that size to kill people. Or maybe he'd seen it in a television adaptation of an old Indiana Jones movie. He'd worry about it later. If he had a later.

He was big enough that stomping the archers into the ground became a viable option if he could just overcome a lifetime of conditioning. He lifted his foot and with *"Pick on someone your own size,"* ringing in his ears, put it down again.

For obvious reasons, no one stood directly in front of the ridge leading up to the dragon's cave. Colin threw himself through the gap, the closest archers diving away from his charge, and scrambled at panicked speed up the rocky slope.

Behind him, he heard Sir Jorrin scream, "Fire!"

It felt like he'd been stung by wasps a half a dozen times in each buttock. Yelping in pain, he leapt forward and got both hands onto the lip of the dragon's ledge just in time to hear the knight admonishing his men to fire at will. A few arrows thudded into the thick, ridged rubber sole of his shoe but the rest fell short as, with strength he never knew he had, he dragged herself up onto the ledge and out of immediate danger.

Inching towards the cave mouth on his stomach, he paused a moment before entering to reach around and pluck out the arrows still quivering in his flesh. They hurt more coming out than they did going in but he supposed that if he *had* to be shot with poisoned arrows then he couldn't think of a place more insulated from anything vital. The pounding of his heart, the multiple trickles of sweat, and his ragged breathing were probably the result of adrenaline. Probably.

Down in the meadow, he could hear Sir Jorrin ordering the archers to storm the cave. From the sounds of it, the archers were objecting.

Tossing aside the handful of arrows, Colin crawled into the mountain and rose to his knees, breath hissing through his teeth at the movement. Curled up on its hoard, the dragon hissed back.

"They tried to kill me!" he told it, still not quite believing in spite of the punctures. "Really kill me!"

The dragon lowered its wedge-shaped head and regarded him through slitted topaz eyes.

"Sir Jorrin's a bigoted thug, the king makes promises like its an election year, fairy tale cities stink, and I've got a dozen poisoned arrow holes in my butt." He sighed and shook his head. This last bit was going to need editing before he could share it with Alison. Heavy editing.

"I'm sorry, dragon. I *tried* to save you but nothing's changed. Any day now, some knight, maybe even Sir Jorrin, will challenge you and you'll have to answer and..."

And all at once, Colin realized that the bits of metal scattered throughout the horde were actually bits of miniature armour and that lying in the curve of the dragon's emerald green tail was a tiny human skull with the top bitten off. "And you'll eat him," he finished. Somehow, after everything he'd been through, it didn't even surprise him much.

"You never needed my help, did you? You probably think the challenge is a call for dinner." It was definitely time to go home. "Oh well, at least you act in self-defense which is more than can be said for Sir Jorrin and company."

He remembered the king telling him that he had *encouraged* Sir Jorrin to challenge the dragon.

"Because Sir Jorrin is young and strong and ambitious and deserves a chance to win a Dukedom."

"Young, strong, ambitious and stupid. His Majesty probably *encourages* everyone he'd like to get rid of. So much for Camelot." With one last rub of his aching bottom, he shuffled over to the quartz passage and began working his way into the narrow opening, eyes squinted almost shut against the shimmer of light.

It'll be just my luck to get stuck here...

But the rainbows were still dancing so they should send him home.

The way the day's been going, I'll probably find out this was a side effect from underground testing and I'm going to end up glowing in the dark.

His lower legs were still in the dragon's cave when he heard it slither off its hoard and across the floor. He couldn't stop himself from chuckling as its forked tongue danced over the inside of one ankle and he felt himself relax as the feathery touch continued. Maybe things weren't so bad. *At least I can tell Alison there's a* little *magic left.* He held perfectly still so as not to scare it away and got his reward when a soft, warm nose lightly pressed against his skin.

Then it bit him on the calf.

His head jerked up, slamming painfully into the top of the passage. Whimpering, he scuttled forward, through the moment of vertigo thinking of nothing but getting home. The walls crumbled behind him during the vertical scrabble up the rock chimney but he ignored them as he struggled towards the smell of rotting vegetation wafting down from the forest floor above.

Finally, his head emerged into the shadows of dusk and he managed to drag his body out after it. Without the energy remaining for contortions, he rolled out from under the fallen tree and lay for a moment breathing heavily on a leafy cushion of ground cover.

He began to itch on the way home. He'd been lying in poison ivy.

Alison stared sleepily up at him, a battered teddy bear clutched under one chubby arm. "Why'd you stop him from fighting the dragon, Daddy?"

Colin blinked. And tried not to scratch. "But honey, surely you wouldn't want the dragon to be killed?"

"But that's what knights *do* with dragons." Her voice held the same matter-of-fact protest Sir Jorrin's had.

"Daddy!" Alison called from the kitchen. "Guess what?"

Colin glanced up from his magazine. The poison ivy blisters had nearly healed, the swelling from the arrows had gone down enough so that he could sit comfortably again, and the new medicine had pretty much taken care of the nasty intestinal parasite he'd picked up from drinking that half barrel of water. "What?" he asked, making the effort to sound interested and involved.

"There's a unicorn in the garden eating the tops off the carrots."

A unicorn in the garden. His mouth went dry. Easy to believe she saw a deer, or a goat, but he knew better.

In spite of everything, there *was* still magic in the world. Still wonderful, mystical, mythical things.

His heart began to pound. Ignoring a sharp pain from the scabbed over dragon bite, he got to his feet and hobbled into the kitchen.

"What ho, magic!" he called softly.

Alison, her nose pressed against the window, watched as the unicorn moved over one row and began eating the lettuce. "What did you say, Daddy?"

Colin smiled down at the back of his daughter's head. "I said, that's nice, dear."

But he said it like he meant it.

Picking up the bottle of calamine lotion, he went back to the livingroom.

Because it was nice.

Wincing only slightly, he settled back into his chair.

And *this* time, it was going to stay that way.

This story is loosely based on the Westray mine disaster (May 9th, 1992, Pictou County, Nova Scotia) where negligence at all levels, from the mine supervisors to the Federal government, resulted in the deaths of twenty-six men. Because conditions underground were so bad, they had to call off rescue/recovery attempts with ten of the twenty-six men still unaccounted for.

A DEBT UNPAID

"Don't...bzzzt...too deep. Over."
Noting the continuing absence of a methane level, Stuart Bell slipped the methanometer into the front pocket of his heavy jacket and unclipped the walkie talkie from his belt. "Say again, surface. We're getting breakup down here. Over."

"I...bzzt...don't go too deep. The last...bzzt...we need is another incident. Over."

Incident. Stuart curled his lip at the euphemism. Eight months before, eleven men had died when a methane explosion had flattened the lower two drifts of the Imap Mine. Only five bodies had been found. Rescue efforts for the other six had been called off after four days when, as the official statement had it, conditions determined no one could have survived and further attempts would put the rescue workers at risk. *Although for a change,* Stuart mused grimly, *the official statement was bang on.* He'd led the crew in and they'd damned near lost one of the younger brothers of the men they were searching for when a ceiling collapsed.

"...bzzt...hear me, Bell?! Over!"

"No need to panic, surface. I'm barely down a hundred meters and I'm going to work my way out to the end of this drift before I go deeper. Try to remember gas rises. Out."

"You ought to know that, you asshole," he added, clipping the walkie talkie back onto his belt. Alex Brekenfield fit the profile of a company mouthpiece completely; a clean cut, articulate chameleon, capable of projecting sincerity regardless of the bullshit he spouted. No one at Imap liked him, a few actively hated him, and Stuart Bell hated him most of all.

"Look, Stuart, we've got the powdered limestone you wanted, six hundred and sixty bags of it." Brekenfield flashed a capped smile and spread his hands. Clean hands. Hands that had never had coal dust ground into the creases. "The problem has been taken care of."

"The problem has not been taken care of until the limestone's been applied. You've got highly combustible coal dust building up down there..."

"And a tight economic situation up here," Brekenfield interrupted. "Production is way behind where it should be and head office is chewing on my butt. We'll shut down operations and give that mine a thorough rock dusting the moment we can afford it."

"Mr. Brekenfield, as the safety engineer on site..."

"You want to keep the mine open don't you? If we fall too far behind in production, head office'll close us down. You know Toronto only cares about the bottom line. And what would happen to this area if the jobs provided by the mine are lost?"

Bottom line, eleven men were dead and eight months later they were trying to open the mine up again because the chance of ending up dead and abandoned, three hundred and fifty meters underground meant little against the systemic unemployment that was the norm in Atlantic Canada. Financially, between private donations and compensation packages, the families of the dead were better off than the miners beginning to wonder how they were going to feed their kids.

"Financially better off," Stuart snarled, kicking at a chunk of gob with the steel toes of his hip waders. "So lets ask any one of those families if they'd rather have the money or their men back? And here I am, helping to open this fucking tomb up again!"

Breathing heavily, helmet light rising and falling in the dark, he pulled out the methanometer and took another reading. Still zero. Hand half way back to his pocket, a sound froze him in place.

Picks?

Imap might use considerably less than state of the art equipment but, even here, power cutters and blasting separated the coal from the face. Not picks.

Head cocked, he moved carefully forward, towards the sound. Ten meters along the drift, he knelt and laid his bare hand against the damp rock. Faintly, very faintly, he could feel a regular vibration.

"But there's nothing down there," he muttered sitting awkwardly back on his heels. "It's solid goddamned rock for almost fifty meters."

The impact of the picks grew louder, a distinct and unmistakable rhythm.

Frowning, Stuart took off his helmet and propped it up so that the light shone on the rock in front of him. Then he laid his ear against the stone.

It was damp. And cold.

The sound stopped.

He was almost positive he could hear voices.

The next impact nearly deafened him.

"God damn it!" He jerked up, cupping his left ear and noticed that the angle of the light threw a tiny line of shadow across the stone. "There wasn't a crack there..." Then his gaze happened to fall on the methanometer still in his right hand. He had just enough time to see the needle flip up into the red before, with a tortured roar, the floor of the tunnel dropped out from underneath him and the world fell on his head.

Someone was singing a Rita McNeil song. Badly. Stuart groaned, opened his eyes and realized it made no difference to the darkness.

"Shut your gob, McIsaac, he's awake." The voice, for all its genial good humor held an unmistakable note of command.

The singing stopped.

"Is he alive?" asked a third voice.

"Heart's beating," replied the first, "so I guess he is."

Stuart wasn't so sure but a quick inventory seemed to indicate that all parts were working. He tried to sit up and fell back gasping for breath as the edges of a broken rib ground together.

"Bet that hurt."

It took him a moment to find his voice and a moment after that to manage a coherent word. "Wh...wh...who?"

"Christ, you sound like an asthmatic owl. Don't you know who we are, Stuart?"

"I was...supposed to be...alone."

"What do mean, you want to reopen the mine?"

Alex Brekenfield looked sincerely concerned. "It's 275 jobs, Stuart. Jobs this county could desperately use. But in order to start the ball rolling, we need a safety check and you are our safety engineer."

Two hundred and seventy-five jobs. Two hundred and seventy-four, plus his. Somehow, Stuart managed to unlock his jaw. "All right. You'll get your safety check. But the first time I go down, I go down by myself."

"Are you sure that's wise?"

"There's eleven dead already. Lets try not to go over an even dozen." He ground his heel into the thick carpet as he turned but the hinging mechanism on the office door defeated his best effort to slam it hard enough to bring the ceiling down on Brekenfield's head.

"You were alone. Technically speaking, you're still the only living man in this mine."

"...and feel the wind beneath my wing!"

"Shut your gob, McIsaac. Isn't it enough you slaughter the tune without screwing up the words as well?"

Waiting for the rest of his shift to come up out of the new crosspiece, Robert McIsaac leaned back against the mantrip and crossed his arms. "You know what your problem is, Harry? You don't appreciate music."

"How the hell would you know?" Harry asked mildly, folding his six foot four inches onto the seat beside Stuart. "You wouldn't know music if it bit you on the ass."

Stuart's sudden struggle to breath had nothing to do with broken ribs. "You're...dead."

"You're right." Harry's chuckle was as unmistakable as McIsaac's singing.

He couldn't stop the scream. The callused hand gripping his chin was not the hand of a living man. "Please..." Terror dropped his voice to a suppliant whisper, "...let me go."

Lifeless fingers gently shook his head back and forth. "Well now, that's the question isn't it? See, me and the boys, when we heard you come down, we decided that we needed to have a little talk, you and us." The hand fell away and a sudden clattering rattled around in the darkness. "Is that your teeth Stuart?"

Stuart clenched his jaw so tightly his temple throbbed and a warm line of blood dribbled into his ear.

"Have we frightened you, Mr. Safety Engineer?" McIsaac's voice was closer than it had been. "That's good. 'Cause you killed us."

"There should never have been a mine here." The new voice belonged to Eugene Short. Stuart didn't know much about him except that his death had left two little girls without a daddy. "The whole damned area's too unstable, the seam itself has too many fault lines, and there's too damned much gas. We all knew it. But the company said the technology could handle it and we believed the company."

"Silly us," said Harry. "We worked up quite a hate list once we realized what had happened. It went right up to the right honorable asshole who approved the government loans that got this mine working; but it started with you."

"You were supposed to be looking out for our safety, Stu." Eugene's wife had begged the rescue crews to go back down just one time. One more time. Once more. "You did a piss poor job."

"I did my job the best I could!" The words jerked out before Stuart could stop them. "The company never listened to me!"

"Uhhhh. Uhhhh. Uh." The sound was pure inarticulate rage.

"That's Phil Lighthouse. You remember Phil don't you? Rock landed on Phil's face, smashed it all to hell and gone. Phil doesn't talk much now." Clothing rustled as Harry settled back. "Most of us are in better shape although I had to splint a knee to keep it from bending both ways and Bobby's ribs kinda grind together when he moves."

They were dead. They'd been dead for eight months. "H, h, how?"

"Well, we've thought about that too. You remember that explosion at Albion? About eight years ago? It was eleven days before they got the last three bodies out and all that time, even though logic said the men had to be dead, people kept believing in the possibility of a miracle. You see, Stuart, when something like this happens and there's no body to prove that death's won, a lot of folk'll keep believing their men are alive and waiting for help. I figure that me and McIsaac and Phil and Eugene here, well, we had folks topside believing in us long enough that we just kinda were forced to hang around."

Stuart wet lips gone dry in spite of the damp. "We didn't...find Al Harris or Peter...Talbot."

"Proves my point." He could feel the darkness thicken as Harry leaned towards him. "Harris has no family around here and Talbot's old lady would believe the worst if you told her she'd won a lottery."

"She's sure gonna look hot in black though," McIsaac observed with a sigh. There was an answering murmur of agreement from the other three men.

Stuart, who had a sudden vision of the widow at the funeral service, where she seemed barely confined by her clothing, wondered how the hell he could think of a thing like that at a time like this.

"Anyway," Harry continued, "we spent the first few months bitchin' and bellyachin' about being stuck haunting this shit hole and then we thought, hey, we're miners, we've got plenty of time, why not dig our way out. Eugene remembered where someone had left a couple of picks—technology often responds to a good kick in the ass—and we headed for the surface."

"It's been eight months. You should've…"

"Decomposed?"

With the condition of his ribs, puking would probably kill him. Stuart swallowed bile and tried not to think of rotting faces appearing out of the darkness.

"Haven't. Aren't. But…" Harry's hand clamped around his arm. Even through his jacket, a sweater, and a flannel shirt, Stuart could feel the cold. "…we can't leave either. We broke out at the bottom of ventilation shaft three and couldn't go any further. That pissed us off some, you bet. Then Eugene had his brilliant idea. Tell him, Eugene."

"I wanted to see how my daughters were doing so I figured even if we couldn't leave the mine, there wasn't anything stopping us from taking the mine with us."

Eugene lived in Ridgeway, in one of the seven houses clustered up tight to the Imap fence. It was plausible they could get that far but…"How could you find them?"

"I'm their father," Eugene said as though it should be obvious. "They're a part of me."

"Had to stop the stupid son-of-a-bitch from breaking right through into the recroom," muttered McIsaac.

"Who're you calling a stupid son-of-a-bitch! That room's underground. It would've counted as part of the mine!"

"And I'm sure the girls would've loved a visit from their dead daddy."

"Asshole!"

"Butthead!"

"Can you imagine an eternity of that crap?" Harry gave Stuart's arm a little squeeze. "Anyway, it seems we can find our families and dig our way close enough to hear what's going on in their lives but we can't find the bastards who put us down here. Which was why we were so glad to hear you were coming for a visit."

"It was an accident!" The beginnings of hysteria ripped a ragged edge off the protest.

"An accident waiting to happen," McIsaac snarled.

Somewhere in the dark, Phil Lighthouse grunted an emphatic agreement.

"I wasn't my fault!" He could hear his own terror bouncing back at him off the rock. "I did everything I could!"

"Stuart. Stuart. Stuart." With each repetition of his name, Harry gave his arm a shake sending hot needles of pain into his right side. "You were the safety engineer. If you'd done everything you could, we'd still be alive. We're not, so you didn't. So now, you're going to die too. Maybe you'll join us. Maybe you won't. Frankly, we don't give a flying fuck, as long as you die."

"Someone has to pay," McIsaac growled. "And you're the only someone we've got."

He was going to die. He could almost deal with that. But they'd never find his body, and maybe, just maybe Kathy and the kids wouldn't be able to let go. Maybe they'd believe he was still alive, waiting for help and maybe they'd believe long enough and hard enough that he'd be trapped forever in the darkness with four men who hated him. Maybe they'd trap him for eternity in his own personal hell. "Noooo…"

"'Fraid so, bud."

Then he had an idea. It fought its way up through the fear and he spat it out before he could change his mind. "I could bring you the others."

For a long moment, he could hear nothing beyond his own tortured breathing then Harry muttered, "Go on."

"You said I was at the bottom of the list. There's got to be guys you want more than me. But you can only find your families so you can't get to those guys. I could bring them to the mine."

"You'd throw another seven…"

Phil Lighthouse grunted.

"Sorry, Phil, I forgot. You'd throw another *eight* guys to our vengeance in order to save your own miserable life?"

No. He couldn't. He wouldn't. But he heard himself say, "Yes."

"Tempting. But how do we know you'll keep your end of the deal?"

"I'll swear."

"On what? We've got a distinct shortage of bibles down here, Stuart."

"On, uh, on..." On what? He rocked his head, back and forth, trying to think and another warm trickle ran into his ear. "On blood."

"Blood, eh?" Harry sat back, releasing his arm. "What do you think, boys?"

"There's power in blood," Eugene admitted. "It took us to my girls."

"There are guys I'd rather have down here than him," McIsaac pointed out. "As murdering assholes go, Stu here's small change."

"Uhhhh. Uh."

"Sorry Phil, you're out-voted. Three to one we let our boy buy his way out. Okay Stuart, put your thinking cap on 'cause you've got eight names to remember."

The pain kept distracting him.

"One more time, Stuart. You're not leaving until you get it right."

He had to get out. Nothing else mattered.

"About fucking time," McIsaac grumbled when he finally got all eight right.

The unmistakable sound of a knife blade snapping open almost stopped Stuart's heart. "This is definitely going to hurt you more than it hurts us," Harry told him cheerfully.

The pain of the knife slicing his palm was only a smaller pain buried in the greater. He bit his lip and endured. Anything to get out. Anything. Then dead flesh pressed against the cut, not once but four times. By the end, he couldn't stop gibbering as his whole body shook, protesting the contact.

"Okay boys, lets get him to where they can find him before he dies on us anyway."

"He's pissed himself, Harry."

"What do you care? You're dead."

When they picked him up, merciful darkness claimed him.

* * *

"Stuart? Stuart, honey? Can you hear me?"

He felt a warm hand gripping his and his fingers tightened around it. "Kathy?"

"Yeah, baby, it's me. Everything's going be all right."

"Kathy, they're dead." He forced his eyes open in time to catch her exchanging a worried glance with the white-coated doctor standing at the foot of his bed. "Kath?"

Her smile held comfort and concern in spite of the exhaustion that painted grey shadows on her face. "Everything's going to be all right," she repeated, but there was more hope than certainty in her voice.

"What's wrong?"

The doctor stepped forward. "You broke a rib, Mr. Bell," she said. "Cracked the two on either side and got a nasty bump on the head."

"No." His throat felt as if he'd been swallowing chunks of coal. "There's something else." Dragging his free hand up onto his chest, he stared at the bandage wrapped around his palm. "Something else."

Something dead.

"Stuart! Stuart stop it! You're out! You're safe!"

His wife's fear reached him in the darkness and he stopped trying to dig his way back through the hospital bed. Slowly, his vision cleared and his heartbeat calmed. "They're down there, Kath. Harry Frazer, Robert McIsaac, Eugene Short, Phil Lighthouse. Down in the mine. Trapped. Dead. Not dead." Another eight names echoed in the confines of his head. He tried to tell her about the promise he made, but he couldn't get the words past the shame.

He saw her swallow. It looked as though she was searching for words of comfort she couldn't find. "You're not surprised," he said slowly.

"You've been repeating their names since they brought you up." Tears spilled over the curve of her cheeks and her nose started to run. "And when they tried to work on your hand you screamed it wasn't your fault. They had to sedate you to put the stitches in."

The doctor perched on the edge of an orange vinyl chair and scooted it up close to the bed. "Mr. Bell, are you familiar with the phrase, survivor guilt?"

He stared at her suspiciously. "Doesn't it have something to do with the holocaust?"

"It is a condition that has been linked with holocaust survivors, yes, but it can occur any time some people die and some people don't."

"Like in the mine?"

"Exactly."

"And you think that's what I've got? Survivor guilt?"

She smiled professionally at him. "It would help explain why you seem to be haunted by those four men."

Haunted. Four dead men, trapped by the hope of their families. Under the harsh hospital fluorescent lights it seemed like a crazy idea. The kind of an idea a guilty mind could come up with while lying in the dark. But he could still feel Harry's cold fingers grasping his jaw and with the memory of the dead man's touch, he could smell his own fear. "What about the cut on my hand?"

"What about it, Mr. Bell?"

"I didn't cut it on a rock, did I?"

"No. You didn't." The doctor exchanged her smile for a slight frown, equally meaningless. "You cut your hand on a sharp piece of metal. I'm sure there's plenty of that down where you were."

There was. The explosion had twisted the roof supports out of place and blown shrapnel all over the tunnels. Stuart stared at the bandage. "Survivor guilt," he murmured at last. "They aren't trapped down in the mine. I made it up to punish myself for letting them down."

"That's right." The doctor stood. "We'll be setting up some counseling sessions for you while you're here with us but I think you'll be fine." She nodded at them both and strode purposefully from the room.

Still clutching his unbandaged hand, Kathy whispered, "Everything's going to be all right."

* * *

"Daddy's coming home today!"

"I know, stupid." Tod Bell shoved his little sister with a six year old's finely tuned instinct for just how much violence he could inflict on a sibling half his age.

Looking harassed, Kathy dragged them apart. "Stop it you two, or Daddy'll wish I'd left you at home."

"Daddy wants *me* here." Lindsey leaned up against her father's legs. "Doncha Daddy?"

"Of course, I want you here, Lindsey-lee." Stuart smiled down at his daughter then swept the smile over wife and son as well. "I want you all here." He was feeling pretty good. The physical injuries were healing and the hospital therapist assured him that the nightmares would stop in time. Zipping shut his overnight bag, he slung it over his shoulder and held out a hand to each child. "Come on, lets go home."

"No." Shaking her head, Lindsey backed away, wide eyes locked on the bandage wrapped around her father's palm.

"It's okay, sweetheart, you won't hurt me." He stretched just a little and gently caught her hand in his.

She screamed.

"The bandage is gone, the stitches are out, and she still won't let me touch her with my left hand." He worked his palm, working flexibility into the scar. "What am I supposed to do?"

"Give her time," the therapist advised. "Your daughter sees that injury as a symbol of how close she came to losing you. This kind of accident can be very traumatic for a child but once she believes you're not going to leave her, she'll be fine."

"You think?"

"I'm positive. How are the nightmares?"

Stuart shrugged. "I've pretty much stopped dreaming about being trapped in the mine."

"Good, good."

Now my head repeats eight names at me, over and over all night. I wake up shouting, go back to sleep, and it happens all over again. Kathy's spent the last two nights on the couch. But he couldn't tell the therapist that because he'd have to explain whose eight names they were and what he'd promised to do in order to get out of the mine alive. What difference that he'd made the promise to phantoms created out of guilt; he couldn't bear that anyone would know how low he'd been willing to crawl.

"Kath, have you seen Lindsey?"

"I think she's in the recroom watching TV." His wife's eyes were shadowed. Obviously she hadn't been sleeping well either. "Why?"

"The therapist suggested I spend some quiet time with her." He started down the basement stairs. "God, I hope it's not time for Barney."

The television was off and the room was empty.

"Lindsey?"

Sometimes she liked to play under the laundry tubs in a space too small for her brother to invade.

"Lindsey?"

Down on one knee, he scooped up a plastic pony and wondered where she could've got to.

Then he heard the unmistakable sound of a pick striking stone.

"Stuart? Stuart, what is it?" Kathy ran into the laundry room, hands covered in dish soap.

He stared at her, back pressed up against the far wall. He couldn't remember moving.

"Stuart?" She took a cautious step towards him. "You shrieked..."

He couldn't remember shrieking but when he swallowed it felt as though the inside of his throat had been flayed. "Can't you hear it?" The sound of the pick was a distant tick, tick. Like a clock. Like a clock he'd set in motion and time was running out.

"Hear what?"

If he told her what, he'd have to tell her why. "Nothing. It's nothing." Grabbing her arm, he dragged her towards the stairs. "Don't you have things to finish in the kitchen?" The kitchen could, in no way, be considered part of the mine.

"Stuart!"

She struggled, but he got her up the stairs and slammed the basement door. He could hear Lindsey out playing in the yard and Tod was still at school. Everyone was safe. "I don't want anyone going downstairs."

"Are you out of your mind?"

He'd frightened her and, as he watched, the fear turned to anger.

"What is going on, Stuart?"

If he told her, she'd despise him and that wouldn't stop the dead. He couldn't explain so there was only one thing he could do.

"Thank you for meeting me out here, Mr. Brekenfield."

"The company appreciates your discretion, Stuart." Alex Brekenfield flashed him a we're-all-in-this-together smile. "The last thing Imap Mines needs right now is bad publicity."

"So no one knows you're here?" Stuart's head jerked from side to side as he scanned the area around the headframe. "'Cause I'd hate for the press to get wind of this."

"No one knows. What did you want to tell me?"

"I think you'll understand the problem better if I show you." He took hold of the other man's elbow, the scar on his palm throbbing against the tweed jacket. "It's over by number three ventilation shaft."

"Wasn't that near where they dug you out?"

"Yes."

"So how're you feeling, Stuart?"

"Fine."

"I uh, meant to visit you in the hospital, but you know how things come up. As I'm sure you've heard, we're still intending to reopen the mine. I've got an incredible workload right now."

"It's okay."

"Isn't this a long way around to number three?"

"A little, but this way the ground's solid." He twisted enough to see they were leaving no tracks.

Brekenfield misunderstood. "Good thinking. I'd hate to have an accident out here."

The housing had been taken off the shaft when the rescue crew had pulled Stuart out. It had never been replaced. Dropping to one knee, Stuart pointed down into the darkness. "There."

Grunting, Brekenfield knelt beside him. "I don't see anything."

"Wait a minute. Your vision has to adjust to the lack of light."

"I still don't see anything."

Stuart closed his eyes. He could hear the picks approaching. "You will." The scar felt hot and cold and, pressed against Brekenfield's back, it pulsed in time to Brekenfield's heart. One-two. One-two. One.

He forced himself to listen to the impact. It was softer than he thought it would be. And wetter.

After a moment, the sound of the picks stopped and the screaming started. Stuart scrambled to his feet and ran for the fence. Retching. Crying. Afraid of what he'd hear if he stayed.

Afraid they might thank him.

"Lindsey! How many times have I told you not to play under there!" He grabbed her arm, his hand wrapped all the way around the soft child flesh, and dragged her out from under the laundry tubs.

She stared at him for a moment, too frightened to react, then the moment passed and she started to sob.

"Oh sweetheart." Stuart dropped to his knees on the concrete floor and gathered the terrified three year old into his arms. "I'm sorry, sweetheart. I didn't mean to scare you. Daddy's just...

"Daddy's just..."

He could hear the picks. He could hear McIsaac singing. Still holding his daughter, he twisted and stared under the tubs. The naked bulb that hung from the laundry room ceiling painted the shadow of a tiny crack.

"NO!" Stuart dove, rolled, and clawed his way over the crumbling floor to the basement stairs, Lindsey's arms clutched desperately around his neck. Darkness yawned suddenly under the bottom step but he raced it to the kitchen finding strength in the precious life he had to save. Three steps from the door, the stairs dropped out from under his feet.

He threw Lindsey onto the linoleum and flung himself after her but too much of his body remained over the pit.

"NO!"

He began to fall back. Caught the doorframe and fought for life. Then Kathy was there. And Tod. They grabbed his arms and pulled, panic lending strength.

His torso was in the kitchen. His legs; his legs were in the mine.

Then his knees cleared the threshold. He kicked up, caught the edge of the door with one foot, and slammed it shut.

It was surprisingly quiet in the kitchen.

Breathing heavily, Kathy sank down onto the floor beside him. "Jesus God, Stuart. What happened?"

They'd had him memorize eight names. There were seven still to go.

"We're moving," he said.

Stuart got a job in Halifax, working for the provincial Industry Minister. Her predecessor was one of the seven but as she'd only just taken over the portfolio her name wasn't on the list. They lived in a flat on the second floor of an old frame house in what was once the monied section of the city. Tod settled into a new school and Lindsey adopted the elderly couple who lived on the first floor as surrogate grandparents. Kathy was sharing his bed again.

The worst thing that happened over the winter was Lindsey's inexplicable delight in Don Cherry's Coach's Corner. Fortunately, it faded with the end of the hockey season.

He wasn't sure what woke him. Bare feet whispering against the carpet, he padded first into Lindsey's room and then Tod's. Both kids were sound asleep.

Frowning, he slid back under the sheet. Then he grinned. Faintly, through the hot air duct beside the bed, he could hear old Mr. Verge bellowing out a Rita MacNeil tune.

Probably serenading the missus before a bit of the old in and out. Still smiling he settled back against the pillow and closed his eyes.

And opened his eyes.

It wasn't old Mr. Verge's voice coming up through the furnace ducts.

The furnace was in the basement.

When they moved to Toronto, they stayed for a few months with Kathy's brother and his family in Don Mills before renting a ninth floor apartment at York Mills and Leslie. Kathy found a part-time job at a day care center and Stuart tried to line up consulting contracts. Unfortunately, there weren't a lot of jobs for mining engineers in this part of the country. Tod hated his new school and Lindsey started wetting the bed.

It took just over a year for things to improve but Kathy finally found a full time job with great pay and better benefits. Stuart threw himself into being a full-time house husband. Tod started little league. Lindsey got her first permanent tooth.

He was down in the building's laundry room, folding the laundry, when he heard the picks.

He moved to Thunder Bay by himself. He would've gone further but the car died just outside the old Port Arthur city limits and he couldn't afford to either fix or replace it.

He got a job with a maintenance firm and lost it because he wouldn't go into basements.

He got a job with the parks department and lost it when he ran screaming from a co-worker who'd intended to take a pick to a hardhead on a park road.

It took them three years to find him.

He went over the seven names and returned to Nova Scotia, stood on the sidewalk outside a pretty white frame house as the sun was setting, watched the ex-Industry Minister pull the living room curtains, and couldn't do it.

He bought the rope with the last of his money, tied one end of it very carefully to a safety railing on the Angus L. Macdonald bridge and put a slip knot in the other. The Halifax/Dartmouth authorities made it as difficult as they could for jumpers but short of closing the bridge between the cities to pedestrian traffic they couldn't do quite enough.

Someone yelled as he jumped. A car horn honked. Tires squealed. He could see the harbor ferry down below. As the knot jerked tight, he smiled. Just let them try to find him here.

Someone was singing a Rita McNeil song. Badly. Stuart groaned and opened his eyes. It took a moment's concentration but he managed to focus on the people standing around him although there wasn't much light and he couldn't seem to straighten his head.

"Where's Brekenfield?" he asked, when the singing stopped and the mine was quiet.

Eugene shrugged. "I guess no one believed in him."

"No one believes in me…"

"That's where you're wrong, Stuart." Harry smiled and patted his cheek so that his head flopped onto his other shoulder. "*We* believe in you. Welcome to Hell."

The challenge with this story was to accept all the mythic information as fact and then present it updated for the nineties. They really were a highly dysfunctional family…

FEBRUARY THAW

Scuffing across the rec room floor in a pair of well-worn fuzzy slippers, Demeter, Goddess of the Harvest, pulled open the door to her small wine cellar, took a bottle of wine from the rack and held it up to the light. A Tignanello, 1990; lovely vintage. Most of the family didn't think much of Dionysus but she rather liked him. Not only did he do very nice things with the grapes she provided but, in his other guise as God of Theatrical Arts, he saw to it that she got complimentary tickets to all the big shows.

She'd seen *Cats* half a dozen times before the novelty wore off.

Tucking the bottle under her arm, she scuffed back to her chair and settled into the overstuffed cushions with a satisfied sigh. One thumb popped the cork—there were perks to being an immortal goddess after all—and she settled back with a glass of wine in one hand and the television remote in the other.

Demeter loved winter. Not so much because she had nothing to do after the rush of planting, tending and harvesting, but because her house was her own again. She could eat what she wanted, she could drink what she wanted, she could wear what she wanted, and, most importantly she could watch what she wanted. During the winter, she wore stretchy fabrics and watched absolutely nothing with socially redeeming value.

"I admit it," she announced to the fat, disinterested tabby sprawled in the middle of a braided rug. "I was an overprotective mother. Well, what do you expect? I was a single, working mom. He was never around. Still…" She took a long, contented swallow of the wine and turned on the first of the afternoon's talk shows. "...if I had it to do over, I'd give them a nice set of salad bowls and my blessing."

"Mom?"

Having just taken another drink, Demeter choked.

"Mom? Where are you?" Fashionably high heels brushing against the worn carpeting on the stairs, Persephone descended into the rec room to find her mother dabbing at the stains on her turquoise track suit with one hand and trying to fish a tissue out of the box with the other. "Mother! Honestly!" She shoved a tissue into Demeter's searching fingers. "It's the middle of the afternoon!"

Wiping at the wine dribbling out her nose, the goddess glared up at her only daughter. "What," she demanded, "are you doing here? There's two more months until spring."

"Two more months?" Persephone repeated, volume rising with every word. "Two more months? I couldn't stay with that man two more minutes!"

While she had every intention of being supportive, Demeter couldn't help looking a little wistfully toward the muted TV as she asked, "What did he do?"

"What didn't he do?" Throwing herself down on the sofa, Persephone ran a slender hand through corn-silk blonde hair. "He leaves his socks and underwear on the floor, he never gets any exercise..."

Just why the Lord of the Underworld, who was not only slender bordering on downright skinny but also an immortal god, needed to exercise, Demeter had no idea.

"...he spends all his time playing poker with Minos, Rhadamanthys, and Aeacus, and he lets that stupid dog up on the furniture."

"Sephie, these don't sound like reasons for you to leave a god you've been married to for millennia. In fact, they sound an awful lot like the things you complain about every spring." She leaned forward and patted her daughter's knee with one plump hand, trying to sound more sympathetic than she felt. "What's the real reason you're here when you shouldn't be?"

In the silence between question and answer, the cat wisely got up and left the room.

"We had a fight."

"What about?"

"Pomegranates."

"What, again?"

"This was a different fight." Her face crumpled. "Hades doesn't love me anymore!"

Picking up the box of tissues, Demeter moved to the sofa beside Persephone. "Of course, he loves you, sweetie."

"No, he used to but now he doesn't." She blew her nose vigorously. "And I'm never going back to him."

"Never?" Demeter repeated. She reached for her wine.

Outside the cozy, country cottage, the snow—currently, the goddess' preferred symbolism of her time off—began to melt.

"Is that what you're having for breakfast?"

Demeter sighed and paused, fork halfway to her mouth. "What's wrong with my breakfast?"

"Eggs, sausages, and homefries? Not to mention toast and beans? Mom, you've got enough bad fats in front of you to kill you, and trust me, I *know* what can kill you." Before Demeter could secure it, she whisked the plate away. "I'll make you some whole grain porridge, just like I do in the summer. No saturated fats, plenty of fruits and vegetables; we'll get that extra weight off you in no time."

"Sephie, I'm the goddess of the harvest, I'm supposed to be ample. And trust me, you can't get ample on fruits and vegetables."

Persephone shot her a glittering smile. "Isn't that a bit of a contradiction?"

"Trust me, dear, I've learned to live with it."

A sheet of snow slid off the steeply raked roof and landed on the burlap wrapped foundation plantings, crushing them under the wet weight.

Demeter stared into her whole-wheat pita stuffed with alfalfa sprouts, hummus and god knew what else because the goddess certainly didn't. "I wonder what Hades is eating right now."

"I don't care."

"Probably something greasy and bad for him."

"I know what you're trying to do, Mom, and I appreciate it, but my marriage can not be saved." Persephone bit the top three inches off a raw carrot with more enthusiasm than was strictly necessary. "After we eat, I've got a new low-impact aerobic workout that I want you to try."

"Sephie, I usually rest in the winter."

"If you mean you usually spend the winter in front of the television, well, that's not resting."

"It's not?"

"It's vegetating. And you won't have to do it this winter because I'm here. Think of it, we'll have such fun. Just like we do in the summer."

"Oh, I'm thinking of it sweetie…"

Out in the garden, a confused iris stuck its head above ground.

"I'm going for a walk, Mom. Do you want to come?"

"No, dear. I thought I'd…" Demeter racked her brain for something that her daughter couldn't object to. "…chop up some vegetables for a salad."

Persephone sniffed disapprovingly. "How can you stand being stuck inside on such a beautiful day? You're not like this in the summer."

"It's not summer, Sephie."

"Hades and I walk all over the Underworld in the winter: through the Asphodel Fields, along the Styx, and back home to Erebus by way of the Lethe. We walk…" The second sniff was much moister. "…and we talk and then, later, we curl up in front of the fire."

Encouraged by the longing in Persephone's voice, Demeter dared to suggest that her husband probably missed her very much.

"Good."

"Maybe you should just talk to him."

"No."

"But…"

"You don't understand, Mother."

Demeter smiled tightly. "That's because you haven't told me anything, dear. If I knew what the fight was about, maybe I could help."

"It's between Hades and me, Mother." Throwing an elegant sweater over slender shoulders, Persephone opened the back door. "I'm going for my walk now."

"Put on a coat, Sephie."

"I don't need one."

Glancing over at the calendar, Demeter sighed.

A few days later, standing in the kitchen making a cup of tea while Persephone went through her winter wardrobe and got rid of everything comfortable—as Queen of the Underworld, she favored haut couture—Demeter stared out the window at the bare lawn and wondered what she should try next. Nothing she'd said so far had made any difference; although she cried herself to sleep every night, Persephone was not going back to her husband and that was that.

"There's a robin on your lawn."

Sighing deeply, the goddess dumped an extra spoonful of sugar in her cup and turned to face the man sitting at her kitchen table. "I figured it would only be a matter of time before you showed up."

Zeus squared massive shoulders and laid both hands flat on the tabletop. "Spring seems to be early this year."

"No shit. What was your first clue?" The head of the pantheon was still an impressive looking god and certainly well suited to populating Olympus but, in Demeter's opinion, he'd never been that bright.

"In fact, spring appears to have arrived two months early."

And he had a way of making pompous pronouncements that really ticked her off. "Persephone's had a fight with her husband and come home."

"I can not allow the seasons to messed up in this manner." Folding his arms, Zeus leaned back in the chair, grey eyes stormy. "Send her back."

"It's not that easy…"

"Why not?" he demanded. "You're her mother."

Demeter smiled and stood. "You're her father. You send her back." Pitching her voice to carry to the second floor, she headed for the rec room, ignoring Zeus' panicked protests. "Persephone! Your father wants to talk to you!"

She kept the volume on the television turned low so she could listen to the ebb and flow of the argument. It seemed to be mostly ebb. A very short time later, quick, angry footsteps headed upstairs and slow, defeated ones headed down.

"Well?" she asked.

"She said, no." Zeus dropped onto the recliner and dug both hands into the luxuriant curls of his beard.

"She said, no?" Demeter repeated with heavy sarcasm. "The Father of Heaven unsuccessful with a woman?"

"She cried, Demi. What could I do?"

"Did you ask her what was wrong?"

He looked indignant. "You told me they had a fight."

Demeter sighed. "Did you ask her what the fight was about?"

"What difference does that make?" His full lips moved into what was perilously close to a pout. "She has to go back and I told her so."

In spite of his many opportunities for practice, Zeus had never been, by any stretch of the imagination, a good father. More of a realist than most of the pantheon, Demeter recognized that they were all in part responsible for that. He'd been the youngest in a wildly dysfunctional family and they'd all indulged him. She'd been just as bad as the rest of their siblings but she'd long ago stopped indulging him where their daughter was concerned. "Well," she said dryly, "that was stupid, wasn't it?"

All things considered, he took it rather well. Thunder rumbled in the distance but nothing in the immediate area got destroyed.

"Demi, it can't be spring yet. When it's this early, it screws everything up."

"Zeus." She leaned forward. She would've patted his leg except that he took physical contact as an invitation and this was not the time for fertility rites. "I know."

"What are we going to do now?" he sighed.

Demeter grabbed her favorite lamp as it blew by on the gust of his exhalation and placed it on the floor by her chair. "We?"

Heaving himself up onto his feet, the ruler of Olympus had grace enough to look sheepish. "Deal with it, would you, Demi?"

She sighed in turn. "Don't I always?"

Having sluffed off responsibility once again, Zeus grew more cheerful and his step was light as he headed for the stairs. "You should visit Olympus more often. We miss you."

"No, you don't. Whenever I'm there, Hera and I fight then you go off and do one of those swan, shower of gold, quail things and we all know how *that* ends up—Hera blames me since she can't seem to blame you, I get ticked off and crops fail over half of the southern hemisphere. Better I just stay here."

He threw her a brilliant smile. "I miss you."

"No, you don't." In spite of everything, she couldn't help adding, "But it's sweet of you to say so."

At the bottom of the stairs, he paused and half turned back to face her as another thought occurred to him. "Oh by the way, what's Iaachus up to these days?"

"How should I know, I'm only his mother." And her son was a great deal like his father. "If you see him, tell him to call."

"Sephie, what are you doing?"

Persephone rubbed at a smudge of dirt on one peaches and cream cheek and looked up at her mother, her other hand continuing to vehemently, almost violently, poke seeds into the ground. "Planting radishes."

"Now?"

"We've got the year off to an early start." She frowned, suddenly noticing the jacket and boots. "Where are you going?"

"Eleuis," lied the goddess. "For the Mysteries."

"Now?"

"You've got the year off to an early start," Demeter reminded her. "We've had to make a few changes because of it." The Eleusinian Mysteries had always been a convenient way to ditch a grown, and often disapproving, daughter for more, as it were, fruitful company. Being Mysteries, they never had to be explained. Patting Persephone fondly on one shoulder, she continued down the garden path. "I won't be long."

"Evenin' yer Ladyship." Boat at the dock, Charon rested on his oar as Demeter approached. "Haven't seen you in these parts since the wedding."

"I try not to interfere in the lives of my children." She glanced down at a full load of the dead. "Do you have room for one more?"

"Well now, I'd have to say that depends."

Demeter sighed and rummaged through a change purse full of breath mints, jiffy pots, and wildflower seeds, finally pulling out a coin. The ferryman reached for it but she held it back. "When we reach the other side."

"Good enough, yer Ladyship." Reaching down, he grabbed his nearest passenger by the head and tossed him overboard. "Fool already paid me," he explained as he held out a hand to help the goddess over the gunnel.

It was a quiet trip across the Styx. Charon didn't encourage chatter and Demeter had a lot on her mind. Not far from the landing, she frowned, suddenly unable to ignore the tormented screaming any longer. "Is it just me or are the cries from Tartarus louder than they should be."

"They're louder," Charon agreed. "He's been depressed since she left. Makes him cranky."

The newly dead, sitting shoulder to shoulder on a triple row of uncomfortable benches, shuddered as a group.

Stepping out onto more or less dry land—it squelched underfoot a great deal less since she'd recommended they have it tile drained—Demeter braced herself.

"Down, Cerberus! Down! Good dog." She scratched the center head behind the ears as the other two stretched around her body and snarled at the disembarking spirits. When one or two hung back, Charon smacked them with his oar. "Oh for pity's sake," she snapped. "He won't bother you if you're supposed to be here. Who's a good boy? Who's Demeter's favorite puppy?"

Tail whipping from side to side, the tapered back end of his body moving back and forth in time, Cerberus drooled happily on the goddess' feet.

Glad she'd worn her wellies, and beginning to realize why Persephone didn't want the dog up on the couch, or on anything else that couldn't be hosed down immediately afterward, Demeter gave all three heads a final scratch and started toward the Asphodel Fields. Winter or not, she didn't intend staying in the Underworld for too long. Cerberus bounded along beside her for half a dozen steps then the wind shifted and he took off downstream, howling, snarling, and barking furiously.

Pulling her jacket more closely around her, she hurried along the path toward Erebus trying to ignore the grey and boring landscape and the incessant twittering of the undistinguished dead. Although a few of those who'd known her in life waved a limp hand in greeting, most ignored her.

Most.

"Greetings rich-haired Demeter, awful goddess, lady of the golden sword and glorious fruits."

"Hello, Orion." The ghost standing on the path before her, the son of Poseidon and the gorgon Euryale, had been the handsomest man alive until he'd taken up with Artemis and run afoul of an over-protective Apollo. As she'd often thought it unfair the way the Olympian powers fell, Demeter smiled kindly on her nephew. "Still hunting the shadow deer?" She nodded toward his bow.

"The hunt is all I have." He paused and then continued ponderously, "The Queen is gone early from Erebus."

"Yes, she is, isn't she."

"She has returned to your hearth?"

"Oh, yes." *My cold hearth*, the goddess added silently. *And I still don't believe gas fireplaces give off unhealthy fumes.*

Orion nodded. "Good. I am glad she is safe. Do you now descend to see the Lord Hades, your brother?"

"Not exactly," Demeter told him tightly. "I descend to see the Lord Hades, my son-in-law."

The hero's eyes widened and his adam's apple bobbed in the muscular column of his throat. "Oh," he said, and stepped off the path. "Look, uh, don't let me get in your way, Aunt Demi." He faded back toward the trees. "And, uh, if there's anything I can do, don't hesitate to call."

Picking up her pace again, Demeter rolled her eyes. *Honestly; men,* she thought. *Even dead ones. And Hera wonders why I never married.*

There were gardens down the middle of the wide avenue that lead to the palace. In spite of the inarguable presence of the pomegranates, Demeter hadn't expected that. If they'd been in place during the wedding, she hadn't noticed them but then as mother of the bride, not to mention sister of the groom, she'd had other things on her mind.

All the flowers were black—except for one corpse-lavender rose she was fairly certain she'd seen in the upper world—and the beds had been edged in giant uncut diamonds. She could see her daughter's taste in the design. Persephone had always loved order. A closer look and she realized that the flowers desperately needed dead-heading and everything wanted water. Sighing deeply, Demeter reached under the lip of a black marble fountain and turned on the irrigation system.

"This is her garden," said a gardener, who'd been standing so quietly she hadn't noticed him. "His Majesty said we weren't to foul it with our touch."

"Hades said that?"

"Yes ma'am."

Demeter smiled. This might be easier than she'd thought.

The palace was a mess.

Demeter had no idea how it could have gotten so bad in only eight days. Then she remembered how it had gotten at her house in those same eight days and tried to be less critical. It wasn't easy.

The servants, drawn from the ranks of the dead, huddled confused and insubstantial in corners. She could feel them watching her hopefully as she passed. Well, with any luck, their ordeal and hers would soon be over.

She found the King of the Dead in a small room he used for a den, slumped in chair mournfully eating peanut butter straight from the jar. His clothes were wrinkled, he didn't smell very good, and it looked like he hadn't shaved in about three days.

He looked up when Demeter came in, too far-gone in misery to be surprised. "Have you come for her things?"

"I've come for an explanation."

His gesture took in the drifts of potato chip bags in the immediate area as well as the chaos in the rest of the palace. "She's left me, Demi."

"I know that, you idiot. Where did you think she'd gone?"

"To you?"

"That's right. To me." She kicked a pizza box out of her way. "And do you know what happens up above when Persephone comes home to me?"

"The upper world is not my concern." If he'd intended to sound regal, he didn't quite make it past petulant.

"This time it is, because it's spring up there." Demeter's voice grew sharper as she put both fists on the back of the couch and leaned toward her son-in-law. "And it's not supposed to be spring for another two months! I want to know what happened and I want to know right now!"

A single tear rolled down along side Hades' aquiline nose. "She's left me, Demi."

Even the most gentle goddess had a line that shouldn't be crossed.

When the dust settled, He Who Has Many Names picked himself up off the floor and lowered himself gently back into his chair. "You blasted me," he said, shaking his head in disbelief, slightly singed black hair falling over his eyes. "In my realm. In my palace. In my den."

"That's right. And I'm going to do it again if I don't start getting some answers that make sense."

Scratching at the stubble on his chin, Hades sighed. "We had a fight," he said in a small voice.

"What about, and don't say pomegranates because I know that much."

"But it *was* about pomegranates, Demi. I had the tree cut down."

Demeter took a deep breath and counted to ten. "What tree?"

"The pomegranate tree." When she made it clear she needed more information and what the consequences would be if she didn't get it, he went on. "You remember back when I was courting Persephone..."

The goddess snorted.

A patch of color stained the son of Chronos' pale cheeks. "Yeah, well, do you remember how Zeus said she didn't have to stay with me if she hadn't eaten anything?"

"I remember."

Hades took a hint from her tapping fingers and began to speak faster. "Well, as it turned out she'd eaten those seven pomegranate seeds. Anyway, we worked all that out years ago and I thought we were happy but in the midst of a small disagreement about saturated fats, one of the servants put a bowl of pomegranates on the table. She said I was trying to run roughshod over her feelings just like before and I said I wasn't then, to prove it, I had the gardeners cut down the tree."

Demeter stared silently down at him. "The tree that bore the fruit that she'd eaten from to become your bride?" she asked when she finally found her voice.

"Well, yeah, but..."

"You putz! For her that tree was a symbol of your union and you got miffed and cut it down to prove a point."

"I didn't want her to be reminded of less happy times," Hades protested indignantly.

"Did you tell her that? Of course not," she went on before he had a chance to answer. "No wonder she thinks you don't love her anymore. That you regret marrying her."

"How can she think that?" He started to pace, kicking accumulated flotsam out of his way with every step. "Persephone is the only bright light in my world. While she's here with me, she rules over all. Without her, I dwell in darkness. I adore her. I always have and I always will." Face twisted in anguish, he turned toward the goddess. "You've got to talk to her, Demi. You've got to."

"Oh no," Demeter shook her finger at him. "I'm not the one who has to talk to her. You go up top right now and you tell all this to my daughter."

Hades stopped pacing so suddenly Demeter thought at first he'd walked through some spilled chip dip and glued his feet to the floor. "I can't."

"You what?"

"I can't go up top. It goes on too far." Glancing up at the ceiling, he looked beyond it to the arcing dome of rock that covered the Underworld. "There's no roof."

"Don't start making excuses, Host of Many, Brain of Pea," Demeter snarled. "You went up there to get her originally."

"That was a long time ago."

"So?"

"I've got agoraphobia."

"So stay out of the marketplace. Or don't you want her back?"

"I want her back more than anything!"

Not more than I want to get rid of her. "Then get off your skinny butt and do something about it. And speaking of getting off your butt, why is this place such a pigsty? You've got servants."

"Persephone always dealt with them. I don't know what to say."

"She's with me half the year." Which was quite long enough. "You can't possibly live like this for all that time."

"She always leaves lists." The King of the Dead bent down and pulled a piece of cold pizza out from under the sofa cushions. "Very precise lists."

Demeter sighed. She knew she was enabling his helplessness, but she couldn't have her daughter return to this mess. "Would you like me to take care of it?"

"Could you?"

The goddess put two fingers in her mouth and whistled. Almost instantly, as though they'd been waiting for a signal, a crowd of worried spirits wafted into the room. Demeter waved at the mess. "Compost this crap," she told them.

Hades frowned as the mess began to disappear. "I'm pretty sure that's not how Persephone does it."

Remembering that his argument with her daughter had started over saturated fats and fully aware of what side of the issue Persephone came down on, Demeter looked more kindly on him than she had. "You're probably right."

"Did you have a nice Mystery, Mother?"

Demeter stuck her heel in the bootjack and pulled off her boot. "I planted a seed, time will tell if anything comes of it."

"I hate it when you've been off talking to your priests," Persephone sniffed. "You get all obscure." She patted a pile of paper before her on the table. "While you were gone I worked up a plan to redecorate the kitchen."

"But I like my kitchen."

"Our kitchen. It's hopelessly old fashioned. The microwave still has dials."

"I only use it to reheat tea," the goddess protested.

"The kitchen in the palace has all the most modern equipment. Very high tech."

"Yes, well Hades is God of Wealth," Demeter muttered. "He can afford to get every new piece of junk that comes out."

Persephone ignored her. "And we'll have to get some servants." She smiled brittlely at her mother's aghast expression. "Mother, we're goddesses. Cook-outs and things are all very well in the summer…"

Demeter had long suspected Persephone regarded the seasons spent with her as an extended visit to Guide camp.

"…but it's not something we should have to live with year round."

"Sephie, when you're with me, it is summer year round."

"That's no reason why we shouldn't have servants. We can add on a wing out back." Rummaging through the pile, she held up a sheet of paper. "I drew a sketch. What the…?"

Both women stared at the paper, trembling like an aspen leaf in Persephone's hand.

Suddenly concerned, Demeter reached for her daughter. "You're shaking."

"No, I'm not." A mug fell off its peg and crashed into a thousand pieces against the floor. "The whole house is shaking."

"Earthquake?" Demeter pressed her lips together. "When I get my hands on the god who's doing this, he'll get a piece of my mind and boot in the backside!"

"Not now, Mother." Grabbing the goddess' shoulders, Persephone pushed her toward the door. "We've got to get outside. This whole place could come down any moment."

"If it does," the goddess promised, "I'm going to be very angry."

They'd got only as far as the porch when the lawn erupted. Four black horses, nostrils flared and eyes wild, charged up from the depths of the earth pulling behind them a golden chariot. In the chariot, stood Hades, ebony armor gleaming, the reins in one hand, a black rose in the other.

Demeter had to admit the rose was a nice touch.

His eyes beneath the edge of his helm almost as wild as those of his horses, Hades turned toward the cottage. "Persephone, this time I do not pull you from your mother's arms but implore you for the sake of love to come home with me."

"Very prettily said. Almost classical." Demeter poked her daughter in the hip. "Well?"

Persephone folded her arms. "You cut down my tree."

"And I have caused another seven to grow in its stead. One for each of the seeds you ate so that you can see how much my love has multiplied."

"I ate?" Persephone repeated, her voice rising dramatically. "You fed them to me."

"I only offered them to you," Hades protested. "You ate them."

Her chin rose. "I didn't know what it meant."

"And now you do." He opened the hand that held the rose and, like drops of blood against his pale skin, were seven pomegranate seeds.

Persephone gave a little cry Demeter wasn't quite able to interpret but her eyes were dewy and that seemed a good sign.

"Please come back to me, Sephie. The Underworld is empty without you. All my wealth is meaningless. I'll stop spending so much time with the guys. I'll cut out saturated fats. I..." The horses jerked forward. Muscles straining, Hades brought them back under control. "I love...Damn it, you four, stop it! I love you, Persephone.."

Could have been a more polished declaration, Demeter acknowledged, but not more sincere. "Well?" she said again, this time with a little more emphasis.

"But spring...?"

The goddess smiled, trying not to let the relief show. "Spring can wait two months."

With a glad cry, Persephone ran forward and leapt into both the chariot and Hades' arms. Finding no hand on the reins, both of the god's hands being otherwise occupied, the team did what horses always do under similar, if less mythic, circumstances. Hoofs striking sparks against the air, they bolted down toward their stable carrying their two oblivious passengers back to the Underworld with them.

The last Demeter saw of her daughter and her son-in-law, they were feeding each other the pomegranate seeds and murmuring things she was just as glad she couldn't hear.

"Happy endings all around," she muttered, and added as she went to work tucking the spring growth back into bed, "I have no idea how Aphrodite puts up with this kind of nonsense day in and day out."

With Persephone back in the loving arms of her husband, it didn't take long for Demeter to return the season to normal. She felt a little bad about the radishes.

When Dusk approached, the goddess wandered down to the rec room and poured herself a glass of wine. The house was blessedly quiet. Even the cat had returned from wherever he'd hidden himself.

Slippered feet up on a hassock, she picked up the remote. Maybe she'd heat up a frozen pizza for dinner.

The lawn was a disaster. In the spring, the actual spring, it would have to be rolled.

It seemed a small price to pay.

Outside the cottage, it began to snow.

When I agreed to do a story for *Tarot Fantastic*, I agreed because the editor, Lawrence Schimel is a friend—at the time, I had no idea of what I'd write. Searching for ideas, I threw myself into a few of the many, many books that have been written about the tarot. They all agreed that the tarot is not meant to be taken literally; we use it as a symbolic key to open the way to higher consciousness.

What, I began to wonder, would happen if that higher consciousness used the tarot as a symbolic key to open the way to us?

And I had my story.

SYMBOLS ARE A PERCUSSION INSTRUMENT

Her cel phone rang just as they were passing through the gates. As the imperious trill rose over the noise of the fair and people began turning to look, David Franklin put one hand over his eyes and sighed. "Cyn, why didn't you leave it in the car?"

"Are you nuts? Do you know how much this thing cost me?"

"Then why not leave it at home?"

"Because I feel naked without it."

"Naked might do you good."

"Don't start," she warned him as they made their way out of the stream of pedestrian traffic to the relative quiet by the chain-link fence. "This'll only take a minute."

David watched her flick the phone open and muttered, "Beam me up, Scotty," under his breath.

"Augustine Textiles, Cynthia Augustine speaking."

Turning to watch a group of shrieking children race toward the merry-go-round, David grinned as their mother—Babysitter? Teacher?—yelled that Stuart was to keep hold of his little brother.

The little brother in question was about four, wearing the remains of a candy apple, and swinging from the reins of a turquoise stallion. Stuart, his own Power Rangers t-shirt none too
clean, solved the problem by simply sitting on the smaller child
and ignoring all protests.

"Cute kids."

"Where?" Cynthia glanced toward the merry-go-round and
frowned. "I wonder who does those banners. We could prob…"
The phone rang again before she finished. "Augustine Textiles,
Cynthia Augustine speaking."

Not even remotely surprised that she'd seen the banners and
not the kids, David waited until she disconnected then held out
his hand.

"Aha." Triumphant, she passed the cel phone over. "You
complain until you suddenly need to make a call and…what are
you doing!?"

He stuffed the battery into one of the outside pockets on his
black leather knapsack and handed back the rest. "This is our
day off. And that means, we don't work."

Her eyes narrowed. "This is a recession. If the company
goes under, that means, you don't work."

"You have so little faith in your business that you can't leave
it for a few hours?"

"Faith has nothing to do with business." She looked down at
the useless plastic in her hand then up at the man who was not
only the company's entire design department but also her best
friend. "All right. For you. Two hours then you give me back
my battery."

David checked his watch. "Three and I'll drive home so you
can talk."

"Deal."

The fair mixed traditional agriculture and current trends. Ten
feet from the ring where yearling beef cattle stood placidly beside their young handlers, a sign proclaimed that for a small fee
attendees could have their picture and comments added to the
fair's web page.

Farmers in co-op baseball hats watched the circulating crowds of wide-eyed city tourists with amusement or disdain, depending on their natures. The tourists, in turn, considered the farmers part of the ambiance and, when they weren't taking pictures, ignored them.

"Ridiculous leash laws in this part of the country," Cynthia murmured as the cattle left the ring, each dragging a child dressed head to toe in white.

"I think it's wonderful these kids have a chance to be part of the whole farming experience."

"Oh yeah, great experience. Today a beloved pet wins a ribbon, tomorrow it's in the freezer, wrapped in brown paper and labeled hamburger."

David winced. "Do you have to?"

"I call 'em like I see 'em." She tucked her hand in his elbow and propelled him toward the open doors of the hockey arena. "Come on, this was your idea, let's go see the rest of it."

The arena had been equally divided between tables of produce brought in to be judged and commercial booths. With the fair only a two-hour drive from Toronto, most venders were pushing variations on the country chic theme.

Throwing himself into the experience, David examined every fruit, vegetable, and flower, comparing those that wore ribbons with those that didn't, asking questions of anyone who seemed like they might have an answer. By the time he reached *five tomatoes on a plate*, he'd charmed an honor guard of little old ladies.

Cynthia lost interest by *two ripe cucumbers over nine inches*, and followed blindly, wondering if she could get her phone back in time to call one of their eastern suppliers. Her wandering attention returned with a snap as David stopped in front of a commercial booth selling decorative door stops.

"David, put that down."

"Don't you like it?"

"No."

"I think it's cute."

"For chrissakes, David, it's a cow in a dress!"

He grinned impishly at her. "Drew wouldn't let me have it in the house but I could always use it at the office."

"Over my dead body."

Tucking it back in with the rest of the sartorial herd, he pulled her back outside. "Come on, let's try the midway."

A few moments later, Cynthia stared up at the double ferris wheel and then down at David. "I was kidding about that over my dead body thing."

"It's perfectly safe. Look, people are letting their kids ride."

"These people have kids to spare. I'm not getting on that death trap."

From the top of the ferris wheel, it was possible to see not only the entire fair ground but a good piece of the surrounding town as well.

"They've got a scrambler!" The basket rocked as David leaned forward and pointed. "It's been years since I've been on one!"

Cynthia tried to work out the tensile strength of the pair of steel pins that seemed to be all that were holding the basket to the ride. "I wonder how often they check for stress fractures," she muttered as they circled around again.

"Hey! There's a fortune teller!"

"David, if you don't stop rocking this thing, I'm going to do something violent."

"I think the sign says she's a card reader."

"Great, maybe we can find a fourth for bridge, now SIT STILL!"

Under normal circumstances, Cynthia wouldn't have gone within a hundred feet of a fortune teller but with a ride on the scrambler—something she clearly remembered as being nauseating and mildly painful—as the immediate alternative, having cards read—whatever that meant in the real world—became the lesser of two evils.

"So, what do you get when you cross a travel agent with an ophthalmologist?" she asked as they approached the tent. Pointing at the sign, she answered her own question. "Let Madame

Zora Help You See the World Through New Eyes. David, you know I don't deal well with this New Age crystal wearing crap."

"Then you're in luck because tarot cards aren't New Age. They're derived from the oldest book in the world; the Egyptian Book of Thoth by Hermes Trismegistus, councilor of Osiris, King of Egypt."

She turned to stare at him in amazement. "I don't *believe* you know all that stuff."

"I don't; it's in the small print on the sign but I consider myself open to extreme possibilities."

"I get it." Cynthia's voice rose in exaggerated outrage. "This is an X-File." She began to turn. "I'm out of here."

David blocked the path. "Oh no you're not. You agreed to have your cards read and, a promise is a promise."

"Don't," Cynthia snarled, "quote Disney at me."

The tent was army surplus. An unsuccessful attempt had been made to dress up the drab canvas by stringing lines of plastic pennants along the guy wires.

Her hands stuffed in the front pockets of her jeans, Cynthia glanced down at the crushed grass path leading under the flap then around at the fair. They stood in a pocket of quiet, the music from the midway seemed muffled and the crowds parted well in advance of the tent. "Now what? Do we wait to be seated?"

"You enter."

The speaker was non-apparent but the tent flap folded back as they watched.

"Here goes nothing," Cynthia murmured, adding to David's back as he hurried past her, "And I mean that literally by the way."

Inside, plastic yard lights pushed into the ground between the patterned carpets and the billowing walls created alternating bands of light and shadow. It would have been a more successful effect had the burning incense been able to overcome the musty smell of canvas stored too long in a damp basement.

A rectangular table with three high-backed chairs lined up behind it stood under the center peak of the tent. The figure in the middle chair had a familiar, if not cliched, silhouette.

"Come closer, seekers."

As they stepped forward, a pair of hanging lights came on over the table, banishing shadows and throwing Madame Zora into hard-edged relief.

David made a small noise of appreciation.

Hundred watt floods, Cynthia thought as the fortuneteller lifted a beringed hand and beckoned them closer still.

"Have you a question for Madame Zora?" Somewhere past forty, she looked exactly how a fortuneteller should look, from the shawls to the jewelry to the heavily kohled eyes.

David gave her his best smile. "Only those questions that every seeker has," he said, matching her dramatics.

Madame Zora responded to the smile and nodded toward the chair to her right. "Then come, sit."

"Wait a minute," Cynthia grabbed David's arm as he started to move away. "I have a question. Do you actually believe that pieces of cardboard can tell the future?"

Dark eyes lifted and met hers. "No. That's not what they're for. The value of the tarot is to make people think, to weigh the pros and cons of a situation." Her voice picked up a new cadence. "The true tarot is symbolism. It speaks no other language and presents no other signs. A. E. Waite."

Cynthia's lip curled. "What you see is what you get. Yacko Warner."

"Symbols are the picture forms of hidden thought, the door leading to the hidden chambers of the mind."

"Give me a break; what hidden chambers?"

"If you want…" Madame Zora indicated the chair on her left. "…I'll let the cards answer your question when I'm finished with your friend."

"I don't believe in fortune telling."

"You don't have to. Your belief or disbelief makes as little difference to the cards as it would to the weather."

"My friend doesn't believe either."

Grabbing her arm, David hauled her around the corner of the table. "Just sit," he hissed. "You're embarrassing me."

As he pushed her into her chair and went to take his own, Cynthia locked the rest of her opinions behind her teeth. The whole old-as-new-spirituality, Mother Goddess, tofu, wheat germ, candle burning sort of thing she saw as a last refuge for those who couldn't cut it in the real world, but if her apparent compliance in this charade made David happy, then she supposed it wouldn't hurt her to play a...

Which was when she became aware of the denomination of the bill changing hands. "Twenty bucks!?"

The money disappeared into a definitively real world cash box. "I have a sliding scale," Madame Zora explained, snapping the lid closed.

"Sliding from where? What makes you think he can afford twenty bucks to have his fortune told?"

"His two hundred and fifty dollar leather backpack."

Behind the curve of Madame's broad back, David shot her a look that clearly said, *Any other objections?*

She glanced from him to the pack now on the floor behind his chair, sighed, and shook her head.

"First, we will remove your significator card." Madame Zora flipped the deck and deftly fanned it. "I would say, the Knight of Cups; a young man with light brown hair and hazel eyes, emotional, imaginative, and skilled in the arts. If you will shuffle the deck..."

Leaning to her right, as though she wanted a better view of the pattern being laid out on the table, Cynthia slowly stretched her arm behind Madame Zora's chair and hooked one finger through a leather loop. If she could just get her hands on her battery...

"You have a high proportion of cups showing, that indicates good news. Here, in the first position..."

The pack slid noiselessly over the short nap of the carpet. Surreptitiously patting each outside pocket, she finally felt a familiar lump.

"...and the happy conclusion of a task. The six of wands, in the fifth position symbolizes what will happen—victory will be achieved and success will be obtained through labor. These two cards obviously support each..."

It wasn't easy opening the buckle one handed but Cynthia eventually worked the battery free. Dropping it into her lap, she returned the pack to its original position.

"...symbolizing your own hopes and ideals on the matter. It's interesting that this is your only pentacle..."

Under the cover of the table, the battery slid into her phone with a gratifying ease. She sagged back against her chair, feeling the tension leave her shoulders.

When David's reading ended, Madame Zora pulled out a second deck of cards. "To allow the others to clear," she explained. "I never use the same deck twice in a row.

"Normally," she continued, fanning the cards, "the significator for a blonde woman with grey eyes would be the Queen of Wands but in this instance I think the Devil might be more suitable."

Cynthia frowned down at the card lying alone on the table. "I don't think I like that..."

"It has nothing to do with the devil as you perceive him, nothing to do with the evil of the Christian religion. The card symbolizes the domination of matter over spirit. Apt enough, I think? Shuffle, please."

Amazed she was actually going through with it, actually giving implied approval to occult psychology, Cynthia shuffled and split the deck as instructed.

Madame Zora laid out cards with firm, no nonsense movements of her hands, the rings flashing in the light. "Oh. My. Four of the Major Arcana. There are powerful outside forces at work here. Look at the pattern please and tell me what you see."

"Words," Cynthia muttered. "Words. Words. Words."

"I beg your pardon?"

"Polonius asked Hamlet what he was reading and Hamlet answered, *Words*." She waved a hand over the cards. "In this instance, however, *Pictures*, might be more appropriate."

Cocking her head slightly, Madame Zora kept her gaze on the cards. "That's all that you see?" she asked, her tone so explicitly neutral it lifted David's brows. "Pictures?"

Cynthia studied the pattern for a moment before she answered. "There isn't anything else," she said at last. "Pretty pictures that don't symbolize anything but a way for you to make a living which, I assure you, I'm not against but I believe in what I can see and..."

The phone cut her off.

"Cynthia!" David could've managed more outrage if he hadn't been so relieved to have the impending rant cut short.

"Augustine Textiles, Cynthia Augustine speaking. What's that? I'm sorry, could you hang on a moment until I get outside?" Scrabbling to her feet she headed for the tent flap. "I'm sorry, but I've got to take this call."

David closed his eyes in embarrassment. When he opened them again, Madame Zora was watching him, her expression unreadable.

"I'm so sorry," he began but she cut him off.

"No need. *I* am sorry for your friend." Her gesture bracketed the pattern. "I see transformation in these cards."

"By powerful outside forces?"

"By, because of, for; who can say. If they feel it necessary, certain *things* will go to extremes to attract attention."

"But you said they were just symbols."

"Symbols," said Madame Zora with ponderous emphasis, "are shortcuts to more complicated meanings."

"I can *not* believe you did that!"

Looking like the cat who swallowed the canary, Cynthia slipped her phone back in its pouch. "Did what?"

"Broke our agreement, went through my stuff, stole your battery back, and interrupted the reading!"

"We got the hotel job."

David choked as he attempted to change responses in mid word. Cheerfully thumping him on the back, Cynthia reassured a number of anxious by-standers that he was fine, just a little overcome with the afternoon's excitement. Several mothers of small children nodded in weary understanding.

"The hotel job?" he repeated when he could speak. "The whole hotel?" Cynthia nodded and he grabbed her arm. "This is exactly what Madame Zora said would happen; victory will be achieved and success will be obtained through labor."

"Co-incidence." She tucked her hand in the crook of his elbow and propelled him toward the parking lot. "Come on, we've got a lot to do."

Digging in his heels, he dragged her to a stop. "I really think you ought to go back and let Madame Zora interpret your cards. Remember those powerful outside forces, Cyn." He repeated his final conversation with the fortuneteller. It had, as he'd expected, no effect.

"David, there's nothing to interpret."

"You've got to admit she did a fine reading for me."

"Well, considering she started with a knight instead of a queen..." Placing her hand in the small of his back, Cynthia shoved him forward, moving him another four feet towards the exit. "Now, can we go?"

She managed to keep him moving until a small crowd stopped them both just inside the perimeter fence. In front of a small pond artistically pierced with jagged rock, two men, in a mix of medieval armor and hockey equipment, were beating on each other with rattan swords. On a bench to one side, sat a young woman, blindfolded and holding a pair of swords aloft.

Separated from David and caught up in the crowd, Cynthia found herself beside the bench without really understanding how she got there. She staggered, stretched out a hand, and managed to stop herself at the last minute from grabbing one of the two swords.

"You may have a well developed sense of balance but you're definitely in need of direction."

"I beg your pardon."

"No need. I'm here to help." Lifting the blindfold with an extended thumb, the girl peered up at Cynthia with dark eyes. "Would you mind holding one of these for a moment?"

There didn't seem to be a polite way to refuse so Cynthia gingerly took the closer of the two swords. It was much heavier than she expected.

"Thanks." Reaching into a side-pocket, the girl pulled out a familiar white rectangle. "My card. For later."

"For later," Cynthia repeated, habit extending her free hand. She'd barely returned the sword when the crowd surged past, caught her up again, and deposited her back by David's side. "Is there a reason you've got your mouth open?"

"That girl!"

"What about her?" She shoved the business card in her back pocket without looking at it.

"Two swords! The pond! The rocks! The bench! The moon!"

Cynthia glanced up at the crescent moon barely visible in the afternoon sky and shrugged. "So?"

"The tarot!"

"A verb, David. Try a verb."

He grabbed her shoulders and shook her. "That's the second card in your tarot reading! The Two of Swords!"

"Do you have any idea how ridiculous that sounds?"

"Yes!" He paused. His cheeks flushed as he released her. "Really ridiculous. I think, I think I got too much sun."

"I think you're right." She tucked her arm into the bend of his elbow. "Come on. Let's go home."

Augustine Textiles was in the lower, not quite basement, level of an old red brick building on King Street West, a neighborhood working toward trendy—by the time the higher rents arrived, Cynthia planned on being able to afford them. Over the years they'd seen a number of spectacular accidents from their vantage point a sidewalk's width from the street but nothing like the accident the morning after the trip to the fair.

"I didn't know there was a circus in town," David declared, his ears ringing in the post-crash quiet.

"I don't think there is." Cynthia found it impossible not to tilt her head to try to bring the view into a normal perspective.

A tractor-trailer, its sides open ironwork, had jackknifed making the turn off Spadina. When the far wheels hit the curb, it had flipped over onto its back.

"Maybe it's a publicity stunt for Beauty and the Beast."

In the trailer, a woman in a long white dress with flowers in her hair and around her waist held closed the mouth of a male lion. Both woman and lion were, at the moment, suspended upside down.

The moment ended. Neither appeared too badly hurt by the fall.

Using language totally at odds with her appearance, the woman untangled herself from her skirts and got, somewhat shakily, to her feet. The lion shook itself, squeezed between two twisted bars and took off down the street. Approaching sirens became quickly overlaid with startled screaming.

Fully aware that the most helpful thing she could do was to stay put, Cynthia yanked open the door and raced out onto street. "Are you all right!?" She rocked to a halt when she saw that the woman, taking the lion's route out of the destroyed truck, was fine—which left her nothing to do but stand and feel embarrassed.

The woman reached back through the hole to pick up a bronze figure eight then turned and smiled kindly at her. "Never fear passion," she said. "Now, if you'll excuse me." Pushing a crushed bloom up off her face, she strode purposefully toward the corner where half a dozen police officers had the lion more-or-less cornered. "Here, let me. Brute force will get you nowhere with him."

"Well?" David demanded when Cynthia came back inside.

"She's fine. And, although several members of Toronto's finest are going to need to have their trousers dry-cleaned, the lion's fine. Let's get back to work."

"That's it?"

"There's nothing we can do out there and there's plenty we can do in here."

David stood a while longer, staring out the window, watching a pair of tow trucks try and pull the trailer away. All at once, he paled. "Cyn?"

"Um."

"What did she say to you?"

Deep in a new database, it took Cynthia a moment to realize what David was talking about. "Something about never fearing passion. Why?"

"That was the third card in your reading. Strength, reversed."

"Strength *reversed*?" Both brows lifted. "You're out of your mind."

"Oh yeah? How many times have you seen a woman and a lion upside down in the fashion district? Remember what Madame Zora said, certain things will go to extremes to attract attention."

"What things?"

"Well, we'd know if you'd finished the reading, wouldn't we!"

"David, you're getting hysterical."

"No, not yet." He crossed the room and leaned over her desk. "You haven't seen hysterical yet. The tarot is coming to life, forcing you to recognize it the only way it can. Do you remember what your last card was?"

"Of course I don't. And neither do you."

"Oh yes, I do. I may not remember the middle of the pattern but I remember that last card. It was a Ten of Swords, Cynthia. And you know what that means!"

She rolled her eyes and sat back. "No, David, what does that mean?"

"It means that sooner or later you're going to be explaining a dead body with ten swords in it to the police."

"If you don't go back to your desk," she reminded him pointedly, "we're going to lose the best contract we've ever had and it's going to be your body."

"Cynthia, please. You know I'm right."

"And what am I, chopped liver?"

"Well, no, you're right too but…"

"Then please, get back to work." She watched him cross back to his desk and shook her head. His sudden obsession with a not terribly successful midway attraction was beginning to worry her.

Out on the street, the lion roared.

"David? Cynthia. Sorry I woke you but I've got a problem."

"Problem. Right. It's two in the morning. It'll keep."

"David, don't hang up!" Pulling back her kitchen curtains, she took another look out the window. "What was the next card in that tarot reading?" The silence on the other end of the phone was so complete she figured he'd gone back to sleep. "David?"

He hadn't. "The next card?"

"Did it look like a dog and a wolf—although it's probably a coyote—bracketed by a pair of upright things—in this particular case the old bridge abutments—howling at a full moon with some real weird shadow patterns on it while a lobster crawls up out of the water?"

"Uh, hang on a minute."

She flinched as the howling began again. "Don't take too long." One of the Garibaldis in the apartment upstairs, yelled for quiet and threw a boot out the window towards the river. The lobster turned toward the noise but the howling continued.

"Cyn? The card's called The Moon. It stands for the influence just passed away. And Cyn, it's the card of the psychic."

Madame Zora. Damn. "How the hell do you know?"

"I bought a book on the way home. You'd better come over." Sleepy protests in the background were quickly hushed. "Just out of curiosity, what convinced you I was right?"

Sighing, she let the curtain drop. "David, I can rationalize upside down lions but trust me, there's no way a lobster could survive in the Humber."

David answered the door to the condo with a slim paperback in one hand and a finger over his lips. "Shhh. Drew's gone back to sleep. We can talk in the den." Ushering her in front of him, he closed the door and relaxed. "How was the trip over?"

Cynthia snorted. "Weird. I stopped at the bottom of the Casa Loma hill to untie a young woman standing blindfolded surrounded by eight swords. She thanked me, picked up her swords, and said she'd have done it herself except she was afraid of moving out of a situation of bondage." She dropped onto one end of a leather couch. "They, whoever they are, are not very subtle."

"We knew that; they dropped a lion on its head to make a point." Sinking down onto the other end of the couch, David flipped through the book. "The Eight of Swords. Your fifth card. Something that may happen in the future."

"David, pay attention please. It already happened."

"It symbolizes what may happen to you."

Her lips pressed into a thin line. "If somebody tries that on me..."

David sighed. "Symbolizes. You may be bound by indecision."

"The only thing I can't decide is whether or not I should look up Madame Zora and slap her with a lawsuit."

"For what?"

It was Cynthia's turn to sigh. "Good point. So what comes next?"

"I don't remember."

"You're a lot of help." He looked so hurt she flushed and gripped his shoulder. "I'm sorry I'm being such a bitch. This has got me a little shaken."

One corner of his mouth hooked up. "Cyn, you're always a bitch, I've gotten used to it. Now, let's go over what we know. Madame Zora said it was a pattern of transformation and, counting the significator, you've seen the first five cards. You've got four to go and then the Ten of Swords—the Final Outcome."

"I wish you wouldn't say it like that," Cynthia muttered, sinking down into the cushions. "It makes me think that I might be the body under the swords—my reading, my Final Outcome."

"We're not even going to think that." But they both were. "Don't put your feet on the coffee table."

"Sorry."

"According to this book, the Ten of Swords symbolizes sudden misfortune…"

"Well, duh."

"…and in spiritual matters, the end of delusion."

She straightened. "I am not deluded. I'm practical. I've kept a small business afloat in a lingering recession and…business…" Reaching into her back pocket she pulled out a creased card. "The girl with the swords said she was here to help and gave me this for later."

The card was blank except for a phone number; a 555 number, an exchange used only by long distance directory assistance and the screen writers' guild. After two rings, an answering machine clicked on and a familiar voice declared, "A changed concept of self automatically alters our future. All outer change takes place in consciousness. If you leave a message after the tone, you'll be wasting your time."

It wasn't so much a tone as the theme from Close Encounters.

"Well, I think the solution's obvious."

Cynthia started at him in wide-eyed disbelief. "Obvious?"

"You've got to learn to see the symbolism before the reality kills you. You've got to get in touch with your spiritual side."

"With my what?"

"You'd better stay here tonight. We can get started in the morning."

She felt each of the ten swords as it pierced her body, nailing her to the floor. Closing her eyes against the pain, she muttered, "The stains are never going to come out of this carpet."

From far away, she heard a familiar voice intone, "Look beyond to the symbolism."

"Symbolism? David, this carpet was hand-tied in Morocco!"

When she opened her eyes, it was morning.

"What is this?"

"Granola."

Cynthia poked at the whole wheat, dried dates and who knew what else in the hand thrown pottery bowl. "I never realized roughage was spiritual."

Before David could offer reassurance, Drew yelled from the next room that they should look out the window. "Some idiot's gone bungee jumping off his balcony."

"He probably jumped rather than eat tree bark for breakfast," Cynthia muttered as she peered over David's shoulder at the building across the courtyard.

The jumper had anchored his cable on one of the trees that crowded the edge of the penthouse garden. As the bounce wore off, he swung by one leg, hands folded behind his back, free leg crossed back behind the other knee.

"He must've threaded fiber optics through his hair. Look at the way his head's glowing."

"Seems perfectly content though, doesn't he." As David moved out of the way, Cynthia pressed against the window and frowned. "You know, physics was never my strong suit, but shouldn't he have swung back and hit the building?" When she heard pages turning behind her, she sighed and closed her eyes. "Don't tell me…"

"The Hanged Man. Representing things that are before you; self-surrender to a higher wisdom."

"Higher wisdom?" Pivoting on one heel, she stared at David in astonishment. "So far they've created a major traffic hazard, turned a lion loose downtown, tossed a crustacean into a hostile environment, tied someone up in the middle of the night surrounded by illegal weapons, and jumped off a balcony! That doesn't sound like a higher wisdom to me!"

"The cards aren't the wisdom, they're pointing the way."

"Oh puh-leez."

"Just eat the cereal. We've got a lot to do."

David felt that bicycling to work would've been more spiritual but they ended up taking Cynthia's car. Fortunately, it had a tape deck.

"What's that?"

"It's a tape called Distant Angels; new age instrumental music. According to the box, it's the music of transformation and it's supposed to break through your inner resistance leaving a state of relaxation and attunement."

As the sound of a single flute filled the car, Cynthia's scowl softened. "Very pretty. Very relaxing." She slumped behind the wheel only to jerk erect as a transport nearly ran them off the road. "But do you really think I should be listening to it during morning rush hour?"

There were no surprises waiting for them at the office.

"I'm just glad the Devil was out of the pack," David declared standing a safe distance away as Cynthia unlocked the door. "That would've made life interesting."

They ate lunch in a tiny park off Spadina. Except for a small disagreement over the burning of some incense—"And what exactly is oxygen deprivation supposed to symbolize?"—the morning had been an uneventful, and unsuccessful, attempt to help Cynthia see beyond the obvious.

"All right, look at this deep, rich red. What does this red symbolize to you?"

"It's a color, David. And I think it's too dark for the hotel."

"Are you doing this on purpose?"

"Doing what?"

A number of other people were also out enjoying the sunshine. Mothers with small children, junior executives with oxford cloth sleeves rolled up, teenagers grouped defensively by the fountain, and the ubiquitous variety of buskers.

David pointed out that the buskers could symbolize artistic freedom, unwilling to be confined by a nine to five world.

"Unable to be confined, you mean." Cynthia winced as a young woman with yards of orange hair delivered an extraordinarily off-key performance of Joni Mitchell's Big Yellow Taxi. "I'm not throttling her. That must count for something."

"But *why* aren't you throttling her? Because her music touched you?"

"Because I don't want to face an assault charge."

David sighed and stood. "Close. But not quite."

Dropping empty juice bottles into the recycling barrels, they started back to the office.

Removing his high crowned hat, one of the buskers balanced carefully on his head and began performing a complicated juggling act with two discs and a piece of hose tied into a figure eight.

As they passed, Cynthia's cel phone rang, the shrill twitter cutting through the ambient noise.

The busker jerked and one of the discs went flying into traffic.

Closest to the curb, and feeling a bit guilty, Cynthia ran out after it, half her attention on the phone—"Augustine Textiles, Cynthia Augustine speaking"—half on the disc.

David grabbed her shirt and yanked her back just as the Spadina bus roared by in a cloud of blue exhaust. When the smoke had cleared, the disc lay in pieces. Checking carefully up street before he bent forward, David picked up the largest shard. Silently, he held it out to the young busker who sighed and shook his head.

"Man, I was afraid that was going to happen. That's no use to me now, you can keep it if you want it."

"No thanks, I…" Then he took a good look at what he held. As the busker headed off, he waved the shard in Cynthia's face.

"…get back to you tomorrow. That right. Thanks for calling. David, that was a business call and…is that part of a broken pentacle?"

He nodded and pulled the slender book out of his back pocket. "Two of Pentacles. Reversed. Your seventh card representing your fears. Oh gee, big surprise—you're afraid you're having difficulty handling your problems."

"There's no need to be sarcastic."

Ignoring her, he went on. "And it seems like you got a double whammy because they also just reminded you that your fears can kill you."

"I think you're reading too much into it."

"The Ten of Swords. The Final Outcome."

She had a sudden memory of the way the carpet felt pressed warm and sticky against her cheek. Dry cleaning was not going to be enough. "Okay, okay, you win. What now?"

"I don't know but I'll think of something. There's only two cards to go and they seem to be coming closer together."

"That's not very reassuring."

"I know." David glanced around and suddenly smiled. "I've got it. This is an easy one." Grabbing Cynthia's shoulders he turned her toward the waterfront. "What does the CN Tower symbolize to you?"

She squinted at the familiar landmark and shrugged. "Radio towers?"

"No, that what it is. Try again."

"Revolving restaurants?"

"Cynthia!"

"I don't know!" Her voice had picked up a slightly desperate tone. "What?"

"It's the world's tallest, freestanding, phallic symbol."

"But they're not shaped anything like that."

David sighed and considered giving up the fight. "Maybe we're going about this the wrong way. Let's go back to work, I'll put on the Benedictine monks and while you try to step beyond reality, I'll try to think up a new angle."

"I think we've been beyond reality since we talked to Madame Zora," Cynthia muttered. The thought of falling swords made the skin between her shoulder blades itch.

"I haven't been inside a church for years."

"Nothing does symbolism better." David pushed open the heavy wooden door of St. Michael's Cathedral. "Come on."

"We can't just *wander* in."

"We're not just wandering. Now, come on."

It was cool and quiet inside the church. Aside from a few elderly women praying in the first couple of rows, they had the place to themselves. In a low voice, David began pointing out the various symbols of his faith.

"I know all this stuff, David. I haven't spent my life in a closet, if you'll pardon the expression."

"You know it here." He touched her forehead then tapped on her sternum. "But not here. You have to believe that some things stand for things that are bigger than they are."

"Would now be a good time to tell you *why* I stopped going to church?"

They were turning to leave when a figure leaned out of one of the alcoves and beckoned.

Cynthia frowned. "Okay, it was a long time ago and it *was* a United Church but isn't that guy just a little overdressed?"

The alcove held a low dias, a throne, and two pillars. A pair of monks in robes embroidered with roses and lilies knelt before the throne. Between them, was a pair of crossed keys. Seated on the throne, was a priest.

"What's with the Carmen Miranda hat?"

"It's not a hat," David hissed looking up from the book. "It's a three tiered crown."

"Don't tell me…"

"It's the Hierophant. Your eighth card. The seeker's environment or the fears of your family and friends."

"If you don't mind, young man." The priest said snippily. "I can speak for myself."

"Sorry."

"I should think so." He cleared his throat. "Your family and friends, my dear, are afraid you're overly concerned with a need to conform. That you are bound too tightly to convention."

Cynthia's lip curled. "First, I'm not your *dear*. Second, you're wrong. Tell him he's wrong, David."

"Uh…"

"So who says I have to be wild and crazy," she snarled. She glared down at the monks. "Do you two have anything to add?"

"No," said the monk on the left.

"We're just here for effect," added the monk on the right.

Absolutely furious, Cynthia stomped out of the church—modifying her step when she heard the slap of her shoes echoing against the stone. When David caught up with her on the sidewalk outside, she whirled around to face him.

"Why me, that's what I want to know? Why put all this effort into changing me? Am I such a horrible person?"

"No. You're not. You're just…" He searched for a polite way to put it. "…a little narrowly focused."

"Is that such a bad thing? I'm not hurting anyone!'

His voice gentled. "Except maybe yourself."

The anger left her as suddenly as it had appeared. She clutched at David's arm. "We haven't much time, have we? One more card and then…"

"We'll beat it, Cyn, you'll see. But maybe you should stay home until you've made a breakthrough, that way no one can drop swords on you."

"No, but my building will collapse in an unexpected earthquake and I'll be found in the rubble wearing Mr. Garabaldi's collection of medieval weaponry."

"Mr. G. has a collection of swords?"

"Not that I know of *now*. Anyway, I can't be responsible for that, think of what an earthquake would do to the property values in my neighborhood." When she caught his expression, she almost grinned. "Kidding." The grin slipped. "Mostly."

They came out onto Yonge Street in the midst of a crowd of street venders. Forward progress meant carefully picking a path through merchandise stacked precariously on rickety tables and spread out on the sidewalk. Her mind replaying the dream of the swords, over and over, Cynthia moved blindly toward disaster.

Her foot struck something hard and cold. Which struck something else. Which struck something else. Metal rang against concrete.

When she looked down, she realized she'd kicked over three brass goblets, spilling their contents. The vendor, his skinny form wrapped head to toe in a black cloak, stared down at them in despair as other pedestrians stepped fastidiously over the spreading liquid.

"I'm so sorry."

"Accidents happen," he allowed mournfully.

"I'll pay you for what I spilled."

He sighed deeply. "No point. What's done, is done."

Done.

Done.

Done.

Cynthia suddenly needed to out-run the word echoing in her head, suddenly needed to get out of the crowds. David found her two blocks away, leaning up against a store window, staring at but not seeing the display.

"There were two cups still standing," he said.

"Doesn't matter. That was the ninth card."

"How do you know?"

"Oh come on, David. Cups. A guy in a full cloak making enigmatic statements—what else could it be. You might want to stand back; you'll never get blood stains out of that shirt, it's silk."

Flipping through the book, David ignored the suggestion. "Okay, if it was your ninth card, then it represents your hopes and fears."

"I think the fears part is pretty damned obvious!"

"But there were two cups still full! You can break through this Cyn if you just try!"

"I AM trying but face it, it's not working!" Her words had picked up a panicked cadence. "So something wants to broaden my viewpoint but suppose I don't want my viewpoint broadened!"

"I don't think you have a choice."

"There's always a choice, David. I can choose to stand here and become some sort of symbolic pincushion!" The look on his face stopped her cold. "All right. No, I can't. But only because it would upset you." She took a deep breath and let it out slowly. "We're almost out of time. What do we do?"

They were standing in front of a shoe store. David peered through the glass and, unexpectedly, he smiled. "Lets buy you some sandals."

"Sandals?" She blinked. "That's your solution?"

"When I was younger, I took riding lessons. When I started I didn't have the right clothes because well, they were expensive and I couldn't see how they'd make a difference. When I finally broke down and bought a pair of breeches and some boots, my riding improved. What you're wearing can affect your state of mind. Sandals can be very spiritual. Christ wore sandals. Come on."

Shaking her head, but with no better idea, Cynthia followed him into the store.

The pattern of the carpet looked familiar.

Eyes locked on the loops and swirls, she heard nothing of what either the salesman or David said as they picked and fitted and boxed her cowboy boots. Moving numbly to the counter on the unfamiliar slabs of cork, she pulled out her wallet and muttered, "How much?" A moment later she repeated the question considerably louder. "HOW MUCH!?"

"Cyn, they're made in Germany..."

"So what! I'm not taking them on the autobahn!"

"Think of it as an investment in your state of mind!"

She looked down at her toes, pale and naked, and past them to the carpet. "Oh well, I probably won't have to wear them for long." Handing over her gold card, she signed where indicated, picked up the piece of plastic...

...and froze, credit card clutched in one hand.

"Cyn?"

"This isn't money!"

"No but..."

"But it symbolizes money! In a way, it symbolizes a standard of living I couldn't achieve on cash alone! Do you hear music?" Without waiting for an answer, she whirled around. "Those shoes with the three inch heels, they not only symbolize the patriarchy's effort to keep women helpless but also women taking charge of and flaunting their own sexuality!"

David felt a little the way Henry Higgins must have when the rain finally fell in Spain.

"And red!" Grabbing his shoulders, she shook him back and forth. "Red symbolizes blood and blood symbolizes sacrifice and sacrifice symbolizes passion so red symbolizes passion!" Releasing him, she spun away, eyes gleaming.

The salesman leaned over the counter. "Is she all right?"

"She's having an epiphany." Trust Cynthia to have an epiphany with a credit card.

"These shoes symbolize a dream of playing like Michael Jordon!"

"Is it going to make a mess on the carpet?"

"I don't think so." He was smiling so broadly his cheeks hurt. She'd done it, she'd managed to acknowledge a greater reality. There would be no tenth card. No swords. No body. It would be enough to know what the meaning was.

"Symbols, symbols tap into the collective unconscious! All of a sudden, poetry makes sense, although," she added throwing herself back into one of the chairs, "I still don't understand Shirley Maclaine." The chair, made for more sedate landings, tipped backwards. "Oh shit!"

Watching her hit the floor, head down and feet in the air, David had an epiphany of his own. As the chair landed solidly on top of her, he wondered if he should say anything. The Ten of Swords had been reversed. Realistically, there wasn't a lot of difference between being stabbed and being impaled but symbolically...

He checked the new meaning as the salesman—torn between laughter and fear of being sued—helped her up.

The Ten of Swords, reversed. In spiritual matters, the Seeker may now turn to higher powers for help.

He closed the book before Cynthia turned to face him. Higher powers. It was out of his hands. And thank God, ghod, gods, or whoever for that.

Rubbing one buttock, Cynthia limped over to the counter. "I think," she said, enthusiasm muted slightly, "I'll consider that a warning. The spiritual must be balanced with the practical."

Before David could agree, the cel phone rang.

"Augustine Textiles, Cynthia Augustine speaking."

Eyes locked on her face, David searched for an outward manifestation of the inner change. He couldn't see one and, as she frowned, his heart started to pound uncomfortably hard. Perhaps it *wasn't* over.

"That," Cynthia said as she tucked the phone back in the belt pouch, "was Madame Zora."

David started breathing again. "She wants to congratulate you on reaching enlightenment?"

"Not exactly. She wants her twenty bucks."

The letter asking me to do a story for *Elf Fantastic* allowed as how their only criteria was that it be about High Elves. Now, you may have noticed that I don't do mythic, on that level, particularly well so I wasn't certain I could come up with a story that fit those parameters. High elves.

Then, while watching the summer Olympics from Atlanta, I saw the Sprite commercial with the basketball players in silhouette walking down a hallway and the announcer explaining how people look up to these guys—which is when one of them hits his head on the door—because they're tall. Real tall.

High elves. Real tall.

The story grew organically out of the title and presented one of those wonderful opportunities to skew reality just slightly off center.

I really love this story.

A MIDSUMMER NIGHT'S DREAM TEAM

Long years ago, when lesser were the shadow veils
That hang 'tween this world
And the courts of proud Oberon,
Who rules the spirits with fair Titania by his side,
Men oft times saw the elven folk.
Saw them in the waters,
And riding beasts of bone or horned head,
Saw them duel each other and more than saw;
Battles there were in those days, great battles.
Blood did spill red and hot upon the ground
As immortal warriors challenged mortals of renown.

But Gentles, times do change,
Though slow within the Faerie court,
And battles now must be a different sort.

"One hundred and ninety-seven countries, ten thousand, seven hundred athletes; we've been at this for two hours and we're only at Belize!" Sam Gilburne squinted through the viewfinder on her camera, saw that the entrance to the stadium was still perfectly framed and leaned back. "We're going to be here for-fucking-ever." The camera went live as the director cut to her wide shot but the red light blinked off again almost immediately when they went in for a close up on one of a multitude of mobile units. "Mobile. Yeah right. If you're a steroid carrying member of the weight lifting team." Fixed positions might be boring—all right, fixed positions were inevitably boring—but boredom never produced a hernia.

She checked her shot again, made a miniscule adjustment in focus just for something to do, and wiped at the sweat dribbling down her neck. Years of practice blocked out the steady chatter in her headphones; when they wanted her, she'd hear them. A number of the European countries were using computer controlled units in their fixed positions but the Canadian Broadcasting Corporation, while as fascinated by high tech as anyone in the industry, recognized two very important things. The first; even the best computer couldn't respond to the unexpected the way a trained operator could. And the second; since, this time, they had lots of room on the trucks, people were cheaper.

Although she swore to deny it later if anyone asked, Sam found herself caught up in the excitement as the Canadian team entered.

"Camera one, when they all get down into the bowl of the stadium, I want you to give me a long, sweeping shot. Start at the flag and move back. I want to see happy faces."

"I thought three was doing the happy faces."

"Just give me the shot, Sam."

As the last of the Canadian team stepped off the ramp, Sam unlocked her camera.

"Just keep it moving. Ready one…"

By the time she got to the end of the team, she'd grown heartily sick of all that smiling. There were those around the CBC, those who'd worked with her for almost twenty years, who believed Sam herself never smiled. That wasn't entirely true, although it was highly possible that they'd never seen her actually do it.

When she finally managed to reframe her establishing shot, the Ethiopian team had almost reached the bottom of the ramp. Behind them, heat shimmered up off the concrete.

Shimmered in the gap between Ethiopia and Fiji.

"Camera one, what are you doing?"

"There's something wrong with my focus."

"There's nothing wrong with your focus, lock it and leave it."

Sam locked the camera in place and squinted around it toward the stadium entrance. Ethiopia. One of the irritatingly frequent empty spaces. Fiji.

She took another look through the viewfinder.

The heat shimmer maintained a careful distance behind the Ethiopian team. Within it, under a gossamer flag, shapes with flowing edges took form for a heartbeat then faded, replaced by others, who were replaced by others in their turn. Some bordered on the grotesque. Some on the beautiful. But they were all tall.

Real tall.

"Swimming?" Sam glared up at the assignment board. "Why swimming?"

One of the technical directors handed her a cardboard cup of coffee. "Why not swimming?"

"Chlorine makes me itch."

"You're not going to be in the pool, Sam." He nodded at the board. "You're up by the booth."

"Great. Announcers make me itch."

"Camera one, what are you doing?"

Sam frowned and flipped her microphone back around in front of her mouth. "I'm establishing the venue. What does it look like I'm doing?"

"If I knew, I wouldn't have asked. I want the pool framed, one. You've got way too much deck at the bottom of the shot. There's only eight lanes."

In the ninth lane, naked women, with flowing hair the color of a sun-lit sea, swam lazy circles and waited.

Many of the men, irrespective of country, swam a personal best that day. Personally, Sam was amazed that none of them drowned.

"Horse Park?" When she got an affirmative, Sam climbed onto the bus and collapsed into the first empty seat. Because daily temperatures were expected to climb into and then out of the thirties, Equestrian events started at seven am. In order to have everything ready in time, crews were pulled out of bed at five. Sam didn't do so well at five. "What the hell is a three day event," she muttered darkly.

Her seat mate stared at her in astonishment. "You don't know horses?"

"Not biblically, no. I'm just filling in for Burbadge; he's down with heat exhaustion. Don't look so worried, I can fake it if I have to."

She didn't have to fake it; she had to remember not to follow the horned horses, the skeletal horses, or the horses who left flaming hoof prints on the course.

"Do you hear dogs baying?" one of the Irish sound techs asked, fiddling with the bass gain.

"I don't think they're dogs," Sam said.

"So, how'd your day at fencing go, Sam?"

Sam shook her head as she swallowed a mouthful of beer. "Can't say as I'm surprised we only had one camera there. It's either so complicated it's beyond me or it's just plain old fucking dull."

One of the gaffers laughed. "Got that in one."

"What do you think it needs to jazz it up, Sam?"

"How about two guys, six and a half, seven feet tall, with hair down to their butts, wearing thigh-high boots, skin-tight pants, no shirts, and lotsa jewelry, hacking at each other with great bloody swords until one of them falls to his knees and begs for mercy."

The din in the bar dropped by about two decibels as everyone in earshot fell into a thoughtful silence.

"I'd watch that," a video editor muttered at last.

Sam finished her beer. "Damn right."

On the second last day of the games, the crowd around the assignment board seemed more animated than usual. As Sam approached, one of the younger cameramen exploded out of the group and grabbed her arm. "We've got the two CBC spots at the basketball finals, Sam! You and me! Gold medal round! Do you know what that means?"

"It's almost over?"

"It's the US against Yugoslavia! It's *the* game to see! You'll be able to tell everyone back home you were there!" He paused, actually focused on her, and released her arm. "Okay, maybe not."

"You're John Lowine, right?"

"The very lucky John Lowine, that's me. I don't believe I'm going to be shooting this game!"

Sam studied his face for a moment, wondered how much of these Olympics he'd been aware of, and had no chance to ask as the rest of the team descended.

Assignments were non-negotiable. Those were the rules. In spite of the rules, Sam could've retired on what she was offered for her spot. Another time, other games, she might've been tempted.

"You've been at this a long time, haven't you?" John asked as they started their equipment check.

"Long enough," Sam agreed.

"I bet you've seen pretty much everything."

"I used to think so."

Tucked into the bottom third of an enormous stadium packed with over 35,000 screaming fans, the game turned out to be unexpectedly exciting basketball. The Yugoslavian team stubbornly refused to fold and stayed to within two points until the US center finally kicked it into high gear in the last thirteen minutes.

Not all the sweat dripping off the US team had to do with exertion. Losing would be an embarrassment none of them would ever live down. In the end, they managed to fulfill expectations— if not as easily as they'd all believed they would.

"Camera one, what are you doing?"

Sam zoomed back until she had the whole court in focus. "Waiting."

"For what?"

"Something's going to happen." All the hair on the back of her neck was standing on end. The static electricity was so high she wouldn't have been surprised to see lightning jump from rafter to rafter, run down the bleachers, off the backboard, and hit nothing but net.

"It's already happened, one. Get in close and lets get some shots of those idiots sniffing the sho…"

Then another team appeared at center court.

Their bodies were too perfectly in proportion, their movements too sensuous, their faces too eerily similar for them to be human. And, if all that wasn't proof enough, beneath meters of multi-colored hair clubbed back with gold and silver bands, their ears came to graceful and prominent points.

The audience, the players, the officials, who had all one short moment before been hooting and hollering and just generally carrying on, stared in silence. Even Sam, who'd expected an appearance of some kind, found herself at a loss for words.

"What are you guys, Vulcans?" one of the US players demanded at last.

"This isn't some freakin' Star Trek episode," the man beside him added.

And pandemonium broke loose as people discovered they couldn't leave their seats.

"I find it absolutely appalling how no one seems to get a classical education anymore."

Sam, not at all surprised that her headphones were dead, turned to see a curly haired young man dressed all in brown—

shorts, t-shirt, running shoes—perched on the light standard beside her.

He grinned and leapt down. "Robin Goodfellow. And you must be Sam, no one calls you Samantha, Gilburne. How've you been enjoying the games?"

"They've been…interesting."

"Haven't they just."

"My gentle Puck! Come hither!"

Sighing, he turned to go. "Our Faerie captain calls and when fell Oberon doth summon, I must move my butt." He tossed a grin back over his shoulder. "I'll be back."

Oberon wore a gold circlet around silver hair and a golden "C" on a leaf green jersey. His voice carried. "This fool pretends to understand me not." A long, pale finger poked a trembling games official in the chest. "Explain, good Puck, the terms on which we play."

Sam couldn't hear the explanation but it involved a great deal of arm waving, consulting of clipboards, and ended with the young man in brown turning the official to face a glowering Oberon.

The crack of thunder shut everyone up again. Hysterics screeched to a halt all over the stadium. As the official was carried off the court, Puck turned to face the US bench. "My lord challenges those proven best in the world to play for the gold. What say you?"

Arms folded and eyes narrowed to disapproving slits, the coach shook his head. "I say that you can all just go back where you came from. My boys don't have to prove anything."

Puck favored him with an extraordinarily rude gesture. "Who asked you?" All at once, the stadium lights seemed to shine brighter over and around the twelve members of the US team. "I was talking to them."

The team milled about for a moment as a single unit then spit out a spokesman.

"He's challenging us?"

Oberon answered for himself. "I am."

"Then we say, let's play ball!"

"They might as well play," Puck said a moment later, back by Sam's side. "He wasn't going to let anyone leave until he got his game. Me, I blame television."

"For what?" The two men—*Well, two males*, Sam amended—stood eye to eye at center court.

"The shorter attention span of children, the sudden popularity of orange bathing suits, the inexplicable interest in Snack Masters…"

Oberon won the jump off.

"You watch our television?"

"Sure. Everything but Fox scrys in beautifully."

"What about the CBC?"

Puck shrugged. "It comes in, but no one watches it. All *this* started when his Majesty discovered the symbolic warfare channel."

One of the elves took a three point shot. It hit the rim, rolled, and dropped through.

3 - 0, Faerie.

"Discovered the what?"

"Oh, sorry. Sports. This specifically…" He waved at hand at the action on the court. "…I blame myself for. His Majesty asked if I thought he should take up the game; I said, why not; you're tall, you're arrogant. The rest, as they say, is mythology."

3 - 4, USA.

Oberon went down with an elbow in the throat and made both foul shots.

5 - 4, Faerie.

Thirty-one seconds later, it happened again.

7 - 6, Faerie.

"That's a man who likes to live dangerously," Puck observed with glee. "Oberon is not going to take kindly to a third foul."

Twelve seconds later, a terrified rooster raced under the USA bench.

After that, the game settled down. Sam, who'd never much cared for basketball and had not been thrilled at the prospect of having to watch a second competition, found herself enjoying the show. The elves made no sound as they ran, their feet only barely touched the floor, and more than one US player lost the ball when he turned suddenly and came face to face with an unexpected feral grin.

Sam had a strong suspicion that no one on the court was named Mustard Seed.

38 - 35, Faerie at half time.

Early in the second half, an elf took a rebound and immediately stepped to the other end of the court. During the time-out, the officials huddled by the scorekeeper and after a moment declared seven league boots to be illegal. The US made both their shots.

38 - 37, Faerie.

Finally realizing that the opposition wasn't going to give them this game either, the US team started to play basketball the way only they could, matching Faerie's ruthless calm with a near telepathic sense of precision teamwork.

65 - 68, USA with three minutes to go.

"Up and down! Up and down!" Puck screamed, balancing on the back of two chairs. "You've got to chase them up and down! This is no time to play defensively!"

He wasn't the only one rooting for the elves, Sam noticed. The Yugoslavian team and their fans seemed solidly on Oberon's side—considering how close they'd come only to lose to a stacked deck, she couldn't blame them.

Impossibly graceful, eyes glittering with an emerald light, Oberon swept past the US defense and took a shot from just outside the line.

Tie game.

Twelve seconds to play.

"What happens if he loses?" Sam wondered.

Puck shrugged. "Ass-heads all around, I'm afraid. He doesn't like losing."

The US got the ball on the turnover. At the elven net, a guard with raven hair and ice blue eyes blocked the shot.

Five seconds. Four.

A green-haired elf took the pass at center court, ducked under the long, sweaty arm of a US player, and on a single bounce got the ball back to Oberon.

Three. Two.

He leapt. Higher. Higher. His arm rose over his head, the ball held balanced on fingertips, and, at the apex of his flight...

...slam dunk.

The buzzer sounded.

70 - 68, Faerie.

Astonished to find herself on her feet, stamping and cheering, Sam fell silent as Oberon walked slowly toward the exhausted US team. By the time the elven lord stood an armslength away, his court behind him, an eerie quiet had settled over the entire stadium.

For a heart beat, great branching antlers rose above a golden crown, and robes, in colors almost painful to mortal eyes, swept the floor.

"Good game," he said.

And they were gone.

"Could someone please tell me *why* I am under this bench!?"

Frowning, Sam watched and listened and realized...

"They remember nothing; not the challenge nor how the challenge ended," Puck told her.

"I do."

"Someone must. What point our being here if no one makes a story of it?"

"Why me?"

"Why not you? You had the eyes to see." He held out his hand. "I must be off, Night's swift dragons cut the clouds full fast and my lord will want his Puck to share the revels."

Half expecting a joy-buzzer, Sam was relieved to note that a firm grip contained nothing more than calluses.

Stepping back, Puck spread his arms and grinned. "Time to party!"

"Camera one? You sleeping up there, Sam? I told you to get me the reactions to that shoe!"

She swung the camera around and panned the strangely subdued crowds. "What shoe?" The shoe had been tossed back for the Faerie game and now covered the foot it belonged on. While the control room argued over just where the alleged shoe should

be, Sam turned back to Puck, saying, as she turned, "Still, it's a
pity you won't get your medals."

"What was that, one?"

Robin Goodfellow had disappeared.

"Nothing."

Later that evening, as they played the anthem they'd had cued
up and ready before the final game began, Sam peered through
her camera at the athletes on the podium.

And she smiled.

On the morrow, many voices were in rage and wonder raised
As the twelve who met the challenge
Of proud Oberon and his court
Did find a leaf against their breasts
Instead of that which they believed they'd won.
Silently, were medals struck again
And those who witnessed never told
How sunlight acts on Faerie gold.

The Blood Books (*Blood Price*, *Blood Trail*, *Blood Lines*, *Blood Pact*, *Blood Debt*) are a series (that really need a series title) about Vicki Nelson, an ex-Metropolitan Toronto police detective now private investigator, Detective-Sergeant Michael Celluci still on the force, and Henry Fitzroy, the bastard son of Henry VIII, romance writer and vampire. Although each book has a self-contained plot, the characters develop through out the series. While you can read them out of order, they work better if you don't.

I originally intended to end the series with *Blood Pact* but it turned out I had a few more things I wanted to say about the characters so I wrote *Blood Debt*. I've now said everything I need to at novel length and there will be no more *Blood* books. None.

Zip. Zilch. Nada.

But I'm not closing the door entirely. I may spin Tony off into his own investigations of the weird and for those of you who can't wait for something so nebulous, there have been, and will be, short stories.

"This Town Ain't Big Enough" is a direct sequel to *Blood Pact* and is referred to in *Blood Debt*.

THIS TOWN AIN'T BIG ENOUGH

"Ow! Vicki, be careful!"

"Sorry. Sometimes I forget how sharp they are."

"Terrific." He wove his fingers through her hair and pulled just hard enough to make his point. "Don't."

"Don't what?" She grinned up at him, teeth gleaming ivory in the moonlight spilling across the bed. "Don't forget or don't..."

The sudden demand of the telephone for attention buried the last of her question.

Detective-Sergeant Michael Celluci sighed. "Hold that thought," he said, rolled over, and reached for the phone. "Celluci."

"Fifty-two division just called. They've found a body down at Richmond and Peter they think we might want to have a look at."

"Dave, it's..." He squinted at the clock. "...one twenty-nine in the am and I'm off duty."

On the other end of the line, his partner, theoretically off duty as well, refused to take the hint. "Ask me who the stiff is?"

Celluci sighed again. "Who's the stiff?"

"Mac Eisler."

"Shit."

"Funny, that's exactly what I said." Nothing in Dave Graham's voice indicated he appreciated the joke. "I'll be there in ten."

"Make it fifteen."

"You in the middle of something?"

Celluci watched as Vicki sat up and glared at him. "I was."

"Welcome to the wonderful world of law enforcement."

Vicki's hand shot out and caught Celluci's wrist before he could heave the phone across the room. "Who's Mac Eisler?"

she asked as, scowling, he dropped the receiver back in its cradle and swung his legs off the bed.

"You heard that?"

"I can hear the beating of your heart, the movement of your blood, the song of your life." She scratched the back of her leg with one bare foot. "I should think I can overhear a lousy phone conversation."

"Eisler's a pimp." Celluci reached for the light switch, changed his mind, and began pulling on his clothes. Given the full moon riding just outside the window, it wasn't exactly dark and given Vicki's sensitivity to bright light, not to mention her temper, he figured it was safer to cope. "We're pretty sure he offed one of his girls a couple weeks ago."

Vicki scooped her shirt up off the floor. "Irene Macdonald?"

"What? You overheard that too?"

"I get around. How sure's pretty sure?"

"Personally positive. But we had nothing solid to hold him on."

"And now he's dead." Skimming her jeans up over her hips, she dipped her brows in a parody of deep thought. "Golly, I wonder if there's a connection."

"Golly yourself," Celluci snarled. "You're not coming with me."

"Did I ask?"

"I recognized the tone of voice. I know you, Vicki. I knew you when you were a cop, I knew you when you were a P.I. and I don't care how much you've changed physically, I know you now you're a...a..."

"Vampire." Her pale eyes seemed more silver than grey. "You can say it, Mike. It won't hurt my feelings. Bloodsucker. Nightwalker. Creature of Darkness."

"Pain in the butt." Carefully avoiding her gaze, he shrugged into his shoulder holster and slipped a jacket on over it. "This is police business, Vicki, stay out of it. Please." He didn't wait for a response but crossed the shadows to the bedroom door. Then he paused, one foot over the threshold. "I doubt I'll be back by dawn. Don't wait up."

Vicki Nelson, ex of the Metropolitan Toronto Police Force, ex private investigator, recent vampire, decided to let him go. If he could joke about the change, he accepted it. And besides, it was always more fun to make him pay for smart-ass remarks when he least expected it.

She watched from the darkness as Celluci climbed into Dave Graham's car, then, with the tail-lights disappearing in the distance, she dug out his spare set of car keys and proceeded to leave tangled entrails of the Highway Traffic Act strewn from Downsview to the heart of Toronto.

It took no supernatural ability to find the scene of the crime. What with the police, the press, and the morbidly curious, the area seethed with people. Vicki slipped past the constable stationed at the far end of the alley and followed the paths of shadow until she stood just outside the circle of police around the body.

Mac Eisler had been a somewhat attractive, not very tall, white male caucasian. Eschewing the traditional clothing excesses of his profession, he was dressed simply in designer jeans and an olive-green raw silk jacket. At the moment, he wasn't looking his best. A pair of rusty nails had been shoved through each manicured hand, securing his body upright across the back entrance of a trendy restaurant. Although the pointed toes of his tooled leather cowboy boots indented the wood of the door, Eisler's head had been turned completely around so that he stared, in apparent astonishment, out into the alley.

The smell of death fought with the stink of urine and garbage. Vicki frowned. There was another scent, a pungent predator scent that raised the hair on the back of her neck and drew her lips up off her teeth. Surprised by the strength of her reaction, she stepped silently into a deeper patch of night lest she give herself away.

"Why the hell would I have a comment?"

Preoccupied with an inexplicable rage, she hadn't heard Celluci arrive until he greeted the press. Shifting position slightly, she watched as he and his partner moved in off the street and got their first look at the body.

"Jesus H. Christ."

"On crutches," agreed the younger of the two detectives already on the scene.

"Who found him?"

"Dishwasher, coming out with the trash. He was obviously meant to be found; they nailed the bastard right across the door."

"The kitchen's on the other side and no one heard hammering?"

"I'll go you one better than that. Look at the rust on the head of those nails—they haven't *been* hammered."

"What? Someone just pushed the nails through Eisler's hands and into solid wood?"

"Looks like."

Celluci snorted. "You trying to tell me that Superman's gone bad?"

Under the cover of their laughter, Vicki bent and picked up a piece of planking. There were four holes in the unbroken end and two remaining three-inch spikes. She pulled a spike out of the wood and pressed it into the wall of the building by her side. A smut of rust marked the ball of her thumb but the nail looked no different.

She remembered the scent.

Vampire.

"...unable to come to the phone. Please leave a message after the long beep."

"Henry? It's Vicki. If you're there, pick up." She stared across the dark kitchen, twisting the phone cord between her fingers. "Come on, Fitzroy, I don't care what you're doing, this is important." Why wasn't he home writing? Or chewing on Tony. Or something. "Look, Henry, I need some information. There's another one of, of us, hunting my territory and I don't know what I should do. I know what I want to do..." The rage remained, interlaced with the knowledge of *another*. "...but I'm new at this bloodsucking undead stuff, maybe I'm over-reacting. Call me. I'm still at Mike's."

She hung up and sighed. Vampires didn't share territory. Which was why Henry had stayed in Vancouver and she'd come back to Toronto.

Well, all right, it's not the only reason I came back. She tossed Celluci's spare car keys into the drawer in the phone table and wondered if she should write him a note to explain the mysterious emptying of his gas tank. "Nah. He's a detective, let him figure it out."

Sunrise was at five twelve. Vicki didn't need a clock to tell her that it was almost time. She could feel the sun stroking the edges of her awareness.

"It's like that final instant, just before someone hits you from behind, when you know it's going to happen but you can't do a damn thing about it." She crossed her arms on Celluci's chest and pillowed her head on them adding, *"Only it lasts longer."*

"And this happens every morning?"

"Just before dawn."

"And you're going to live forever?"

"That's what they tell me."

Celluci snorted. "You can have it."

Although Celluci had offered to light-proof one of the two unused bedrooms, Vicki had been uneasy about the concept. At four and a half centuries, maybe Henry Fitzroy could afford to be blasé about immolation but Vicki still found the whole idea terrifying and had no intention of being both helpless and exposed. Anyone could walk into a bedroom.

No one would accidentally walk into an enclosed plywood box, covered in a blackout curtain, at the far end of a five foot high crawl space—but just to be on the safe side, Vicki dropped two by fours into iron brackets over the entrance. Folded nearly in half, she hurried to her sanctuary, feeling the sun drawing closer, closer. Somehow she resisted the urge to turn.

"There's nothing behind me," she muttered, awkwardly stripping off her clothes. Her heart slamming against her ribs, she crawled under the front flap of the box, latched it behind her, and squirmed into her sleeping bag, stretched out ready for the dawn.

"Jesus H. Christ, Vicki," Celluci had said, squatting at one end while she'd wrestled the twin bed mattress inside. *"At least a coffin would have a bit of historical dignity."*

"You know where I can get one?"

"I'm not having a coffin in my basement."

"Then quit flapping your mouth."

She wondered, as she lay there waiting for oblivion, where the *other* was. Did they feel the same near panic knowing that they had no control over the hours from dawn to dusk? Or had they, like Henry, come to accept the daily death that governed an immortal life? There should, she supposed, be a sense of kinship between them but all she could feel was a possessive fury. No one hunted in *her* territory.

"Pleasant dreams," she said as the sun teetered on the edge of the horizon. "And when I find you, you're toast."

Celluci had been and gone by the time the darkness returned. The note he'd left about the car was profane and to the point. Vicki added a couple of words he'd missed and stuck it under a refrigerator magnet in case he got home before she did.

She'd pick up the scent and follow it, the hunter becoming the hunted and, by dawn, the streets would be hers again.

The yellow police tape still stretched across the mouth of the alley. Vicki ignored it. Wrapping the night around her like a cloak, she stood outside the restaurant door and sifted the air.

Apparently, a pimp crucified over the fire exit hadn't been enough to close the place and Tex Mex had nearly obliterated the scent of a death not yet twenty-four hours old. Instead of the predator, all she could smell was fajitas.

"God damn it," she muttered, stepping closer and sniffing the wood. "How the hell am I supposed to find..."

She sensed his life the moment before he spoke.

"What are you doing?"

Vicki sighed and turned. "I'm sniffing the door frame. What's it look like I'm doing?"

"Let me be more specific," Celluci snarled. "What are you doing *here*?"

"I'm looking for the person who offed Mac Eisler," Vicki began. She wasn't sure how much more explanation she was willing to offer.

"No, you're not. You are not a cop. You aren't even a P.I. anymore. And how the hell am I going to explain you if Dave sees you?"

Her eyes narrowed. "You don't have to explain me, Mike."

"Yeah? He thinks you're in Vancouver."

"Tell him I came back."

"And do I tell him that you spend your days in a box in my basement? And that you combust in sunlight? And what do I tell him about your eyes?"

Vicki's hand rose to push at the bridge of her glasses but her fingers touched only air. The retinitis pigmentosa that had forced her from the Metro Police and denied her the night had been reversed when Henry'd changed her. The darkness held no secrets from her now. "Tell him they got better."

"RP doesn't get better."

"Mine did."

"Vicki, I know what you're doing." He dragged both hands up through his hair. "You've done it before. You had to quit the force. You were half-blind. So what? Your life may have changed but you were still going to prove that you were "Victory" Nelson. And it wasn't enough to be a private investigator. You threw yourself into stupidly dangerous situations just to prove you were still who you wanted to be. And now your life has changed again and you're playing the same game."

She could hear his heart pounding, see a vein pulsing, framed in the white vee of his open collar, feel the blood surging just below the surface in reach of her teeth. The Hunger rose and she had to use every bit of control Henry had taught her to force it back down. This wasn't about that.

Since she'd returned to Toronto, she'd been drifting; feeding, hunting, relearning the night, relearning her relationship with Michael Celluci. The early morning phone call had crystallized a subconscious discontent and, as Celluci pointed out, there was really only one thing she knew how to do.

Part of his diatribe was based on concern. After all their years together playing cops and lovers she knew how he thought; if something as basic as sunlight could kill her, what else waited to strike her down? It was only human nature for him to want to protect the people he loved—for him to want to protect her.

But, that was only the basis for *part* of the diatribe.

"You can't have been happy with me lazing around your house. I can't cook and I don't do windows." She stepped towards him. "I should think you'd be thrilled that I'm finding my feet again."

"Vicki."

"I wonder," she mused, holding tight to the Hunger, "how you'd feel about me being involved in this if it wasn't your case. I am, after all, better equipped to hunt the night than, oh, detective-sergeants."

"Vicki…" Her name had become a nearly inarticulate growl.

She leaned forward until her lips brushed his ear. "Bet you I solve this one first." Then she was gone, moving into shadow too quickly for mortal eyes to track.

"Who you talking to Mike?" Dave Graham glanced around the empty alley. "I thought I heard…" Then he caught sight of the expression on his partner's face. "Never mind."

Vicki couldn't remember the last time she felt so alive. *Which, as I'm now a card-carrying member of the bloodsucking undead, makes for an interesting feeling.* She strode down Queen Street West, almost intoxicated by the lives surrounding her, fully aware of crowds parting to let her through and the admiring glances that traced her path. A connection had been made between her old life and her new one.

"You must surrender the day," Henry had told her, *"but you need not surrender anything else."*

"So what you're trying to tell me," she'd snarled, *"is that we're just normal people who drink blood?"*

Henry had smiled. *"How many* normal *people do you know?"*

She hated it when he answered a question with a question but now, she recognized his point. Honesty forced her to admit that Celluci had a point as well. She did need to prove to herself that she was still herself. She always had. The more things changed, the more they stayed the same.

"Well, now we've got that settled..." She looked around for a place to sit and think. In her old life, that would have meant a donut shop or the window seat in a cheap restaurant and as many cups of coffee as it took. In this new life, being enclosed with humanity did not encourage contemplation. Besides, coffee, a major component of the old equation, made her violently ill—a fact she deeply resented.

A few years back, CITY TV, a local Toronto station, had renovated a deco building on the corner of Queen and John. They'd done a beautiful job and the six story, white building, with its ornately molded modern windows, had become a focal point of the neighborhood. Vicki slid into the narrow walkway that separated it from its more down-at-the-heels neighbor and swarmed up what effectively amounted to a staircase for one of her kind.

When she reached the roof a few seconds later, she perched on one crenellated corner and looked out over the downtown core. These were her streets; not Celluci's and not some out of town bloodsucker's. It was time she took them back. She grinned and fought the urge to strike a dramatic pose.

All things considered, it wasn't likely that the Metropolitan Toronto Police Department—in the person of Detective-Sergeant Michael Celluci—would be willing to share information. Briefly, she regretted issuing the challenge then she shrugged it off. As Henry said, the night was too long for regrets.

She sat and watched the crowds jostling about on the sidewalks below, clumps of color indicating tourists amongst the Queen Street regulars. On a Friday night in August, this was the place to be as the Toronto artistic community rubbed elbows with wanna-bes and never-woulds.

Vicki frowned. Mac Eisler had been killed before midnight on a Thursday night in an area that never completely slept. Someone had to have seen or heard something. Something they probably didn't believe and were busy denying. Murder was one thing, creatures of the night were something else again.

"Now then," she murmured, "where would a person like that—and considering the time and day we're assuming a regular not a tourist—where would that person be tonight?"

She found him in the third bar she checked, tucked back in a corner, trying desperately to get drunk, and failing. His eyes darted from side to side, both hands were locked around his glass, and his body language screamed *I'm dealing with some bad shit here, leave me alone.*

Vicki sat down beside him and for an instant let the Hunter show. His reaction was everything she could have hoped for.

He stared at her, frozen in terror, his mouth working but no sound coming out.

"Breathe," she suggested.

The ragged intake of air did little to calm him but it did break the paralysis. He shoved his chair back from the table and started to stand.

Vicki closed her fingers around his wrist. "Stay."

He swallowed and sat down again.

His skin was so hot it nearly burned and she could feel his pulse beating against it like a small wild creature struggling to be free. The Hunger clawed at her and her own breathing became a little ragged. "What's your name?"

"Ph...Phil."

She caught his gaze with hers and held it. "You saw something last night."

"Yes." Stretched almost to the breaking point, he began to tremble.

"Do you live around here?"

"Yes."

Vicki stood and pulled him to his feet, her tone half command half caress. "Take me there. We have to talk."

Phil stared at her. "Talk?"

She could barely hear the question over the call of his blood. "Well, talk first."

"It was a woman. Dressed all in black. Hair like a thou-sand strands of shadow, skin like snow, eyes like black ice. She chuckled, deep in her throat, when she saw me and licked her lips. They were painfully red. Then she vanished, so quickly that she left an image on the night."

"Did you see what she was doing?"

"No. But then, she didn't have be doing anything to be ter-rifying. I've spent the last twenty-four hours feeling like I met my death."

Phil had turned out to be a bit of a poet. And a bit of an athlete. All in all, Vicki considered their time together well spent. Working carefully after he fell asleep, she took away his memory of her and muted the meeting in the alley. It was the least she could do for him.

Description sounds like someone escaped from a Hammer film; The Bride of Dracula Kills a Pimp.

She paused, key in the lock, and cocked her head. Celluci was home, she could feel his life and if she listened very hard, she could hear the regular rhythm of breathing that told her he was asleep. Hardly surprising as it was only three hours to dawn.

There was no reason to wake him as she had no intention of sharing what she'd discovered and no need to feed but, after a long, hot shower, she found herself standing at the door of his room. And then at the side of his bed.

Mike Celluci was thirty-seven. There were strands of grey in his hair and although sleep had smoothed out many of the lines, the deeper creases around his eyes remained. He would grow older. In time, he would die. What would she do then?

She lifted the sheet and tucked herself up close to his side. He sighed and without completely waking scooped her closer still.

"Hair's wet," he muttered.

Vicki twisted, reached up, and brushed the long curl back off his forehead. "I had a shower."

"Where'd you leave the towel?"

"In a sopping pile on the floor."

Celluci grunted inarticulately and surrendered to sleep again. Vicki smiled and kissed his eyelids. "I love you too."

She stayed beside him until the threat of sunrise drove her away.

"Irene Macdonald."

Vicki lay in the darkness and stared unseeing up at the plywood. The sun was down and she was free to leave her sanctuary but she remained a moment longer, turning over the name that had been on her tongue when she woke. She remembered facetiously wondering if the deaths of Irene Macdonald and her pimp were connected.

Irene had been found beaten nearly to death in the bathroom of her apartment. She'd died two hours later in the hospital.

Celluci said that he was personally certain Mac Eisler was responsible. That was good enough for Vicki.

Eisler could've been unlucky enough to run into a vampire who fed on terror as well as blood—Vicki had tasted terror once or twice during her first year when the Hunger occasionally slipped from her control and she knew how addictive it could be—or he could've been killed in revenge for Irene.

Vicki could think of one sure way to find out.

"Brandon? It's Vicki Nelson."

"Victoria?" Surprise lifted most of the Oxford accent off Dr. Brandon Singh's voice. "I thought you'd relocated to British Columbia."

"Yeah, well, I came back."

"I suppose that might account for the improvement over the last month or so in a certain detective we both know."

She couldn't resist asking. "Was he really bad while I was gone?"

Brandon laughed. "He was unbearable and, as you know, I am able to bear a great deal. So, are you still in the same line of work?"

"Yes, I am." Yes, she was. God, it felt good. "Are you still the Assistant Coroner?"

"Yes, I am. As I think I can safely assume you didn't call me, at home, long after office hours, just to inform me that you're back on the job, what do you want?"

Vicki winced. "I was wondering if you'd had a look at Mac Eisler."

"Yes, Victoria, I have. And I'm wondering why you can't call me during regular business hours. You must know how much I enjoy discussing autopsies in front of my children."

"Oh God, I'm sorry Brandon, but it's important."

"Yes. It always is." His tone was so dry it crumbled. "But since you've already interrupted my evening, try to keep my part of the conversation to a simple yes or no."

"Did you do a blood volume check on Eisler?"

"Yes."

"Was there any missing?"

"No. Fortunately, in spite of the trauma to the neck the integrity of the blood vessels had not been breached."

So much for yes or no; she knew he couldn't keep to it. "You've been a big help, Brandon, thanks."

"I'd say *any time*, but you'd likely hold me to it." He hung up abruptly.

Vicki replaced the receiver and frowned. She—the *other*—hadn't fed. The odds moved in favor of Eisler killed because he murdered Irene.

"Well, if it isn't Andrew P." Vicki leaned back against the black Trans Am and adjusted the pair of non-prescription glasses she'd picked up just after sunset. With her hair brushed off her face and the window-glass lenses in front of her eyes, she didn't look much different than she had a year ago. Until she smiled.

The pimp stopped dead in his tracks, bluster fading before he could get the first obscenity out. He swallowed, audibly. "Nelson. I heard you were gone."

Listening to his heart race, Vicki's smile broadened. "I came back. I need some information. I need the name of one of Eisler's other girls."

"I don't know." Unable to look away, he started to shake. "I didn't have anything to do with him. I don't remember."

Vicki straightened and took a slow step towards him. "Try, Andrew."

There was a sudden smell of urine and a darkening stain down the front of the pimp's cotton drawstring pants. "Uh, D...D...Debbie Ho. That's all I can remember. Really."

"And she works?"

"Middle of the track." His tongue tripped over the words in the rush to spit them at her. "Jarvis and Carlton."

"Thank you." Sweeping a hand towards his car, Vicki stepped aside.

He dove past her and into the driver's seat, jabbing the key into the ignition. The powerful engine roared to life and with one last panicked look into the shadows, he screamed out of the driveway, ground his way through three gear changes, and hit eighty before he reached the corner.

The two cops, quietly sitting in the parking lot of the donut shop on that same corner, hit their siren and took off after him.

Vicki slipped the glasses into the inner pocket of the tweed jacket she'd borrowed from Celluci's closet and grinned. "To paraphrase a certain adolescent crime-fighting amphibian, I *love* being a vampire."

"I need to talk to you Debbie."

The young woman started and whirled around, glaring suspiciously at Vicki. "You a cop?"

Vicki sighed. "Not any more." Apparently, it was easier to hide the vampire than the detective. "I'm a private investigator and I want to ask you some questions about Irene Macdonald."

"If you're looking for the shithead who killed her, you're too late. Someone already found him."

"And that's who I'm looking for."

"Why?" Debbie shifted her weight to one hip.

"Maybe I want give them a medal."

The hooker's laugh held little humor. "You got that right. Mac got everything he deserved."

"Did Irene ever do women?"

Debbie snorted. "Not for free," she said pointedly.

Vicki handed her a twenty.

"Yeah, sometimes. It's safer, medically, you know?"

Editing out Phil's more ornate phrases, Vicki repeated his description of the woman in the alley.

Debbie snorted again. "Who the hell looks at their faces?"

"You'd remember this one if you saw her. She's..." Vicki weighed and discarded several possibilities and finally settled on, "...powerful."

"Powerful." Debbie hesitated, frowned, and continued in a rush. "There was this person Irene was seeing a lot but she wasn't charging. That's one of the things that set Mac off, not that the shithead needed much encouragement. We knew it was gonna happen, I mean we've all felt Mac's temper, but Irene wouldn't stop. She said that just being with this person was a high better than drugs. I guess it could've been a woman. And since she was sort of the reason Irene died, well, I know they used to meet in this bar on Queen West. Why are you hissing?"

"Hissing?" Vicki quickly yanked a mask of composure down over her rage. The other hadn't come into her territory only to kill Eisler—she was definitely hunting it. "I'm not hissing. I'm just having a little trouble breathing."

"Yeah, tell me about it." Debbie waved a hand ending in three inch scarlet nails at the traffic on Jarvis. "You should try standing here sucking carbon monoxide all night."

In another mood, Vicki might have re-applied the verb to a different object but she was still too angry. "Do you know which bar?"

"What, now I'm her social director? No, I don't know which bar." Apparently they'd come to the end of the information twenty dollars could buy as Debbie turned her attention to a prospective client in a grey sedan. The interview was clearly over.

Vicki sucked the humid air past her teeth. There weren't that many bars on Queen West. Last night she'd found Phil in one. Tonight; who knew.

* * *

Now that she knew enough to search for it, minute traces of the other predator hung in the air—diffused and scattered by the paths of prey. With so many lives masking the trail, it would be impossible to track her. Vicki snarled. A pair of teenagers, noses pierced, heads shaved, and Doc Martin's laced to the knee, decided against asking for change and hastily crossed the street.

It was Saturday night, minutes to Sunday. The bars would be closing soon. If the other was hunting, she would have already chosen her prey.

I wish Henry had called back. Maybe over the centuries they've—we've—evolved ways to deal with this. Maybe we're supposed to talk first. Maybe it's considered bad manners to rip her face off and feed it to her if she doesn't agree to leave.

Standing in the shadow of a recessed storefront, just beyond the edge of the artificial safety the street-light offered to the children of the sun, she extended her senses the way she'd been taught and touched death within the maelstrom of life.

She found Phil, moments later, lying in yet another of the alleys that serviced the business of the day and provided a safe haven for the darker business of the night. His body was still warm but his heart had stopped beating and his blood no longer sang. Vicki touched the tiny, nearly closed wound she'd made in his wrist the night before and then the fresh wound in the bend of his elbow. She didn't know how he had died but she knew who had done it. He stank of the *other*.

Vicki no longer cared what was traditionally "done" in these instances. There would be no talking. No negotiating. It had gone one life beyond that.

"I rather thought that if I killed him you'd come and save me the trouble of tracking you down. And here you are, charging in without taking the slightest of precautions." Her voice was low, not so much threatening as in itself a threat. "You're hunting in my territory, child."

Still kneeling by Phil's side, Vicki lifted her head. Ten feet away, only her face and hands clearly visible, the other vampire stood. Without thinking—unable to think clearly through the red rage that shrieked for release—Vicki launched herself at the snow-white column of throat, finger hooked to talons, teeth bared.

The Beast Henry had spent a year teaching her to control, was loose. She felt herself lost in its raw power and she reveled in it.

The *other* made no move until the last possible second then she lithely twisted and slammed Vicki to one side.

Pain eventually brought reason back. Vicki lay panting in the fetid damp at the base of a dumpster, one eye swollen shut, a gash across her forehead still sluggishly bleeding. Her right arm was broken.

"You're strong," the other told her, a contemptuous gaze pinning her to the ground. "In another hundred years you might have stood a chance. But you're an infant. A child. You haven't the experience to control what you are. This will be your only warning. Get out of my territory. If we meet again, I *will* kill you."

Vicki sagged against the inside of the door and tried to lift her arm. During the two and a half hours it had taken her to get back to Celluci's house, the bone had begun to set. By tomorrow night, provided she fed in the hours remaining until dawn, she should be able use it.

"Vicki?"

She started. Although she'd known he was home, she'd assumed—without checking—that because of the hour he'd be asleep. She squinted as the hall light came on and wondered, listening to him pad down the stairs in bare feet, whether she had the energy to make it into the basement bathroom before he saw her.

He came into the kitchen, tying his bathrobe belt around him, and flicked on the overhead light. "We need to talk," he said grimly as the shadows that might have hidden her fled. "Jesus H. Christ. What the hell happened to you?"

"Nothing much." Eyes squinted nearly shut, Vicki gingerly probed the swelling on her forehead. "You should see the other guy."

Without speaking, Celluci reached over and hit the play button on the telephone answering machine.

"Vicki? Henry. If someone's hunting your territory, whatever you do, don't challenge. Do you hear me? *Don't* challenge. You can't win. They're going to be older, able to overcome the instinctive rage and remain in full command of their power. If you won't surrender the territory…" The sigh the tape played back gave a clear opinion of how likely he thought that was to occur. "…you're going to have to negotiate. If you can agree on boundaries there's no reason why you can't share the city." His voice suddenly belonged again to the lover she'd lost with the change. "Call me, please, before you do anything."

It was the only message on the tape.

"Why," Celluci asked as it rewound, his gaze taking in the cuts and the bruising and the filth, "do I get the impression that it's "the other guy" Fitzroy's talking about?"

Vicki tried to shrug. Her shoulders refused to co-operate. "It's my city, Mike. It always has been. I'm going to take it back."

He stared at her for a long moment then he shook his head. "You heard what Henry said. You can't win. You haven't been…what you are, long enough. It's only been fourteen months."

"I know." The rich scent of his life prodded the Hunger and she moved to put a little distance between them.

He closed it up again. "Come on." Laying his hand in the center of her back, he steered her towards the stairs. *Put it aside for now*, his tone told her. *We'll argue about it later.* "You need a bath."

"I need…"

"I know. But you need a bath first. I just changed the sheets."

The darkness wakes us all in different ways, Henry had told her. *We were all human once and we carried our differences through the change.*

For Vicki, it was like the flicking of a switch; one moment she wasn't, the next she was. This time, when she returned from the little death of the day, an idea returned with her.

Four hundred and fifty odd years a vampire, Henry had been seventeen when he changed. The *other* had walked the night for perhaps as long—her gaze had carried the weight of several life-times—but her physical appearance suggested that her mortal life had lasted even less time than Henry's had. Vicki allowed that it made sense. Disaster may have precipitated her change but passion was the usual cause.

And no one does that kind of never-say-die passion like a teenager.

It would be difficult for either Henry or the other to imagine a response that came out of a mortal not a vampiric experience. They'd both had centuries of the latter and not enough of the former to count.

Vicki had been only fourteen months a vampire but she'd been human thirty-two years when Henry'd saved her by draw-ing her to his blood to feed. During those thirty-two years, she'd been nine years a cop—two accelerated promotions, three cita-tions, and the best arrest record on the force.

There was no chance of negotiation.

She couldn't win if she fought.

She'd be damned if she'd flee.

"Besides..." For all she realized where her strength had to lie, Vicki's expression held no humanity. "...she owes me for Phil."

Celluci had left her a note on the fridge.

Does this have anything to do with Mac Eisler?

Vicki stared at it for a moment then scribbled her answer underneath.

Not anymore.

It took three weeks to find where the *other* spent her days. Vicki used old contacts where she could and made new ones where she had to. Any modern Van Helsing could have done the same.

For the next three weeks, Vicki hired someone to watch the *other* come and go, giving reinforced instructions to stay in the car with the windows closed and the air conditioning running. Life had an infinite number of variations but one piece of machinery smelled pretty much like any other. It irritated her that she couldn't sit stakeout herself but the information she needed would've kept her out after sunrise.

"How the hell did you burn your hand?"

Vicki continued to smear ointment over the blister. Unlike the injuries she'd taken in the alley, this would heal slowly and painfully. "Accident in a tanning salon."

"That's not funny."

She picked the roll of gauze up off the counter. "You're losing your sense of humor, Mike."

Celluci snorted and handed her the scissors. "I never had one."

"Mike, I wanted to warn you, I won't be back by sunrise."

Celluci turned slowly, the TV dinner he'd just taken from the microwave held in both hands. "What do you mean?"

She read the fear in his voice and lifted the edge of the tray so that the gravy didn't pour out and over his shoes. "I mean I'll be spending the day somewhere else."

"Where?"

"I can't tell you."

"Why? Never mind." He raised a hand as her eyes narrowed. "Don't tell me. I don't want to know. You're going after that other vampire aren't you? The one Fitzroy told you to leave alone."

"I thought you didn't want to know."

"I already know," he grunted. "I can read you like a book. With large type. And pictures."

Vicki pulled the tray from his grip and set it on the counter. "She's killed two people. Eisler was a scumbag who may have deserved it but the other…"

"Other?" Celluci exploded. "Jesus H. Christ, Vicki, in case you've forgotten, murder's against the law! Who the hell painted a big vee on your long-johns and made you the vampire vigilante?"

"Don't you remember?" Vicki snapped. "You were there. I didn't make this decision, Mike. You and Henry made it for me. You'd just better learn to live with it." She fought her way back to calm. "Look, you can't stop her but I can. I know that galls but that's the way it is."

They glared at each other, toe to toe. Finally Celluci looked away.

"I can't stop you, can I?" he asked bitterly. "I'm only human after all."

"Don't sell yourself short," Vicki snarled. "You're quintessentially human. If you want to stop me, you face me and ask me not to go and *then* you remember it every time *you* go into a situation that could get your ass shot off."

After a long moment, he swallowed, lifted his head, and met her eyes. "Don't die. I thought I lost you once and I'm not strong enough to go through that again."

"Are you asking me not to go?"

He snorted. "I'm asking you to be careful. Not that you ever listen."

She took a step forward and rested her head against his shoulder, wrapping herself in the beating of his heart. "This time, I'm listening."

The studios in the converted warehouse on King Street were not supposed to be live-in. A good seventy-five percent of the tenants ignored that. The studio Vicki wanted was at the back on the third floor. The heavy steel door—an obvious upgrade by the occupant—had been secured by the best lock money could buy.

New senses and old skills got through it in record time.

Vicki pushed open the door with her foot and began carrying boxes inside. She had a lot to do before dawn.

"She goes out every night between ten and eleven then she comes home every morning between four and five. You could set your watch by her."

Vicki handed him an envelope.

He looked inside, thumbed through the money, then grinned up at her. "Pleasure doing business for you. Any time you need my services, you know where to call."

"Forget it," she told him.

And he did.

Because she expected her, Vicki knew the moment the *other* entered the building. The Beast stirred and she tightened her grip on it. To lose control now would be disaster.

She heard the elevator, then footsteps in the hall.

"You know I'm in here," she said silently, *"and you know you can take me. Be overconfident, believe I'm a fool and walk right in."*

"I thought you were smarter than this." The *other* stepped into the apartment then casually turned to lock the door. "I told you when I saw you again I'd kill you."

Vicki shrugged, the motion masking her fight to remain calm. "Don't you even want to know why I'm here?"

"I assume, you've come to negotiate." She raised ivory hands and released thick, black hair from its bindings. "We went past that when you attacked me." Crossing the room, she preened before a large ornate mirror that dominated one wall of the studio.

"I attacked you because you murdered Phil."

"Was that his name?" The other laughed. The sound had razored edges. "I didn't bother to ask it."

"Before you murdered him."

"Murdered? You *are* a child. They are prey, we are predators—their deaths are ours if we desire them. You'd have learned that in time." She turned, the patina of civilization stripped away. "Too bad you haven't any time left."

Vicki snarled but somehow managed to stop herself from attacking. Years of training whispered, *Not yet.* She had to stay exactly where she was.

"Oh yes." The sibilants flayed the air between them. "I almost forgot. You wanted me to ask you why you came. Very well. Why?"

Given the address and the reason, Celluci could've come to the studio during the day and slammed a stake through the *other's* heart. The vampire's strongest protection would be of no use against him. Mike Celluci believed in vampires.

"I came," Vicki told her, "because some things you have to do yourself."

The wire ran up the wall, tucked beside the surface mounted cable of a cheap renovation, and disappeared into the shadows that clung to a ceiling sixteen feet from the floor. The switch had been stapled down beside her foot. A tiny motion, too small to evoke attack, flipped it.

Vicki had realized from the beginning that there were a number of problems with her plan. The first involved placement. Every living space included an area where the occupant felt secure—a favorite chair, a window...a mirror. The second problem was how to mask what she'd done. While the *other* would not be able to sense the various bits of wiring and equipment, she'd be fully aware of Vicki's scent *on* the wiring and equipment. Only if Vicki remained in the studio, could that smaller trace be lost in the larger.

The third problem was directly connected with the second. Given that Vicki had to remain, how was she to survive?

Attached to the ceiling by sheer brute strength, positioned so that they shone directly down into the space in front of the mirror, were a double bank of lights cannibalized from a tanning bed. The sun held a double menace for the vampire— its return to the sky brought complete vulnerability and its rays burned.

Henry had a round scar on the back of one hand from too close an encounter with the sun. When her burn healed, Vicki would have a matching one from a deliberate encounter with an imitation.

The *other* screamed as the lights came on, the sound pure rage and so inhuman that those who heard it would have to deny it for sanity's sake.

Vicki dove forward, ripped the heavy brocade off the back of the couch, and burrowed frantically into its depths. Even that instant of light had bathed her skin in flame and she moaned as for a moment the searing pain became all she was. After a time, when it grew no worse, she managed to open her eyes.

The light couldn't reach her, but neither could she reach the switch to turn it off. She could see it, three feet away, just beyond the shadow of the couch. She shifted her weight and a line of blister rose across one leg. Biting back a shriek, she curled into a fetal position, realizing her refuge was not entirely secure.

Okay genius, now what?

Moving very, very carefully, Vicki wrapped her hand around the one by two that braced the lower edge of the couch. From the tension running along it, she suspected that breaking it off would result in at least a partial collapse of the piece of furniture.

And if it goes, I very well may go with it.

And then she heard the sound of something dragging itself across the floor.

Oh shit! She's not dead!

The wood broke, the couch began to fall in on itself, and Vicki, realizing that luck would have a large part to play in her survival, smacked the switch and rolled clear in the same motion.

The room plunged into darkness.

Vicki froze as her eyes slowly readjusted to the night. Which was when she finally became conscious of the smell. It had been there all along but her senses had refused to acknowledge it until they had to.

Sunlight burned.

Vicki gagged.

The dragging sound continued.

The hell with this! She didn't have time to wait for her eyes to repair the damage they'd obviously taken. She needed to see *now*. Fortunately, although it hadn't seemed fortunate at the time, she'd learned to maneuver without sight.

She threw herself across the room.

The light switch was where they always were, to the right of the door.

The thing on the floor pushed itself up on fingerless hands and glared at her out of the blackened ruin of a face. Laboriously it turned, hate radiating off it in palpable waves and began to pull itself towards her again.

Vicki stepped forward to meet it.

While the part of her that remembered being human writhed in revulsion, she wrapped her hands around its skull and twisted it in a full circle. The spine snapped. Another full twist and what was left of the head came off in her hands.

She'd been human for thirty-two years but she'd been fourteen months a vampire.

"No one hunts in *my* territory," she snarled as the *other* crumbled to dust.

She limped over to the wall and pulled the plug supplying power to the lights. Later, she'd remove them completely—the whole concept of sunlamps gave her the creeps.

When she turned, she was facing the mirror.

The woman who stared out at her through bloodshot eyes, exposed skin blistered and red, was a hunter. Always had been really. The question became, who was she to hunt?

Vicki smiled. Before the sun drove her to use her inherited sanctuary, she had a few quick phone calls to make. The first to Celluci; she owed him the knowledge that she'd survived the night. The second to Henry for much the same reason.

The third call would be to the eight hundred line that covered the classifieds of Toronto's largest alternative newspaper. This ad was going to be a little different than the one she'd placed upon leaving the force. Back then, she'd been incredibly depressed about leaving a job she loved for a life she saw as only marginally useful. This time, she had no regrets.

Victory Nelson, Investigator: Otherworldly Crimes a Specialty.

I'm a huge fan of Georgette Heyer's regency novels so when Pat Elrod asked me to do a story for a historical vampire anthology she was editing, I asked, in turn, if I could use Regency England. Pat was agreeable and so Henry Fitzroy sat down to play cards.

WHAT MANNER OF MAN

Shortly after three o'clock in the morning, Henry Fitzroy rose from the card table, brushed a bit of ash from the sleeve of his superbly fitting coat and inclined his head toward his few remaining companions. "If you'll excuse me, gentlemen, I believe I'll call it a night."

"Well, I won't excuse you." Sir William Wyndham glared up at Fitzroy from under heavy lids. "You've won eleven hundred pounds off me tonight, damn your eyes, and I want a chance to win it back."

His gaze flickering down to the cluster of empty bottles by Wyndham's elbow, Henry shook his head. "I don't think so, Sir William, not tonight."

"You don't think so?" Wyndham half rose in his chair, dark brows drawn into a deep vee over an aristocratic arc of nose. His elbow rocked one of the bottles. It began to fall.

Moving with a speed that made it clear he had not personally been indulging over the course of the evening's play, Henry caught the bottle just before it hit the floor. "Brandy," he chided softly, setting it back on the table, "is no excuse for bad manners."

Wyndham stared at him for a moment, confusion replacing the anger on his face, instinct warning him of a danger reason couldn't see. "Your pardon," he said at last. "Perhaps another night." He watched as the other man bowed and left, then muttered, "Insolent puppy."

"Who is?" asked another of the players, dragging his attention away from the brandy.

"Fitzroy." Raising his glass to his mouth, his hand surprisingly steady considering how much he'd already drunk, Wyndham tossed back the contents. "He speaks to me like that again and he can name his seconds."

"Well, *I* wouldn't fight him."

"No one's asking you to."

"He's just the sort of quiet chap who's the very devil when pushed too far. I've seen that look in his eyes, I tell you—the very devil when pushed too far."

"Shut up." Opening a fresh deck, Wyndham sullenly pushed Henry Fitzroy from his thoughts and set about trying to make good his losses.

His curly brimmed beaver set at a fashionably rakish angle on his head, Henry stood on the steps of his club and stared out at London. Its limits had expanded since the last time he'd made it his principal residence, curved courts of elegant townhouses had risen where he remembered fields, but, all in all, it hadn't changed much. There was still something about London—a feel, an atmosphere—shared by no other city in the world.

One guinea-gold brow rose as he shot an ironic glance upward at the haze that hung over the buildings, the smoke from a thousand chimney pots that blocked the light of all but the brightest stars. Atmosphere was, perhaps, a less than appropriate choice of words.

"Shall I get you a hackney or a chair, Mr. Fitzroy?"

"Thank you, no." He smiled at the porter, his expression calculated to charm, and heard the elderly man's heart begin to beat a little faster. The Hunger rose in response but he firmly pushed it back. It would be the worst of bad ton to feed so close to home. It would also be dangerous but, in the England of the Prince Regent, safety came second to social approval. "I believe I'll walk."

"If you're sure, sir. There's some bad'uns around after dark."

"I'm sure." Henry's smile broadened. "I doubt I'll be bothered."

* * *

The porter watched as the young man made his way down the stairs and along St. James Street. He'd watched a lot of gentlemen during the years he'd worked the clubs—first at Boodles, then at Brook's, and finally here at White's—and Mr. Henry Fitzroy had the unmistakable mark of Quality. For all he was so polite and soft-spoken, something about him spoke strongly of power. It would, the porter decided, take a desperate man, or a stupid one, to put Mr. Fitzroy in any danger. *Of course, London has no shortage of either desperate or stupid men.*

"Take care, sir," he murmured as he turned to go inside.

Henry quelled the urge to lift a hand in acknowledgement of the porter's concern, judging that he'd moved beyond the range of mortal hearing. As the night air held a decided chill, he shoved his hands deep in the pockets of his many-caped greatcoat, even though it would have to get a great deal colder before he'd feel it. A successful masquerade demanded attention to small details.

Humming under his breath, he strode down Brook Street to Grosvenor Square, marveling at the new technological wonder of the gaslights. The long lines of little brightish dots created almost as many shadows as they banished but they were still a big improvement over a servant carrying a lantern on a stick. That he had no actual need of the light, Henry considered unimportant in view of the achievement.

Turning toward his chambers in Albany, he heard the unmistakable sounds of a fight. He paused, head cocked, sifting through the lives involved. Three men beating a fourth.

"Not at all sporting," he murmured, moving forward so quickly that, had anyone been watching, it would have seemed he simply disappeared.

"Be sure that he's dead." The man who spoke held a narrow sword in one hand and the cane it had come out of in the other. The man on the ground groaned and the steel point moved around. "Never mind, I'll take care of it myself."

Wearing an expression of extreme disapproval, Henry stepped out of the shadows, grabbed the swordsman by the back of his coat, and threw him down the alley. When the other two whirled to face him, he drew his lips back off his teeth and said, in a tone of polite, but inarguable menace, "Run."

Prey recognized predator. They ran.

He knelt by the wounded man, noted how the heartbeat faltered, looked down, and saw a face he knew. Captain Charles Evans of the Horse Guards, the nephew of the current Earl of Whitby. Not one of his few friends—friends were chosen with a care honed by centuries of survival—but Henry couldn't allow him to die alone in some dark alley like a stray dog.

A sudden noise drew his attention around to the man with the sword-cane. Up on his knees, his eyes unfocused, he groped around for his weapon. Henry snarled. The man froze, whimpered once, then, face twisted with fear, scrambled to his feet and joined his companions in flight.

The sword had punched a hole high in the captain's left shoulder, not immediately fatal but bleeding to death was a distinct possibility.

"Fitz...roy?"

"So you're awake are you?" Taking the other man's chin in a gentle grip, Henry stared down into pain-filled eyes. "I think it might be best if you trusted me and slept," he said quietly.

The captain's lashes fluttered then settled down to rest against his cheeks like fringed shadows.

Satisfied that he was unobserved, Henry pulled aside the bloodstained jacket—like most military men, Captain Evans favored Scott—and bent his head over the wound.

"You cut it close. Sun's almost up."

Henry pushed past the small, irritated form of his servant. "Don't fuss, Varney, I've plenty of time."

"Plenty of time is it?" Closing and bolting the door, the little man hurried down the short hall in Henry's shadow. "I was worried sick, I was, and all you can say is don't fuss?"

Sighing, Henry shrugged out of his greatcoat—a muttering Varney caught it before it hit the floor—and stepped into his sitting room. There was a fire lit in the grate, heavy curtains over the window that opened onto a tiny balcony, and a thick oak slab of a door replacing the folding doors that had originally led to the bedchamber. The furniture was heavy and dark, as close as Henry could come to the furniture of his youth. It had been purchased in a fit of nostalgia and was now mostly ignored.

"You've blood on your cravat!"

"It's not mine," Henry told him mildly.

Varney snorted. "Didn't expect it was but you're usually neater than that. Probably won't come out. Blood stains, you know."

"I know."

"Mayhap if I soak it…" The little man quivered with barely concealed impatience.

Henry laughed and unwound the offending cloth, dropping it over the offered hand. After thirty years of unique service, certain liberties were unavoidable. "I won eleven hundred pounds from Lord Wyndham tonight."

"You and everyone else. He's bad dipped. Barely a feather to fly with so I hear. Rumor has it, he's getting a bit desperate."

"And I returned a wounded Charlie Evans to the bosom of his family."

"Nice bosom so I hear."

"Don't be crude, Varney." Henry sat down and lifted one foot after the other to have the tight Hessians pulled gently off. "I think I may have prevented him from being killed."

"Robbery?"

"I don't know."

"How many did you kill?"

"No one. I merely frightened them away."

Setting the gleaming boots to one side, Varney stared at his master with frank disapproval. "You merely frightened them away?"

"I did consider ripping their throats out but as it wasn't actually necessary, it wouldn't have been…" he paused and smiled. "…polite."

"Polite!? You risked exposure so as you can be polite?"

The smile broadened. "I am a creature of my time."

"You're a creature of the night! You know what'll come of this? Questions, that's what. And we don't need questions!"

"I have complete faith in your ability to handle whatever might arise."

Recognizing the tone, the little man deflated. "Aye and well you might," he muttered darkly. "Let's get that jacket off you before I've got to carry you in to your bed like a sack of meal."

"I *can* do it myself," Henry remarked as he stood and turned to have his coat carefully peeled from his shoulders.

"Oh, aye, and leave it lying on the floor no doubt." Folding the coat in half, Varney draped it over one skinny arm. "I'd never get the wrinkles out. You'd go about looking like you dressed out of a ragbag if it wasn't for me. Have you eaten?" He looked suddenly hopeful.

One hand on the bedchamber door, Henry paused. "Yes," he said softly.

The thin shoulders sagged. "Then what're you standing about for?"

A few moments later, the door bolted, the heavy shutter over the narrow window secured, Henry Fitzroy, vampire, bastard son of Henry the VIII, once Duke of Richmond and Somerset, Earl of Nottingham, and Lord President of the Council of the North, slid into the day's oblivion.

"My apologies, Mrs. Evans, for not coming by sooner, but I was out when your husband's message arrived." Henry laid his hat and gloves on the small table in the hall and allowed the waiting footman to take his coat. "I trust he's in better health than he was when I saw him last night?"

"A great deal better, thank you." Although there were purple shadows under her eyes and her cheeks were more than fashionably pale, Lenore Evans' smile lit up her face. "The doctor says he lost a lot of blood but he'll recover. If it hadn't been for you…"

As her voice trailed off, Henry bowed slightly. "I was happy to help." Perhaps he *had* taken a dangerous chance. Perhaps he should have wiped all memory of his presence from the Captain's mind and left him on his own doorstep like an oversized infant. Having become involved, he couldn't very well ignore the message an obviously disapproving Varney had handed him at sunset with a muttered, *I told you so.*

It appeared that there were indeed going to be questions.

Following Mrs. Evans up the stairs, he allowed himself to be ushered into a well-appointed bedchamber and left alone with the man in the bed.

Propped up against his pillows, recently shaved but looking wan and tired, Charles Evans nodded a greeting. "Fitzroy. I'm glad you've come."

Henry inclined his own head in return, thankful that the bloodscent had been covered by the entirely unappetizing smell of basilicum powder. "You're looking remarkably well, all things considered."

"I've you to thank for that."

"I really did very little."

"True enough, you *only* saved my life." The captain's grin was infectious and Henry found himself returning it in spite of an intention to remain aloof. "Mind you, Dr. Harris did say he'd never seen such a clean wound." One hand rose to touch the bandages under his nightshirt. "He said I was healing faster than any man he'd ever examined."

As his saliva had been responsible for that accelerated healing, Henry remained silent. It had seemed foolish to resist temptation when there'd been so much blood going to waste.

"Anyway..." The grin disappeared and the expressive face grew serious. "I owe you my life and I'm very grateful you came along but that's not why I asked you to visit. I can't get out of this damned bed and I have to trust someone." Shadowed eyes lifted to Henry's face. "Something tells me that I can trust you."

"You barely know me," Henry murmured, inwardly cursing his choice of words the night before. He'd told Evans to trust him and now it seemed he was to play the role of confidant. He could remove the trust as easily as he'd placed it but something in the man's face made him hesitate. Whatever bothered him, involved life and death—Henry had seen the latter too often to mistake it now. Sighing, he added, "I can't promise anything, but I'll listen."

"Please." Gesturing at a chair, the captain waited until his guest had seated himself, then waited a little longer, apparently searching for a way to begin. After a few moments, he lifted his chin. "You know I work at the Home Office?"

"I had heard as much, yes." In the last few years, gossip had become the preferred entertainment of all classes and Varney was a devoted participant.

"Well, for the last little while—just since the start of the Season, in fact—things have been going missing."

"Things?"

"Papers. Unimportant ones for the most part, until now." His mouth twisted up into a humorless grin. "I can't tell you exactly what the latest missing document contained—in spite of everything we'd still rather it wasn't common knowledge—but I can tell you that if it gets into the wrong hands, into French hands, a lot of British soldiers are going to die."

"Last night you were following the thief?"

"No. The man we think is his contact. A french spy named Yves Bouchard."

Henry shook his head, interested in spite of himself. "The man who stabbed you last night was no Frenchman. I heard him speak, and he was as English as you or I. English, and though I hesitate to use the term, a Gentleman."

"That's Bouchard. He's the only son of an old emigre family. They left France during the revolution—Yves was a mere infant at the time and now he dreams of restoring the family fortunes under Napoleon."

"One would have thought he'd be more interested in defeating Napoleon and restoring the rightful king."

Evans shrugged, winced and said, "Apparently not. Anyway, Bouchard's too smart to stay around after what happened last night. I kept him from getting his hands on the document, now we have to keep it from leaving England by another means."

"We?" Henry asked, surprised into ill-mannered incredulity. "You and I?"

"Mostly you. The trouble is, we don't know who actually took the document although we've narrowed it down to three men who are known to be in Bouchard's confidence and who have access to the Guard's offices."

"One moment, please." Henry raised an exquisitely mani- cured hand. "You want me to find your spy for you?"

"Yes."

"Why?"

"Because I can't be certain of anyone else in my office and because I trust you."

Realizing he had only himself to blame, Henry sighed. "And I suppose you can't bring the three in for questioning because two of them are innocent?"

Evans' pained expression had nothing to do with his wound. "Only consider the scandal. I will if I must but, as this is Wednes- day and the information must be in France by Friday evening or it won't get to Napoleon in time for it to be of any use, one of those three will betray himself in the next two days."

"So the document must be recovered with no public outcry?"

"Exactly."

"I would have thought, the Bow Street Runners…"

"No. The Runners may be fine for chasing down highway men and murderers, but my three suspects move in the best circles. Only a man of their own class could get near them with- out arousing suspicion." He lifted a piece of paper off the table beside the bed and held it out to Henry, who stared at it for a long moment.

Lord Ruthven, Mr. Maxwell Aubrey, and Sir William Wyndham. Frowning, Henry looked up to meet Captain Evans' weary gaze. "You're sure about this?"

"I am. Send word when you're sure, I'll do the rest."

The exhaustion shading the other man's voice reminded Henry of his injury. Placing the paper back beside the bed, he stood. "This is certainly not what I expected."

"But you'll do it?"

He could refuse, could make the captain forget that this conversation had ever happened, but he had been a prince of England and, regardless of what he had become, he could not stand back and allow her to be betrayed. Hiding a smile at the thought of what Varney would have to say about such melodrama, he nodded. "Yes, I'll do it."

The sound of feminine voices rising up from the entryway caused Henry to pause for a moment on the landing.

"…so sorry to arrive so late, Mrs. Evans, but we were passing on our way to dinner before Almack's and my uncle insisted we stop and see how the Captain was doing."

Carmilla Amworth. There could be no mistaking the faint country accent not entirely removed by hours of lessons intended to erase it. She had enough fortune to be considered an Heiress and that, combined with a dark-haired, pale-skinned, waif-like beauty, brought no shortage of admirers. Unfortunately, she also had a disturbing tendency to giggle when she felt herself out of her depth.

"My uncle," she continued, "finds it difficult to get out of the carriage and so sent me in his place."

"I quite understand." The smile in the answering voice suggested a shared amusement. "Please tell your uncle that the captain is resting comfortably and thank him for his consideration."

A brief exchange of pleasantries later, Miss Amworth returned to her uncle's carriage and Henry descended the rest of the stairs.

Lenore Evans turned and leapt backwards, one hand to her heart, her mouth open. She would have fallen had Henry not caught her wrist and kept her on her feet.

He could feel her pulse racing beneath the thin sheath of heated skin. The Hunger rose and he hurriedly broke the contact. Self-indulgence, besides being vulgar, was a sure road to the stake.

"Heavens, you startled me." Cheeks flushed, she increased the distance between them. "I didn't hear you come down."

"My apologies. I heard Miss Amworth and didn't wish to break in on a private moment."

"Her uncle works with Charles and wanted to know how he was but her uncle is *also* a dear friend of his Royal Highness and is, shall we say, less than able to climb in and out of carriages. Is Charles...?"

"I left him sleeping."

"Good." Her right hand wrapped around the place where Henry had held her. She swallowed, then, as though reminded of her duties by the action, stammered, "Can I get you a glass of wine?"

"Thank you, no. I must be going."

"Good. That is, I mean..." Her flush deepened. "You must think I'm a complete idiot. It's just that with Charles injured..."

"I fully understand." He smiled, careful not to show teeth.

Lenore Evans closed the door behind her husband's guest and tried to calm the pounding of her heart. Something about Henry Fitzroy spoke to a part of her she'd thought belonged to Charles alone. Her response might have come out of gratitude for the saving of her husband's life, but she didn't think so. He was a handsome young man, and she found the soft curves of his mouth a fascinating contrast to the gentle strength in his grip.

Shaking her head in self-reproach, she lifted her skirts with damp hands and started up the stairs. "I'm beginning to think," she sighed, "that Aunt Georgette was right. Novels are a bad influence on a young woman."

What she needed now was a few hours alone with her husband but, as his wound made that impossible, she'd supposed she'd have to divert her thoughts with a book of sermons instead.

Almack's Assembly Rooms were the exclusive temple of the Beau Monde and vouchers to the weekly ball on Wednesday were among the most sought after items in London. What matter that the assembly rooms were plain, the dance floor inferior, the anterooms unadorned, and the refreshments unappetizing—this was the seventh heaven of the fashionable world and to be excluded from Almack's was to be excluded from the upper levels of society.

Henry, having discovered that a fashionable young man could live unremarked from dark to dawn, had effortlessly risen to the top.

After checking with the porter that all three of Captain Evans' potential spies were indeed in attendance, Henry left hat, coat and gloves and made his way up into the assembly rooms. Avoiding the gaze of Princess Esterhazy, who he considered to be rude and overbearing, he crossed the room and made his bow to the Countess Lieven.

"I hear you were quite busy last night, Mr. Fitzroy."

A little astonished by how quickly the information had made its way to such august ears, he murmured he had only done what any man would have.

"Indeed. Any *man*. Still, I should have thought the less of you had you expected a fuss to be made." Tapping her closed fan against her other hand, she favored him with a long, level look. "I have always believed there was more to you than you showed the world."

Fully aware that the Countess deserved her reputation as the cleverest woman in London, Henry allowed a little of his mask to slip.

She smiled, satisfied for the moment with being right and not overly concerned with what she had been right about. "Appearances, my dear Mr. Fitzroy, are everything. And now, I believe they are beginning a country-dance. Let me introduce you to a young lady in need of a partner."

Unable to think of a reason why she shouldn't, Henry bowed again. A few moments later, as he moved gracefully through the pattern of the dance, he wondered if he should pay the Countess a visit some night, had not made a decision by the time the dance ended, and put it off indefinitely as he escorted the young woman in his care back to her waiting mama.

Well aware that he looked, at best, in his early twenties, Henry could only be thankful that a well-crafted reputation as a man who trusted to the cards for the finer things in life took him off the Marriage Mart. No matchmaking mama would allow her daughter to become shackled to someone with such narrow prospects.

As he had no interest in giggling young damsels just out of the schoolroom, he could only be thankful. The older women he spent time with were much more...appetizing.

Trying not to stare, one of the young damsels so summarily dismissed in Henry's thoughts leaned toward a second and whispered, "I wonder what Mr. Fitzroy is smiling about."

The second glanced up, blushed rosily, and ducked her head. "He looks *hungry*."

The first, a little wiser in the ways of the world than her friend, sighed and laid silent odds that the curve of Mr. Henry Fitzroy's full lips had nothing to do with bread and butter.

Hearing a familiar voice, Henry searched through the moving couples and spotted Sir William Wyndham dancing with Carmilla Amworth. Hardly surprising if he'd lost as much money lately as Varney suggested. While Henry wouldn't have believed the fragile, country-bred heiress to his taste—it was a well known secret that he kept a yacht off Dover for the express purpose of entertaining the women of easy virtue he preferred—upon reflection he supposed Sir William would consider her inheritance sufficiently alluring. And a much safer way of recovering his fortune than selling state secrets to France.

With one of Captain Evans' suspects accounted for, Henry began to search for the other two, moving quietly and unobtrusively from room to room. As dancing was the object of the club and no high stakes were allowed, the card rooms contained only dowagers and those gentlemen willing to play whist for pennies. Although he found neither of the men he looked for, he did find Carmilla Amworth's uncle, Lord Beardsley. One of the Prince Regent's cronies, he was a stout and somewhat foolish middle-aged gentleman who smelled strongly of scent and creaked alarmingly when he moved. Considering the bulwark of his stays, Henry was hardly surprised that he'd been less than able to get out of the carriage to ask after Captain Evans.

"...cupped and felt much better," Lord Beardsley was saying as Henry entered the room. "His Royal Highness swears by cupping, you know. Must've had gallons taken out over the years."

Henry winced, glanced around, and left. As much as he deplored the waste involved in frequent cupping, he had no desire to avail himself of the Prince Regent's blood—which he strongly suspected would be better than ninety percent Madeira.

When he returned to the main assembly room, he found Aubrey on the dance floor and Lord Ruthven brooding in a corner. Sir William had disappeared but he supposed a two for one trade couldn't be considered bad odds and wondered just how he was expected to watch all three men at once. Obviously, he'd have to be more than a mere passive observer. The situation seemed to make it necessary he tackle Ruthven first.

Dressed in funereal black, the peer swept the room with a somber gaze. He gave no indication that he'd noticed Henry's approach and replied to his greeting with a curt nod.

"I'm surprised to see you here, Lord Ruthven." Henry locked eyes with the lord and allowed enough power to ensure a reply. "It is well known you do not dance."

"I am here to meet someone."

"Who, if I may be so bold as to ask. I've recently come from the card rooms and may have seen him."

A muscle jumped under the sallow skin of Ruthven's cheek. To Henry's surprise, he looked away, sighed deeply, and said, "It is of no account as he is not yet here."

Impressed by the man's willpower—if unimpressed by his theatrical melancholy—Henry bowed and moved away. The man's sullen disposition and cold, corpse-grey eyes isolated him from the society his wealth and title gave him access to. Could he be taking revenge against those who shunned him by selling secrets to the French? Perhaps. This was not the time, nor the place, for forcing an answer.

Treading a careful path around a cluster of turbaned dowagers—more dangerous amass than a crowd of angry peasants with torches and pitchforks—Henry made his way to the side of a young man he knew from White's and asked for an introduction to Mr. Maxwell Aubrey.

"Good lord, Henry, whatever for?"

Henry smiled disarmingly. "I hear he's a damnably bad card player."

"He is, but if you think to pluck him, you're a year too late or two years too early. He doesn't come into his capital until he's twenty-five and after the chicken incident, his trustees keep a tight hold of the purse strings."

"Chicken incident?"

"That's right, it happened before you came to London. You see, Aubrey fell in with this fellow named Bouchard."

"Yves Bouchard?"

"That's right. Anyway, Bouchard had Aubrey wrapped around his little finger. Dared him to cluck like a chicken in the middle of the dance floor. I thought Mrs. Drummond-Burrell was going to have spasms. Neither Bouchard nor Aubrey were given vouchers for the rest of the Season."

"And this Season?"

He nodded at Aubrey who was leading his partner off the dance floor. "This Season, all is forgiven."

"And Bouchard?" Henry asked.

"Bouchard too. Although he doesn't seem to be here tonight."

So Aubrey was wrapped around Bouchard's little finger. *Wrapped tightly enough to spy for the French?* Henry wondered.

The return of a familiar voice diverted his attention. He turned to see Sir William once again playing court to Carmilla. When she giggled and looked away, it only seemed to inspire Sir William the more. Henry moved closer until he could hear her protests. She sounded both flattered and frightened.

Now that's a combination impossible to resist, Henry thought, watching Wyndham respond. With a predator's fluid grace, he deftly inserted himself between them. "I believe this dance is mine." When Carmilla giggled but made no objection, there was nothing Wyndham could do but quietly seethe.

Once on the floor, Henry smiled down into cornflower blue eyes. "I hope you'll forgive me for interfering, Miss Amworth, but Sir William's attentions seemed to be bothering you."

She dropped her gaze to the vicinity of his waistcoat. "Not bothering, but a bit overwhelming. I'm glad of the chance to gather my thoughts."

"I feel I should warn you, he has a sad reputation."

"He is a very accomplished flirt."

"He is a confirmed rake, Miss Amworth."

"Do you think he is more than merely flirting then?" Her voice held a hint of hope.

Immortality, Henry mused, *would not provide time enough to understand women.* Granted, Sir William had been blessed with darkly sardonic good looks and an athletic build but he was also—the possibility of his being a spy aside—an arrogant, self-serving libertine. Some women were drawn to that kind of danger; he had not thought Carmilla Amworth to be one of them. His gaze dropped to the pulse beating at an ivory temple and he wondered just how much danger she dared to experience.

Obviously aware that she should be at least attempting conversation, she took a deep breath and blurted, "I hear you saved Captain Evans last night."

Had everyone heard about it? Varney would not be pleased. "It was nothing."

"My maid says that he was set upon by robbers and you saved his life."

"Servants' gossip."

A dimple appeared beside a generous mouth. "Servants usually know."

Considering his own servant, Henry had to admit the truth of that.

"Were they robbers?"

"I didn't know you were so bloodthirsty, Miss Amworth." When she merely giggled and shook her head, he apologized and added, "I don't know what they were. They ran off as I approached."

"Surely Captain Evans knew."

"If he did, he didn't tell me."

"It must have been so exciting." Her voice grew stronger and her chin rose, exposing the soft flesh of her throat. "There are times I long to just throw aside all this so-called polite society."

I should have fed before I came. After a brief struggle with his reaction, Henry steered the conversation to safer grounds. It wasn't difficult as Carmilla, apparently embarrassed by her brief show of passion, answered only yes and no for the rest of the dance.

As he escorted her off the floor, Wyndham moved possessively toward her. While trying to decide just how far he should extend his protection, Henry saw Aubrey and Ruthven leave the room together. He heard the younger man say "Bouchard" and lost the rest of their conversation in the surrounding noise.

Good lord, are they both involved?

"My dance this time, I believe, Fitzroy." Shooting Henry an obvious warning, Sir William captured Carmilla's hand and began to lead her away. She seemed fascinated by him and he, for his part, clearly intended to have her.

Fully aware that the only way to save the naive young heiress was to claim her himself, Henry reluctantly went after Aubrey and Ruthven.

By the time he reached King Street, the two men were distant shadows, almost hidden by the night. Breathing deeply in an effort to clear his head of the warm, meaty odor of the assembly rooms, Henry followed, his pace calculated to close the distance between them without drawing attention to himself. An experienced hunter knew better than to spook his prey.

He could hear Aubrey talking of a recent race meeting, could hear Ruthven's monosyllabic replies, and heard nothing at all that would link them to the missing document or to Yves Bouchard. Hardly surprising. Only fools would speak of betraying their country so publicly.

When they went into Aubrey's lodgings near Portman Square, Henry wrapped himself in darkness and climbed to the small balcony off the sitting room. He felt a bit foolish, skulking about like a common housebreaker. Captain Evans' desire to avoid a scandal, while admirable, was becoming irritating.

"Here it is."

"Are you sure?" Ruthven's heart pounded as though he'd been running. It all but drowned out the sound of paper rustling.

"Why would Bouchard lie to me?"

Why indeed? A door opened, and closed, and Henry was on the street waiting for Ruthven when he emerged from the building. He was about to step forward when a carriage rumbled past, reminding him that, in spite of the advanced hour, the street was far from empty.

Following close on Ruthven's heels—and noting that wherever the dour peer was heading it wasn't toward home—Henry waited until he passed the mouth of a dark and deserted mews then made his move. With one hand around Ruthven's throat and the other holding him against a rough stone wall, his lips drew back off his teeth in involuntary anticipation of the other man's terror.

To his astonishment, Ruthven merely declared with gloomy emphasis. "Come Death, strike. Do not keep me waiting any longer."

His own features masked by the night, Henry frowned. Mouth slightly open to better taste the air, he breathed in an acrid odor he recognized. "You're drunk!" Releasing his grip, he stepped back.

"Although it is none of your business, I am always drunk." Under his customary scowl Ruthven's dull grey eyes flicked from side to side, searching the shadows.

That explained a great deal about Ruthven's near legendary melancholy and perhaps it explained something else as well. "Is that why you're spying for France?"

"The only thing I do for France is drink their liquor." The peer drew himself up to his full height. "And Death or not, I resent your implication."

His protest held the ring of truth. "Then what do you want with Yves Bouchard?"

"He said he could get me..." All at once he stopped and stared despondently into the night. "That also is none of your business."

Beginning to grow irritated, Henry snarled.

Ruthven pressed himself back against the wall. "I ordered a cask of brandy from him. Don't ask me how he smuggles it through the blockade because I don't know. He was to meet me tonight at Almack's but he never came."

"What did Maxwell Aubrey give you?"

"Bouchard's address." As the wine once again overcame his fear—imitation willpower, Henry realized—Ruthven's scowl deepened. "I don't believe you are Death. You're nothing but a common-cutpurse." His tone dripped disdain. "I shall call for the Watch."

"Go right ahead." Henry's hand darted forward, patted Ruthven's vest, and returned clutching Bouchard's address. Slipping the piece of paper into an inner pocket, he stepped back and merged with the night.

Varney would probably insist that Ruthven should die but Henry suspected that nothing he said would be believed. Besides, if he told everyone he'd met Death in an alley, he wouldn't be far wrong.

As expected, Bouchard was not in his rooms.

And neither, upon returning to Portman Square, was Maxwell Aubrey. Snarling softly to himself, Henry listened to a distant watchman announce it was a fine night. At just past two, it was certainly early enough for Aubrey to have gone to one of his clubs, or to a gaming hell, or to a brothel. Unfortunately, all Henry knew of him was that he was an easily influenced young man. Brow furrowed, he'd half decided to head back toward St. James Street when he heard the crash of breaking branches coming from the park the square enclosed.

Curious, he walked over to the wrought iron fence and peered up into an immense old oak. Believing himself familiar with every nuance of the night, he was astonished to see Aubrey perched precariously on a swaying limb, arms wrapped tightly around another, face nearly as white as his crumpled cravat.

"What the devil are you doing up there?" Henry demanded, beginning to feel that Captain Evans had sent him on a fool's mission. The night was rapidly taking on all the aspects of high farce.

Wide-eyed gaze searching the darkness for the source of the voice, Aubrey flashed a nervous smile in all directions. "Seeber dared me to spend a night in one of these trees," he explained ingenuously. Then he frowned. "You're not the Watch are you?"

"No, I'm not the Watch."

"Good. That is, I imagine it would hard to explain this to the Watch."

"I imagine it would be," Henry repeated dryly.

"You see, it's not as easy as it looks like it would be." He shifted position slightly and squeezed his eyes closed as the branch he sat on bobbed and swayed.

The man was an idiot and obviously not capable of being a French spy. Bouchard would have to be a greater idiot to trust so pliable a tool.

"I don't suppose you could help me down."

Henry considered it. "No," he said at last and walked away.

He found Sir William Wyndham, the last name on the list, and therefore the traitor by default, at White's playing deep basset. Carefully guarding his expression after Viscount Hanely had met him in a dimly lit hall and leapt away in terror, Henry declined all invitations to play. Much like a cat at a mouse hole, he watched and waited for Sir William to leave.

Unfortunately, Sir William was winning.

At five, lips drawn back off his teeth, Henry left the club. He could feel the approaching dawn and had to feed before the day claimed him. He had intended to feed upon Sir William, leaving him weak and easy prey for the captain's men—but Sir William obviously had no intention of leaving the table while his luck held.

The porter who handed Mr. Fitzroy his greatcoat and hat averted his gaze and spent the next hour successfully convincing himself that he hadn't seen what he knew he had.

Walking quickly through the dregs of the night, Henry returned to Albany but, rather than enter his own chambers, he continued to where he could gain access to the suite on the second floor. Entering silently through the large window, he crossed to the bed and stared down at its sleeping occupant.

George Gordon, the 6th Lord Byron, celebrated author of *Childe Harold's Pilgrimage*, was indeed a handsome young man. Henry had never seen him as having the ethereal and poignant beauty described by Caroline Lamb but then, he realized, Caro Lamb had never seen the poet with his hair in paper curlers.

His bad mood swept away by the rising Hunger, Henry sat down on the edge of the bed and softly called Byron's name, drawing him up but not entirely out of sleep.

The wide mouth curved into an anticipatory smile, murmuring "Incubus" without quite waking.

"I don't like you going to see that poet," Varney muttered, carefully setting the buckled shoes to one side. "You're going to end up in trouble there, see if you don't."

"He thinks I'm a dream." Henry ran both hand back through his hair and grinned, remembering the curlers. So much for Byron's claim that the chestnut ringlets were natural. "What could possibly happen?"

"You could end up in one of his stories, that's what." Unable to read, Varney regarded books with a superstitious awe that bordered on fear. "The secret'd be out and some fine day it'd be the stake sure as I'm standing here." The little man drew himself up to his full height and fixed Henry with an indignant glare. "I told you before and I'll tell you again, you got yourself so mixed up in this society thing you're forgetting what you are! You got to stop taking so many chances." His eyes glittered. "Try and remember, most folks don't look kindly on the bloodsucking undead."

"I'll try and remember." Glancing up at his servant over steepled fingers, Henry added, "I've something for you to do today. I need Sir William Wyndham watched. If he's visited by someone named Yves Bouchard, go immediately to Captain Evans; he'll know what to do. If he tries to leave London, stop him."

Brows that crossed above Varney's nose in a continuous line, lifted. "How stopped?"

"Stopped. Anything else, I want to be told at sunset."

"So, what did this bloke do that he's to be stopped?" Varney raised his hand lest Henry get the wrong idea. "Not that I won't stop him, mind, in spite of how I feel about you suddenly taking it into your head to track down evil doers. You know me, give me an order and I'll follow it."

"Which is why I found you almost dead in a swamp outside Plassey while the rest of your regiment was *inside* Plassey?"

"Not the same thing at all," the ex-soldier told him, pointedly waiting for the answer to his question.

"He sold out Wellington's army to the French."

Varney grunted. "Stopping's too good for him."

"Sir William Wyndham got a message this afternoon. Don't know what was in it, but he's going to be taking a trip to the coast tonight."

"Damn him!" Henry dragged his shirt over his head. "He's taking the information to Napoleon *himself!*"

Varney shrugged and brushed invisible dust off a green striped waistcoat. "I don't know about that but, if his coachman's to be trusted, he's heading for the coast right enough, soon as the moon lights the road."

Henry stood on the steps of Sir William's townhouse, considered his next move and decided the rising moon left him no time to be subtle.

The butler who answered the imperious summons of the polished brass knocker, opened his mouth to deny this inopportune visitor entry but closed it again without making a sound.

"Take me to Sir William," Henry commanded.

Training held, but only just. "Very good, sir. If you would follow me." The butler's hand trembled sightly but his carefully modulated voice gave no indication that he had just been shown his own mortality. "Sir William is in the library, sir. Through this door here. Shall I announce you?"

With one hand on the indicated door, Henry shook his head. "That won't be necessary. In fact, you should forget I was ever here."

Lost in the surprisingly dark depths of the visitor's pale eyes, the butler shuddered. "Thank you, sir. I will."

Three sets of branched candelabra lit the library, more than enough for Henry to see that the room held two large leather chairs, a number of hunting trophies, and very few books.

Sir William, dressed for travel in breeches and top boots, stood leaning on the mantelpiece reading a single sheet of paper. He turned when he heard the door open and scowled when he saw who it was. "Fitzroy! What the devil are you doing here? I told Babcock I was not to be..."

Then his voice trailed off as he got a better look at Henry's face. There were a number of men in London he considered to be dangerous but until this moment, he would not have included Henry Fitzroy among them. Forcing his voice past the growing panic he stammered, "W,what?"

"You dare to ask when you're holding *that*!" A pale hand shot forward to point at the paper in Wyndham's hand.

"This?" Confusion momentarily eclipsed the fear. "What has this to do with you?"

Henry charged across the room, grabbed a double handful of cloth and slammed the traitor against the wall. "It has everything to do with me!"

"I didn't know! I swear to God I didn't know!" Hanging limp in Henry's grasp, Sir William made no struggle to escape. Every instinct screamed "RUN!" but a last vestige of reason realized he wouldn't get far. "If I'd known you were interested in her..."

"Who?"

"Carmilla Amworth."

Sir William crashed to his knees as Henry released him and stepped back. "So that's how you were going to hide it," he growled. "A seduction on your fabled yacht. Was a French boat to meet you in the channel?"

"A French boat?"

"Or were you planning on finding sanctuary with Napoleon? And what of Miss Amworth, compromised both by your lechery and your treason?"

"Treason?"

"Forcing her to marry you would gain you her fortune but tossing her overboard would remove the only witness." Lips drawn back off his teeth, Henry buried his hand in Sir William's hair and forced his head back. Cravat and collar were thrown to the floor, exposing the muscular column of throat. "I don't know how you convinced her to accompany you, but it doesn't really matter now."

With the last of his strength, Sir William shoved the crumpled piece of paper in Henry's face, his life saved by the faint scent of a familiar perfume clinging to it.

Henry managed to turn aside only because he'd fed at dawn. His left hand clutching the note, his right still holding Sir William's hair, he straightened.

"*...I can no longer deny you but it must be tonight for reasons I can not disclose at this time.*" It was signed, C. Amworth.

Frowning, he looked down into Sir William's face. If Carmilla had insisted that they leave for the yacht tonight there could be only one answer. "Did Yves Bouchard suggest you seduce Miss Amworth?"

"I do not seduce young woman on the suggestion of acquaintances," Sir William replied as haughtily as possible under the circumstances. "However," he added hurriedly as the hazel eyes locked onto his began to darken, "Bouchard may have mentioned she was not only rich but ripe for the plucking."

So, there was the Bouchard connection. Caught between the two men, Carmilla Amworth was being used by both. By Bouchard to gain access to Wyndham's yacht and therefore France. By Wyndham to gain access to her fortune. And that seemed to be all that Sir William was guilty of. Still frowning, Henry stepped back. "Well, if you didn't steal the document," he growled, "who did?"

"I did." As he turned, Carmilla pointed a small but eminently serviceable pistol at him. "I've been waiting in Sir William's carriage these last few moments and when no one emerged, I let myself in. Stay right where you are, Mr. Fitzroy," she advised, no longer looking either fragile or waif-like. "I am held to be a very good shot." Her calm gaze took in the positions of the two men and she suddenly smiled, dimples appearing in both cheeks. "Were you fighting for my honor?"

Lips pressed into a thin line, Henry bowed his head. "Until I discovered you had none."

The smile disappeared. "I was raised a republican, Mr. Fitzroy, and I find the thought of that fat fool returning to the throne of France to be ultimately distasteful. In time..." Her eyes blazed. "...I'll help England be rid of her own fat fool."

"You think the English will rise and overthrow the royal family?"

"I know they will."

"If they didn't rise when m..." About to say, *my father*, he hastily corrected himself. "...when King Henry burned Catholic and Protestant indiscriminately in the street what makes you think they'll rise now?"

Her delicate chin lifted. "The old ways are finished. It's long past time for things to change."

"And does your uncle believe as you do?"

"My uncle knows nothing. His little niece would come visiting him at his office and little bits of paper would leave with her." The scornful laugh had as much resemblance to the previous giggles as night to day. "I'd love to stand around talking politics with you, but I haven't the time." Her lavender kid glove tightened around the butt of one of Manton's finest. "There'll be a French boat meeting Sir William's yacht very early tomorrow morning and I have information I must deliver."

"You used me!" Scowling, Sir William got slowly to his feet. "I don't appreciate being used." He took a step forward but Henry stopped him with a raised hand.

"You're forgetting the pistol."

"The pistol?" Wyndham snorted. "No woman would have the fortitude to kill a man in cold blood."

Remembering how both his half-sisters had held the throne, Henry shook his head. "You'd be surprised. However," he fixed Carmilla with an inquiring stare, "we seem to be at a stand-still as you certainly can't shoot both of us."

"True. But I'm sure both of you *gentlemen*..." The emphasis was less than complimentary. "...will co-operate lest I shoot
the other."

"I'm afraid you're going to shoot no one." Suddenly behind
her, Henry closed one hand around her wrist and the other around
the barrel of the gun. He had moved between one heartbeat and
the next; impossible to see, impossible to stop.

"What are you?" Carmilla whispered, her eyes painfully
wide in a face blanched of color.

His smile showed teeth. "A patriot." He'd been within a
moment of killing Sir William, ripping out his throat and feast-
ing on his life. His anger had been kicked sideways by Miss
Amworth's entrance and he supposed he should thank her
for preventing an unredeemable faux pas. "Sir William, if
you could have your footman go to the house of Captain
Charles Evans on Clarges Street, I think he'll be pleased to
know we've caught his traitor."

"...so they come and took the lady away but that still doesn't
explain where you've been 'til nearly sunup."

"I was with Sir William. We had unfinished business."

Varney snorted, his disapproval plain. "Oh. It was like that,
was it?"

Henry smiled as he remembered the feel of Sir William's
hair in his hand and the heat rising off his kneeling body.

Well aware of what the smile meant, Varney snorted again.
"And did Sir William ask what you were?"

"Sir William would never be so impolite. He thinks we fought
over Carmilla, discovered she was a traitor, drank ourselves
nearly senseless, and parted the best of friends." Feeling the sun
poised on the horizon, Henry stepped into his bedchamber and
turned to close the door on the day. "Besides, Sir William doesn't
want to know what I am."

"Got some news for you." Varney worked up a lather on the
shaving soap. "Something happened today."

Resplendent in a brocade dressing gown, Henry leaned back

in his chair and reached for the razor. "I imagine that something happens every day."

"Well *today*, that Carmilla Amworth slipped her chain and run off."

"She escaped from custody?"

"That's what I said. Seems they underestimated her, her being a lady and all. Still, she's missed her boat so even if she gets to France she'll be too late. You figure that's where she's heading?"

"I wouldn't dare to hazard a guess." Henry frowned and wiped the remaining lather off his face. "Is everyone talking about it?"

"That she was a French spy? Not likely, they're all too busy talking about how she snuck out of Lady Glebe's party and into Sir William's carriage." He clucked his tongue. "The upper classes have got dirty minds, that's what I say."

"Are you including me in that analysis?"

Varney snorted. "Ask your poet. All I say about you is that you've got to take more care. So you saved Wellington's Army. Good for you. Now…" He held out a pair of biscuit colored pantaloons. "…do you think you could act a little more suitable to your condition?"

"I don't recall ever behaving *unsuitably*."

"Oh, aye, dressing up so fine and dancing and going to the theater and sitting about playing cards at clubs for *gentlemen*." His emphasis sounded remarkably like that of Carmilla Amworth.

"Perhaps you'd rather I wore grave clothes and we lived in a mausoleum?"

"No, but…"

"A drafty castle somewhere in the mountains of eastern Europe?"

Varney sputtered incoherently.

Henry sighed and deftly tied his cravat. "Then let's hear no more about me forgetting who and what I am. I'm very sorry if you wanted someone a little more darkly tragic. A brooding, mythic personae who only emerges to slake his thirst on the fair throats of helpless virgins…"

"Here now! None of that!"

"But I'm afraid you're stuck with me." Holding out his arms, he let Varney help him into his jacket. "And I am almost late for an appointment at White's. I promised Sir William a chance to win back his eleven hundred pounds."

His sensibilities obviously crushed, Varney ground his teeth. "Now, what's the matter?"

The little man shook his head. "It just doesn't seem right that you, with all you could be, should be worried about being late for a card game."

His expression stern, Henry took hold of Varney's chin, and held the servant's gaze with his. "I think you forget who I am." His fingertips dimpled stubbled flesh. "I am a Lord of Darkness, a Creature of the Night, an Undead Fiend with Unnatural Appetites, indeed a *Vampyre*; but all of that…" His voice grew deeper and Varney began to tremble. "…is no excuse for bad manners."

This story also takes place between *Blood Pact* and *Blood Debt*. The blue van Vicki is driving in *Debt* makes its first appearance here.

THE CARDS ALSO SAY

Surveying Queen Street West from her favorite perch on the roof of the six story CITY TV building, Vicki Nelson fidgeted as she watched the pre-theater crowds spill from trendy restaurants. Usually able to sit, predator patient, for hours on end, she had no idea why she was suddenly so restless.

Old instincts honed by eight years with the Metropolitan Toronto Police and two years on her own as a PI suggested there was something wrong, something she'd seen or heard. Something was out of place and it nagged at her subconscious, demanding first recognition then action.

Apparently, observation wouldn't tell her what she needed to know; she had to participate in the night.

Crossing to the rear of the building, she climbed swiftly down the art-deco ornamentation until she could drop the last ten feet into the alley below. Barely noticing the familiar stink of old urine, she straightened her clothes and stepped out onto John Street.

A dark haired young man who'd been leaning on the side of the building, straightened and turned toward her.

Hooker, Vicki thought, then, as she drew closer and realized there was nothing of either sex or commerce in the young man's expression, revised her opinion.

"My grandmother wants to see you," he said matter-of-factly as she came along beside him.

Vicki stopped and stared. "To see me?"

"Yeah. You." Running the baby fingernail on his right hand over the fuzzy beginning of a mustache, he avoided her gaze and in a bored tone recited, "Tall, fair, dressed like a man…"

Brows raised, Vicki glanced down at her black corduroy jacket, faded jeans and running shoes.

"…coming out of the alley behind the white TV station." Finished, he shrugged and added, "Looks like you. Looks like the place. You coming or not?" His posture clearly indicated that he didn't care either way. "She says if you don't want to come with me, I've got to say night walker."

Not night walker as he pronounced it, two separate words, but Nightwalker.

Vampire.

"Do you have a car?"

In answer, he nodded toward an old Camaro parked under the no parking sign, continuing to avoid her gaze so adroitly, it seemed he'd been warned.

They made the trip up Bathurst Street to Bloor in complete silence. Vicki waited until she could ask her questions of some-one more likely to know the answers. The young man seemed to have nothing to say.

He stopped the car just past Bloor and Euclid and, oblivious to the horns beginning to blow behind him, jerked his head to-ward the north side of the street. "In there."

At the other end of the gesture was a small store front. Painted in brilliant yellow script over a painting of a classic horse-drawn Gypsy caravan were the words: *Madame Luminitsa, Fortune Teller. Sees Your Future in Cards, Palms, or Tea Leaves.* Behind the glass, a crimson curtain kept the curious from attempting to glimpse the future for free.

The door was similarly curtained and held a sign that listed business hours as well as an explanation that Madame Luminitsa dealt only in cash having seen too many bad credit cards. As Vicki pushed it open and stepped into a small waiting room, she heard a buzzer sound in the depths of the building.

The waiting room reminded her of a baroque doctor's office with, she noted glancing down at the glass topped coffee table, one major exception—the magazines were current. The place was empty not only of customers but also of the person who usually sat behind the official looking desk in the corner of the room. There were two interior doors; one behind the desk, one in the middle of the back wall. Soft background music with an Eastern European sound, combined with three working incense burners, set the mood.

Vicki sneezed and listened for the nearest heartbeat.

A group in the back of the building caught her attention but couldn't hold it when she became aware of the two lives just behind the back wall. One beat slowly and steadily, the other raced, caught in the grip of some strong emotion. As Vicki listened, the second heartbeat began to calm.

It sounded very nearly post-coital.

"Must've got good news," she muttered, crossing to the desk.

The desk top had nothing on it but a phone and half a pad of yellow legal paper. About to start searching the drawers, Vicki moved quickly away when she heard the second door begin to open.

A slim man with a distinctly receding hair line and slightly protuberant eyes emerged first, a sheet of crumpled yellow paper clutched in one hand. "You don't know what this means to me," he murmured.

"I have a good idea." The middle-aged woman behind him smiled broadly enough to show a gold-capped molar. "I'm pleased that I could help."

"Help?" he repeated. "You've done more than help. You've opened my eyes. I've got to get home and get started."

He rushed past Vicki without seeing her. As the outer door closed behind him, she took a step forward. "Madame Luminitsa, I presume?"

Flowered skirt swirling around her calves, the woman strode purposefully toward the desk. "Do you have an appointment?" Vicki shook her head. Under other circumstances, she'd have been amused by the official trappings to what was, after all, an elaborate way to exploit the unlimited ability of people to be self-deluded. "Someone's grandmother wants to see me."

"Ah. So you're the one." She showed no more interest than the original messenger had. "Wait here."

Since it seemed to be the only way she'd find out what was going on, Vicki dropped down onto a corner of the desk and waited while Madam Luminitsa went back into the rear of the building. Although strange things seemed to be afoot, she'd learned to trust her instincts and she didn't think she was in danger.

The Romani, as a culture, were more than willing to exploit the greed and/or stupidity of the *gadje*, or non-Rom, but they were also culturally socialized to avoid violence whenever possible. During the eight years she'd spent on the police force, Vicki had never heard of an incident where one of Toronto's extensive Romani communities had started a fight. Finished a couple, well, yes, but never started one.

Still, someone here had named her Nightwalker.

When the door opened again, the woman framed within it bore a distinct family resemblance to Madame Luminitsa. There were slight differences in height and weight and coloring—a little shorter, a little rounder, a little greyer—but a casual observer would have had difficulty telling them apart. Vicki was not a casual observer and she slowly stood as the dark gaze swept over her. The Hunger rose in recognition of a challenging power.

"Good. Now we know who we are, we can put it aside and get on with things." The woman's voice held a faint trace of Eastern Europe. "You'd best come in." She stepped aside leaving the way to the inner room open.

Curiosity overcoming her instinctive reaction, Vicki slipped a civilized mask back into place and did as suggested.

The inner room was a quarter the size of the outer. The ceiling had been painted navy blue and sprinkled with day-glo stars. Multicolored curtains fell from the stars to the floor and on each wall an iron bracket supporting a round light fixture thrust through the folds. In the center of the room, taking up most of the available floor space was a round table draped in red between two painted chairs. Shadows danced in every corner and every fold of fabric.

"Impressive," Vicki acknowledged. "Definitely sets the mood. But I'm not here to have my fortune told."

"We'll see." Indicating the second chair, the woman sat down.

Vicki sat as well. "Your grandson neglected to give me your name."

"You can call me Madame Luminitsa."

"Another one?"

The fortune teller shrugged. "We are all Madame Luminitsa if business is good enough. My sister, our daughters, their daughters…"

"You?"

"Not usually."

"Why not?" Vicki asked dryly. "Your predictions don't come true?"

"On the contrary." She folded her hands on the table, the colored stones in the rings that decorated six of eight fingers flashing in the light. "Some people can't take a dump without asking advice—Madame Luminitsa gives them a glimpse of the future they want. *I* give them the future they're going to get."

Arms crossed, Vicki snorted. "You're telling me, you can really see the future?"

"I saw you, Nightwalker. I saw where you'd be this evening. I sent for you and you came."

Which was, undeniably, unpleasantly, true. "For all that, you seem pretty calm about *what* I am."

"I'm used to seeing what others don't." Her expression darkened again for a moment as though she were gazing at a scene she'd rather not remember, then she shook her head and half-smiled. "If you know your history, Nightwalker—my people and your people have worked together in the past."

Vicki had a sudden vision of Gypsies filling boxes of dirt to keep their master safe on his trip to England. The memory bore the distinctive stamp of an old Hammer film. She returned the half-smile, another fraction of trust gained. "The one who changed me said that Bram Stoker was a hack."

"He got a few things right. The Romani were enslaved in that part of the world for many years and we had masters who made Bram Stoker's Count seem like a lovely fellow." Her voice held no bitterness at the history. It was over, done; they'd moved on and wouldn't waste the energy necessary to hold a grudge. "I've seen you're no danger to me, Nightwalker. As for the others…" The deliberate pause held a clear warning. "…they don't know.

"All right." It was an acknowledgement more than agreement. "So, why did you send for me?"

"I saw something."

"In my future?"

"Yes."

Vicki snorted, attempting to ignore the hair lifting off the
back of her neck. "A tall, dark stranger?"

"Yes."

Good cops learned to tell when people were lying. It wasn't
a skill vampires needed; no one lied to them. So far, Vicki had
been told only the truth—or at least the truth as Madame
Luminitsa believed it. Unfortunately, truth tended to be just a
tad fluid when spoken Romani to *gadje*.

The other woman sighed. "Would you feel better if I said a
I saw a short, fair stranger?"

"Did you?"

"No. The stranger that I saw was tall, and dark, and he is
dangerous. To you and to my family."

Now this meeting began to make sense. Intensely loyal to
their extended families and clans, the Romani would never go to
this much trouble for a mere *gadje* even, or especially, if that
gadje was a member of the bloodsucking undead. Self-interest,
however, Vicki understood. "I'm listening."

"It isn't easy to always see so I look only enough to keep
my family safe. This afternoon I laid out the cards and I saw
you and I saw danger approaching as a tall, dark man. Cliche,"
she shrugged, "but true. If you fall, this stranger will grow so
strong that when he turns his hate on other targets, he will be
almost invincible."

"And the danger to you?"

"He hates you because you're different. You haven't hurt
him or anyone near him but neither are you like him." Madame
Luminitsa paused, glanced around the room, and spread her
hands. "We are also different, we work hard at keeping it that
way. In the old days, we could have taken to the roads but now
we, as much as you, are sitting targets."

"You're sure he's just a man?" Vicki asked, twisting a pinch of the table cloth between thumb and forefinger. She'd met a demon once and didn't want to again.

"Men do by choice what demons do by nature."

Vicki'd spent too much time in Violent Crimes to argue with that. "You've got to give me more to go on than tall, dark and male."

From a pocket in her skirt or perhaps a shelf under the table, Madame Luminitsa pulled out a deck of tarot cards. "I can."

"Oh come on..."

Shuffling the cards with a dexterity that spoke of long practice, the older woman ignored her. She placed the shuffled deck in the center of the table. "With your left hand, cut the cards into three piles to your left," she said.

Vicki stared down at the cards then up at the fortune-teller. "I don't think so."

"Cut the cards if you want to live."

Put like that, it was pretty hard to refuse.

Tarot cards had made a brief surge into popular culture while Vicki'd been attending university. A number of the girls she knew laid out patterns at every opportunity. Vicki'd considered it more important to maintain her average than to take the time to learn the symbolism. She also considered most of the kerchiefed, sandaled, skirted amateur fortune tellers to be complete flakes. As a history major, she was fully aware of the persecutions the Romani had gone through for centuries, persecutions that had started up with renewed vigor after the fall of the iron curtain, and she was at a loss to understand why anyone would consider the life of the caravans to be romantic.

The pattern Madame Luminitsa laid out was a familiar one. "Aren't you supposed to start by picking a card out to stand for me?"

"Do I tell you your business?"

"Uh, no."

"Then don't tell me mine." She laid down the tenth card, set the unused part of the deck carefully to one side and sat back in her chair, her eyes never leaving the brightly colored rectangles spread out in front of her. "The three of swords sets an atmosphere of loss. Reversed, the Emperor covers it; a weak man but one who will take action. In his past, the star reversed; physical or mental illness."

"Wait a minute, I thought this was my reading."

"It's a reading to help you find the stranger before he can strike."

"Oh." Vicki reached into the inside pocket of her jacket for the small notebook and pen. She carried the old massive shoulder bag less and less these days. Somehow a purse, even one of luggage dimensions, just didn't seem vampiric. "Maybe I should be writing this down."

Madame Luminitsa waited until the first three cards had been recorded and then went on. "He has just set aside his material life."

"Fired from his job?"

"I don't know, but now he does other, more spiritual things."

"How can destroying me be spiritual?"

"He believes he's removing evil from the world."

"And what will he believe when he goes after your people?"

"For some, different is enough to be considered evil. He's about to come to a decision, you haven't much time."

"Or much information."

"You're here, in his recent past. I suspect you took his blood and the mental illness kept the shadows you command from blotting the memory. The Page of Swords—here—means he's watching you. Spying, learning your patterns before he strikes."

She remembered the feeling that something was wrong, out of place. "Great. Like I've only ever fed off one tall dark man, unstable and unemployed."

"There's only one watching you."

"That makes me feel so much better."

"Ace of wands, reversed. He's likely to make one unsuccessful attempt before you're in any actual danger. He's afraid of being alone and he's created this purpose to fill the void. He has no family. No friends. But look here…"

Vicki obediently bent forward.

"…the nine of wands. He has prepared for this. In the final outcome, he is dead to reason. Don't argue with him, stop him."

"Kill him?"

Madame Luminitsa shuffled the cards back into the deck. "That's up to you, Nightwalker."

Tapping her pen against the paper, Vicki glanced over her list. "So I'm looking for a tall, dark, unstable, unemployed, lonely man with sawdust in his cuffs from sharpening stakes who remembers me feeding from him and has been spying on me ever since. He'll make an attempt he won't carry through all the way but when push comes to shove I won't be able to talk him out of destroying me and may have to destroy him first." When she looked up, her eyes had silvered slightly. "How do I know you're not setting me up to destroy an enemy of yours?"

"You don't."

"How do I know you didn't deliberately mislead me so that you can destroy me yourself?"

"You don't."

"So, essentially, what you're saying is, I have to trust that you, and this whole fortune-telling thing, are on the level."

The Romani's eyes reflected bits of silver, the physical manifestation of Vicki's power stopped at the surface. "Yes."

"Vicki, get real! These are Gypsies, they live for the elaborate scam."

"Not this time, Mike." Swiveling out into the room, she tipped her desk chair back and frowned up at him. "Even if your stereotyping *was* accurate, this wasn't a scam. Madame Luminitsa needs me to protect her family. That's the only possible reason strong enough for her to even deal with me. If my danger wasn't her danger too, I'd be facing it on my own."

"So she wants something from you."

Beginning to wish she'd never told him how she'd spent her evening, Vicki closed her eyes and counted to ten. "Yes, she does. And so she's no different than any of my other clients who want something from me except that she's paid in full, in advance, by warning me of the danger that I'm in."

"You want to know what danger you're in?" Detective-Sergeant Michael Celluci stopped pacing and turned to glare at the woman in the chair. He'd loved her when they'd been together with police, he'd loved her when a degenerative eye disease had forced her to quit a job she'd excelled at and start over as a private investigator, and he'd continued to love her even after she'd become an undead, bloodsucking, creature of the night but there were times, and this was one of them, when he wanted to wring her neck. "This fortune teller knows what you are and what one Gypsy knows, they all do."

"Romani."

"What?"

"Most prefer to be called Romani, not Gypsy."

He threw up his hands. "What difference does that make!?"

"Well, let's see…" Her voice dripped sarcasm. "How would you like to be called a dumb, bigoted Wop?"

Celluci's eyes narrowed and, over the angry pounding of his heart, Vicki could hear him breathing heavily through his nose. "Fine. Romani. Whatever. They still know what you are and therefore they know you're completely helpless during the day. I want you to move back in with me."

"So you can protect me?"

"Yes!" He spat the word out, defying the reaction he knew she'd have.

To his surprise, there was no explosion.

As much touched as irritated by his concern, Vicki sighed impatiently and said, "Mike, do you honestly think that a plywood box in your basement is safer than this apartment?" The converted warehouse space boasted a barred window, a steel door, industrial strength locks, and an enclosed loft with an access so difficult even Celluci didn't attempt it on his own. The safety features had been designed by a much older vampire who'd made one, fatal error—she hadn't realized that the territory was already taken.

Slowly, Celluci sank down onto the arm of the sofa. "No. I don't."

"And it's not like you're home all day."

"I know. It's just…"

Vicki rolled her office chair out from under the edge of the loft, stopping only when they were knee to knee. She reached out and pushed an over-long curl of hair back off his face. "I'm not saying that I won't ever move back, Mike, just not now. Not because a mentally unstable, unemployed blood-donor thinks he's a modern Van Helsing."

He caught her hand, the skin cool against his palm. "And the Gy...Romani?"

"From what I understand about their culture, Madame Luminitsa's abilities make her a bit of an outsider already and she won't risk being named *marhime*...a kind of social/cultural exile," she added when Mike's brows went up, "...by telling her family she's dealing with a vampire."

"All right." Releasing his grip, he pushed her chair far enough away to give him room to stand. "So how do we stop this Van Helsing of yours?"

"I love it when you get all macho," she purred, rubbing her foot up his inseam. Befor he could react, she scooted back to the office, the chair's wheels protesting her speed. "According to the cards, he's prepared. You could check with the B&E guys to see if anyone's reported stolen Holy Water."

"Holy Water?"

"Madam Luminitsa said he thinks of me as evil and Holy Water is one of the traditional, albeit ineffectual, ways to melt a vampire."

"How the hell would someone steal Holy Water?"

"Don't you ever watch movies, Mike?" She mimed filling a water pistol. "Ask them about communion wafers too."

"Communion wafers?" He sighed and looked at his watch. "Fine. Whatever. Patterson's on evenings this week and he owes me a favor. It's only a quarter past eleven so if I leave in the next few minutes I'll catch him at Headquarters before he heads home."

"Great—I'll make this next bit quick. Since the cards also pointed out that our stalker's recently unemployed, a homicide detective with an open case involving the shooting of two counselors at a Canada Manpower center last month would have a reason to ask for a printout of everyone who'd recently applied for unemployment insurance."

"The guy who did the shooting could've been unemployed for years."

"You don't know that."

"Okay, let's say I come up with a plausible story and get the list—would you recognize the name of a..." He paused. This aspect of her life wasn't something they spoke about. Intellectually, Celluci knew he couldn't fulfill all her needs but he chose to ignore what that actually meant. "...dinner companion?"

"I don't know. Do you remember what you had for dinner every night for the last month?"

His lip curled into an expression approximating a smile. "Any other time, I'd be pleased you thought so little of them; this time, it's damned inconvenient. If you won't recognize his name, why do you want to see the list?"

"I *might* recognize his name," Vicki corrected. "But mostly I want to see the list to compare it to..." She paused and decided Detective-Sergeant Michael Celluci would be happier not knowing about the list she planned on comparing it to.

Unlike the unemployment office, the Queen Street Mental Health Center was open more or less twenty-four hours a day— recent government cutbacks having redefined the word open.

Vicki watched from the shadows as the old woman wearing a plastic hospital bracelet shuffled into the circle of light by the glass doors, cringed as the streetcar went by, pushed a filthy palm against the buzzer, and left it there. She'd been easy enough to find—this part of the city had an embarrassment of riches when it came to the lost—but less than easy to control. Those parts of the human psyche that responded to the danger, to the forbidden sensuality that the vampire represented, were so inaccessible they might as well not have existed. Vicki'd finally given her ten bucks and told her, in words of one syllable, what she needed done.

Sometimes, the old ways worked best.

Eventually, an orderly appeared, shaking his head as if the motion would disconnect the incessant buzzing. Peering through the wired glass, his frown segued into annoyed recognition. "Damn it, Helen," he muttered as he opened the door. "Stop leaning on the fucking buzzer."

Vicki slipped inside while he dealt with the old woman.

When he turned, the door closing behind him, she was there; her eyes silver, her smile very white, the Hunger rising.

"I need you to do me a favor," she said.

He swallowed convulsively as she ran her thumb lightly down the muscles of his throat.

Sometimes, the new ways worked best.

When the approaching dawn drove her home, Vicki carried a list of recent discharges from Queen Street and a similar list from the Clark Institute. All she needed was Celluci's list from UIC to make comparisons. With luck there'd be names in common, names with addresses she could visit until she recognized the distinctive signature of a life she'd fed on.

Her pair of lists were depressingly long and, given the current economic climate in Mike Harris' Ontario, she expected the third to be no shorter. Searching them would take most of a night and checking the names in common could easily take another two or three nights after that.

Unlocking her door, Vicki hoped they'd have the time. Madame Luminitsa had seemed convinced the wacko in the cards was about to make his move.

The apartment was dark but the shadows were familiar. Nothing lurked in the corners except dust bunnies not quite big enough to be a danger.

After locking and then barring the door with a two by four painted to match the wall—unsophisticated safety measures were often the most effective—Vicki hurried toward the loft, fighting to keep her shoulders from hunching forward as she felt the day creep up behind her. Almost safe within her sanctuary, she looked down and saw the light flashing on her answering machine. She hesitated. The sun inched closer toward the horizon.

"Oh damn…" Unable to let it go, she swung back down to the floor.

"Vicki, Mike. St. Paul's Anglican on Bloor reported a break-in last Tuesday afternoon. The only thing missing was a box of communion wafers. If he drained the Holy Water as well, they didn't bother reporting it. Looks like you were right." His sigh seemed to take up a good ten seconds of tape. "There's no point in telling you to be careful but could you please…"

She couldn't wait for the end of the message. The sun was too close. Throwing herself up and into the loft, she barred that door as well and sank back onto the bed.

The seconds, moving so quickly a moment before, slowed.

There were sounds, all around her Vicki couldn't remember ever hearing before. Outside, in the alley—was that someone climbing toward her window?

No. Pigeons.

That vibration in the wall—a drill?

No. The distant ring of a neighbor's alarm.

In spite of her vulnerability, she had never faced the dawn wondering if she'd see the dusk—until today. She didn't like the feeling.

"Maybe I *should* move back into Celluci's ba…"

Vicki hated spending the day in her clothes. She had a long hot shower to wash the creases away and listened to another message from Celluci suggesting she check out the church as he'd be at work until after midnight. "…and don't bother feeding, you can grab a bite when I get there."

"Like *that's* going to speed things up?" she muttered, shrugging into her jacket as the tape rewound. "Feeding from you isn't exactly fast food."

Quite the contrary.

Deciding to grab a snack on the street, or they'd never get to those lists, Vicki set the two by four aside and opened her door. Out in the hallway, key in hand, she stared down at the lower of the two locks. It smelled like latex. Like a glove intended to hide fingerprints.

She jumped as the door opened across the hall.

"Hey, sweetie. Did he scratch the paint?"

"Did who scratch the paint, Lloyd?"

"Well, when I got home this pm, I saw some guy on his knees foolin' with your lock. I yelled and he fled." Ebony arms draped in a blue silk kimono, crossed over a well muscled chest. "I knocked but you didn't wake up."

"I've told you before Lloyd, I work nights and I'm a heavy sleeper." It seemed that pretty soon she'd have re-enforce the message. "Can you tell me what this guy looked like?"

Lloyd shrugged. "White guy. Tall, dark, dressed all in black but not like he was makin' a fashion statement, you know? I didn't get a good look at his face but I can tell you, I've never seen him before." He paused and suddenly smiled. "I guess he was a tall, dark stranger. Pretty funny, eh?"

"Not really."

"He's likely to make one unsuccessful attempt before you're in any actual danger."

He'd made his attempt.

"The Page of Swords—here—means he's watching you."

He knew what she was and he knew where she lived.

"Well, that sucks," Vicki muttered, standing on the front step of the converted factory, scanning the street.

Something was out of place and it nagged at her subconscious, demanding first recognition then action.

At some point during the last few nights, she'd seen him, or been aware of him watching her. A little desperately, she searched for the touch of a life she'd shared, however briefly, but the city defeated her. There were a million lives around and such a tenuous familiarity got lost in the roar.

Another night, she'd have walked to St. Paul's. Tonight, she flagged a cab and hoped her watching stranger had to run like hell to keep up.

It had been some years since churches in the city had been able to leave their doors unlocked after dark; penitent souls looking for God had to make do with twenty-four hour donut shops.

Ignoring the big, double doors that faced the bright lights of Bloor Street, Vicki slipped around to the back of the old stone building and one of the less obvious entrances. To her surprise, the door was unlocked.

When she pulled it open, she realized why. Choir practice. Keeping to shadows, she made her way up and into the back of the church. There were bodies in the pews, family and friends of those singing, and, standing off to one side an elderly minister—or perhaps St. Paul's was high enough Anglican that they called him a priest.

Vicki waited until the hymn ended then she tapped the minister on the shoulder and asked if she could have a quiet word. She used only enough power to get the information she wanted—when he assumed she was with the police, she encouraged him to think it.

The communion wafers had been kept in a locked cupboard in the church office. Time and use had erased any scent Vicki might have recognized.

"No, nothing else," the minister said confidently when she asked if anything else had been taken.

"What about Holy Water?"

He glanced up at her in some surprise. "Funny you should mention that." Relocking the cupboard, he lead the way out of the office. "We had a baptism on Thursday evening—three families, two babies and an adult—or I might never have noticed. When I took the lid off the font, just before the service, the water level was lower than it should have been—I knew because I'd been the one to fill it, you see—and I found a cuff button caught on the lip." Opening the door to his own office, he crossed to the desk. "It's a heavy lid and anyone trying to scoop the water out, for heaven only knows what reason why, would have to hold it up one-handed. Easy enough to get your shirt caught, I imagine. Ah, here it is."

Plucking a white button out of an empty ashtray, he turned and dropped it in Vicki's palm. "The sad thing is, you know, this probably makes the thief one of ours."

"Why?"

"Well, the Catholics keep Holy Water by the door, it's a whole lot easier to get to. If he went to all this trouble, he was probably on familiar ground. Will that button help you catch him, do you think?"

Vicki smiled, forgetting for a moment the effect it was likely to have. "Oh yes, I think it will."

She had the cab wait out front while she ran into her apartment for the pair of lists then had it drop her off in front of Madame Luminitsa's.

Which was closed.

Fortunately, there were lights on upstairs and there could be no mistaking the unique signature of the fortune-teller's life. Fully aware she was not likely to be welcomed with open arms and not really caring, Vicki went around back.

She'd never seen so many large cars in so many states of disrepair as were parked in the alley that theoretically provided delivery access for the stores. Squeezing between an old blue delivery van and a cream colored Caddy, she stood at the door and listened, eight heart beats, upstairs and down, three of them children, one of them the woman she was looking for. There were a number of ways she could gain an audience—Stoker had been wrong about that, she no more needed to be invited in than an encyclopedia salesman—but, deciding it might be best to cause the least amount of offense, she merely knocked on the door.

The man who opened it was large. Not tall exactly, nor exactly fat—large. A drooping mustache, almost too black to be real, covered his upper lip and he stroked it with the little finger of his right hand as he looked her up and down, waiting for her to speak.

"I'm looking for Madame Luminitsa," Vicki told him, masks carefully in place. "It's very important."

"Madame Luminitsa is not available. The shop is closed."

She could feel the Hunger beginning to rise, remembered she'd intended to feed and hadn't. "I saw her last night, she sent for me."

"Ah. You." His expression became frankly speculative and Vicki wondered just how much Madame Luminitsa had told her family. Without turning his head, he raised his voice. "One of you, fetch your grandmother."

Vicki heard a chair pushed out and the sound of small feet running up a flight of stairs. "Thank you."

He shrugged. "She may not come. In the meantime, do you own a car?"

"Uh, no."

"Then I can sell you one of these." An expansive gesture and a broad smile reserved for prospective customers, indicated the vehicles crowding the alley. "You won't find a better price in all of Toronto and I will personally vouch for the quality of each and every one." A huge hand reached out and slapped the hood of the blue van. "Brand new engine, six cylinders, more power than..."

"Look, I'm not interested." Not unless that tall, dark stranger gave her a chance to run him over.

"Later then, after the cards have been played out."

A small, familiar hand covered in rings, reached out into the doorway and shoved the big man aside. He glanced down at the woman Vicki knew as Madame Luminitsa and hurriedly stepped back into the building, closing the door behind him.

"You haven't stopped him," the fortune-teller said bluntly.

"Give me a break," Vicki snorted. "I have to find him first. And, I think you can help me with that."

"The cards..."

"Not the cards." She pulled the lists from her shoulderbag and fished the button out of a pocket. "This was his. If his name's here shouldn't it help you find him?"

The dark brows rose. "You watch too much television, Nightwalker." But she took the pile of fan-fold and the button. "Has he made his first attempt?"

"Yeah. He has."

"Then there's a need to hurry."

"No shit, Sherlock," Vicki muttered as the fortune teller slipped back inside.

She acted as though she hadn't heard, declaring imperiously as the door closed. "I'll let you know what I find."

The door was unlocked but since Vicki could hear Celluci's heart beat inside her apartment, she wasn't concerned. She *was* surprised to hear another life besides his, both hearts beating hard and fast. They'd obviously been arguing; not an unusual occurrence around the detective.

He'd probably pulled a late duty and when she hadn't answered his calls had thought she was in trouble and brought his partner in with him for backup, just in case. It wasn't hard for Vicki to follow his logic. If they were too late to save her, explanations wouldn't matter. If they were in time, she could easily clear up the confusion he'd caused poor Detective-Sergeant Graham.

Stepping into the apartment, she froze just over the threshold, eyes widening in disbelief. "You've got to be kidding."

"Snuck up on me in the parking lot," Celluci growled, glaring up at the man holding his own gun to his head. "Shoved a pad of chloroform under my nose and jabbed me with a pin so I'd inhale." Muscles strained as he fought to free his hands from the frame of the chair. "Used my own god-damned handcuffs too."

"Shut up! Both of you!" He was probably in his mid forties, short black hair and beard lightly dusted with grey, tall enough from the fortune-teller's point of view. White showed all around the brown eyes locked on Vicki's face. His free hand pointed toward the door, trembling slightly with the effect of strong emotions. "Close it."

Without turning, she pushed it shut, gently so that the latch didn't quite catch, then she let the Hunger rise. He'd made a big mistake not attacking her in the day when she was vulnerable. Her eyes grew paler than his and her voice went past command to compulsion. "Let him go."

Celluci shuddered but the man with the gun only laughed shrilly. "You have no power over me! You never have! You never will!" He met her gaze and, even through the Hunger, she saw that he was right. Like the woman she'd used to gain access to Queen Street, he had no levels of darkness or desire she could touch. Everything inside his head had been locked tightly away and she didn't have the key. She couldn't command him so, in spite of Madame Luminitsa's belief she couldn't reason with him, she reined in the Hunger and let the silver fade from her eyes.

"Let him go," she said again, "you have me."

"But I can't keep you without him." The muzzle of the gun dug a circle into Celluci's cheek. "You can't leave or I'll blow his freakin' head off."

She'd forgotten that she had another vulnerability besides the day. "If you kill him, I'll rip your living heart out of your chest and I'll make you eat it while you di…"

"Vicki…"

He laughed again as Celluci protested. "You can't get to me, before I can pull the trigger. As long as I have him, I have you."

"So we have a stand-off," she said. The silver rose unbidden to her eyes. "Do you think you can out wait *me*?"

His teeth flashed in the shadow of his beard. "I know I can. I only have to wait until dawn."

And he would too. It was the one certainty Vicki could read in his eyes. She took an involuntary step forward.

He lifted a bright green water pistol. "Hold it right there, or I'll shoot."

"I don't think so." She took another step.

The Holy Water hit her full in the face. He was a good shot, she had to give him that—although under the circumstances there wasn't much chance of him missing the target that mattered. Wiping the water from her eyes, she growled. "If this is how you plan to kill me, there's a flaw in the plan."

Appalled that the water hadn't had its intended effect, he recovered quickly. Throwing the plastic pistol onto the sofa, he reached down beside him and brought up a rough hewn wooden stake. "The water was only intended to slow you down. *This* is what I'll kill you with."

Celluci cursed and began to struggle again.

The man with the gun ignored him, merely keeping the muzzle pressed tight into his face.

Vicki had no idea of how much damage she could take and survive but a stake through the heart had to count as a mortal wound, especially since he seemed to be the type to finish the job with a beheading and a mouthful of garlic. "What happens *after* I'm dead?"

"After?" He looked confused. "Then you'll be dead. And it'll be over." He checked his watch. "Less than five hours."

Desperately trying to remember everything she'd ever learned about defusing a hostage situation, Vicki took a deep breath and spread her arms, trying to appear as non-threatening as possible. "Since we're going to be together for those five hours," she said quietly, forcing her lips down over her teeth, "why don't you explain why you've decided to kill me. I've never hurt you."

"You don't remember me, do you?"

"Not remember as such, no." She knew she'd fed from him, and she knew how long it had been but that was all.

"Do you spread your evil over so many?"

"What evil?" Vicki asked trying to keep her tone level. It wasn't easy when all she could think of was rushing forward and ripping the hand holding the gun right off the end of his arm.

"You are evil by existing!" Tears glimmered against his lower lids and spilled over to vanish in his beard. "You mock their deaths by not dying."

"The three of swords sets an atmosphere of loss."

"Whose deaths?"

"My Angela, my Sandi."

Vicki exchanged a puzzled look with Celluci. "Whoever they are, I'm sorry for your loss but I didn't kill them."

"Of course you didn't kill them." He had to swallow sobs before he could go on. In spite of his anguish, the hand holding the gun never wavered. "It was a car accident. They died and were buried and now the worms devour their flesh but you…" His voice rose to a shriek. "…you live on, mocking their death with infinity. You will never die." Drawing in a long shuddering breath, he checked his watch again. "God sent you to me and gave me the power to resist you so I could kill you and set things right."

"God doesn't work that way," Celluci objected.

His smile was almost beatific. "Mine does."

Uncertain of where to go next, Vicki was astonished to hear footsteps stop outside her door. A soft touch eased it open just enough for a breath to pass through.

"Nightwalker, his name is James Wause."

Then the footsteps went away again.

There was power in a name. Power enough to reach through the madness? Vicki didn't know but it was their only chance. She let the Hunger rise again, this time let it push away the masks of civilization, and when she spoke, her voice had all the primal cadences of a storm.

"James Wause."

He jerked and shook his head. "No."

She caught his gaze with hers, saw the silver reflected in the dilated pupils as his madness kept her out, then saw it abruptly vanish as she called his name again and it gave her the key to the locked places inside. The cards had said she couldn't reason with him so she stopped trying. She called his name a third and final time. When he crumbled forward, she caught him. When he lifted his chin, she brought her teeth down to his throat.

"Vicki."

There was power in a name.

But his blood throbbed warm and red beneath his skin, and sobbing in a combination of sorrow and ecstasy he was begging her to take him.

"Vicki, no."

More importantly, he had threatened one of hers.

"Vicki! Hey!" Celluci head-butted her in the elbow, about all the contact the handcuffs allowed. "Stop it! Now."

There was also power in the sheer pig-headed unwillingness that refused to allow her to lose the humanity she had remaining. Forcing the Hunger back under fingertip control, she dropped the man she held and turned to the one beside her. The cards hadn't counted on Detective-Sergeant Michael Celluci.

Ignoring the Hunter still in her expression, he snorted. "Nice you remembered I'm here. Now do you think you could do something about the nine millimeter automatic—with, I'd like to add, the safety off—that Mr. Wause dropped into my lap?"

Later, after Celluci had been released and James Wause laid out on the sofa, put to sleep by a surprisingly gentle command, Vicki leaned against the loft support and tried not to think of how close it had all come to ending.

When Celluci picked up the phone, she reached out and closed her hand around his wrist. "What are you doing?"

He looked at her, sighed, and set the receiver back in its cradle. "No police, right?"

"Would the courts understand what I am any better than he did?" She nodded toward Wause who stirred in his sleep as though aware of her regard.

Celluci sighed again and gathered her into the circle of his arms. "All right," he said resting his cheek against her hair. "What do we do with him?"

"I've got an idea."

This time the back door was locked but Vicki quickly picked the lock, slung James Wause over her shoulder, and carried him into the church. Celluci had wanted to come, but she'd made him wait in the car.

Laying him out in a front pew, she tucked the box of unused communion wafers under his hands and stepped back. His confession would be short a few details—this time she'd successfully removed all memory of her existence from his mind—but she hoped she'd opened the way for him to get the help he needed to cope with his grief.

"The vampire as therapist," she sighed and nodded toward the altar as she passed. "So if he's one of yours, you deal with him."

It didn't surprise her to see the beat up old Camaro out in the church parking lot when she emerged. Lifting a hand to let

Celluci know he should stay where he was, she walked over to the passenger side door.

"Did the cards tell you I'd be here?"

Madame Luminitsa nodded toward the church. "You gave him to God?"

"Seems like it."

"Alive."

"Didn't the cards say?"

"The cards weren't sure."

On the other side of the car, the grandson snorted.

Both women ignored him.

"Did the cards tell you where I lived?" Vicki asked.

"If they did, are you complaining?"

Without his name, she'd have never stopped him. "No. I guess I'm not."

"Good. You've less blood on your hands than I feared," the fortune-teller murmured taking Vicki's hands in hers and turning them. "Some day, I'll have to read your palms."

Vicki glanced over at Celluci, who was making it plain he wasn't going to wait patiently in the car much longer. "I'll bet I have a really long life line."

An ebony brow rose as, across the parking lot, the car door opened. "How much?"

This is the original story for this book; you'll notice as short sto- ries go, it isn't very short. I got the idea while visiting a time- share resort down in Florida last fall and the tale grew in telling as I began to research the weird and wonderful possibilities in deep water lakes. If any of you want to know what's REALLY going on here, pick up a copy of Michael Bradley's fascinating book, *More Than a Myth: The Search for the Monster of Muskrat Lake*. It's certainly changed my mind about swimming after dark...

THE VENGEFUL SPIRIT OF LAKE NEPEAKEA

"Camping?"

"Why sound so amazed?" Dragging the old turquoise cooler behind her, Vicki Nelson, once one of Toronto's finest and cur- rently the city's most successful paranormal investigator, backed out of Mike Celluci's crawl space.

"Why? Maybe because you've never been camping in your life. Maybe because your idea of roughing it is a hotel without room service. Maybe..." He moved just far enough for Vicki to get by then followed her out into the rec room. "...because you're a..."

"A?" Setting the cooler down beside two sleeping bags and a pair of ancient swim fins, she turned to face him. "A *what*, Mike?" Gray eyes silvered.

"Stop it."

Grinning, she turned her attention back to the cooler. "Be- sides, I won't be on vacation, I'll be working. You'll be the one enjoying the great outdoors."

"Vicki, my idea of the great outdoors is going to the Skydome for a Jay's game."

"No one's forcing you to come." Setting the lid to one side, she curled her nose at the smell coming out of the cooler's depths. "When was the last time you used this thing?"

"Police picnic, 1992. Why?"

She turned it up on its end. The desiccated body of a mouse rolled out, bounced twice and came to rest with its sightless little eyes staring up at Celluci. "I think you need to buy a new cooler."

"I think I need a better explanation than *'I've got a great way for you to use up your long weekend,'*" he sighed, kicking the tiny corpse under the rec room couch.

"So this developer from Toronto, Stuart Gordon, bought an old lodge on the shores of Lake Nepeakea and he wants to build a rustic, time-share resort so junior executives can relax in the woods. Unfortunately, one of the surveyors disappeared and local opinion seems to be that he's pissed off the lake's protective spirit..."

"The what?"

Vicki pulled out to pass a transport and deftly reinserted the van back into her own lane before replying. "The protective spirit. You know, the sort of thing that rises out of the lake to vanquish evil." A quick glance toward the passenger seat brought her brows in. "Mike, are you all right? You're going to leave permanent finger marks in the dashboard."

He shook his head. The truck load of logs coming down from Northern Ontario had missed them by inches. Feet at the very most. *All right, maybe meters but not very many of them.* When they'd left the city, just after sunset, it had seemed logical that Vicki, with her better night sight, should drive. He was regretting that logic now but, realizing he didn't have a hope in hell of gaining control of the vehicle, he tried to force himself to relax. "The speed limit isn't just a good idea," he growled through clenched teeth, "it's the law."

She grinned, her teeth very white in the darkness. "You didn't used to be this nervous."

"I didn't used to have cause." His fingers wouldn't release their grip so he left them where they were. "So this missing surveyor, what did he..."

"She."

"...she do to piss off the protective spirit?"

"Nothing much. She was just working for Stuart Gordon."

"The same Stuart Gordon you're working for."

"The very one."

Right. Celluci stared out at the trees and tried not to think about how fast they were passing. *Vicki Nelson against the protective spirit of Lake Nepeakea. That's one for pay for view...*

"This is the place."

"No. In order for this to be 'the place' there'd have to be something here. It has to be *'a place'* before it can be *'the place'.*"

"I hate to admit it," Vicki muttered, leaning forward and peering over the arc of the steering wheel, "but you've got a point." They'd gone through the village of Dulvie, turned right at the ruined barn and followed the faded signs to The Lodge. The road, if the rutted lanes of the last few kilometers could be called a road, had ended, as per the directions she'd received, in a small gravel parking lot—or more specifically in a hard packed rectangular area that could now be called a parking lot because she'd stopped her van on it. "He said you could see the lodge from here."

Celluci snorted. "Maybe *you* can."

"No. I can't. All I can see are trees." At least she assumed they were trees, the high contrast between the area her headlights covered and the total darkness beyond made it difficult to tell for sure. Silently calling herself several kinds of fool, she switched off the lights. The shadows separated into half a dozen large evergreens and the silhouette of a roof steeply angled to shed snow.

Since it seemed they'd arrived, Vicki shut off the engine. After a heartbeat's silence, the night exploded into a cacophony of discordant noise. Hands over sensitive ears, she sank back into the seat. "What the hell is that?"

"Horny frogs."

"How do you know?" she demanded.

He gave her a superior smile. "PBS."

"Oh." They sat there for a moment, listening to the frogs. "The creatures of the night," Vicki sighed, "what music they make." Snorting derisively, she got out of the van. "Somehow, I expected the middle of nowhere to be a lot quieter."

Stuart Gordon had sent Vicki the key to the lodge's back door and once she switched on the main breaker, they found themselves in a modern, stainless steel kitchen that wouldn't have looked out of place in any small, trendy restaurant back in Toronto. The sudden hum of the refrigerator turning on momentarily drowned out the frogs and both Vicki and Celluci relaxed.

"So now what?" he asked.

"Now we unpack your food from the cooler, we find you a room, and we make the most of the short time we have until dawn."

"And when does Mr. Gordon arrive?"

"Tomorrow evening. Don't worry, I'll be up."

"And I'm supposed to do what, tomorrow in the daytime?"

"I'll leave my notes out. I'm sure something'll occur to you."

"I thought I was on vacation?"

"Then do what you usually do on vacation."

"Your foot work." He folded his arms. "And on my last vacation—which was also your idea—I almost lost a kidney."

Closing the refrigerator door, Vicki crossed the room between one heartbeat and the next. Leaning into him, their bodies touching between ankle and chest, she smiled into his eyes and pushed the long curl of hair back off of his forehead. "Don't worry, I'll protect you from the spirit of the lake. I have no intention of sharing you with another legendary being."

"Legendary?" He couldn't stop a smile. "Think highly of yourself, don't you?"

"Are you sure you'll be safe in the van?"

"Stop fussing. You know I'll be fine." Pulling her jeans up over her hips, she stared out the window and shook her head. "There's a whole lot of nothing out there."

From the bed, Celluci could see a patch of stars and the top of one of the evergreens. "True enough."

"And I really don't like it."

"Then why are we here?"

"Stuart Gordon just kept talking. I don't even remember saying yes but the next thing I knew, I'd agreed to do the job."

"He pressured you?" Celluci's emphasis on the final pronoun made it quite clear that he hadn't believed such a thing was possible.

"Not pressured, no. Convinced with extreme prejudice."

"He sounds like a prince."

"Yeah? Well, so was Machiavelli." Dressed, she leaned over the bed and kissed him lightly. "Want to hear something romantic? When the day claims me, yours will be the only life I'll be able to feel."

"Romantic?" His breathing quickened as she licked at the tiny puncture wounds on his wrist. "I feel like a box luuu…ouch! All right. It's romantic."

Although she'd tried to keep her voice light when she'd mentioned it to Celluci, Vicki really didn't like the great outdoors. Maybe it was because she understood the wilderness of glass and concrete and needed the anonymity of three million lives packed tightly around hers. Standing by the van, she swept her gaze from the first hints of dawn to the last lingering shadows of night and couldn't help feeling excluded, that there was something beyond what she could see that she wasn't a part of. She doubted Stuart Gordon's junior executives would feel a part of it either and wondered why anyone would want to build a resort in the midst of such otherness.

The frogs had stopped trying to get laid and the silence seemed to be waiting for something.

Waiting…

Vicki glanced toward Lake Nepeakea. It lay like a silver mirror down at the bottom of a rocky slope. Not a ripple broke the surface. Barely a mile away, a perfect reflection brought the opposite shore closer still.

Waiting…

Whippoor-will!

Vicki winced at the sudden, piercing sound and got into the van. After locking both outer and inner doors, she stripped quickly—if she were found during the day, naked would be the least of her problems—laid down between the high, padded sides of the narrow bed and waited for the dawn. The bird call, repeated with Chinese water torture frequency, cut its way through special seals and interior walls.

"Man, that's annoying," she muttered, linking her fingers over her stomach. "I wonder if Celluci can sleep through…"

As soon as he heard the van door close, Celluci fell into a dreamless sleep that lasted until just past noon. When he woke, he stared up at the inside of the roof and wondered where he was. The rough lumber looked like it'd been coated in creosote in the far distant past.

"No insulation, hate to be here in the winter…"

Then he remembered where *here* was and came fully awake.

Vicki had dragged him out to a wilderness lodge, north of Georgian Bay, to hunt for the local and apparently homicidal protective lake spirit.

A few moments later, his sleeping bag neatly rolled on the end of the old iron bed, he was in the kitchen making a pot of coffee. That kind of a realization upon waking needed caffeine.

On the counter next to the coffee maker, right where he'd be certain to find it first thing, he found a file labeled Lake Nepeakea in Vicki's unmistakable handwriting. The first few pages of glossy card stock had been clearly sent by Stuart Gordon along with the key. An artist's conception of the timeshare resort, they showed a large L-shaped building where the lodge now stood and three dozen "cottages" scattered through the woods, front doors linked by broad gravel paths. Apparently, the guests would commute out to their personal chalets by golf cart.

"Which they can also use on…" Celluci turned the page and shook his head in disbelief. "…the nine hole golf course." Clearly, a large part of Mr. Gordon's building plan involved bulldozers. And right after the bulldozers would come the cappuccino. He shuddered.

The next few pages were clipped together and turned out to be photocopies of newspaper articles covering the disappearance of the surveyor. She'd been working with her partner in the late evening, trying to finish up a particularly marshy bit of shore destined to be filled in and paved over for tennis courts, when, according to her partner, she'd stepped back into the mud, announced something had moved under her foot, lost her balance, fell, screamed, and disappeared. The OPP, aided by local volunteers, had set up an extensive search but she hadn't been found. Since the area was usually avoided because of the sink holes, sink holes a distraught Stuart Gordon swore he knew nothing about—"Probably distraught about having to move his tennis courts," Celluci muttered—the official verdict allowed that she'd probably stepped in one and been sucked under the mud.

The headline on the next page declared DEVELOPER ANGERS SPIRIT, and in slightly smaller type, Surveyor Pays the Price. The picture showed an elderly woman with long gray braids and a hawklike profile staring enigmatically out over the water. First impressions suggested a First Nations elder. In actually reading the text, however, Celluci discovered that Mary Joseph had moved out to Dulvie from Toronto in 1995 and had become, in the years since, the self-proclaimed keeper of local myth. According to Ms. Joseph, although there had been many sightings over the years, there had been only two other occasions when the spirit of the Lake had felt threatened enough to kill. *"It protects the lake,"* she was quoted as saying, *"from those who would disturb its peace."*

"Two weeks ago," Celluci noted, checking the date. "Tragic but hardly a reason for Stuart Gordon to go to the effort of convincing Vicki to leave the city."

The final photocopy included a close-up of a car door that looked like it had been splashed with acid. *SPIRIT ATTACKS DEVELOPER'S VEHICLE.* During the night of May 13th, the protector of Lake Nepeakea had crawled up into the parking lot of the lodge and secreted something corrosive and distinctly fishy against Stuart Gordon's brand new Isuzu trooper. *A trail of dead bracken, a little over a foot wide and smelling strongly of rotting fish, led back to the lake.* Mary Joseph seemed convinced it was a manifestation of the spirit, the local police were looking for anyone who might have information about the vandalism, and Stuart Gordon announced he was bringing in a special investigator from Toronto to settle it once and for all.

It was entirely probable that the surveyor had stepped into a mud hole and that local vandals were using the legends of the spirit against an unpopular developer. Entirely probable. But living with Vicki had forced Mike Celluci to deal with half a dozen improbable things every morning before breakfast so, mug in hand, he headed outside to investigate the crime scene.

Because of the screen of evergreens—although given their size 'barricade' was probably the more descriptive word—the parking lot couldn't be seen from the lodge. Considering the impenetrable appearance of the overlapping branches, Celluci was willing to bet that not even light would get through. The spirit could have done anything it wanted to, up to and including changing the oil, in perfect secrecy.

Brushing one or two small insects away from his face, Celluci found the path they'd used the night before and followed it. By the time he reached the van, the one or two insects had become twenty-nine or thirty and he felt the first bite on the back of his neck. When he slapped the spot, his fingers came away dotted with blood.

"Vicki's not going to be happy about that," he grinned wiping it off on his jeans. By the second and third bites, he'd stopped grinning. By the fourth and fifth, he really didn't give a damn what Vicki thought. By the time he'd stopped counting, he was running for the lake, hoping that the breeze he could see stirring its surface would be enough to blow the little bastards away.

The faint but unmistakable scent of rotting fish rose from the dead bracken crushed under his pounding feet and he realized that he was using the path made by the manifestation. It was about two feet wide and led down an uncomfortably steep slope from the parking lot to the lake. But not exactly all the way to the lake. The path ended about three feet above the water on a granite ledge.

Swearing, mostly at Vicki, Celluci threw himself backwards, somehow managing to save both his coffee and himself from

taking an unexpected swim. The following cloud of insects effortlessly matched the move. A quick glance through the bugs
showed the ledge tapering off to the right. He bounded down it
to the water's edge and found himself standing on a small, man-
made beach staring at a floating dock that stretched out maybe
fifteen feet into the lake. Proximity to the water *had* seemed to
discourage the swarm so he headed for the dock hoping that the
breeze would be stronger fifteen feet out.

It was. Flicking a few bodies out of his coffee, Celluci took
a long grateful drink and turned to look back up at the lodge.
Studying the path he'd taken, he was amazed he hadn't broken
an ankle and had to admit a certain appreciation for who or what
had created it. A graying staircase made of split logs offered a
more conventional way to the water and the tiny patch of gritty
sand, held in place by a stone wall. Stuart Gordon's plans had
included a much larger beach and had replaced the old wooden
dock with three concrete piers.

"One for papa bear, one for mama bear, and one for baby
bear," Celluci mused, shuffling around on the gently rocking
platform until he faced the water. Not so far away, the far shore
was an unbroken wall of trees. He didn't know if there *were*
bears in this part of the province but there was certainly bathroom facilities for any number of them. Letting the breeze push
his hair back off his face, he took another swallow of rapidly
cooling coffee and listened to the silence. It was unnerving.

The sudden roar of a motor boat came as a welcome relief.
Watching it bounce its way up the lake, he considered how far
the sound carried and made a mental note to close the window
should Vicki spend any significant portion of the night with him.

The moment distance allowed, the boat's driver waved over
the edge of the cracked windshield and, in a great, banked turn
that sprayed a huge fantail of water out behind him, headed toward the exact spot where Celluci stood. Celluci's fingers tightened around the handle of the mug but he held his ground. Still
turning, the driver cut his engines and drifted the last few meters
to the dock. As empty bleach bottles slowly crumpled under the
gentle impact, he jumped out and tied off his bow line.

"Frank Patton," he said, straightening from the cleat and holding out a callused hand. "You must be the guy that developer's brought in from the city to capture the spirit of the lake."

"Detective Sergeant Mike Celluci." His own age or a little younger, Frank Patton had a working man's grip that was just a little too forceful. Celluci returned pressure for pressure. "And I'm just spending a long weekend in the woods."

Patton's dark brows drew down. "But I thought..."

"You thought I was some weirdo phychic you could impress by crushing his fingers." The other man looked down at their joined hands and had the grace to flush. As he released his hold, so did Celluci. He'd played this game too often to lose at it. "I suggest, if you get the chance to meet the actual investigator, you don't come on quite so strong. She's liable to feed you your preconceptions."

"She's..."

"Asleep right now. We got in late and she's likely to be up...investigating tonight."

"Yeah. Right." Flexing his fingers, Patton stared down at the toes of his workboots. "It's just, you know, we heard that, well..." Sucking in a deep breath, he looked up and grinned. "Oh hell, talk about getting off on the wrong foot. Can I get you a beer, Detective?"

Celluci glanced over at the Styrofoam cooler in the back of the boat and was tempted for a moment. As sweat rolled painfully into the bug bites on the back of his neck, he remembered just how good a cold beer could taste. "No, thanks," he sighed with a disgusted glare into his mug. "I've, uh, still got coffee."

To his surprise, Patton nodded and asked, "How long've you been dry? My brother-in-law gets that exact same look when some damn fool offers him a drink on a hot almost-summer afternoon," he explained as Celluci stared at him in astonishment. "Goes to AA meetings in Bigwood twice a week."

Remembered all the bottles he'd climbed into during those long months Vicki had been gone, Celluci shrugged. "About two years now—give or take."

"I got generic cola..."

He dumped the dregs of cold bug infested coffee into the lake. The Ministry of Natural Resources could kiss his ass. "Love one," he said.

"So essentially everyone in town and everyone who owns property around the lake and everyone in a hundred kilometer radius has reason to want Stuart Gordon gone."

"Essentially," Celluci agreed, tossing a gnawed chicken bone aside and pulling another piece out of the bucket. He'd waited to eat until Vicki got up, maintaining the illusion that it was a ritual they continued to share. "According to Frank Patton, he hasn't endeared himself to his new neighbors. This place used to belong to an Anne Kellough who...What?"

Vicki frowned and leaned toward him. "You're covered in bites."

"Tell me about it." The reminder brought his hand up to scratch at the back of his neck. "You know what Nepeakea means? It's an old Indian word that translates as 'I'm fucking sick of being eaten alive by black flies; let's get the hell out of here.'"

"Those old Indians could get a lot of mileage out of a word."

Celluci snorted. "Tell me about it."

"Anne Kellough?"

"What, not even one poor sweet baby?"

Stretching out her leg under the table, she ran her foot up the inseam of his jeans. "Poor sweet baby."

"That'd be a lot more effective if you weren't wearing hiking boots." Her laugh was one of the things that hadn't changed when she had. Her smile was too white and too sharp and it made too many new promises but her laugh remained fully human. He waited until she finished, chewing, swallowing, congratulating himself for evoking it, then said, "Anne Kellough ran this place as sort of a therapy camp. Last summer, after ignoring her for 13 years, the Ministry of Health people came down on her kitchen. Renovations cost more than she thought, the bank foreclosed, and Stuart Gordon bought it twenty minutes later."

"That explains why she wants him gone—what about everyone else?"

"Lifestyle."

"They think he's gay?"

"Not his, theirs. The people who live out here, down in the village and around the lake—while not adverse to taking the occasional tourist for everything they can get—like the quiet, they like the solitude and, god help them, they even like the woods. The boys who run the hunting and fishing camp at the west end of the lake…"

"Boys?"

"I'm quoting here. The boys," he repeated, with emphasis, "say Gordon's development will kill the fish and scare off the game. He nearly got his ass kicked by one of them, Pete Wegler, down at the local gas station and then got tossed out on said ass by the owner when he called the place quaint."

"In the sort of tone that adds, and a Starbucks would be a big improvement?" When Celluci raised a brow, she shrugged. "I've spoken to him, it's not that much of an extrapolation."

"Yeah, exactly that sort of tone. Frank also told me that people with kids are concerned about the increase in traffic right through the center of the village.

"Afraid they'll start losing children and pets under expensive sport utes?"

"That, and they're worried about an increase in taxes to maintain the road with all the extra traffic." Pushing away from the table, he started closing plastic containers and carrying them to the fridge. "Apparently, Stuart Gordon, ever so diplomatically, told one of the village women that this was no place to raise kids."

"What happened?"

"Frank says they got them apart before it went much beyond name calling."

Wondering how far 'much beyond name calling' went, Vicki watched Mike clean up the remains of his meal. "Are you sure he's pissed off more than just these few people? Even if this was already a resort and he didn't have to rezone, local council must've agreed to his building permit."

"Yeah, and local opinion would feed local council to the spirit right along side Mr. Gordon. Rumor has it, they've been bought off."

Tipping her chair back against the wall, she smiled up at him. "Can I assume from your busy day that you've come down on the mud hole/vandals side of the argument?"

"It does seem the most likely." He turned and scratched at the back of his neck again. When his fingertips came away damp, he heard her quick intake of breath. When he looked up, she was crossing the kitchen. Cool fingers wrapped around the side of his face.

"You didn't shave."

It took him a moment to find his voice. "I'm on vacation."

Her breath lapped against him, then her tongue.

The lines between likely and unlikely blurred.

Then the sound of an approaching engine jerked him out of her embrace.

Vicki licked her lips and sighed. "Six cylinder, sport utility, four wheel drive, *all* the extras, black with gold trim."

Celluci tucked his shirt back in. "Stuart Gordon told you what he drives."

"Unless you think I can tell all that from the sound of the engine."

"Not likely."

"A detective sergeant? I'm impressed." Pale hands in the pockets of his tweed blazer, Stuart Gordon leaned conspiratorially in toward Celluci, too many teeth showing in too broad a grin. "I don't suppose you could fix a few parking tickets."

"No."

Thin lips pursed in exaggerated reaction to the blunt monosyllable. "Then what do you do, detective sergeant?"

"Violent crimes."

Thinking that sounded a little too much like a suggestion, Vicki intervened. "Detective Celluci has agreed to assist me this weekend. Between us, we'll be able to keep a 24 hour watch."

"Twenty four hours?" The developer's brows drew in. "I'm not paying more for that."

"I'm not asking you to."

"Good." Stepping up onto the raised hearth as though it were a stage, he smiled with all the sincerity of a television infomercial. "Then I'm glad to have you aboard Detective, Mike—can I call you Mike?" He continued without waiting for an answer. "Call me Stuart. Together we'll make this a safe place for the weary masses able to pay a premium price for a premium week in the woods." A heartbeat later, his smile grew strained. "Don't you two have detecting to do?"

"Call me Stuart?" Shaking his head, Celluci followed Vicki's dark on dark silhouette out to the parking lot. "Why is he here?"

"He's bait."

"Bait? The man's a certified asshole, sure, but we are not using him to attract an angry lake spirit."

She turned and walked backward so she could study his face. Sometimes he forgot how well she could see in the dark and forgot to mask his expressions. "Mike, you don't believe that call-me-Stuart has actually pissed off some kind of vengeful spirit protecting Lake Nepeakea?"

"You're the one who said bait..."

"Because we're not going to catch the person, or persons, who threw acid on his car unless we catch them in the act. He understands that."

"Oh. Right."

Feeling the bulk of the van behind her, she stopped. "You didn't answer my question."

He sighed and folded his arms, wishing he could see her as well as she could see him. "Vicki, in the last four years I have been attacked by demons, mummies, zombies, werewolves..."

"That wasn't an attack, that was a misunderstanding."

"He went for my throat, I count it as an attack. I've offered my blood to the bastard son of Henry VIII and I've spent two years watching you hide from the day. There isn't anything much I don't believe in anymore."

"But..."

"I believe in you," he interrupted, "and from there, it's not that big a step to just about anywhere. Are you going to speak with Mary Joseph tonight?"

His tone suggested the discussion was over. "No, I was going to check means and opportunity on that list of names you gave me." She glanced down toward the lake then up at him, not entirely certain what she was looking for in either instance. "Are you going to be all right out here on your own?"

"Why the hell wouldn't I be?"

"No reason." She kissed him, got into the van, and leaned out the open window to add, "Try and remember, Sigmund, that sometimes a cigar is just a cigar."

Celluci watched Vicki drive away and then turned on his flashlight and played the beam over the side of Stuart's car. Although it would have been more helpful to have seen the damage, he had to admit that the body shop had done a good job. And to give the man credit, however reluctantly, developing a wilderness property did provide more of an excuse than most of his kind had for the four wheel drive.

Making his way over to an outcropping of rock where he could see both the parking lot and the lake but not be seen, Celluci sat down and turned off his light. According to Frank Patton, the black flies only fed during the day and the water was still too cold for mosquitoes. He wasn't entirely convinced but since nothing had bitten him so far the information seemed accurate. "I wonder if Stuart knows his little paradise is crawling with blood suckers." Right thumb stroking the puncture wound on his left wrist, he turned toward the lodge.

His eyes widened.

Behind the evergreens, the lodge blazed with light. Inside lights. Outside lights. Every light in the place. The harsh yellow-white illumination washed out the stars up above and threw everything below into sharp such sharp relief that even the lush, spring growth seemed manufactured. The shadows under the distant trees were now solid, impenetrable sheets of darkness.

"Well at least Ontario Hydro's glad he's here." Shaking his head in disbelief, Celluci returned to his surveillance.

Too far away for the light to reach it, the lake threw up shimmering reflections of the stars and lapped gently against the shore.

Finally back on the paved road, Vicki unclenched her teeth and followed the southern edge of the lake toward the village. With nothing between the passenger side of the van and the water but a whitewashed guard rail and a few tumbled rocks, it was easy enough to look out the window and pretend she was driving on the lake itself. When the shoulder widened into a small parking area and a boat ramp, she pulled over and shut off the van.

The water moved inside its narrow channel like liquid darkness, opaque and mysterious. The part of the night that belonged to her ended at the water's edge.

"Not the way it's supposed to work," she muttered, getting out of the van and walking down the boat ramp. Up close, she could see through four or five inches of liquid to a stony bottom and the broken shells of fresh water clams but beyond that, it was hard not believe she couldn't just walk across to the other side.

The ubiquitous spring chorus of frogs suddenly fell silent, drawing Vicki's attention around to a marshy cove off to her right. The silence was so complete she thought she could hear a half a hundred tiny amphibian hearts beating. One. Two...

"Hey, there."

She'd spun around and taken a step out into the lake before her brain caught up with her reaction. The feel of cold water filling her hiking boots brought her back to herself and she damped the hunter in her eyes before the man in the canoe had time to realize his danger.

Paddle in the water, holding the canoe in place, he nodded down at Vicki's feet. "You don't want to be doing that."

"Doing what?"

"Wadding at night. You're going to want to see where you're going, old Nepeakea drops off fast." He jerked his head back toward the silvered darkness. "Even the ministry boys couldn't tell you how deep she is in the middle. She's got so much loose mud on the bottom it kept throwing back their sonar readings."

"Then what are you doing here?"

"Well, I'm not wading, that's for sure."

"Or answering my question," Vicki muttered stepping back out on the shore. Wet feet making her less than happy, she half hoped for another smart ass comment.

"I often canoe at night. I like the quiet." He grinned in at her, clearly believing he was too far away and there was too little light for her to see the appraisal that went with it. "You must be that investigator from Toronto. I saw your van when I was up at the lodge today."

"You must be Frank Patton. You've changed your boat."

"Can't be quiet in a 50 horsepower Evinrude can I? You going in to see Mary Joseph?"

"No. I was going in to see Anne Kellough."

"Second house past the stop sign on the right. Little yellow bungalow with a carport." He slid backward so quietly even Vicki wouldn't have known he was moving had she not been watching him. He handled the big aluminum canoe with practiced ease. "I'd offer you a lift but I'm sure you're in a hurry."

Vicki smiled. "Thanks anyway." Her eyes silvered. "Maybe another time."

She was still smiling as she got into the van. Out on the lake, Frank Patton splashed about trying to retrieve the canoe paddle that had dropped from nerveless fingers.

"Frankly, I hate the little bastard, but there's no law against that." Anne Kellough pulled her sweater tighter and leaned back against the porch railing. "He's the one who set the health department on me you know."

"I didn't."

"Oh yeah. He came up here about three months before it happened looking for land and he wanted mine. I wouldn't sell it to him so he figured out a way to take it." Anger quickened her breathing and flared her nostrils. "He as much as told me, after it was all over, with that big shit-eating grin and his, 'Rough luck, Ms. Kellough, too bad the banks can't be more forgiving.' The patronizing asshole." Eyes narrowed, she glared at Vicki. "And you know what really pisses me off? I used to rent the lodge out to people who needed a little silence in their lives; you know, so they could maybe hear what was going on inside their heads. If Stuart Gordon has his way, there won't be any silence and the place'll be awash in brand names and expensive dental work."

"If Stuart Gordon has his way?" Vicki repeated, brows rising.

"Well, it's not built yet, is it?"

"He has all the paperwork filed; what's going to stop him?"

The other woman picked at a flake of paint, her whole attention focused on lifting it from the railing. Just when Vicki felt she'd have to ask again, Anne looked up and out toward the dark waters of the lake. "That's the question, isn't it," she said softly, brushing her hair back off her face.

The lake seemed no different to Vicki than it ever had. About to suggest that the question acquire an answer, she suddenly frowned. "What happened to your hand? That looks like an acid burn."

"It is." Anne turned her arm so that the burn was more clearly visible to them both. "Thanks to Stuart fucking Gordon, I couldn't afford to take my car in to the garage and I had to change the battery myself. I thought I was being careful..." She shrugged.

"A new battery, eh? Afraid I can't help you miss." Ken, owner of Ken's Garage and Auto Body, pressed one knee against the side of the van and leaned, letting it take his weight as he filled the tank. "But if you're not in a hurry I can go into Bigwood tomorrow and get you one." Before Vicki could speak, he went on. "No wait, tomorrow's Sunday, place'll be closed. Closed Monday too seeing as how it's Victoria Day." He shrugged and smiled. "I'll be open but that won't get you a battery."

"It doesn't have to be a new one. I just want to make sure that when I turn her off on the way home I can get her started again." Leaning back against the closed driver's side door, she gestured into the work bay where a small pile of old batteries had been more or less stacked against the back wall. "What about one of them?"

Ken turned, peered, and shook his head. "Damn but you've got good eyes, miss. It's dark as bloody pitch in there."

"Thank you."

"None of them batteries will do you any good though, cause I drained them all a couple of days ago. They're just too dangerous, eh? You know, if kids get poking around?" He glanced over at the gas pump and carefully squirted the total up to an even thirty-two dollars. "You're that investigator working up at the lodge, aren't you?" he asked as he pushed the bills she handed him into a greasy pocket and counted out three loonies in change. "Trying to lay the spirit?"

"Trying to catch whoever vandalized Stuart Gordon's car."

"He, uh, get that fixed then?"

"Good as new." Vicki opened the van door and paused, one foot up on the running board. "I take it he didn't get it fixed here?"

"Here?" The slightly worried expression on Ken's broad face vanished to be replaced by a curled lip and narrowed eyes. "My gas isn't good enough for that pissant. He's planning to put his own tanks in if he gets that god damned yuppie resort built."

"If?"

Much as Anne Kellough had, he glanced toward the lake. "If."

About to swing up into the van, two five gallon glass jars sitting outside the office caught her eye. The lids were off and it looked very much as though they were airing out. "I haven't seen jars like that in years," she said, pointing. "I don't suppose you want to sell them?"

Ken turned to follow her finger. "Can't. They belong to my cousin. I just borrowed them, eh? Her kids were supposed to come and get them but, hey, you know kids."

According to call-me-Stuart, the village was no place to raise kids.

Glass jars would be handy for transporting acid mixed with fish bits.

And where would they have gotten the fish, she wondered, pulling carefully out of the gas station. *Maybe from one of the boys who runs the hunting and fishing camp.*

Pete Wegler stood in the door of his trailer, a slightly confused look on his face. "Do I know you?"

Vicki smiled. "Not yet. Aren't you going to invite me in?"

Ten to twelve. The lights were still on at the lodge. Celluci stood, stretched, and wondered how much longer Vicki was going to be. *Surely everyone in Dulvie's asleep by now.*

Maybe she stopped for a bite to eat.

The second thought followed the first too quickly for him to prevent it so he ignored it instead. Turning his back on the lodge, he sat down and stared out at the lake. Water looked almost secretive at night, he decided as his eyes readjusted to the darkness.

In his business, secretive meant guilty.

"And if Stuart Gordon has gotten a protective spirit pissed off enough to kill, what then?" he wondered aloud, glancing down at his watch.

Midnight.

Which meant absolutely nothing to that ever expanding catalogue of things that went bump in the night. Experience had taught him that the so called supernatural was just about as likely to attack at two in the afternoon as at midnight but he couldn't not react to the knowledge that he was as far from the dubious safety of daylight as he was able to get.

Even the night seemed affected.

Waiting...

A breeze blew in off the lake and the hair lifted on both his arms.

Waiting for *something* to happen.

About fifteen feet from shore, a fish broke through the surface of the water like Alice going the wrong way through the

Looking Glass. It leapt up, up, and was suddenly grabbed by the end of a glistening, gray tube as big around as his biceps. Teeth, or claws or something back inside the tube's opening sank into the fish and together they finished the arch of the leap. A hump, the same glistening gray, slid up and back into the water, followed by what could only have been the propelling beat of a flat tail. From teeth to tail the whole thing had to be at least nine feet long.

"Jesus H. Christ." He took a deep breath and added, "On crutches."

"I'm telling you, Vicki, I saw the spirit of the lake manifest."

"You saw something eat a fish." Vicki stared out at the water but saw only the reflection of a thousand stars. "You probably saw a bigger fish eat a fish. A long, narrow pike leaping up after a nice fat bass."

About to deny he'd seen any such thing, Celluci suddenly frowned. "How do you know so much about fish?"

"I had a little talk with Pete Wegler tonight. He provided the fish for the acid bath, provided by Ken the garageman, in glass jars provided by Ken's cousin, Kathy Boomhower—the mother who went much beyond name calling with our boy Stuart. Anne Kellough did the deed—she's convinced Gordon called in the Health Department to get his hands on the property—having been transported quietly to the site in Frank Patton's canoe." She grinned. "I feel like Hercule Poirot on the Orient Express."

"Yeah? Well, I'm feeling a lot more Stephen King than Agatha Christie."

Sobering, Vicki laid her hand on the barricade of his crossed arms and studied his face. "You're really freaked by this aren't you?"

"I don't know exactly what I saw, but I didn't see a fish get eaten by another fish."

The muscles under her hand were rigid and he was staring past her, out at the lake. "Mike, what is it?"

"I told you, Vicki. I don't know exactly what I saw." In spite of everything, he still liked his world defined. Reluctantly transferring his gaze to the pale oval of her upturned face, he sighed. "How much, if any, of this do you want me to tell Mr. Gordon tomorrow?"

"How about none? I'll tell him myself after sunset."

"Fine. It's late, I'm turning in. I assume you'll be staking out the parking lot for the rest of the night."

"What for? I guarantee the vengeful spirits won't be back." Her voice suggested that in a direct, one-on-one confrontation, a vengeful spirit wouldn't stand a chance. Celluci remembered the thing that rose up out of the lake and wasn't so sure.

"That doesn't matter, you promised 24 hour protection."

"Yeah, but…" His expression told her that if she wasn't going to stay, he would. "Fine, I'll watch the car. Happy?"

"That you're doing what you said you were going to do? Ecstatic." Celluci unfolded his arms, pulled her close enough to kiss the frown lines between her brows, and headed for the lodge. *She had a little talk with Pete Wegler, my ass.* He knew Vicki had to feed off others, but he didn't have to like it.

Should never have mentioned Pete Wegler. She settled down on the rock still warm from Celluci's body heat and tried unsuccessfully to penetrate the darkness of the lake. When something rustled in the underbrush bordering the parking lot, she hissed without turning her head. The rustling moved away with considerably more speed than it had used to arrive. The secrets of the lake continued to elude her.

"This isn't mysterious, it's irritating."

As Celluci wandered around the lodge, turning off lights, he could hear Stuart snoring through the door of one of the two mainfloor bedrooms. In the few hours he'd been outside, the other man had managed to leave a trail of debris from one end of the place to the other. On top of that, he'd used up the last of the toilet paper on the roll and hadn't replaced it, he'd put the almost empty coffee pot back on the coffee maker with the machine still on so that the dregs had baked onto the glass, and he'd eaten a piece of Celluci's chicken, tossing the gnawed bone back into the bucket. Celluci didn't mind him eating the piece of chicken but the last thing he wanted was Stuart Gordon's spit over the rest of the bird.

Dropping the bone into the garbage, he noticed a crumpled piece of paper and fished it out. Apparently the resort was destined to grow beyond its current boundaries. Destined to grow all the way around the lake, devouring Dulvie as it went.

"Which would put Stuart Gordon's spit all over the rest of the area."

Bored with watching the lake and frightening off the local wildlife, Vicki pressed her nose against the window of the sports ute and clicked her tongue at the dashboard full of electronic displays, willing to bet that call-me-Stuart didn't have the slightest idea of what most of them meant.

"Probably has a trouble light if his air freshener needs...hello."

Tucked under the passenger seat was the unmistakable edge of a lap top.

"And how much to you want to bet this thing'll scream bloody blue murder if I try and jimmy the door..." Turning toward the now dark lodge, she listened to the sound of two heartbeats. To the slow, regular sound that told her both men were deeply asleep.

Stuart slept on his back with one hand flung over his head and a slight smile on his thin face. Vicki watched the pulse beat in his throat for a moment. She'd been assured that, if necessary she could feed off lower lifeforms—pigeons, rats, developers—but she was just as glad she'd taken the edge off the Hunger down in the village. Scooping up his car keys, she went out of the room as silently as she'd come in.

Celluci woke to a decent voice belting out a Beatles tune and came downstairs just as Stuart came out of the bathroom finger combing damp hair.

"Good morning, Mike. Can I assume no vengeful spirits of Lake Nepeakea trashed my car in the night?"

"You can."

"Good. Good. Oh, by the way…" His smile could have sold attitude to Americans. "…I've used all the hot water."

"I guess it's true what they say about so many of our boys in blue."

"And what's that?" Celluci growled, fortified by two cups of coffee made only slightly bitter by the burned carafe.

"Well you know, Mike." Grinning broadly, the developer mimed tipping a bottle to his lips. "I mean, if you can drink that vile brew, you've certainly got a drinking problem." Laughing at his own joke, he headed for the door.

To begin with, they're not your boys in blue and then, you can just fucking well drop dead. You try dealing with the world we deal with for a while asshole, it'll chew you up and spit you out. But although his fist closed around his mug tightly enough for it to creak, all he said was, "Where are you going?"

"Didn't I tell you? I've got to see a lawyer in Bigwood today. Yes, I know what you're going to say, Mike; it's Sunday. But since this is the last time I'll be out here for a few weeks, the local legal beagle can see me when I'm available. Just a few loose ends about that nasty business with the surveyor." He paused, with his hand on the door, voice and manner stripped of all pretensions. "I told them to be sure and finish that part of the shoreline before they quit for the day—I know I'm not, but I feel responsible for that poor woman's death and I only wish there was something I could do to make up for it. You can't make up for someone dying though, can you, Mike?"

Celluci growled something non-committal. Right at the moment, the last thing he wanted was to think of Stuart Gordon as a decent human being.

"I might not be back until after dark but hey, that's when the spirit's likely to appear so you won't need me until then. Right, Mike?" Turning toward the screen where the black flies had settled, waiting for their breakfast to emerge, he shook his head. "The first thing I'm going to do when all this is settled is drain every stream these little blood suckers breed in."

The water levels in the swamp had dropped in the two weeks since the death of the surveyor. Drenched in the bug spray he'd found under the sink, Celluci followed the path made by the searchers, treading carefully on the higher hummocks no matter how solid the ground looked. When he reached the remains of the police tape, he squatted and peered down into the water. He didn't expect to find anything but after Stuart's confession, he felt he had to come.

About two inches deep, it was surprisingly clear.

"No reason for it to be muddy now, there's nothing stirring it…"

Something metallic glinted in the mud.

Gripping the marsh grass on his hummock with one hand, he reached out with the other and managed to get thumb and forefinger around the protruding piece of…

"Stainless steel measuring tape?"

It was probably a remnant of the dead surveyor's equipment. One end of the six inch piece had been cleanly broken but the other end, the end that had been down in the mud, looked as though it had been dissolved.

When Anne Kellough had thrown the acid on Stuart's car, they'd been imitating the spirit of Lake Nepeakea.

Celluci inhaled deeply and spit a mouthful of suicidal black flies out into the swamp. "I think it's time to talk to Mary Joseph."

"Can't you feel it?"

Enjoying the first decent cup of coffee he'd had in days, Celluci walked to the edge of the porch and stared out at the lake. Unlike most of Dulvie, separated from the water by the road, Mary Joseph's house was right on the shore. "I can feel *something*," he admitted.

"You can feel the spirit of the lake, angered by this man from the city. Another cookie?"

"No, thank you." He'd had one and it was without question the worst cookie he'd ever eaten. "Tell me about the spirit of the lake, Ms. Joseph. Have you seen it?"

"Oh yes. Well, not exactly it, but I've seen the wake of its passing." She gestured out toward the water but, at the moment, the lake was perfectly calm. "Most water has a protective spirit you know. Wells and springs, lakes and rivers, it's why we throw coins into fountains, so that the spirits will exchange them for luck. Kelpies, selkies, mermaids, Jenny Greenteeth, Peg Powler, the Fideal...all water spirits."

"And one of them, is that what's out there?" Somehow he couldn't reconcile mermaids to that toothed trunk snaking out of the water.

"Oh no, our water spirit is a new world water spirit. The Cree called it a mantouche—surely you recognize the similarity to the word Manitou or Great Spirit? Only the deepest lakes with the best fishing had them. They protected the lakes and the area around the lakes and, in return..."

"Were revered?"

"Well, no actually. They were left strictly alone."

"You told the paper that the spirit had manifested twice before?"

"Twice that we know of," she corrected. "The first recorded manifestation occurred in 1762 and was included in the notes on native spirituality that one of the exploring Jesuits sent back to France."

Product of a Catholic school education, Celluci wasn't entirely certain the involvement of the Jesuits added credibility. "What happened?"

"It was spring. A pair of white trappers had been at the lake all winter, slaughtering the animals around it. Animals under the lake's protection. According to the surviving trapper, his partner was coming out of a highwater marsh, just after sunset, when his canoe suddenly upended and he disappeared. When the remaining man retrieved the canoe he found that bits had been burned away without flame and it carried the mark of all the dead they'd stolen from the lake."

"The mark of the dead?"

"The record says it stank, Detective. Like offal." About to eat another cookie, she paused. "You do know what offal is?"

"Yes, ma'am. Did the survivor see anything?"

"Well, he said he saw what he thought was a giant snake except that it had two stubby wings at the upper end. And you know what that is."

...a glistening, gray tube as big around as his biceps. "No."

"A wyvern. One of the ancient dragons."

"There's a dragon in the lake."

"No, of course not. The spirit of the lake can take many forms. When it's angry, those who facing its anger see a great and terrifying beast. To the trapper, who no doubt had northern European roots, it appeared as a wyvern. The natives would have probably seen a giant serpent. There are many so called serpent mounds around deep lakes."

"But it couldn't just *be* a giant serpent?"

"Detective Celluci, don't you think that if there was a giant serpent living in this lake that someone would have gotten a good look at it by now? Besides, after the second death the lake was searched extensively with modern equipment—and once or twice since then as well—and nothing has ever been found. That trapper was killed by the spirit of the lake and so was Thomas Stebbing."

"Thomas Stebbing?"

"The recorded death in 1937. I have newspaper clippings..."

In the spring of 1937, four young men from the University of Toronto came to Lake Nepeakea on a wilderness vacation. Out canoeing with a friend at dusk, Thomas Stebbing saw what he thought was a burned log on the shore and they paddled in to investigate. As his friend watched in horror, the log "attacked" Stebbing, left him burned and dead, and "undulated into the lake" on a trail of dead vegetation.

The investigation turned up nothing at all and the eyewitness account of a "kind of big worm thing" was summarily dismissed. The final, official verdict was that the victim had indeed disturbed a partially burnt log and, as it rolled over him was burned by the embers and died. The log then rolled into the lake, burning a path as it rolled, and sank. The stench was dismissed as the smell of roasting flesh and the insistence by the

friend that the burns were acid burns was completely ignored—
in spite of the fact he was a chemistry student and should therefore know what he was talking about.

"The spirit of the *lake* came up on *land*, Ms. Joseph?"

She nodded, apparently unconcerned with the contradiction. "There were a lot of fires being lit around the lake that
year. Between the wars this area got popular for a while and
fires were the easiest way to clear land for summer homes.
The spirit of the lake couldn't allow that, hence its appearance
as a burned log."

"And Thomas Stebbing had done what to disturb its peace?"

"Nothing specifically. I think the poor boy was just in the
wrong place at the wrong time. It is a vengeful spirit, you
understand."

Only a few short years earlier, he'd have understood that
Mary Joseph was a total nutcase. But that was before he'd willingly thrown himself into the darkness that lurked behind a pair
of silvered eyes. He sighed and stood. The afternoon had nearly
ended. It wouldn't be long now until sunset.

"Thank you for your help, Ms. Joesph. I…what?"

She was staring at him, nodding. "You've seen it, haven't
you? You have that look."

"I've seen something," he admitted reluctantly and turned
toward the water. "I've seen a lot of thi…"

A pair of jet skis roared around the point and drowned him
out. As they passed the house, blanketing it in noise, one of the
adolescent operators waved a cheery hello.

*Never a vengeful lake spirit around when you really need
one,* he thought.

"He knew about the sinkholes in the marsh and he sent those
surveyors out anyway." Vicki tossed a pebble off the end of the
dock and watched it disappear into the liquid darkness.

"You're sure?"

"The information was all there on his lap top and the file was
dated back in March. Now, although evidence that I just happened to have found in his computer will be inadmissible in court,

I can go to the Department of Lands and Forests and get the dates he requested the geological surveys."

Celluci shook his head. "You're not going to be able to get him charged with anything. Sure, he should've told them but they were both professionals, they should've been more careful." He thought of the crocodile tears Stuart had cried that morning over the death and his hands formed fists by his side. Being a irresponsible asshole was one thing; being a manipulative, irresponsible asshole was on another level entirely. "It's an ethical failure," he growled, "not a legal one."

"Maybe I should take care of him myself then." The second pebble hit the water with considerably more force.

"He's your client, Vicki. You're supposed to be working for him, not against him."

She snorted. "So I'll wait until his check clears."

"He's planning on acquiring the rest of the land around the lake." Pulling the paper he'd retrieved from the garbage out of his pocket, Celluci handed it over.

"The rest of the land around the lake isn't for sale."

"Neither was this lodge until he decided he wanted it."

Crushing the paper in one hand, Vicki's eyes silvered. "There's got to be something we can…Shit!" Tossing the paper aside, she grabbed Celluci's arm and leapt back one section, dragging him with her as the end of the dock bucked up into the air . "What the fuck was that?" she demanded as they turned to watch the place they'd just been standing rock violently back and forth. The paper she'd dropped into the water was nowhere to be seen.

"Wave from a passing boat?"

"There hasn't been a boat past here in hours."

"Sometimes these long narrow lakes build up a standing wave. It's called a seiche."

"A seiche?" When he nodded, she rolled her eyes. "I've got to start watching more PBS. In the meantime…"

The sound of an approaching car drew their attention up to the lodge in time to see Stuart slowly and carefully pull into the parking lot, barely disturbing the gravel.

"Are you going to tell him who vandalized his car?" Celluci asked as they started up the hill.

"Who? Probably not. I can't prove it after all, but I will tell him it wasn't some vengeful spirit and it definitely won't happen again." At least not if Pete Wegler had anything to say about it. The spirit of the lake might be hypothetical but she wasn't.

"A group of villagers, Vicki? You're sure?"

"Positive."

"They actually thought I'd believe it was an angry spirit manifesting all over the side of my vehicle?"

"Apparently." Actually, they hadn't cared if he believed it or not. They were all just so angry they needed to do something and since the spirit was handy... She offered none of that to call-me-Stuart.

"I want their names, Vicki." His tone made it an ultimatum.

Vicki had never responded well to ultimatums. Celluci watched her masks begin to fall and wondered just how far his dislike of the developer would let her go. He could stop her with a word, he just wondered if he'd say it. Or when.

To his surprise, she regained control. "Check the census lists then. You haven't exactly endeared yourself to your neighbors."

For a moment, it seemed that Stuart realized how close he'd just come to seeing the definition of his own mortality but then he smiled and said, "You're right, Vicki, I haven't endeared myself to my neighbors. And do you know what; I'm going to do something about that. Tomorrow's Victoria Day, I'll invite them all to a big picnic supper with great food and fireworks out over the lake. We'll kiss and make up."

"It's Sunday evening and tomorrow's a holiday. Where are you going to find food and fireworks?"

"Not a problem, Mike. I'll email my caterers in Toronto. I'm sure they can be here by tomorrow afternoon. I'll pay through the nose but hey, developing a good relationship with the locals is worth it. You two will stay, of course."

Vicki's lips drew back off her teeth but Celluci answered for them both. "Of course."

"He's up to something," he explained later, "and I want to know what that is."

"He's going to confront the villagers with what he knows, see who reacts and make their lives a living hell. He'll find a way to make them the first part of his expansion."

"You're probably right."

"I'm always right." Head pillowed on his shoulder, she stirred his chest hair with one finger. "He's an unethical, immoral, unscrupulous little asshole."

"You missed annoying, irritating, and just generally unlikable."

"I could convince him he was a combination of Mother Theresa and Lady Di. I could rip his mind out, use it for unnatural purposes, and stuff it back into his skull in any shape I damn well choose, but, unfortunately I won't."

Once you start down the dark side, forever will it dominate your destiny? But he didn't say it aloud because he didn't want to know how far down the dark side she'd been. He was grateful that she'd drawn any personal boundaries at all, that she'd chosen to remain someone who couldn't use terror for the sake of terror. "So what are we going to do about him?"

"I can't think of a damned thing. You?"

Suddenly he smiled. "Could you convince him that you were the spirit of the lake and that he'd better haul his ass back to Toronto unless he wanted it dissolved off?"

She was off the bed in one fluid movement. "I knew there was a reason I dragged you out here this weekend." She turned on one bare heel then turned again and was suddenly back in the bed. "But I think I'll wait until tomorrow night. He hasn't paid me yet."

"Morning, Mike. Where's Vicki?"

"Sleeping."

"Well, since you're up, why don't you help out by carrying the barbecue down to the beach. I may be willing to make amends but I'm not sure they are and since they've already damaged my car, I'd just as soon keep them away from anything valuable. Particularly when in combination with propane and open flames."

"Isn't Vicki joining us for lunch, Mike?"

"She says she isn't hungry. She went for a walk in the woods."

"Must be how she keeps her girlish figure. I've got to hand it to you, Mike, there aren't many men your age who could hold onto such a woman. I mean, she's really got that independent thing going doesn't she?" He accepted a tuna sandwich with effusive thanks took a bite and winced. "Not light mayo?"

"No."

"Never mind, Mike. I'm sure you meant well. Now, then, as it's just the two of us, have you ever considered investing in a time share…"

Mike Celluci had never been so glad to see anyone as he was to see a van full of bleary eyed and stiff caterers arrive at four that afternoon. As Vicki had discovered during that initial phone call, Stuart Gordon was not a man who took no for an answer. He might have accepted "Fuck off and die!" followed by a fast exit, but since Vicki expected to wake up on the shores of Lake Nepeakea, Celluci held his tongue. Besides, it would be a little difficult for her to chase the developer away if they were half way back to Toronto.

Sunset.

Vicki could feel maybe two dozen lives around her when she woke and she laid there for a moment reveling in them. The last two evenings she'd had to fight the urge to climb into the driver's seat and speed toward civilization.

"Fast food."

She snickered, dressed, and stepped out into the parking lot.

Celluci was down on the beach talking to Frank Patton. She made her way over to them, the crowd opening to let her pass without really being aware she was there at all. Both men nodded as she approached and Patton gestured toward the barbecue.

"Burger?"

"No thanks, I'm not hungry." She glanced around. "No one seems to have brought their kids."

"No one wants to expose their kids to Stuart Gordon."

"Afraid they'll catch something," Celluci added.

"Mike here says you've solved your case and you're just waiting for Mr. Congeniality over there to pay you."

Wondering what Mike had been up to, Vicki nodded.

"He also says you didn't mention any names. Thank you." He sighed. "We didn't really expect the spirit of the lake thing to work but…"

Vicki raised both hands. "Hey, you never know. He could be suppressing."

"Yeah, right. The only thing that clown suppresses is everyone around him. If you'll excuse me, I'd better go rescue Anne before she rips out his tongue and strangles him with it."

"I'm surprised she came," Vicki admitted.

"She thinks he's up to something and she wants to know what it is."

"Don't we all," Celluci murmured as he walked away.

The combined smell of cooked meat and fresh blood making her a little light headed, Vicki started Mike moving toward the floating dock. "Have I missed anything?"

"No, I think you're just in time."

As Frank Patton approached, Stuart broke off the conversation he'd been having with Anne Kellough—or more precisely, Vicki amended, at Anne Kellough—and walked out to the end of the dock where a number of large rockets had been set up.

"He's got a permit for the damned things," Celluci muttered. "The son of a bitch knows how to cover his ass."

"But not his id." Vicki's fingers curved cool around Mike's forearm. "He'll get his, don't worry."

The first rocket went up, exploding red over the lake, the colors muted against the evening gray of sky and water. The developer turned toward the shore and raised both hands above his head. "Now that I've got your attention, there's a few things I'd like to share with you all before the festivities continue. First of all, I've decided not to press charges concerning the damage to my vehicle although I'm aware that..."

The dock began to rock. Behind him, one of the rockets fell into the water.

"Mr. Gordon." The voice was Mary Joseph's. "Get to shore, now."

Pointing a finger toward her, he shook his head. "Oh no, old woman, I'm Stuart Gordon..."

No *call-me-Stuart*, tonight, Celluci noted.

"...and you don't tell me what to do, I tell..."

Arms windmilling, he stepped back, once, twice, and hit the water. Arms and legs stretched out, he looked as though he was sitting on something just below the surface. "I have had enough of this," he began...

...and disappeared.

Vicki reached the end of the dock in time to see the pale oval of his face engulfed by dark water. To her astonishment, he seemed to have gotten his cell phone out of his pocket and all she could think of was that old movie cut line, *Who you gonna call?*

One heartbeat, two. She thought about going in after him. The fingertips on her reaching hand were actually damp when Celluci grabbed her shoulder and pulled her back. She wouldn't have done it, but it was nice that he thought she would.

Back on the shore, two dozen identical wide-eyed stares were locked on the flat, black surface of the lake, too astounded by what had happened to their mutual enemy, Vicki realized, to notice how fast she'd made it to the end of the dock.

Mary Joseph broke the silence first. "Thus acts the vengeful spirit of Lake Nepeakea," she declared. Then as heads began to nod, she added dryly, "Can't say I didn't warn him."

Mike looked over at Vicki, who shrugged.

"Works for me," she said.

The following is an excerpt form Tanya's new novel from DAW Books in 1999.

Revelry was not the best thing to have reverberating through one's skull after a night of too much and too little in various combinations. Making a mental note to change the program to something less painfully intrusive, Torin tongued the implant and tried to remember how to open her eyes during the five blessed seconds of silence before the first of her messages came in.

At the chime, it will be 0530.

The chime set up interesting patterns on the inside of her lids. What had she been drinking?

Your liberty will be over at 0600.

Which might be a problem considering how much trouble she was having with basic bodily functions. Groping for the panel beside the bed, she applied what she hoped was enough pressure for dim lighting and cautiously cracked an eye. From the little she could see, these were not her quarters. The less than state of the art wall utility suggested station guest quarters—for a not particularly important guest.

Finally managing to sort current sensation from memory, she turned her head toward the warm body pressed up against her side. The Taykan's short lilac hair swayed gently in response to her exhalation, the pointed tip of an ear covered and uncovered by the moving strands.

A Taykan.

That explained things. It wasn't a hangover, she had pheromone head.

Sliding out from under the blanket, Torin stood, stretched carefully and filled her lungs with air that hadn't been warmed by the Taykan's body heat. As memories returned, she smiled. Not only did Humans find the Taykan incredibly attractive but a Taykan in the di' phase was one of the most indiscriminately enthusiastic lifeforms in the Galaxy and offered the perfect and uncomplicated way to chase the memories of that last, horrible planetfall right back to the galactic core.

Captain Rose wants to see you in his office at 0800.

There were two piles of clothing on the room's one chair; both folded into neatly identical piles. Wondering if the Taykan had been taught by a particularly strict sheshan as a child—name, if not manner indicated di' Ka Darnayal came from one of the old aristocratic families—she scooped up hers and ducked into the bathroom. When she emerged a few moments later, fully dressed, all she could see of her companion was a lithe lump under the blanket and a moving fringe of uncovered hair.

Relieved, she moved silently toward the door, pausing only long enough to turn the lights off. A di' Taykan considered, "Once more before breakfast?"

to be a reasonable substitute for "Good morning." and as she had no time, she was just as happy not to have to test her willpower.

Outside in the corridor, the familiar "something's leaking somewhere" smell of the station's recycled air drove the last of the pheromone-induced haze from her head.

0547 the implant told her when she prodded. Thirteen minutes before her liberty ended and her flasher came back up on screen. Thirteen minutes to get to a part of the station that wouldn't incite purient speculation among the duty staff.

"I should've reset wakeup for five. What was I thinking?" she muttered diving into the vertical—fortunately empty at this hour—and freefalling two levels. Grabbing a handhold, she swung out the lock level. Easy answer, actually. She'd been thinking that she needed to forget the carnage, forget those they lost limping back to the station on a ship that had won its battle but nearly lost its own little slice of the war, forget the messages she'd sent to family and friends, and forget that new faces, always new faces, arriving to replace those they'd lost.

And she had been able to forget. For a while.

A di' Taykan wouldn't feel used. She didn't think they could.

Considering the time, it was a damned good thing station guest quarters were on the same side of the core as the barracks. Another vertical, another lock and she was in NCO country.

0600

Heading for her own quarters, Staff Sergeant Torin Kerr had her implant scan the night's reports for any of the names she kept flagged. Apparently, no one had died and no one had gotten arrested.

Things hadn't fallen apart while she was gone.

No harm done and it wasn't as if she'd ever see the Taykan again...

At 0758, showered, changed, and carrying her slate, Torin approached the captain's door turning over the possible reasons he'd moved their morning meeting up an hour. As senior surviving NCO, she'd been his acting First Sergeant since the battered remnant of Sh'quo Company had arrived back at the station. Clearly that wasn't going to last but it was unlikely Battalion HQ would send out a new First before the recruits needed to bring the company up to strength—unlikely but possible, she admitted after a moment's reflection. Battalion HQ had shown what could only be called unique leadership in the past.

It was also possible that they were promoting her and the captain needed to tell her in time for her to make the 1000 shuttle. With a war on, it didn't take long to make sergeant but after that, promotions tended to slow down, common wisdom suggesting that by the time a grunt got that third chevron, they'd learned to duck. Still, with the company losing their First there'd be a Gunny moving up and that'd leave room for her.

She'd have rather had First Sergeant Chigma back. The few Krai who went into the Marines usually opted for armored platoons or air support—their feet just weren't built for infantry—so those few who not only chose to be grunts but rose in the ranks left pretty big shoes to fill. Unfortunately, since Chigma had ended up on the wrong end of an enemy projectile weapon their last planetfall...

0759

Maybe the med-op had scheduled the captain for new treatments at nine.

Look at the bright side, she reminded herself, laying her palm against the door, we're in no condition to be sent back out.

The presence of a two star general in the captain's office did not come as a pleasant surprise. In Torin's experience, when generals ignored the chain of command to speak directly to sergeants, it was never good news. And smiling generals were the worst kind.

"You must be Staff Sergeant Kerr."

"Sir."

"Staff, this is General Morris." The regeneration tank around the lower half of his left leg kept Captain Rose from standing but his voice, unexpectedly deep from a such a small man, was enough to stop the general's advance. "He has new orders for you."

"Say rather an opportunity. But don't let me interrupt." He gestured at the slate under Torin's arm. "I understand you've been acting First. We'll talk once you've finished your morning report."

"Sir." Her face expressionless under the general's smiling regard, she crossed to the desk and downloaded the relevant files. Right now, with no more information to go on than his smile and two dozen words delivered in an annoying we're-all-in-this-together tone, she'd be willing to bet that General Morris had never seen combat and that Captain Rose liked him even less than she did. As the captain appeared to know what was going on, her sense of impending disaster strengthened.

"Doctorow's no longer critical?"

"Regained consciousness at 0300. Woke up and demanded to know what..." Given the general's presence, she rephrased the quote. "...idiot had taken his implant off line."

"Good news." Quickly scanning the rest of the report, the captain looked up, brows rising. "No one got arrested?"

"Apparently some vacuum jockeys off The Redoubt got into a disagreement with some of our air support in Haligan's and betting on the fight provided a sufficient diversion."

"Wait a minute," the general interrupted, one hand raised as if to physically stop further discussion. "Am I to understand that you expected your people to get arrested?"

Together, Torin and the captain turned, Torin shifting position slightly, unable to move to the captain's side but making it quite clear where she stood as he answered. "I'm sure I don't need to tell the general what kind of planetfall we had. After something like that, I expect my people to need to blow off."

The general's broad cheeks flushed. "You've been on station for six days."

"Half of us have. Sir." Like many combat officers, Captain Rose had come up through the ranks and he'd retained the NCO's ability to place inflection.

The two men locked eyes.

General Morris looked away first. "They say another company wouldn't have got that many out," he admitted.

"I have good people, sir. And I lost good people." The quiet reminder drew Torin's gaze down to the captain's face and she frowned slightly. He looked tired, his fair skin had developed a greyish cast and there were dark circles under his eyes. Had they been alone, she'd have asked how the regeneration was going; as it was, she made a mental note to check his condition with med-op as soon as possible. As acting First, he was as much her concern as the company.

"Yes. Good people." General Morris straightened and cleared his throat. "Which leads us nicely into what I'm here for."

Oh shit. Here it comes. Torin braced herself as he aimed that *I'm looking for someone to get their tail shot off* smile directly at her.

"I need a platoon for a special duty, shipping out ASAP."

"I haven't got a platoon, sir."

He looked momentarily nonplused and then the smile returned. "Of course, I see. I should have said, I need you to put together a platoon out of the available Marines."

"Out of what's left of Sh'quo Company, sir?"

"Yes."

"Out of the survivors, sir?"

"Yes." The general's smile had begun to tighten.

Torin figured she'd gotten as much satisfaction from that line of inquiry as she was likely to. "A lot of them have leave coming, sir, but we should have new recruits arriving shortly."

"No. Even if I had time to wait for new recruits, I couldn't use them." Folding his hands behind his back in what Torin thought she recognized as parade ground rest—it had been a damned long time since she'd seen a parade ground—the general fixed her with an imposing stare. "I'm full aware of your situation, Staff Sergeant Kerr, yours and Sh'quo Company's and I wouldn't be canceling leaves if it wasn't absolutely necessary. The problem, Sergeant, is this; I'm putting together a very important diplomatic mission intended to convince a new race to join the Confederation and I need an Honor Guard. A military escort is absolutely essential because the new race, the Silsviss, are controlled by a powerful warrior cast that we most certainly do not want to insult. After careful consideration, I've decided that Sh'quo company is the best available unit."

"As an honor guard?" Torin glanced from the general to her captain— who looked so noncommittal that the hope it was some kind of a joke died unborn—and back to the general again. "We're ground combat, sir, not a ceremonial unit."

"You'll do fine. All you have to do, Sergeant, is have the troops apply a little spit and polish then stand around and look menacing. You'll see new worlds, meet new lifeforms, and not shoot at them for a change." He paused for laughter that never came then continued gruffly. "It's a win/win situation. I won't have to pull a company out of their rotation for planetfall— which means Sh'quo Company won't be rotated in before it's their turn. As there's no need for heavy artillery, company equipment can still get the overhaul it requires."

"A full platoon makes quite an honor guard, sir."

"It's essential we make a strong impression, Sergeant." For less than an instant, an honest emotion showed in the general's eyes but before Torin could identify it, he added, "Besides, it'll give you a chance to break in your new 2nd Lieutenant."

"My new..." Unable to think of anything to say to the general that wouldn't get her court martialed, she turned to Captain Rose. "Sir?"

"He arrived yesterday afternoon, I asked him to meet us here at 0900. The general thought you should receive your orders first and then he could give the lieutenant the overview."

Officers handled the big picture, NCO's handled the minutia. Part of a Staff Sergeant's minutia was handling new officers in charge of their first platoon. This would be Torin's third, Staff Sergeants having a slightly longer life expectancy than 2nd Lieutenants.

The captain's door announced an arrival just as her implant proclaimed 0900.

"Open."

The door slid back into the wall and a Taykan wearing the uniform of a 2nd Lieutenant, Confederation Marine Corps, walked into the office pheromone masker prominently displayed at his throat. It could have been any Taykan; Torin was no better than most Humans at telling them apart. Male and female, they were all tall, slender, and pointy and, even when heavily armed, moved like they were dancing. Their "hair" grew a uniform three inches long so they all looked as if they went to the same barber and with their somewhat eclectic taste in clothing removed by the corps...

It could have been any Taykan, but it wasn't.

The lilac eyes, exactly one shade darker than his hair, widened slightly when he saw her and slightly more when he spotted the general. "2nd Lieutenant di'Ka Darnayal, reporting as ordered, Captain."

"Welcome to Sh'quo Company, Lieutenant. General Morris will begin your briefing in a moment but in the meantime, I'd like you to meet Staff Sergeant Kerr. She'll be your senior NCO."

The corners of the wide mouth curled slightly. "Staff."

"Sir." There were a number of things Torin figured she should be thinking about now but all that came to mind was, so that explains why he folded his clothes so neatly which wasn't even remotely relevant. She only hoped she'd managed to control her expression by the time Captain Rose turned his too perceptive attention her way.

"Sergeant, if you could start forming that platoon... see if you can do it without splitting up any fireteams. The three of us..."

She had to admire how that us definitively excluded the general.

"...will go over what you've got this afternoon."

"Yes, sir." Turning toward General Morris, she stiffened not quite to attention. "Begging the general's pardon but if I'm to cancel liberties I need to know exactly how soon ASAP is."

"Forty-eight hours."

She should've known—a desk jockey's version of as soon as possible, or in other words, no real rush. "Thank you, sir." Retrieving her slate from the captain's desk, she nodded at all three officers, turned on her heel, and left the room.

The general's hearty voice followed her out into the corridor.

"Lieutenant, I've got a proposal, I think you'll..."

Then she stepped beyond the proximately grid and the door slid shut.

"Figures," Torin sighed. "Officers get a proposal and the rest of us just get screwed."

Technically, she could've worked at the First's desk in the small office right next to the captain's. All Chigma's personal files had been deleted, every trace of his occupancy removed—it was just a desk. Smarter than any other she'd have access to but still, just a desk. Which was why she didn't want to use it. Sometimes it was just too depressing to contemplate how quickly the Corps moved on.

The verticals were crowded at this hour of the mornings so she grabbed the first available loop for the descent down to C deck, exchanging a disgusted look with a Navy Warrant one loop over; both of them in full agreement that their careful progress represented an irritating waste of time. By the time she finally swung out onto the deck, Torin was ready to kill the idiot in station programming who'd decided to inflict insipid music on trapped personnel.

"'Morning, Staff."

The cheerful greeting brought her up short and she turned toward the Marine kneeling by the edges of the lock with a degrimer, turquoise hair flattened by the vibrations. The grooves could have been scrubbed automatically but on a station designed to house thousands of Marines, manual labor became a useful discipline. "Maintenance duties again, Haysole?"

The Taykan grinned. "I was only cutting across the core. I figured I'd be there and back before anyone noticed I wasn't wearing my masker."

"You crossed the core on a Fivesday evening unmasked and you're only on maintenance?"

"I kept moving, it wasn't too bad." Turquoise eyes sparkled. "Unfortunately, Sergeant Glicksohn was also crossing the core. Uh, Staff..." He paused while a pair of Human engineers came through the lock, waiting until they'd moved beyond their ability to overhear. "...I heard you were seeing stars in the captain's office."

Torin folded her arms around her slate. Many Taykan worked in Intelligence—most species had to make a conscious effort not to confide in them. She had no idea how need-to-know General Morris had intended to keep his visit but it was irrelevant now. "What else have you heard, Haysole."

He grinned, taking her lack of denial for confirmation. "That the stars have risen as high as possible in the political sky and this visit is intended to give them a boost."

"And?"

"And the new trilinshy is a di'Ka."

She frowned and his grin disappeared as he realized she'd translated trilinshy to something approximating its distinctly uncomplimentary meaning.

"That is, the new 2nd Lieutenant is a di'Ka, Staff Sergeant. High family. Not going to be easy to work with."

"For me or for you?" Private First Class Haysole was a di'Stenjic. Five more letters in a Taykan family name made for a considerable difference in class.

His graceful shrug meant absolutely nothing. "You know me, Sarge, I get along with everybody.

"Staff Sergeant Kerr?"

Torin started, suddenly aware she'd been staring at nothing for a few moments too long, the implications of shepherding an aristocratic 2nd Lieutenant and a combat platoon through a planetfall where no one got to shoot anything suddenly sinking in. And just in case that doesn't seem like enough fun, let's not forget you slept with said 2nd Luie. The one bright light in her morning was that that particular little tidbit hadn't been picked up by the gossip net. "You missed a spot," she said pointing, and left him to it.

TANYA HUFF, THE ESSENTIAL BIOGRAPHY

Born in Halifax, Nova Scotia: Although I haven't actually lived "down east" since just before my fourth birthday, I still consider myself a Maritimer. I think it's something to do with being born in sight of the ocean. Or possibly with the fact that almost no one admits to being from Ontario...

Raised, for the most part, in Kingston, Ontario. It was the late sixties, early to mid seventies. Enough said for those of us who lived through it—and those who didn't seem to be getting another chance to fall off platform shoes.

Spent three years in the Canadian Naval Reserve: I was a cook. They'd just opened it up to women and I figured it would be the first trade that would send women to sea. I was right. Unfortunately it happened a year after I left.

Received a degree in RADIO AND TELEVISION ARTS (B.A.A.) from Ryerson Polytechnical Institute: The year I graduated was the year that the CBC laid off 750 employees in Toronto alone. We were competing for jobs with people who had up to five years experience. The cat threw up on my degree.

Spent eight years working at Bakka, North America's oldest surviving science fiction book store: Change Of Hobbit in California was actually a very little bit older but unfortunately it was a casualty of the recession in '91. During those eight years, while working full-time, I wrote seven books (the first seven, except for the original draft of CHILD), and nine short stories.

In 1992, after living in downtown Toronto, a city of nearly three million, for thirteen years, I moved with two large cats, one small psychotic cat, and my partner out to a rented house in the middle of nowhere. In the years since, we've purchased the house, buried two of the original cats, replaced them with three more felines and, unintentionally, acquired a Chihuahua. You're probably wondering how two reasonably intelligent adults can unintentionally acquire a Chihuahua. Please don't ask.

I love living in the country, writing full-time, anything by Charles de Lint, Xena, Hercules, Buffy, and email. I dislike telephones, electric blankets, and bathroom renovations.

I always expect catastrophe; as a result, I'm usually pleasantly surprised.

TODD LOCKWOOD

Before joining the TSR art staff in September of '96, Todd Lockwood was a sixteen year veteran of advertising, with agents in Denver and New York. His work appears on the covers of Advanced Dungeons and Dragons books and products, on the covers of Asimov's, Analog, Dragon, and in the pages of Science Fiction Age and Realms of Fantasy.

Among the many honors his artwork has recieved are two World Fantasy Artshow awards, three Chesleys, and appearances in Spectrum II, III, and IV. In his spare time he is currently designing action figures for Antiquities Vault, for their Middle Earth toy line, and is the Vice-President of ASFA, the Association of Science Fiction/Fantasy Artists.

Todd lives in Washington state with his wife, three children, a mouse, and Spook, the psychotic couch muffin.

Come check out our web site for details on these Meisha Merlin authors!

Kevin J. Anderson
Storm Constantine
Sylvia Engdahl
Jim Grimsley
Keith Hartman
Beth Hilgartner
Tanya Huff
Janet Kagan
Caitlin R. Kiernan
Lee Killough
Lee Martindale
Sharon Lee & Steve Miller
Jim Moore
Adam Niswander
Selina Rosen
Kristine Kathryn Rusch
S. P. Somtow
Allen Steele
Michael Scott

http://www.angelfire.com/biz/MeishaMerlin